I0612967

The Last Child At Versailles

French Legacy Trilogy Book 3

Rose Pascoe

Published by Flax Bay Books, 2021

Copyright

Contents

Prologue.. 5

A Message from the Past 9

A New Family 37

Deep in the Attic... 43

Rural Idyll.. 62

A French Legacy 70

Storm Clouds Gather 96

The Girl with the Cameo 126

Fight or Flight.. 146

A Tourist at Versailles.. 163

The Storm Breaks 192

The Queen's Bedroom.. 204

Eye of the Storm... 221

Dinner for Two 236

Fury Unleashed.. 256

An Issue of Trust 273

Storm Debris... 307

The Jewellery Box 344

Tower of Terror 368

Wild Speculation 386

Behind Locked Doors 410

Champagne 435

Freedom 466

In the Dark 487

Return to Versailles 524

Read on 532

Historical Characters 533

Historical Notes and References...........................535

Acknowledgments 540

About the Author 541

Other Books by Rose Pascoe 542

Prologue

Elisabeth Penrose sat in her wicker chair on the veranda, relishing the warm rays of spring sunshine on her age-dappled face. A song thrush watched her from the kowhai tree, half a world away from his native land. He paused to flaunt his waistcoat of fine brown spots before bursting into song.

The sweet melody took her back to her childhood in France, ripe with the scent of apples and sun-dried hay. She closed her eyes for a moment, hearing the long-ago laughter of her nephew, as he swung upside down from a branch of the ancient oak tree.

She woke with a start when her heart skipped a beat. Despite the sun, she shivered and pulled the homespun blanket tighter around her knees. These moments of slipping away were coming more frequently. Soon, Elisabeth knew she would close her eyes for the last time.

No time to be maudlin, she reminded herself. There was work to be done. Her hand hovered over the pile of documents, which she was intending to put in order for her children, but settled instead on the photograph from her seventieth birthday celebration. Three rows of smiling faces – the family and friends who had filled her life in Wellington with love and joy. So much to be thankful for.

Inevitably, her thoughts turned to those she had left behind. Her fingers reached out for the portrait of her mother, clasping it to her heart, wishing she could have seen her family again, or at least known they were safe.

Her husband's footsteps roused her from her memories, his tread as familiar as her own faltering heartbeat. Elisabeth waited until he was by her shoulder, because his hearing was not so good these days. 'Hello, my love. Did you find it?'

'I hope this is the last time I have to climb that cursed ladder into the attic.' George Penrose eased himself down on the matching chair beside her, a faint sigh and a clicking of joints his only capitulation to age. 'How is it we have only been in this huge house for a few years, yet the attic is already cluttered?'

George toyed with the linen-wrapped bundle in his hands. 'Have you decided whether to give this to the children?'

Elisabeth did not need his tone of voice to tell her his view on the matter. The family heirloom she had reluctantly accepted from her aunt, over fifty years ago, had been far more of a curse than a blessing. Her family had been wrenched apart, her first husband had been killed, and she herself had narrowly escaped death twice – all over that innocent-looking bundle.

So much time had passed that it probably posed no threat now, but why take the risk? She took George's hand and squeezed it gently. 'I have decided our children will be better off without this burden. I wish to have a last look, then you can put it back in the attic forever.'

'Good,' he replied, handing her the bundle without further hesitation.

Under the layer of linen, the polished wood of the jewellery box glowed enticingly, just as it had when she had first laid eyes on it as a carefree girl of eighteen. When she opened the lid and saw the exquisite pearl necklace in its bed of satin, she gasped, as she always did, at the beauty of the pearls.

Her hand reached out to touch the little wooden owl, carved by her father, and more precious to her than the priceless jewellery. When she closed the lid of the box, it was with a certainty that she hadn't felt before. The flood of relief surprised her. The past was the past. By closing the box, she had finally set it to rest.

She smiled at George and handed the package back. He kissed her cheek and then the curve of her neck, in the deliciously familiar way that never ceased to send a quiver of delight through her, even after all these years.

When George had gone, Elisabeth lifted her face to the sun again. Who could know what the future would bring? Perhaps one day, long after the threat had passed, someone would find the old trunk in the attic and wonder why it had been hidden. If only her ever-curious daughter didn't find it first.

As soon as the thought flitted through her mind, she realised she had forgotten to put the letter in the jewellery box. What a foozler I am these days, she thought, searching under the pile of family documents for the single sheet of paper with a new red seal. Hopefully, if Sophie found the necklace, the letter would be sufficient warning of the danger, while satisfying her daughter's thirst for knowledge.

Elisabeth could hear George clambering slowly up the creaking ladder. Too late to call him back. Instead, she reached for the sketchbook he had used on their voyage to New Zealand and tucked the letter into the cover. She put everything back in the box and leaned back into the cushions with a sigh of satisfaction.

A Message from the Past

Wellington, New Zealand, 2019

Sophie West held the palm-sized portrait by the edges. 'Who is this little Botticelli cherub, Auntie?'

Her elderly aunt, Margaret, leaned over her shoulder. 'Family legend has it that this was Elisabeth Penrose's mother, who was supposed to have been French.'

'I'd love to find out more about her.' Sophie did a quick calculation in her head. 'This portrait could date back to the late 1700s. I remember my mother showing it to me as a child, but it didn't mean much to me then.'

Her aunt rummaged around under the piles of paper and boxes on the table, before finding her glasses pushed back on her head. She slipped them down onto her nose and took the portrait from Sophie. 'It's pretty special all right. Our oldest family heirloom. I reckon she looks quite like you did as a child.'

Sophie studied the chubby-cheeked girl with golden-blonde hair and wide blue eyes. The girl was looking to the side, her demure pose belied by the impish grin on her rosebud lips. 'A little, maybe. The unruly waves of hair and the eyes are similar to mine.'

Margaret placed the picture carefully back into its nest of soft velvet. 'You've got the same cheeky grin. How many times did I see that look on your face when you'd raided the biscuit tin or come home caked in mud after one of your expeditions to the bottom of the garden?'

Sophie laughed. 'Yeah, and I'd bet my life savings that you and mum were just the same at that age. Or worse.' She picked up the oldest photo in the box of family treasures, a group shot of the entire family and friends taken at Elisabeth Penrose's seventieth birthday party in 1882, in the front yard of this very house. 'It's so nice that they're all smiling. In most photos of the era, the people look like they're being held at gunpoint.'

'I suppose because they had to sit still while it was taken. By all accounts, the party was a splendid knees-up.' Margaret pointed to the older couple in the centre of the photo. 'That's Elisabeth and her husband, George Penrose, the first of our ancestors to arrive in New Zealand. The woman with her hands on their shoulders is Sophie, their oldest daughter and your namesake.'

Under a magnifying glass, Sophie could see the strong family resemblance between Elisabeth and her daughter, as well as two younger girls, presumably

Sophie's daughters. She couldn't tell the colour of their hair – although it looked pale enough to be blonde – but the shape of the face and the eyes were a giveaway. Not to mention the lack of height, which had travelled down the generations with annoying determination.

Elisabeth was a slip of a woman in a pale shirt and a plain, dark skirt. The sort of woman you might pass on the street without noticing, except for her smile. She'd survived the arduous voyage from England and a gruelling life in the early years of a new colony, yet she sat with a straight back and a slightly tilted chin, a proud matriarch caught in mid-laugh.

'So, why the sudden interest in family history, Sophie?'

'I've decided to go ahead with the trip to Europe we planned before Mike died. Only, to spice it up a bit, I want to visit all the places our various ancestors came from.'

Her aunt wrapped her arms around Sophie's neck and kissed her cheek. 'Sweet petal, that's wonderful news. I know it's been hard since Mike died. It would do you the world of good to do something adventurous, just for you. After all, they say life begins at fifty. Or is it forty?'

'Whatever the age, I can't wait to spread my wings and fly off into the sunset.'

'What have you found out about our ancestors so far?'

'I've tracked down locations for all the family lines except for the mysterious Elisabeth Penrose. Hence my visit to you, the fount of family knowledge.'

'Afraid I can't help you there,' Margaret said. 'I only know that Elisabeth was widowed at a young age and came out from England to New Zealand in 1841, with Anne, the sister of her first husband, John Godwin.'

'The rest is the stuff of family legend – falling in love with the ship's surgeon, George Penrose, and living happily ever after.'

'You might find out more on a computer. I never could figure out how to use the darn things.'

Sophie packed away the treasured mementoes into the Family Box, a solid wooden butter box, which was so old it might well have dated back to Elisabeth's time. 'I've searched online, but Elisabeth is stubbornly elusive, with no hint that she was from France, unfortunately.'

'I take it you're going to fly to England, rather than recreating their voyage to New Zealand by sailing ship? Four months of storms and stodgy food, surrounded by a couple of hundred people sharing a few bars of soap and a toilet bucket.' Margaret shuddered. 'Wouldn't suit me, but it might make a good reality television show, don't you think?'

'Maybe, if the contestants didn't kill each other.' Sophie had read about how hellish the months at sea had been on some voyages – the contestants would probably stage a mutiny within a week. 'Wasn't there a sketchbook of the voyage? I remember seeing one as a kid. I can't believe I've forgotten about it.'

'Golly, you're right. Haven't seen it in years though. I think it's in the other box of family stuff.'

Her aunt disappeared into the hall cupboard, which was bulging with stacks of cartons, old suitcases, discarded sports equipment, and all manner of other things that 'we're sure to need some day'. In a remarkably short space of time, she emerged triumphant.

The two women sat beside each other at the kitchen table with the sketchbook open between them, leafing through page after page of wonderfully intricate drawings, mainly in pencil, with a few in pastels.

'Look at this incredible drawing.' The sketch showed a woman standing by the rails of the ship at sunrise or sunset, in full colour. 'She looks like an angel about to ascend to heaven on the rays of light. And those birds over her head – they're so realistic it seems as if they're about to fly off the page. George

Penrose was an extraordinary artist.' Sophie looked between the photo and the sketch. 'Do you think this could be Elisabeth as a young woman?'

Margaret adjusted her glasses and peered at the drawing. 'Jeepers, I think you're right.'

'I'd forgotten how amazing these sketches were.' Sophie flipped through the pages again, taking a photograph of each sketch. A bustling scene on a wharf, the sailing ship from every angle, sheer cliffs receding in the ship's wake, swooping birds, playful dolphins, and scenes capturing all aspects of life aboard the ship.

'It's a shame Elisabeth didn't keep a diary of the voyage. It would be lovely to know more about her.'

'Unfortunately, I suspect she's always going to remain a mystery.' Sophie got up and helped her aunt repack the box. 'Thanks for all your help, Auntie. I'm going to head home and have one last go on the ancestry websites.'

'Once you get your teeth into something, you'll have it figured out in no time. I can't wait to hear what you find.'

Sophie spent a fascinating, but ultimately fruitless, afternoon browsing family history websites. Why on earth had Elisabeth left her home on a journey to the far side of the world after losing her first husband? Her situation in England must have been dire indeed to take such a risky step.

She flipped through the photos of the sketchbook again, stopping at the drawing of Elisabeth. An odd jolt of connection to this distant ancestor ran through her like an unexpected touch of a hand in the dark. Was it because they looked a little alike? Or was it the element of mystery surrounding her origins?

Whatever it was, Sophie was determined to find out more. No amount of searching uncovered any further information, so she left a series of queries on various ancestry sites, hoping that another genealogist might have some information on Elisabeth. When she finally stopped typing, she realised it was pitch dark outside. Her shoulders ached from hunching over the keyboard, and her stomach howled at her neglect.

She was halfway through eating reheated leftovers with one hand, while scrolling through messages with the other, when a new email pinged.

The subject line read: 'Elisabeth Godwin'. With a tingle of anticipation, she opened it.

'Hello. I am related to Elisabeth Duchamp Godwin, born in France in 1812, who was known to be living in England in the 1830s, where she married John Godwin. She disappeared around 1841. I am eager to find out what happened to her. Warm regards, Lucien Duchamp.'

Incredible! Fate was clearly on her side this time to throw her a lead so quickly. And with a confirmation that Elisabeth was French.

The email listed a web address for Lucien Duchamp, so she held off replying until she checked him out. As she kept reassuring her daughter, who was a technology whizz, just because she had the odd grey hair, didn't mean she was ignorant about the dangers of online scammers.

Lucien Duchamp lived in Paris, where he ran a business researching and collecting historical items from the French Revolution and Restoration periods. She read through his bio, which was impressive. He had studied at the Sorbonne and Cambridge University, then worked for several major museums before starting his own business. Which explained his excellent English. Just as well, given how rusty her French was.

The photo showed a man of perhaps sixty, an academic type with old-fashioned wire-framed glasses and a skewed tie, leaning over an indistinguishable object with a look of total absorption. He looked like someone who might present one of the older BBC documentaries, before all the fancy graphics and focus on mass-market appeal.

She went back to the email and replied: 'Bonjour Monsieur Duchamp, and thank you for your email. I am trying to trace the origins of my ancestor, known to me as Elisabeth Godwin Penrose. All I know about her is that her age tallies with an 1812 birth date and family legend suggests her family was French. Elisabeth Godwin was married to John Godwin in England. She sailed to New Zealand from London in 1841 and married George Penrose here. Looking forward to hearing more about her. Yours in anticipation, Sophie West.'

His reply came back within a minute. Sophie pushed the remains of her meal away and pulled the laptop closer.

'New Zealand!? No wonder I couldn't find her. I would love to hear more about her. Do you have any old diaries or mementoes? You must excuse me if I am being too forward, but I have been trying to find her all my life. Luc.'

Sophie smiled at the old-fashioned phrasing. She was not at all hesitant about using technology, but still disliked the blunt brevity of the email age, let alone the scattergun outpourings of Twitter.

'I have George Penrose's wonderful sketchbook of the voyage (he was the ship's doctor) and memorabilia from their life in New Zealand. His sketches of Elisabeth look a little like me, which might explain why I feel such a strong connection to her. I know nothing of Elisabeth's life before the voyage. Do you?'

'*I have the diary of her nephew, François Duchamp. It's quite a story – I'm sure you will be fascinated. I would love to meet you, but New Zealand appears to be almost exactly on the opposite side of the world to France.*'

Sophie's fingers tapped out a response on impulse. 'As it happens, I'm planning to visit Europe soon. How would it be if I visited you in Paris?'

'*Wonderful! How soon?*'

Sophie tapped her fingers on the table as she went through everything she would have to do before she left. She had a current passport, credit card, no dependents (apart from her garden and pot plants, which her neighbour would see to) and no pressing commitments. Her calendar was filled with social events, but nothing that couldn't be put off for a few weeks.

Honestly, what was to stop her? Before she could chicken out, she typed, 'How about next week? Will check flights and get back to you.'

'*Fantastic. I'll pick you up at the airport and make arrangements here. Au revoir, Luc.*'

The first thing she saw when she opened up her browser again was a special offer on 'Last Minute Travel Deals to Europe'. Despite not being a great believer in fate, this coincidence was too much to resist. A few clicks later, she was booked on a flight leaving in a week's time. Another quick email to Lucien Duchamp to confirm her arrival time in Paris and she was done.

Her nerves tingled with the outrageous spontaneity of her decision, but at least tonight she would go to bed with something thrilling to look forward to. Practical concerns could wait until tomorrow.

Four days later, Sophie was attempting to work her way through the third page of her 'To Do' list, but getting constantly distracted by friends who were dying to know why she was suddenly heading off to France to meet a mystery man. Their views ranged from a couple who were worried she was having a mid-life crisis, to the vast majority who were bubbling with envy. Fortunately, both her adult children were supportive, although worried about her meeting up with a stranger.

Her mobile rang as she was picking it up to call the dentist to cancel her annual check. 'Hi Auntie Margaret, did you get my email about France?'

'I sure did. You're really grabbing the bull by the horns, Sophie. Do be careful, love. This French bloke you're meeting is a stranger after all, even if he looks as harmless as a hamster in his website photo.'

'I will be careful, Auntie. I've done a self-defence course, so he doesn't stand a chance.'

'You have? When?'

Sophie cast her mind back to the two-hour self-defence class, which had been a fundraiser for her children's primary school. 'Umm, a wee while ago.' Only twenty years.

'Well, I have some exciting news. I found an old letter. From the age and the name on it, I think it might be a letter from Elisabeth to her daughter. It dropped out of the sketchbook when I was putting it away.'

'Wow, fantastic.' Sophie jumped out of her chair, grabbing her handbag and keys with one hand and juggling her mobile with the other. 'I'll be there in ten minutes. Don't open it without me!' She glanced at the time and was surprised to find it was nearly three o'clock, which gave her a couple of hours at most. She arrived at her aunt's house eleven minutes later, leaving a patch of rubber on the road.

Margaret had tea made by the time Sophie burst into the kitchen. The letter was sitting exactly halfway between them on the table – a fragile slip of paper with its red wax seal squashed flat, but still intact. '*My darling Sophie*' was written in cursive on the front.

'It gave me quite a start to see your name on it until I realised it must have been intended for the original

Sophie. I think the wax might have been holding it inside the cover of the sketchbook, like glue.'

Sophie touched the letter with the tip of a finger, pushing it a little closer to her aunt. 'Go ahead, open it.'

Margaret shook her head. 'You do it. My fingers are shaking.'

Sophie picked up the letter, slipped a clean knife under the edge of the wax, and eased the seal away from the paper. The writing was in an elegant script, full of extended uprights and long loops, but legible. The hand was precise, although the slight wavering of the letters suggested the writer was elderly. And no wonder, as it was written by Elisabeth Penrose in 1884, when she must have been seventy-two years old – a venerable age in those days.

My darling Sophie,

If you are reading this letter, then you have found my box of treasures in the depths of the attic. I could not bear to throw them away, yet I feared that keeping them would bring danger to my beloved children.

How proud your father would have been to see you now; so clever and brave, making the world a fairer place. George is equally proud, as the only father you have known, who always loved you like his own. You already know the most important truth about John Godwin, which is that he was a fine man and a loving husband. He saved my life the day he agreed to transport me away from France, way back in 1830. What I could never bear to tell you was that his own death was not an accident. I will never overcome the guilt, as it should have been me who died, not John.

Arriving in New Zealand was a new beginning for me; a chance to forget the tragedy that has tailed my family like a hungry wolf. Suffice to say, my mother and I have both paid a high price for our loyalty to the family who adopted her as a child. The jewellery is the last reminder of those dreadful days. I trust you will derive some pleasure from this family legacy, while keeping these precious things safe from prying eyes.

With love for eternity and blessings on all the family,
Your loving mother,
Elisabeth
Wellington, 1884

Sophie and her aunt looked at each other with tears in their eyes, both of them too stunned to speak.

Margaret was the first to recover her wits. 'Good heavens! What a tragedy that the original Sophie never got to read this.'

'What do you make of this bit about the box of treasures in the attic?'

'No idea.' Margaret glanced up at the ceiling. 'If she wrote this in 1884, presumably she meant the attic in this house. I can't imagine they would have left

22

anything valuable up there, but if there is something, it was intended for Sophie and therefore it is rightly yours, as the eldest daughter in a long line of eldest daughters. I wish your mum was here to see this.'

'She did love a mystery, just like me.' Sophie took a couple of photos of the precious letter, then inserted it into an empty slot at the back of the family folder. 'Mum would be so happy knowing you're here looking after me and the old homestead, keeping the memories alive.'

Her mother, her aunt's favourite sister, had passed away when Sophie was only fifteen. Aunt Margaret had been Sophie's anchor, looking after her during school holidays in this house, a second home to her until she had moved away to start her own life. Study, career, husband, children – how quickly the decades had slipped past.

'She'll be looking down from heaven right now, egging you on.' Margaret reached out to squeeze her hand. 'I can see from your far-away expression that you are hatching a plan to search the attic. I should warn you, no one has been up there for years.'

'Why not? Are there ghosts?'

'Worse than that. You know how jam-packed with junk the hall cupboard is? Well, the attic is ten times worse.' Her aunt gave her one of her impish grins, which reminded Sophie so much of her own mother.

'The last person who went up there wasn't found for a week. Eight generations of unwanted family junk lurk up there. Old furniture and boxes of bric-a-brac submerged under a hundred and forty years of dust and spiders' webs. Sometimes I lie in bed at night, terrified the whole lot will come crashing down on me in the next quake.'

'Spiders' webs?' Sophie glanced at the clock on the oven and was surprised to see it was after five o'clock. 'Maybe I'll come back tomorrow with full protective gear and a hard hat. I haven't got time today anyway, as I've got to go out to dinner tonight. I wonder if I could make an excuse and cancel?'

Margaret got up and gave her niece a hug. 'That box has been waiting for you for a very long time. One more night won't make a difference. Go have some fun – you've been skulking at home far too long.'

'The box may be willing to wait, but patience is definitely not my virtue. To be honest, I'd rather face the spiders than a blind date set up by an acquaintance of a colleague of a friend.' She kissed her aunt's wrinkled cheek. 'See you bright and early tomorrow morning. Have a bucket of coffee ready.'

Sophie spent the short drive home cursing her foolishness at getting trapped into a blind date. Even if he turned out to be closer to Prince Charming than Frankenstein, she would far rather be up in the attic all night, delving into her family secrets, than making small talk with a stranger. Truth be told, she'd rather be curled up with a good book and a glass of wine … or even a pile of dirty washing. She was just too old to cope with dating again, and especially the well-meaning efforts of her friends to set her up with 'suitable' men who were anything but.

As she parked beside her little wildflower garden, Sophie reminded herself how lucky she was to be free to do as she wished. Her life had been perfect until two years ago. A happy marriage, two successful children (who actually remembered her birthday and came home for Christmas most years). All the trappings of a comfortable life in a leafy suburb, garnished with laughter and holidays in the great outdoors.

And then, one unexceptional day, while Sophie had been hanging washing on the line and scrubbing moss off the path, her husband had gone out for a Sunday run and had a fatal heart attack. An undiagnosed heart defect in an otherwise trim and healthy man of forty-nine, according to the autopsy report.

His unexpected death had been bad enough, but the aftermath had pushed her close to the edge of despair. Two years it had taken her to pull herself back from the brink to the point where she didn't have to paste on a cheery smile and fake an 'I'm fine' conversation. She had sold their joint business recently, cutting the last strands of the mesh that had held their life together. For better or worse, Mike was gone, and she was determined that the wrongs he had done would die with him. If she had gone through hell and back, at least she hadn't had to watch anyone else go through it too.

Now, with teeth-gritted optimism, she reminded herself that she was a fit, competent woman of fifty, entirely capable of travelling alone to the other side of the world to see London and Paris, or even Timbuktu and Kazakhstan, if she wished.

All she had to do was get through one teeny weeny blind date and three more days of frantic organisation, before she winged her way to adventure.

Four hours later, Sophie slumped into her date's BMW, feeling as if the life had been sucked out of her. The date had not been a complete disaster – maybe about a three on a scale of zero (axe-murdering psychopath) to ten (love at first sight) – but there definitely would not be a second date.

Her first impression of Carl was that he seemed presentable and pleasant, with no obviously obnoxious traits or BO, although the lingering whiff of cigar smoke on his jacket was off-putting. He picked her up on time, complemented her dress, and gently removed the neighbour's cat from the warm bonnet of his car with good humour. A promising start.

Carl chatted easily about the latest appalling gaff by an inept politician, a subject everyone could agree on. If one squinted a bit, there was even a hint of Prince Charming about him, albeit a few decades older, twenty kilograms heavier, and balding.

In the restaurant, he allowed her plenty of time to peruse the menu, while keeping up a monologue about his successful business, which seemed to involve maximising company profits and management salaries by plundering family businesses, slashing the workforce, and rehiring them on zero-hour contracts.

Sophie tried not to cringe at his ethics, instead diverting the conversation to his interests and discovering, with more than a hint of relief, that he had travelled to Europe. She relaxed and settled in for a potentially enjoyable evening of favourite places to go and things to do.

'Did you go to France, Carl? That's where I'm heading in a few days' time.'

Carl scrunched up his mouth and nose as if he'd been served with week-old raw fish. 'Oh, France, you don't want to go there. Don't listen to what the so-called experts say. The food there is atrocious. Honestly Sophie, everything's dripping in butter or cream. You don't want to lose your figure by eating that stuff at your age.'

Fortunately, the waiter delivered his steak in bearnaise sauce and her Thai chicken salad at that moment, saving her from having to reply. She stared at her salad, which smelled divinely of spices and fresh coriander, and wished, perversely, that she had ordered something with lashings of cream. She stabbed her fork into it with a combination of annoyance and relish, trying to ignore the hunk of bloody steak he was hacking off and slathering with buttery sauce.

'I love French food. French women always look fabulous, so it can't be too bad for you.'

With a meat-laden fork waving in the air, Carl continued as if she hadn't spoken. 'And the people – so rude. They refused to speak English to me even though I'm sure they all can, what with the EC and all that. And don't get me started on the plumbing – even the Romans did it better.'

Sophie shifted into that Zen-Dating state of determined chirpiness. 'Luckily, I speak enough French to get by on basics. I find if you try to engage, people are usually pretty good. There are always exceptions, of course, probably people who are fed up with masses of tourists invading their towns.'

'I expect they like to humour the nice-looking gals.' He snared a passing waiter to ask for tomato sauce. 'You have to watch those French fellas – all fake charm and sneaky hands. Honestly Sophie, if you must go to France, the best strategy is to take a tour bus around the sights and stay at a decent English-style hotel. That way, you'll maximise your sightseeing and minimise your interactions with the locals.'

Sophie scooped up a mouthful of salad, to strategically minimise her chances of saying something offensive. When she finished chewing, she smiled at him over the rim of her wineglass. 'But don't you find the best travel memories involve meeting the locals and trying new things? Otherwise, it would be easier to stay home and watch travel documentaries.'

'Now there's a good idea. It's far more fun watching Michael Palin deal with dodgy locals than doing it yourself. And a damn sight cheaper.' He stuffed the final three chips into his mouth with an air of having won the argument.

'Can I ask why you wanted to go to France, Carl?'

'Wife insisted on it. Ex-wife now.' He wiped a glob of tomato sauce off his lips. 'Fancy dessert? Or are you watching your weight?' His gaze slid down her body appraisingly.

Did he just wink at her? Sure, she wasn't quite as slim as the good old days, but she was not the one with the thick roll of flab bulging over his belt. She replied, rather more sharply than was polite, 'To be honest, I'm pretty shattered. My trip is a bit of a last-minute decision, so there has been a lot to do. Let's call it a night.'

Sophie signalled a passing waiter, who accurately diagnosed her frantic plea and returned promptly with the bill, which she insisted on splitting. The last thing she needed was for him to feel that she owed him.

Now, they were standing at her doorstep and Carl was bending forward to kiss her, as she fumbled her keys and hastily wished him goodnight. She turned her head, so the kiss landed on her cheek. For a moment there, she thought she might have to resort to desperate measures to prove she really meant 'goodnight' not 'come in for a shag', but he left quietly, and she closed the door with relief.

Was she being too picky in her expectations, or just too old and ornery to compromise? Both probably. One of the great advantages of middle age is that you learn to accept who you are and work with it, rather than battling to be someone else's definition of normal. What did she care if the things that mattered to her were not what the average person wanted, and vice versa? With a burst of elation, she realised just how much she was enjoying the freedom to follow her own dreams.

Once inside, all she wanted to do was remove her makeup and slide between her electric blanket and her duvet. She had crossed the lounge before the odd feeling that something was wrong sunk into her exhausted brain. Hadn't she left the hall light on when she went out? The cottage around her was utterly silent as she held her breath and listened for strange noises.

Slowly, she scanned the room with a critical gaze. Granted, she wasn't one of those fanatically neat people who have nothing on their coffee tables but designer-store baubles and glitzy magazines arranged in a perfect fan. But she knew her own mess, and this wasn't it. The television and stereo were still there – not surprisingly, as both were so old that they'd hardly be worth the bother of lugging them away.

She'd left a pile of bills on the end of the sofa and now a few of them were on the floor. The table was very slightly pushed out from its usual position, leaving long-established dents in the carpet visible. Had she left her charities folder on top of the other documents she'd been sorting through? Possibly, as she needed to drop it off to another board member tomorrow, with an apology for missing the next meeting.

Thoughts zipped through her mind in quick succession: what else might be missing, thank goodness she had left Elisabeth's letter at her aunt's house, should she phone the police and, finally – far too belatedly – was the burglar still in the house?

The hairs rose on the back of her neck as she tried to decide between running over to her neighbour's house, although the burglar was almost certain to have gone, and checking for herself, with the slim chance he might be lurking behind a door. The thought of fleeing her own domain, her sanctuary, roused the stubborn streak in her. She pulled her mobile from her handbag, found her neighbour's number, and hovered a finger over the call button.

She sniffed the air, as instinctively as a Neanderthal checking for predators. Was there a touch of cologne in the air, or was she being paranoid? With a shock of recognition, she realised it was the same cologne that her husband had used – a spicy vanilla fragrance by Armani.

Grabbing an umbrella from the stand in the hall as a makeshift weapon, Sophie moved from room to room, not finding anything missing, but noticing several subtle indications that someone had been there. The sheets were not quite as neatly stacked as usual in the hall closet. The sticky drawer in the kitchen, which never shut properly unless you got the angle just right, wasn't fully closed. And there was a faint smear of mud under the kitchen door, when the floor had only been mopped yesterday. Although Sophie was sure that was how the intruder had got in, there was no sign of a forced entry, apart from a few faint scratches around the keyhole, which may or may not have been there before.

She locked the door again and put a chair up against it, before double-checking that all the windows were secured. Only two rooms left to check. The study looked the same as usual, but enough items were slightly out of place to suggest it too had been searched. The intruder must have been thorough, as all the books had been pulled out, judging by the scrapes in the dust on the bookshelves. She'd never been one for dusting.

The room had been Mike's 'man-cave' when he was alive, and most of the stuff in it was his. Even after two years, she didn't like coming into this room. When the anguish of the funeral was over, she had had to force herself to come into his territory. Everything had been as expected – life insurance payments up to date, thank goodness, statements from the bank and superannuation investments neatly filed, his will and personal documents in order.

It was only when she checked his laptop that she found she didn't really know her husband at all. A secret online bank account, solely in his name, with abundant evidence of his illicit affairs in the credit card statements. Luxury hotel getaways when she thought he was on work trips, couples' spa retreats he had never shared with her, extravagant lingerie and expensive wines, when they were supposed to be saving money for a trip to Europe.

His duplicity had smashed through the happy façade of their marriage. They had been called 'the perfect couple' by all their friends and she had thought it too for thirty years. After a week of shutting herself off from the world and crying into her pillow at night, Sophie had resolved to put it behind her and forge the life she wanted. No point in blighting everyone else's memory of him, now that he was gone. She steeled herself to empty and close the bank account (donating the money to Women's Refuge), before purging the laptop of every trace of his deceit.

With a start, Sophie realised that Mike's laptop was missing. She'd left her own laptop at Margaret's place, as luck would have it, but his laptop had been sitting on a shelf in the corner until she decided what to do with it. In a way, she was relieved it was gone. It was certainly not worth calling the police over, especially as she was flying out of the country in a couple of days.

The last room she had to check was even harder to face. She dreaded to think of the intruder in her bedroom, rifling through her underwear drawer. Like all the other rooms, there were subtle signs of a search. Her everyday jewellery was all there, but the antique wooden jewellery box her mother had given her for her twenty-first birthday was missing, its contents tipped out. How bizarre that the thief would take the box but leave the jewellery. Not that either was worth much beyond their sentimental value.

The very last place she checked was her wardrobe. The previous owner of the cottage had installed a small safe underneath, hidden by a neatly fitted panel, topped with carpet. A surge of relief washed through her when she saw that the panel was undisturbed. The precious sapphire and diamond necklace, which had been passed down to each eldest daughter since Elisabeth's time, lay tucked up inside, kept safe for her own daughter. She flipped through the other contents: passport, computer backups, her mother's engagement ring, and a few other nice pieces of jewellery – all undisturbed.

When she closed the wardrobe door again, Sophie found she was shaking, the reaction only setting in now that the immediate threat had passed. She made herself a milky hot chocolate, with a generous slosh of brandy, and retreated to the comfort of her warm bed.

To distract herself, she focussed on the excitement of finding Elisabeth's letter and the prospect of finding her box of treasures still in the attic. Her imagination supplied a pirate's treasure chest, but instead of overflowing with gold doubloons and gem-studded cutlasses, there would be a diary of the voyage and the precious heirlooms from her family's past.

The wording of the letter stuck in her mind: *'Tragedy has tailed my family like a hungry wolf. Suffice to say, my mother and I have both paid a high price for our loyalty to the family who adopted her as a child.'*

She longed to find out more about Elisabeth and her parents. Why was her mother adopted and how did it end in tragedy?

A New Family

Versailles, France, 30 April 1788

Two quills scratched across thick paper, forming words simultaneously in near-identical script. Their writing was elegant for nine-year-olds, as required by their strict tutors, although such precision required the kind of painstaking attention that tested their fragile patience.

Strangers were charmed by these two pretty little cherubs, with their curly blonde hair and porcelain skin, although the more astute amongst them were quick to note the spark of mischief in their eyes and the hint of determination in the set of their rosebud lips. They were occasionally mistaken for twins, although they were neither sisters nor even from the same level of society.

Their tutor was an elderly scholar with a penchant for fine wine, who often fell asleep if they were quiet enough, especially if their female attendants were gathered quietly in a corner, gossiping in low voices. Which was always. So, they sat as quietly as two porcelain dolls, communicating only with exaggerated facial expressions and suppressed giggles, until the snoring started.

One girl was tiptoeing across the room to get her favourite doll when the heavy oak door banged open. The tutor awoke with a porcine snort. The attendants rose in alarm, dropping their needlework. For the door to burst open during the children's lessons, or indeed at any time, was an outrage against the strict layers of protocol that ruled every moment of their lives.

The man in the doorway said only one word, 'Come', before whirling around and vanishing again.

The girl at the desk saw the chalk-white face of her father and obeyed his command instantly, dropping her quill in her hurry. A blob of ink spilled onto her work and spread across the page, covering the crude caricature of the tutor, which the girl had just finished drawing, until all that could be seen was the tip of his elongated nose and chin.

Under ordinary circumstances, the ill-mannered interruption would have prompted a stern rebuke from the tutor. But today, with the girl's mother lying gravely ill, he merely waved arthritic fingers to speed her on her way.

The girl hurried in the footsteps of her father, her slight frame floating in a white muslin dress and her blonde curls bouncing out of a loose lilac ribbon as she struggled to keep up. She glanced back at the pale face of her playmate, who was motionless in the doorway with wide eyes mirroring her own fear. The pretty doll slipped from her playmate's fingers, its white silk dress momentarily flaring, before landing on the parquet floor.

The man and his daughter wove through a series of narrow corridors and hidden stairwells, his heavier tread and her pattering slippers causing everyone they passed to look up in surprise at their unseemly haste. One did not run – one glided, slowly, elegantly. When they reached a plain wooden door, her father stopped to draw a deep breath, his head bowed and his knuckles white on the heavy iron handle.

He turned to her and knelt down to her level, his strong hands clasping her slender shoulders. 'Your mother will go to God soon. You must pray for her, my dear, and remember how much she loves you.'

The girl sucked in her cheeks to stop tears flowing and patted her father's trembling arm. Although she was young, she understood what death was and the grief it brought, as her playmate had lost a baby sister not two years ago. She had provided warm arms of comfort then and would again now for her father.

In the dim light of the room, her mother was as still and pale as a wax model. The absence of her usual rosy-cheeked smile rendered the familiar face almost unrecognisable, and the girl's resolve to be strong crumbled away. She reached for her mother's hand, dreading that it would be limp and cold, but felt a weak responding squeeze.

When she moved to kiss her mother's sunken cheek, a voice rasped in her ear so softly, she almost thought she was imagining it. 'My dearest daughter. I am sorry.' The girl leaned in to hear better. '…will be cared for.' Her mother struggled for breath. '…pray for your happiness.'

'*Maman*, don't try to talk if it tires you. Papa and I will look after you and you will get better.'

Her mother shook her head so feebly that the movement was barely discernible. Her fingers tightened for a moment on her daughter's hand, before losing strength and falling open on the quilt.

Her father leaned over, holding his face close to his wife's mouth. His eyes clenched as he felt for her breath on his cheek. 'She is still with us. For how much longer, I do not know.'

Her father did not speak again until his daughter's tears were under control. He drew her over to the two plain wooden chairs in the corner of the room. 'I have something important to tell you.'

She looked up at her father's drawn face, but he would not meet her eyes.

'You have been offered an extraordinary favour. Your mother has agreed that you will be adopted by the family we serve. You will live with them and be given a life beyond anything the daughter of a chambermaid could dream of. A fine education, a good marriage, people to serve you. It is a great opportunity, which will benefit the whole family.'

'Will I still live with you, Papa?'

'No, my dear. You will live with them, although you will still be able to visit me. I will remain in service here.'

'But Papa, why do they want to adopt me?'

'One day I will explain, but for now you must simply be grateful and work as hard as you can to please them.' His lips twisted into an unconvincing smile. 'Won't it be lovely that your friend will now be your sister?'

The girl was silent for a time, wondering what the other girl would think of having to share her life with an adopted sister from such lowly origins. Their friendship was finely balanced, never quite tipping into jealousy or resentment, because each one knew precisely who was the lesser of the two, there to serve the needs of the other.

Another thought struck her, even worse than the first. Would she have to become like her new sister, spending hours learning etiquette and being paraded in front of staring crowds? Her beautiful gowns might look elegant, but the tight bodices and layers of heavy material made them more like instruments of torture.

'Papa, I wouldn't like to be like her. Will I have to dress in uncomfortable gowns and do everything she does?' She paused, uncertain, yet not wanting to sound too ungrateful. 'Will she still order me to fetch and carry for her if I am her sister?'

Her father knew her well enough to understand her fears. 'Well, my dear child, you must accept that you are growing up and can no longer run around like a wild creature in the gardens. But no, you will be her sister only in private. In public, I trust you will remain as you are now – a sweet child of no significance, except to those who love you. You must always be aware of your position and accept that she is the special one, who will be treated as such by everyone, including you.'

Whatever her fate, the girl's only thoughts now were for her ailing mother. 'Should we not get the physician?'

'He has been. There is nothing more to be done, aside from being here with her to ease her passing.'

The girl sank to her knees, her wayward curls falling loose over tightly shut eyes, as she prayed with every shred of her soul for her mother's recovery. Then she curled up on the bed and whispered words of love into her mother's ear.

Once, she thought her mother's lips twitched into a ghost of a smile. But, when the room lit up with the first rays of a new day, the girl awoke to find her mother's hand stiff and cold in her own.

Deep in the Attic

Sophie woke up stiff and cold, having kicked off her duvet during a particularly unpleasant nightmare involving a gigantic spider lurking in a gothic attic. The adrenalin seeped away over a calming cup of tea and toast slathered with her Aunt Margaret's home-made marmalade.

Her excitement at the search for the box in the attic grew as she reread Elisabeth's letter. After all she'd been through, Sophie reckoned she was due a bit of good fortune. The burglary was bad timing and upsetting, but best purged from her thoughts. A quick call to a security company to arrange the installation of new locks and that would be the end of it.

By the time she arrived at her aunt's house, she was buzzing, despite the early hour. Sophie parked in the street and checked for signs of life, as she retrieved her bag from the passenger seat. Her aunt's curly grey hair bobbed back and forth between the half-drawn gingham curtains in the kitchen window, outlined in gold by the first rays of sun streaming through the autumn leaves in the garden.

Margaret looked up and waved, before meeting her at the door, surrounded by the wafting aroma of fresh coffee. 'Come on in, my dear. I've hardly slept a wink.'

Fortified with extra-strength caffeine and armed with a powerful torch, Sophie scrambled up the ladder and through the hatch into the attic. The air was breathable, if rather stale, and there was no apparent sign of Shelob or her massive spidery friends.

A shiver of delicious anticipation went down her spine as she took in the dim outline of mysterious objects, eerily lit by soft, dust-spangled light. She lingered a moment, surveying haphazard piles of every imaginable shape spread out into all four corners from floor to ceiling. A glimpse of a ghostly human figure in one corner sent her pulse racing. Cursing her overactive imagination, she switched the torch on, revealing an old hat stand draped with the filmy fabric of ancient net curtains.

Perhaps it might be best to focus on the furthest points of the attic, which likely contained the oldest items. If she made her way to the far wall, which was stacked with antique chairs, and spiralled around and inward, eventually she would find whatever was there.

In theory. The reality was a little trickier, given the volume of junk and the fact that she had no idea whether she was looking for a shoebox or a shipping container. At least there didn't appear to be too many spiders' webs.

After what seemed like hours of climbing over boxes and stumbling over furniture, she spotted the corner of a wooden trunk under a pile of ancient rugs. Silverfish scuttled for cover as she heaved the rugs aside. Once the haze of dust and her coughing fit had subsided, she got her first good look at the trunk. Her pulse ticked up a notch. It was a beautiful piece of craftsmanship, with solid sides, a gracefully curved top, and an ornate lock. Just the sort of trunk a well-to-do Victorian might take on a voyage.

Sophie proceeded methodically, hanging the torch from a length of twine, clearing the surrounding objects and laying out a clean sheet over the floorboards. She rubbed the dust off the top of the trunk with a soft rag, revealing the rich glow of red-brown mahogany. A broad smile crept over her face. The trunk, polished until gleaming, would look terrific nestled at the end of the bed in her own cottage. She snapped off a few photos for her aunt, who was not up to scaling ladders, although she was pretty spry for eighty.

Thankfully, the key was in the lock. With infinite care, although the trunk appeared robust, she twisted the key and raised the lid, with a creak of hinges and a waft of lavender.

The trunk was filled with clothes, luckily with no smell of mildew. The first items out of the trunk were three floor-length dresses with scooped necks, puffed sleeves and nipped waists, in rich shades of midnight-blue, russet, and forest-green. Holding the green one up, she realised that Elisabeth Penrose would have been about her own less than average height and shared her taste in colours.

The thick layers of silk and cotton sat heavily in her hands as she laid them on the sheet. The dresses appeared to be in good condition, with no insect or water damage. Sophie's concept of fashion leaned more to the 'smart casual' end of the spectrum (or 'sloppy casual', if she was being honest), but even she could admire the exquisite tailoring of these garments, while being grateful she lived in a more modern age of zips and lightweight comfort.

These dresses must have been Elisabeth's best outfits, packed away for protection, as they surely would have been totally impractical for her life in the new colony, especially with six young children. Sophie hoped Elisabeth had had the foresight to pack some sturdy boots and practical work dresses in tough cotton as well.

Discreetly hidden underneath the dresses in the trunk were the more personal items: petticoats, bonnets, underwear, frilly neckpieces. The corset was stiffly reinforced and must have been a nightmare to wear. Heaven help these poor women, wearing this strait jacket every day. It had a rip and a brownish stain under the bustline. On closer inspection, she realised it was not a rip, but a slash-mark made by something sharp. Suddenly, the stain looked a little more ominous.

She put the corset aside with a shiver and dug down to the bottom of the trunk, which was covered with a plethora of decorative combs, hat pins, lacy handkerchiefs, ribbons, delicate shoes, a sewing kit and other paraphernalia of the nineteenth-century lady. Nestled at the very bottom, wrapped in a soft velvet cloth, was a portrait of an elegantly dressed man, of slim build and angular features, who gazed out from the canvas with a serious expression, softened by a glint of humour around his eyes. Elisabeth's first husband, perhaps? Or perhaps her brother or father?

She set the picture down and considered the empty trunk. Wonderful as the finds were, she couldn't help but be disappointed that there were no diaries or documents. The letter had hinted at dangerous family treasures, which surely meant more than clothes.

Sophie sat on a nearby chair with a wobbly leg and richly embroidered upholstery, which was frayed beyond repair. The monotonous hum of Margaret's vacuum cleaner seemed to come from a world away in the muted gloom of the attic, as she contemplated the trunk. But no matter how long she stared at it, it remained stubbornly empty. Which meant she was going to have to steel herself for the mammoth task of searching every box and drawer in the attic.

And yet, she had a strong sense that the trunk was the most likely place to keep a family treasure. She examined it again, patting down the cloth-covered sides – which were marred by several slash-marks – tapping the lid, checking the base. Everything seemed solid. She examined it from all angles, feeling that something was not quite right. Using her arm as a measure, she found the inside was not quite as deep as the outside, suggesting the possibility of a hidden compartment in the thick base.

Not wanting to damage the trunk, she searched for the mechanism to release the bottom panel. After a few minutes, she realised the decorative elements on the inside corners of the trunk could be levered up to unlock the base plate. Once released, the bottom was simple to remove.

Inside, a linen-wrapped bundle, a drawstring bag, and a book nestled perfectly into a shallow cavity. She could scarcely breathe as she gently eased them into the bright beam of the torch.

The book was not much bigger than the size of her extended hand. With trembling fingers, she opened it, letting out a squeak of excitement when she saw it was a diary written in French. So, the family legend was definitely true. Her French was rusty, but good enough to read the title page: 'Diary of Our Voyage on the *Lady Rosalind*, 1841', followed by the name of the writer, Elisabeth Duchamp Godwin.

Eureka, the same name as Lucien Duchamp had mentioned.

She was itching to read the diary from cover to cover, but the tiny, precise, copperplate writing was difficult to read by torchlight and her French was not up to the challenge without help. Leafing through, she found some pages were almost unreadable, due to a thick brown stain. With a shudder, she wondered if it was more blood, then chided herself for being melodramatic. It was probably just the 1840s equivalent of tomato sauce. She set the diary aside and picked up the linen bundle, unwrapping it to reveal a box.

If the mahogany trunk was beautiful, the jewellery box was truly stunning. The rich, dark wood was inset with a design in lighter wood around a floral centrepiece. The edges of the box were reinforced with elaborately worked vines and flowers in gilded metal. It was so exquisite, she could scarcely bring herself to touch it. But the desire to see inside was far too strong. With the tips of her fingers, she released the catch and eased the lid open.

The inside was lined with royal blue satin and divided into several compartments for jewellery. The largest one held a necklace of fat pearls, which glowed in the torchlight like miniature moons, so beautiful they made her gasp.

The other compartments held a selection of period pieces, dominated by a striking cameo brooch, with two heads in profile, carved in milk-white ivory against a dark blue background. One of the smaller compartments contained rings, including one set with a large pearl and another that was probably a gold wedding band, although the engraving was too worn to read. The last compartment contained sparkling hair decorations and a small, intricate carving of an owl.

She shut the box and picked up the last item, a drawstring bag made of dark blue velvet. It appeared to be almost empty, but it clinked when she picked it up and was surprisingly heavy for its size. Inside were four coins, presumably real gold, given their weight. Squinting at one under the beam of her torch, she made out the head of a young Queen Victoria on one side, and a crown and crest on the other, which made sense given the date of their voyage from England.

Sophie sat back on the wobbly chair and marvelled at her finds. How extraordinary that they had remained undiscovered all this time. The jewellery and gold coins were certainly treasure of the conventional sort, but it was not their monetary value that excited her imagination. Every single item seemed filled with a tale begging to be told – a precious insight into the lives of her ancestors and their perilous journey across the oceans. Hopefully, the diary would be the narrator.

Sophie was bursting to show her aunt what she had found, so she carefully packed the valuables into her bag and took photos of everything else before repacking the truck.

Her aunt was in the kitchen, humming a tune from Phantom of the Opera, and stirring a steaming pot. 'Sophie, at last. I thought you might have fallen through a hole into Wonderland.' Margaret turned to her. 'Well, I can see you're grinning like the Cheshire Cat, so I'm guessing you found something.' She plucked a cobweb out of Sophie's hair. 'A rather grubby version of the cat. I really should have cleaned out the attic half a century ago.'

'I imagine our ancestors have been saying the same thing for a hundred and forty years.' Sophie gave her aunt a one-armed hug, while her nose hovered over the pot and her stomach rumbled in a most unladylike manner. 'Mm, soup smells divine. Kumara and ginger, my favourite. You're going to love what I found up there, but first I need a shower and food. No peeking until I get back.'

After lunch, they settled themselves on the sofa to inspect the booty.

'Right at the back of the attic, under a pile of old rugs, I found the most gorgeous old shipping trunk, filled with fancy clothes and personal items.' Sophie flipped through the photos of the gorgeous gowns, drawing oohs and aahs from her aunt (and grimaces for the corset). 'This painting was at the bottom of the trunk.'

Margaret held up the picture. 'Who do you think he is? He does look dreadfully serious, but I suppose that was how portraits were painted back then. I expect most people would get sick of smiling if they had to sit for hours while the artist did his thing.'

'I thought perhaps he might be Elisabeth's first husband, John Godwin, Sophie's father.'

'What a shame you didn't find a diary. That might have shed some light on it.' Margaret saw the wide grin splitting Sophie's face. 'You did find one! How marvellous.'

'I almost missed it. There was a secret compartment in the base of the trunk, very cleverly concealed.' Sophie pulled the diary and jewellery box out of her bag with a flourish. 'Ta-da. It's like the best Christmas ever, times ten.'

Margaret took up the diary with eager fingers. 'Is it just my ancient eyes or is this writing really difficult to make out? Is it French?'

'Yes, so it might take me a while to translate, unless you happen to know someone fluent in French?'

Margaret laughed. 'Café, croissant and sauvignon blanc are about the only French words my friends speak. Anyway, this handwriting is far too small for me to read. I shall expect a full and detailed account the very second you have finished.'

Sophie turned to the title page. 'The writer's name was Elisabeth Duchamp Godwin, so it looks like Lucien Duchamp was right that we are both related to her.'

Her aunt switched her attention to the jewellery box. 'Good heavens, how beautiful! To think it's been sitting up in the attic all these years.' Margaret turned the box over in her hands, examining it in detail. 'The workmanship is absolutely exquisite. They surely don't make them like this anymore.'

Margaret opened the lid and let out a gasp. 'Oh, my goodness, what a stunning necklace! These pearls look too perfectly matched and far too large to be real.'

'Did they have cultured pearls back then? Or fake ones?'

'I don't know.' Margaret took the necklace over to the lamp and examined it minutely. 'When I was a young lass, I stepped out with a young man who worked for a jeweller. He told me how to tell real pearls from fake ones. I seem to recall he even promised to buy me a real pearl necklace. Perhaps I should have married him, but Arnold came along and swept me off my feet.'

'And?'

'I can hardly believe it, but I think they might be real. They have slight imperfections, as they would in nature. Such a shame that a couple of them have deep cut marks in them, but you can see how they are pearl all the way through, not just in an outer layer. Heavens, Sophie, this necklace must be worth an absolute fortune. What are you going to do with it?'

With the burglary so fresh in her mind, Sophie wanted to be extra cautious. 'I haven't time to do anything before I leave. I think it might be best to lock it in my safe and not say a word to anyone, at least until we know more about its history and value.'

'A bank's safe-deposit box might be more secure, if such things still exist.'

'Good idea. I would like to take some of the other items to France though, as Lucien Duchamp is an expert.'

Margaret set the pearls back in the box, easing them gently into a perfect circle. 'Take care, Sophie, you know nothing about this man or his motives.'

'You saw the website photo. He looks like a harmless academic.' She saw the dubious look on her aunt's face. 'Point taken, Auntie. Looks can deceive.

But I haven't felt so enthusiastic about anything since Mike died. I really want to do this.'

'It does sound thrilling. I'd tag along if it wasn't for my dicky heart.'

'I promise I'll take care and message you every day.' Sophie was on the verge of telling her aunt about the burglary but decided to spare her the upset. 'Auntie, please don't tell anyone about any of this, for your own safety, as well as mine.'

'It'll be our secret. Now, are you going to make a start on translating that diary, before I die of suspense?'

Sophie needed no encouragement to snuggle down under a fluffy blanket on the sofa with the diary and a language app on her phone. Reading and translating were frustratingly slow, until she got the hang of the old-fashioned writing and the oddities thrown up by the translation app, which clearly hadn't been designed with a nineteenth-century sailing voyage in mind.

The story of Elisabeth's voyage drew her in, until the sofa became a hard bunk, while the trees rustling in the wind outside the window were massive sails flapping in a storm. Every new peril her ancestor had faced pulled Sophie deeper into a world of mast-high waves and treacherous shipmates.

When she emerged back into the real world, her neck was stiff, and the sun was inexplicably shining at a low angle through the window.

Margaret was standing in front of her with a cup of tea and a worried frown. 'Sophie? Are you okay?'

'Sorry, Auntie, I must have zoned out for a minute.'

'A minute! More like an entire afternoon. I'm dying to hear about the diary, but I didn't want to disturb you.'

'What an amazing journey they had. Elisabeth was a real character – a woman before her time. She was devastated by the tragic death of her first husband, John Godwin, who is almost certainly the man in the portrait, as she mentions it in the diary.'

'How awful to be widowed so young.'

'It must have been a recent bereavement, as her grief fairly pours off the page in places, although mostly she keeps a stiff upper lip and writes about the voyage and her fellow passengers.'

'Do you know what happened to John Godwin?'

'No, but it's all a bit odd, as Elisabeth was forced to leave England soon after his death. She is pretty cagey about the reason, but I get the sense there was some unpleasantness with John's brother. Her sister-in-law, Anne Godwin, was being sent to Canada to marry, but it must have been an undesirable match, as they both escaped by going to New Zealand instead.'

'Intriguing. I can't wait to hear more.'

'Sorry, Auntie, but I really need to get home, because I've still got loads to organise.'

'I can't believe you'll be in Paris in a couple of days. You'll have plenty of time when you get home again to tell me everything.'

At home, there was an email from Luc waiting for her, confirming arrangements. She replied with the good news about finding Elisabeth's diary, without mentioning the other items. Maybe she was being a little paranoid, but the burglary had made her extra careful about how much she disclosed to a stranger. Obviously, it was simply a coincidence, as no one could have known about the treasures in the attic, when she didn't even know herself at the time of the burglary.

Luc's reply came back within an hour, despite it being early in the morning in Paris.

'I can't wait to read the diary. Does she mention anything about her past or her parents? The account written by François is full of intriguing mysteries. His grandparents – Elisabeth's parents – both grew up at Versailles around the time of the 1789 revolution. Elisabeth's father, Pierre Duchamp, was one of the

gardener's lads. I know little about Elisabeth's mother, other than that she was the daughter of two of the servants. Luc.'

Intriguing. She dashed off a quick reply. 'Versailles? Do you mean the palace? My impression from Elisabeth's diary was that she grew up on a farm. Sophie.'

'Yes, to both. Pierre Duchamp's family had an orchard and farm in the Loire Valley, but they struggled to make a living, so Pierre was sent to his uncle at Versailles. Elisabeth's parents returned to the farm around 1795, with enough money to pay off the debt and buy more land. We can visit the farm if you'd like. Luc.'

'I'd love to see where they lived. I know that Elisabeth's mother was adopted into a wealthy family and obviously felt a strong loyalty to them. I gather that is why Elisabeth was sent to England – to return an item that was precious to the family.'

'Interesting. I did wonder if they had come into the money by, how should we say, less legitimate means. Many valuable items disappeared during the chaos of the revolution. Unfortunately, François knew very little for certain, as he was only a young boy when Elisabeth left the farm after the 1830 revolution – or rather, she narrowly escaped after the family was attacked by the new king's soldiers. François lost his

grandparents, his father and his aunt, leaving him as the oldest son to keep the family going.'

'How tragic. I can't wait to hear the full story.'

'Does Elisabeth mention what she took to England? François knew only that it was an item of great value, small enough to be kept in a wooden box that fitted into a saddlebag.'

An item of great value in a wooden box? Surely, that must mean the pearl necklace. Sophie felt a strong urge to tell him about her find in the attic but kept her eagerness in check until she felt more confident of Luc's motives. 'That tallies with comments she made in her diary. Unfortunately, my French is fairly basic, more geared to ordering food and booking hotels than to translating a diary of a voyage in 1841. Must go, loads to do. See you soon, Sophie.'

Sophie shut down her laptop, aware of the rapidly dwindling amount of time she had before she left. Luc seemed genuinely enthusiastic about hearing Elisabeth's story, but she couldn't help wondering whether his interest was in family history or in the valuables Elisabeth had taken to England. She ought not forget that he made his living by finding and selling historic objects, no doubt for a hefty profit.

On the other hand, he seemed genuine and had openly shared his knowledge of their family story. And what an intriguing tale it was turning out to be.

How extraordinary that Elisabeth's parents had both grown up at Versailles, the centre of power for Louis XVI and Marie Antoinette at the time of the French Revolution. But then, if she remembered correctly, several thousand people had lived and worked at the Palace of Versailles during its heyday, including any number of minor aristocrats and officials who might be considered a wealthy family by the daughter of a servant.

Even though she had visited decades ago, on her honeymoon, the immense scale of the palace and gardens was etched into her memory. The Palace of Versailles was one of those larger-than-life places that, once visited, was never forgotten. Who could forget the insane opulence of the Hall of Mirrors? A masterpiece of one-upmanship, with its grand mirrors and windows, gold embellishments, statuary, and rows of enormous crystal chandeliers hanging from a vaulted ceiling.

By the time she and Mike had finished their palace tour, Sophie had been more than ready to stroll through the acres of gardens. She felt some sympathy for Marie Antoinette, who had loved to escape the stifling protocol of the palace for the quiet charms of her own smaller sanctuary, the Petit Trianon. The Queen had transformed the surrounding gardens into a place of natural serenity, mirroring her own opinion that everyone needs a good daily dose of nature to be happy.

Sophie knew enough of French history to know that Marie Antoinette was not quite as bad as she had been painted in popular culture. She had been a victim of a ruthless propaganda campaign, eerily reminiscent of the more vicious forms of fake news which circulate in the modern era, although conducted by pamphlets and coffee-house gossip back then, rather than the social media of today.

Ironically, Marie Antoinette was derided for her extravagance, while at the same time being mocked for wearing simple muslin gowns and pretending to be a peasant in the rustic simplicity of the faux village she had created.

Of course, for the real peasants of the day, nature was not a place for pleasant strolls by a lake and spotless farmyards with groomed livestock, but an unrelenting grind of backbreaking work for little reward.

What had life been like for her own ancestors, as a gardener and servant at Versailles?

Rural Idyll

Everything had changed. They had given her a new name – Ernestine – and a new place to live, complete with lavish gifts and servants to tend to her needs. She knew she should be grateful for this bounty, but her heart was aching from the death of her mother and the separation from her father.

'Ernestine, come on,' her new sister urged. 'It's lovely outside and we're going to have a picnic in the gardens.'

Ernestine forced her lips into a smile. The warm breeze drifting through the open window was alive with the scent of flowers, promising a perfect day for a picnic. A spark of life flickered at the thought of being let loose in the gardens, free from the usual constraints of her new life. She stood still long enough for the maid to tie her hair up with a pink satin ribbon before bounding out the door after the other girl.

By the time the girls reached the meadow, with their red-faced escorts puffing behind them, the servants had already laid out blankets, cushions, chairs and stools. They dodged their way through a stream of men carrying tables, baskets of food, flagons of wine, tablecloths, silverware and platters, running all the way to the tower and up its winding stairs.

From the top of the tower, the girls looked onto the idyllic scene stretched out below. Swallows darted past them, swooping gracefully to pluck the insects above the pond. A dozen ladies were strolling through the little rustic village, stopping to pat the fat lambs being led around with white satin ribbons by liveried footmen. Another gaggle of ladies were wandering around the pond and past the mill, stopping to pick the last of the irises. A few children raced around the meadow and through the surrounding trees, shrieking with the thrill of a day off their lessons.

A ripple of laughter made them turn back to the meadow, where Marie Antoinette and her closest friends were settling themselves under parasols. The Queen was soon in the centre of a merry group, looking radiant in a white muslin gown and a straw hat, sprigged with roses.

She never looked happier than when she was in the gardens and salons of the Petit Trianon. Indeed, the Queen had herself overseen the garden design and construction over the last five years, completely transforming the gardens from their previous formality. Now, she took great delight in sharing her vision of paradise with favoured friends and family.

Ernestine was pleased to see the Queen's sons had joined the picnic. Louis-Joseph, the Dauphin, was a sickly six-year-old, disfigured and debilitated by his illness, which meant he often missed out on the merriment. In stark contrast, three-year-old Louis-Charles was a chubby, happy boy who loved to play outside and pick flowers for his mother. She watched as a servant brought a tray of the most delicious delicacies for the boys, while others moved discreetly amongst the ladies with glasses and platters.

'I'm starving. Race you down.'

The two girls hurtled down the stairs, almost running into a group of strolling women. Unfortunately, one of them was an under-governess, who glared at them sharply. With suppressed giggles, the girls linked arms and glided their way across the meadow at a deliberate snail's pace, with noses elegantly in the air and shoulders pulled back, like the young ladies they were taught to be, rather than the nine-year-old girls they yearned to be.

The children ate their fill and more, until the thought of one more madeleine or another hothouse strawberry made their stomachs beg for mercy. They managed to sit still for a while, listening to the gossip and chatter, but soon grew bored.

Marie-Thérèse turned to an under-governess and tugged on her frilled sleeve. 'May we please have a ride on the ponies?'

Several of the other children perked up and added their voices to the plea.

The Queen turned to see what the commotion was. To their delight, she signalled a footman. 'Have the grooms prepare the children's ponies.' She must have noted the downcast look on Louis-Joseph's face. 'And have them bring the Dauphin's carriage.'

Louis-Joseph gave a little cheer, which brought a tender smile to his mother lips. The Queen's love of children was a joy to them all, especially as she encouraged them to play in the fresh air, often overruling the strict governesses, so that the children might enjoy more vigorous amusements than their ladies felt was appropriate.

After a long delay, a groom appeared with two ponies trailing behind him and a look of panic in his eyes. One of the waiting women went to find out why he had not brought the Dauphin's miniature carriage. After a whispered conversation, the groom disappeared again at a fast trot.

'Your Majesty, the groom says the little goats which pull the Dauphin's carriage are refusing to behave. He has gone to get the gardener's boy, who has a way with them.'

Ten minutes later, a scruffy runt of a lad appeared, his ragged clothes filthy from his work in the gardens. Ernestine was shocked by how thin he was, noting that his collarbone protruded sharply under his threadbare shirt. He stopped some way away from the group, no doubt unsure about how to proceed in such company. His gaze rested for a moment on the tables of food and his eyes widened. Then he recalled his place and made an awkward bow, throwing an unruly mop of coal-black hair over his face.

A buzz of outrage rippled through the crowd. Two of the footmen stepped forward to intercept the boy, lest he come any closer and expose the ladies to his disreputable state.

'Wait,' the Queen commanded. To the horror of her ladies, she walked up to the boy, who was trailed by two goats hitched to the miniature carriage. The goats were nuzzling his hands and behaving like little hairy gentlemen. 'Thank you for bringing the Dauphin's carriage. What is your name?'

'Pierre Duchamp, madame,' the boy replied, looking the Queen directly in the eye, then sketching another awkward bow.

Another gasp from the crowd. It was clear from his manner of address that he had no knowledge of protocol and no idea to whom he was talking.

The groom surged forward and cuffed the back of his head. 'Kneel before Her Majesty, boy.'

The boy shot a petrified glance at the Queen, then fell to his knees, causing the goats to shy sideways, tangling their harness. After a few moments of confusion, the boy calmed them and fixed the harness, never once rising from his knees.

A flicker of a smile played across Marie Antoinette's lips. 'Well, Pierre Duchamp, would you like something to eat?'

Pierre's cheeks flared red, but his eyes flicked to the table and his tongue whipped across his lips before he could gather his wits. 'If it pleases Your Majesty.' He managed another bow, still kneeling.

The Queen turned to one of her ladies and whispered some instructions. The lady turned to another, who turned to a servant, who bowed and went over to the table to pile food onto a plate.

Ernestine watched with fascination as the scene played out. The Queen went up another notch in her estimation for her kind treatment of this poor, terrified boy. She watched with interest as the boy was led to a spot away from the ladies and with fascination as he scooped up every last morsel of bread, cheese and meat on the plate, so fast that it seemed he had inhaled it in a single breath.

Nobody else was watching the boy now, as the ladies had either returned to their chatter or were watching the Dauphin being led around in his carriage by a groom, while Marie-Thérèse rode her pony with perfect grace. Ernestine gathered several sweet treats into a napkin and looped around the back of the crowd to where the boy was sitting.

'Would you like some more?' She opened the napkin to show him the slices of tart and gateau.

He almost dropped his plate, as he tried to balance it on his bony knees and bow his head at the same time. When he looked up, his bright hazel eyes examined her with interest.

'Thank you, mademoiselle.' He selected a large slice of cake, licking his lips again before taking an enormous bite. In four mouthfuls, the cake had vanished. 'Please excuse my rudeness, would you care for a piece?'

'No thank you, I have eaten my fill.' She wanted to laugh at the incongruity between his nice manners and ragged clothes, but she didn't want to offend him. He fascinated her, this gardener's lad who was nothing like the dull oaf she had expected. She laid the napkin down beside him. 'I haven't seen you here before.'

He eyed the sweet offerings, his fingers hovering tentatively, before selecting a slice of strawberry tart. Between mouthfuls, he said, 'I recently arrived from my parent's farm to help my uncle tend the gardens here. I never expected to meet the Queen.'

'And how did you find her?'

'She is very kind. Honestly, when the groom said who she was, I thought I was about to lose my head.'

He nodded toward the ladies. 'It seems they would like you to return, mademoiselle.'

She turned and saw the under-governess stalking in her direction. 'See that tree stump over there? It is hollow inside. If I can, I will leave some food there whenever I am allowed into the gardens. Seems to me you could do with it.'

'Beats the pig slops I usually get fed. I thank you again. May I know your name, mademoiselle?'

'Ernestine. *Au revoir*, Pierre Duchamp.' She skipped off with a light heart, hoping she might meet him again someday.

A French Legacy

Wellington to Paris, 2019

Sophie was buzzing with excitement as she checked in her small suitcase and boarded the Air New Zealand flight. A long haul to London, followed by a quick hop across the Channel, and she would be in Paris, meeting Luc Duchamp.

To her surprise, her economy-class ticket had been upgraded to first class, presumably by Luc. An odd thing for him to do, but she wasn't about to complain as she stretched out in comfort on the luxury seat after a delicious dinner and two glasses of champagne. A far cry from her last flight in economy class, when she had been crammed up against a sweaty, obese man whose wandering elbow knocked a full can of cola off his table and all over her white shirt.

The few passengers who shared her first-class privileges were mostly quietly elegant, dressed down in the designer equivalent of trackpants. The Hermes scarves, Louis Vuitton handbags and twinkling diamonds of the women, and the Rolex watches and array of gadgets of the men were a giveaway of their true status, along with the nonchalance with which they sipped their champagne. Sophie wondered what they thought of her, as she effusively thanked the flight attendant as each new treat was dished out.

People-watching was always so fascinating. She liked to pass the time during long journeys imagining who these strangers were. The game was more fun in economy class, where the range of options was greater. Here, they all looked like business people or wealthy retired couples, with a couple of uber-fashionistas, who might have been anything from minor celebrities to high-flying entrepreneurs.

The only odd one out, apart from herself, was a man in a rumpled suit whose broad shoulders made the generous first-class seat look inadequate. A long flight in economy would have been a nightmare for him and whoever had to sit next to him. He had swarthy skin, a large nose and heavy stubble, which was probably less designer stubble and more travel weariness, judging from his sagging eyelids. If she was casting him for a movie role, he would be a shoo-in for a Godfather remake, although more likely the mafia lawyer character than the brutal enforcer, despite his muscles. He was probably something completely different in real life, like an opera singer or the CEO of an internet start-up.

When she walked past him to get to the bathroom, she caught a hint of the same Armani cologne as she'd smelled in her house on the night of the burglary. On the way back to her seat, another man passed her in the aisle wearing the same scent, dressed in a matching Armani suit. Must be a common fragrance amongst the well-to-do and burgling classes.

She kept half an eye on them, but neither looked her way, so she went back to re-reading Elisabeth's diary. The dire conditions Elisabeth had faced at sea were enough to ensure Sophie would never complain about air travel again. Even the worst economy class flight was a delight compared to the three-and-a-half-month voyage to New Zealand by sailing ship across the wild Southern Ocean.

Sophie felt uplifted by Elisabeth's spirit and courage. At the start of the voyage, she was weighed down by the death of her husband and the betrayal of her brother-in-law. Elisabeth had tried to stay positive and had written of the friendships she and Anne were developing with their fellow passengers, but there were also many darker hints of the troubles she had faced on board.

The origin of the pearl necklace was made no clearer in the diary than it had been in the letter, but she now understood why Elisabeth considered it a threat to her family's safety. A ruthless man had pursued her for years to get his hands on the necklace, nearly killing her during the voyage.

Sophie drifted off to sleep in the comfort of the first-class seat, with her hand curled protectively around the bag containing her family heirlooms, thankful that such dangers were in the distant past.

She stumbled off the plane after thirty-six hours, having been rerouted and delayed due to adverse weather. After an hour of shuffling like a zombie in an endlessly snaking queue, she was perused, stamped and churned out into the maelstrom of the arrivals hall. She had texted Lucien Duchamp from London, at goodness knows what ungodly hour of the morning, and felt sure that he would have given up waiting long ago. But she was wrong.

She recognised him from his website photo – a slim man, average height, with an aquiline nose and wavy black hair liberally sprinkled with grey. Except that now he wasn't wearing glasses and a shapeless tweed jacket, but a casual white shirt, with rolled-up sleeves, and dark grey trousers, which made him look ten years younger and trendier than the dusty academic in the photo. She had an odd feeling of déjà vu, which must have had more to do with lack of sleep than any actual connection.

He stopped scanning the crowd as soon as he saw her, apparently sure it was her without the benefit of a photo. He jumped to his feet and began striding energetically towards her as if she was a long-lost friend. Before she could collect herself, he swooped in and kissed her on both cheeks. I'm really in France now, she thought.

'Sophie West, I presume? At least, I hope so.' He stepped back to examine her with his unusual hazel eyes. One was slightly greener than the other, or perhaps it was just the harsh airport lighting and her state of exhaustion. With a quick nod, as if to confirm his judgement, he said, '*Bienvenue à Paris.* I am Luc Duchamp.'

'Great to meet you, Luc. How did you know me, out of all these passengers?'

'Would you believe I recognised you from a drawing made almost two hundred years ago by my ancestor, François, in his diary?'

Sophie took a step back and searched his face for signs that he was joking, but she didn't know him well enough to judge whether he was smiling in welcome or in jest. 'Really? That's extraordinary.'

The smile jagged up at the ends into a deep dimple. 'Also, you are travelling alone, have an Air New Zealand luggage tag, ignored the walkway to the taxis and trains, and stopped walking when you saw me heading over.'

'Elementary.'

'Ah, another Sherlock fan. Perhaps I should have mentioned the rare perfume derived from a flower known only from the highest valleys of the New Zealand Alps?'

'If only. I think it rather more likely you noticed a bedraggled traveller who looks like someone who has been on a plane for the last day and a half, but you're too polite to say.' And no doubt smelling less like a rare alpine flower than the inside of a gym bag.

Sophie breathed a sigh of relief that she'd had time during her transit through London to change into a clean, if crumpled, shirt and brush her teeth. Still, she felt like a vagrant compared to the chic Parisian women click-clacking across the concourse in their high heels, clutching designer handbags and trailed by men hauling oversized matching suitcases.

'Not at all.' The dimples deepened. 'Well, maybe a little rumpled. Not surprising after travelling halfway around the earth to meet me.'

'So good of you to pick me up when the flight was delayed. I could have taken the train.'

'After so arduous a journey, I think the RER would not have been a pleasant finale.'

Sophie hoisted her handbag onto her shoulder. She didn't want to create a bad first impression by complaining. 'Actually, the flight wasn't too bad at all, thanks to the first-class upgrade. Do I have you to thank for that?'

'No, much as I'd like to claim credit. You must have got lucky and been upgraded by the airline.' He glanced at her suitcase with a frown. 'Did they lose your luggage?'

'No, this is all of it. I like to travel light.'

'Wonderful. The women in my family never travel without the maximum allowed baggage. We used to go on holiday with a trailer.' He picked up her small, travel-worn case. 'Follow me.'

She had to walk at full speed to keep up with his long stride. 'You have a large family, then?'

'No, only two daughters.'

Sophie formed a picture in her mind of two chic girls, dressed in Chanel suits, elegantly standing next to a pile of Louis Vuitton bags. The exact opposite of her present state. At least she didn't have a can of cola all through her clothes this time.

They emerged into the bright light of a warm, cloudless day. After a long walk through a massive carpark, Luc headed towards an old grey Renault, fishing a key fob out of his pocket. Her aunt would applaud his taste as a sign of a solid, dependable character. But the flashing lights activated by the key belonged to the car beyond the Renault – a sleek red convertible, which would have been perfect for an old movie involving the Riviera, beautiful people, big sunglasses, and a headscarf blowing artfully in the breeze.

She mentally readjusted her preconceptions of her host again. 'Wow. Fabulous way to arrive in Paris.'

'1965 Peugeot Cabriolet.' He loaded her luggage, then opened the door for her. 'I promised to give it a regular run for its owner, a friend who is away on business. Nice to look at, but a nightmare for fuel consumption. I feel a pang of guilt for the planet every time I step on the accelerator. My own vehicle is a bicycle these days.'

The drive into the city was reminiscent of most airport runs – a multi-lane motorway surrounded by commercial buildings and high-rise, low-appeal apartment blocks. Although it was the middle of the day, if her watch was set correctly for the time zone, traffic was heavy. Perhaps everyone was heading out for one of those fabled long, relaxed French lunches. If so, they weren't helping the relaxation vibe with their high-speed driving and constant tooting of horns.

Luc drove with a disconcerting nonchalance, pointing out various landmarks with a wave of his hand, while weaving expertly back and forth across lanes of traffic, all on the wrong side of the road from her Anglo-centric point of view.

'Your English is excellent,' Sophie said. 'I can see I won't get a chance to improve my rusty French.'

'We can speak French if you prefer. I have a French father and an English mother, which meant I went to school and university in both countries.'

'Sounds like the best of both worlds.'

'Have you visited France before, Sophie?'

'Only once, thirty-odd years ago, on my honeymoon. We bought an old van and travelled around Europe for a few weeks, having the time of our lives. We'd been planning to come back for a while, but never quite got around to it.'

He nipped into a tiny gap in the next lane, waving at the honking driver behind them, before calmly resuming the conversation. 'Your husband does not mind you travelling alone?'

'He passed away two years ago. Undiagnosed heart defect.' If they didn't get off this motorway soon, she'd be joining him in the cardiac statistics.

'I'm sorry.'

'He would be happy to see me back here again.' She watched the signs go by, indicating they were circling Paris on a ring-road. 'Which part of the city do you live in, Luc?'

'*Quinzieme arrondissment.* Montparnasse. How well do you know Paris?'

'I remember taking the train at Montparnasse station to Versailles. We walked to the Seine via the gardens of the Luxembourg Palace and streets of Saint-Germain. A beautiful part of the city.'

'Then you would have walked very close to where I live, near Montparnasse cemetery.'

Sophie relaxed into the leather seat as happy memories flooded back. 'My favourite part of our visit to Paris was strolling through the streets, early in the morning, watching the cafés opening and the markets in full swing. Fresh-baked bread and coffee, enough bustle to make it interesting, but before the mass of tourists swamped the streets.'

'I agree. I feel sorry for the visitors who are whisked from the Eiffel Tower to the Louvre to the Moulin Rouge by tour bus all in a single day, without ever seeing the true beauty of our city. It cannot be helped on a short vacation, I suppose.'

'To be honest, I've never understood why a tower made of steel struts is such an attraction when there are so many other wonderful places to visit. Notre-Dame, the Pantheon, Orsay Museum – almost any of the old buildings, in fact.'

He shrugged with every muscle in his upper body, from upturned hands to forehead. 'I've no idea. People want to see whatever everyone else is seeing. I must be getting old – I find it increasingly hard to fathom human behaviour.'

'Like the hundreds of people who cram into the Mona Lisa room at the Louvre, when there are thousands of other masterpieces to be seen with no crush whatsoever. I vividly recall standing in a room surrounded by Grand Masters of stunning beauty, wondering how it was possible that I was entirely alone.'

'*Exactement.* Time to leave the *périph* and see the city.'

Luc navigated the car through a bewildering spaghetti junction of roads and overpasses, before popping out on a wide avenue lined with buildings that were quintessentially Parisian. The street was lined with trees, bursting with fresh foliage, adding another layer of beauty to the scene. 'I thought you might like to enter Paris the traditional way, along the route of conquerors.'

A bubble of euphoria rose within her at simply being here, in Paris.

The graceful arch of the Arc de Triomphe stood out above the constant river of vehicles racing towards it. Luc circled it twice, within a herd of stampeding cars zigzagging across the width of the road, before they escaped from the melee and headed down the Champs-Élysées. Terrifying and exhilarating, in equal measure.

The sight of boarded-over shop windows and a fire-damaged restaurant brought her back to reality with a thump.

Luc caught the direction of her gaze. 'A large protest turned violent recently. Rioting, looting, vandalism – as you can see.'

'I remember seeing it on the news. Wasn't it part of the Yellow Vest protests? You'll have to remind me what it was about.'

'Fuel prices, the cost of living, high taxes – the usual suspects. As in most other countries, people are frustrated that the rich keep getting richer, while workers struggle to put food on the table.'

'I know what you mean. It's the same in New Zealand, although without the riots, so far. Must be unsettling for Parisians.'

'No need to worry. The demonstrations are organised and easy to avoid.' He flashed a dimpled smile. 'It's not as bad as the 1789 revolution yet.'

They turned off near the end of the boulevard, heading across the Seine and into the maze of streets beyond. Sophie had lost all sense of direction by the time they pulled into a parking compound on a quiet street, lined with elegant old apartment buildings, which appeared to be a mix of residential and office space.

Luc took her luggage. 'I know you must be feeling exhausted, but it's still too early to check into the hotel. You can relax in my office, or we can have some lunch if you feel like it.' He stopped in front of a tall wooden door in a five-storey building of cream stone. The upper storey windows had classic narrow balconies, held up by scrolls of stone, guarded by elegant wrought-iron railings and decorated with pots of flowers. The epitome of Parisian architectural style.

Sophie expected to step into a cosy antique shop crammed with period pieces. The bright, modern, tall-ceilinged space came as a complete surprise. A workbench ran down one side of the room, while the far corner was filled with a vast desk stacked high with papers and computer equipment. The rest of the room was set out as a sitting area, with sofas arranged around a set of tables and shelves, subtly displaying a variety of *objets d'art*. The colour scheme was a restful neutral, accented with natural furnishings, from cushions of mossy-green linen to a soft rug the colour of river stones. An artful mix of functional and beautiful, reeking subtly of class.

'This is gorgeous. Your interior designer must be in high demand.'

'Yes, she is. I'm very proud of my youngest daughter. She has a real gift for design.' He gestured at the overflowing desk, with books stacked in lopsided piles beside it. 'That's what it would look like if it was left to me.'

She gazed around the light-filled space. 'I guess I expected to see Louis XIV chairs and ornate desks.'

'I probably would have gone that way, but my daughter persuaded me the biggest impact comes from a few exquisite objects from the past displayed in a contrasting environment. There's some psycho-babble name for it, but it seems to work.'

Sophie admired an excessively ornate, gilded clock. Not something she'd want on her own mantelpiece, but obviously old and valuable. And yes, it did appear to greater advantage for not being crammed in amongst other items. 'I'm not quite clear on exactly what it is you do, Luc.'

'If you want a formal title, I go by "Acquisitions Consultant". My clients want exceptional pieces from the revolutionary and restoration periods. They pay me to find what they want and ensure that the provenance is properly established.' He handed her a tall crystal glass of water. 'You must be thirsty.'

'Now you mention it.' Sophie gulped down half of it in one go. 'Private collectors or museums?'

'Most of the money these days is in private hands, but I prefer to work with museums. You would be amazed at how much Asian and American collectors are willing to pay for a porcelain chamber pot that once hosted a royal bottom, let alone a diamond that once graced a crown.'

'When it comes to the tastes of the rich and famous, nothing surprises me anymore.' She sat down on one of the sofas, which were surprisingly comfortable for such a modern design, and stretched out her stiff limbs. 'Why would anyone pay millions of dollars for a painting of a white stripe on a blue background? Or a drawing of a Coke bottle? At least the chamber pot has history.'

'Quite an interesting history, in fact.' He settled down in the armchair opposite her and raised his glass. 'The Palace of Versailles had flushing toilets far earlier than you might imagine, although only for the royals. Yet, it was not uncommon for people of all levels to squat in a corner of the corridor to relieve themselves or empty the chamber pots out the nearest window. Diarists often mention the dreadful smell of the place. People didn't believe in bathing much back in those days, either. Marie Antoinette was considered very odd for wanting regular baths.'

'How extraordinary that a royal palace didn't have better hygiene.' Her own sense of smell was unusually sharp, something of a curse as well as a blessing. The thought of unwashed bodies and corridors used as latrines was gross in the extreme. Time to change the subject. 'It must be hard to see French heritage sold off to overseas buyers.'

'One advantage of age and experience is that I can choose my clients. I much prefer to see important items remain in France, so I work almost exclusively with our local museums and collectors, even if it is less lucrative.'

'I look forward to learning more about your work. New Zealand has only a short history of European settlement. In fact, our ancestor, Elisabeth, arrived in 1841 on one of the first immigrant ships from Britain.'

'I can't imagine living in such a young country.' He sipped the water in silence for a moment, probably trying to image a place without thousand-year-old cathedrals and twenty-thousand-year-old cave paintings. 'Before you contacted me, I knew almost nothing about New Zealand, apart from your country's enthusiasm for rugby and my lingering shame at the French government having blown up a ship in one of your harbours.'

'Not one of France's finest moments, I agree, but I promise not to hold it against you.'

'I haven't even asked what you do, Sophie. I keep having this odd sensation that we are old friends, when actually I know nothing about you.'

'I suppose because we have a distant ancestor in common, we have skipped all the normal introductions.' It really was odd. Here she was, sitting with a total stranger in a foreign land, yet feeling as if she was chatting to someone she knew. Must be some weird side-effect of jetlag.

She suddenly recalled that he had asked a question. 'My career was about as far from this as possible. We had a small environmental monitoring business, mainly testing water quality. I sold it to some of the staff recently, so I'm free to do as I please.'

'So, how's the water?' he asked, holding up his glass.

She closed her eyes and swirled the glass under her nose before taking another taste. 'Not bad. A fair amount of mineral loading, so probably at least partly from underground sources, but a good balance, similar to bottled mineral water. No nasty odour or aftertaste, unlike many cities. Very palatable.'

'You can tell all this without chemical testing?'

'The scientific results are the critical thing for clients, but it does help to be able to sniff out any potential issues quickly.' Sophie shrugged. 'Some people are gifted with great talents, like perfect pitch or leadership skills. I got landed with a decent sense of smell and taste. Not always a positive thing, believe me.'

'Do you also have a nose for wine?'

'Sadly, no. Winemaking is such a speciality, they have their own experts. I have done a bit with dairy though. One of our local organic producers wasn't happy with the taste of their cheese and they thought it might be because of polluted water. Turned out the cows were grazing on a bitter weed through the fence. We got quite a few clients through that. When I go home, I'd like to concentrate on that side of it, working with organic dairy farmers on specialist products.'

'Fascinating. I hope you will enjoy tasting our French cheeses, which are some of the best in the world, if you have time. Which reminds me, I have not asked how long you are you able to spend here.'

'I think I mentioned I was planning to travel anyway, to see where some of my ancestors came from. With no job and my two children independent, I can stay as long as I like. But I won't trespass on your time for more than a day or two, I expect. As I said by email, I know very little of my ancestor Elisabeth's life before she came to New Zealand, so I'm keen to hear what you know.'

'As I am eager to talk about her.' Luc leaned forward as if he was about to launch into a story, then pulled himself back from the brink. 'My apologies. You've just arrived after an extremely long flight and already I'm interrogating you. Perhaps you'd like a chance to freshen up? I have an apartment upstairs if you would like to have a wash or shower.'

'If you wouldn't mind the intrusion, I would give my right arm to have a shower, preferably followed by a strong coffee to keep me awake. It's the middle of the night according to my body clock.'

Sophie followed Luc up the stairs to his apartment, which was exactly what she would have imagined had she not seen the office first. It could easily have been used as a set for a period drama, although it was also warm, unlike many old houses, and blessed with modern plumbing.

Scrubbed up and dressed in a light merino sweater, clean trousers and comfy boots, she felt almost human again. As she left, she couldn't resist a quick peek at the photos lined up along one shelf of a tall bookcase. Most of them were of the same two girls, ranging in age from cute toddlers through to young women who might be in their late twenties or early thirties. They were slim and smiling, clutching bikes, tennis racquets, hiking packs or surfboards, with not a single Chanel suit in evidence. The absence of a woman's touch around the apartment and the lack of a mother in the photos suggested Luc was probably separated.

When she entered the office again, Luc was tapping away at his keyboard with the speed of a touch-typist. 'Thanks, Luc, I really needed that.'

'Why don't you take a seat, and I'll make some coffee.' He gestured towards the sofa.

She watched as he worked a coffeemaker with almost as many dials and levers as an aircraft cockpit.

88

The satisfying sounds of gurgling and steam jets, combined with the heady smell of freshly ground beans, left her feeling desperate for a shot of caffeine.

He handed her an espresso cup of coffee so thick it barely sloshed when she took it. 'I forgot to ask whether you would prefer an American coffee. I can get milk from upstairs.'

'Definitely not. This is exactly what I need after the stewed tar the airlines pass off as coffee. I'm more of an addict than I realised.' The fumes alone were enough to perk her up, while the liquid had the kick of a pacemaker, just as she liked it. 'So, now that my brain is functioning again, I have some things to show you. Or do you have other work to do?'

'I'd love to see what you have. I've hardly slept with the anticipation of finally finding out about Elisabeth. She's the missing piece in a puzzle I've wanted to solve my whole life.' He threw back his shot of coffee. 'When I got your email, I thought one of my friends might be playing a cruel joke. But here you are.' He shook his head as if he still couldn't quite believe it.

'I left my bag upstairs. Back in a minute.' The jewellery box was inside a padded packing cell. Not much of a hiding place, but at least not obvious to anyone glancing through her bag. The customs man had asked to see it, but seemed satisfied in the brusque, passive-aggressive manner they have, which might mean anything from 'you're free to go' to 'show me the drugs or I'll be forced to use the latex gloves.'

She saw no reason not to show Luc the smaller pieces of jewellery, the portrait and other items, but a heightened sense of caution told her to withhold the jewellery box until she was sure of his motives. Besides, the large empty compartment would alert him to the fact that a necklace was missing, and she was reluctant to tell anyone about the exquisite pearl necklace yet.

Sophie removed the items from the jewellery box, each individually wrapped in tissue paper, and slipped them into the velvet bag that had held the coins. The portrait of Elisabeth's mother and diary were wrapped separately in her handbag, which had been super-glued to her side ever since she stepped out of her cottage in Wellington.

As she descended the stairs, she felt butterflies and caterpillars inside – a fluttering of excitement, edged with a gnawing worry that the items were nothing more than common trinkets or, worse, cheap fakes.

Luc had white cotton gloves on, which struck her as amusingly formal, as if he was about to attend an old-time dance, until she realised he was about to handle something that might be wanted by a museum. He put on his glasses and took the velvet bag over to a high bench, which was set out with lights, magnifying lenses, tweezers and soft brushes. She watched nervously as he took out the items, unwrapping each one in utter silence, before placing it on a black velvet cloth.

He picked up the cameo brooch first, examining it minutely under the magnifying lens, looking every bit the professor from his website photo. 'Hmm,' he muttered, after an agonising length of time.

Sophie leaned closer to catch his words, but he put down the cameo and studied the other pieces with the same impressive, but infuriatingly, silent attention to detail. It wasn't until he picked up the little carved owl that he smiled. By now, she was convinced that she had nothing more than a pile of junk on her hands. Oh well, she could still have a lovely holiday and the pleasure of gaining a very distant relative.

'*Un moment, s'il vous plait.*' He vanished up the stairs, so distracted that he was oblivious he had reverted to French.

He returned with a simple wooden box, which he opened to reveal a set of beautifully carved birds, including a spindly legged egret-like bird, a couple of birds of prey with soaring wings, and a tiny robin with a tilted head and a faint smudge of red on its breast. The robins at home were a different species, but she instantly recognised the inquisitive perkiness, which the carver had captured so perfectly in miniature.

An irresistible grin tugged at the corners of her mouth as she looked up to see Luc grinning back. 'The carver had a real gift.'

'Elisabeth's father, Pierre Duchamp, made these for her and François. It looks as if she must have taken her favourite one with her to remind her of her father.'

'Thank you, Luc. I can't tell you how wonderful it feels to see these.' Words could not express the emotion she felt at seeing so tangible a link between them and their past, but she felt sure Luc understood. She held the owl for a moment longer, then placed it in the box. 'Now you have a complete set.'

He looked from the box to her. 'Are you sure?'

'They belong together.'

He was silent for a moment as he took another look at the collection, touching the owl gently with the tip of a finger, before closing the lid. 'You have not asked about the jewellery. Most people would have asked about the valuable items first.'

'You can buy jewellery anywhere, but the birds are unique to our family and thus priceless. Besides, I could tell from your lack of enthusiasm that the pieces were not of interest.'

He looked over the top of his glasses at her, just as her science teacher used to when he was disappointed with her answer. 'Quite the opposite. They are exquisite items deserving of my full concentration.

There can be little doubt that Elisabeth's family was connected to wealth. Come and see.'

As they leaned over the bench together, Sophie listened with fascination as Luc told her how he was able to date these items to eighteenth-century France, describing the specific type and quality of the cameo and the perfection of the tiny diamonds on the hair ornaments.

The gold wedding band was the most ordinary of the pieces, but precious nevertheless, as Luc was able to make out the letters JG and ED on its worn surface under the magnifying lens. John Godwin and Elisabeth Duchamp, her great-great-great-great-great-grandparents.

'The cameo is undoubtedly worthy of further study.' Luc picked up the brooch again, showing her the detail of the carved heads under the magnifying glass. 'I'm sure I've seen one like it before, but I can't quite place it.'

'I'm afraid I know very little about jewellery, although I can see it is beautifully made.' Despite her excitement, Sophie had to stifle a yawn. 'Sorry, the long flight is catching up with me. I'm finding this utterly fascinating and I'm dying to hear everything you know about Elisabeth and François, but right now my brain feels like mush.'

'Perhaps the hotel will let you check in early? Or would you like lunch first? I know what it's like on planes – you get fed breakfast when your stomach is ready for dinner–'

'–and lunch appears in the middle of the night, just as you want to fall asleep. At least the food was worth waking up for in first-class.' She considered the options. 'I think I might skip lunch and try to reset my biological clock by having dinner and an early night. I should probably get some sunlight and exercise too.'

'Why don't you relax on the sofa while I do some research on the cameo. Then we can walk.'

The next thing Sophie knew, she was woken by an 'a-ha' from behind the pile of books on Luc's desk. She sat up, trying to shake off the awful, semi-drugged feeling brought on by an afternoon nap. Until she remembered, with a burst of euphoria, that she was in the City of Light and on the cusp of an unexpected adventure.

She ran a hand through her hair, straightened her rumpled clothes, folded the cashmere throw that he had draped over her, and got herself another glass of water. Only when she felt vaguely human again did she go over to his desk to see what he had found.

'Sorry if I woke you. Have a look at this.'

The picture he had open on his computer screen had more impact than a glass of iced water in the face. The cameo in the picture was definitely of a similar style to the one she had found in Elisabeth's box, except that it was a necklace, not a brooch. But it wasn't the cameo that had her pulse zinging. Her eyes were drawn to the young woman with a sad expression who was wearing it.

Luc must have noted her amazement, because he rocked back on his chair, flashing his dimples as if he'd won a prize. 'Look familiar?'

'The cameo, yes. But that's not the half of it.' She dug into her handbag for the portrait, unwrapping it carefully and holding it out for him to see. 'I haven't had a chance yet to show you the portrait of Elisabeth's mother as a child.'

Luc whistled as he looked from one picture to the other and then at Sophie's face. By no means identical, but certainly a broad resemblance, especially between the two girls. 'Wavy blonde hair and expressive eyes must be dominant genes for women in the family tree.'

'Don't keep me in suspense. Who is this woman?'

'Marie-Thérèse of France, Madame Royale, daughter of Louis XVI and Marie Antoinette.'

Storm Clouds Gather

Versailles, 4 May 1789

'Please be still, Madame Royale.'

Ernestine winced in sympathy as the laces of Marie-Thérèse's undergarments were cinched in.

'I cannot breathe,' the girl wheezed, but she stood as still as a mannequin, as layer after layer was added to the ensemble, the last being an elaborate gown of heavily embroidered silk.

The gown was nearly impossible to move in, except by gliding slowly across the parquet floors like a trussed swan crossing a lake. A curtain of jewels completed the ensemble, the combined weight threatening to bow down the proud head of the royal daughter.

But comfort was not the aim. Today, the royal family – King Louis XVI, Queen Marie Antoinette and their daughter Marie-Thérèse – must be nothing short of resplendent, to demonstrate to all echelons of society their God-given right to rule the people of France. History was about to be made on the grandest of scales.

Today, a grand procession through the streets of Versailles. Tomorrow, the *États-Généraux* would convene for the first time in nearly two hundred years. Thousands of people had flocked to Versailles for this momentous occasion, when over a thousand deputies, including members representing the common people, would meet to shape the future of the nation.

'Ouch! Be careful, or you will have my eye out.'

The attendant blanched and hastily repositioned the sharp end of a diamond-encrusted hairpin.

Ernestine hid a grin behind a delicate handkerchief as her adoptive sister pouted. 'You look truly magnificent, Marie-Thérèse.'

Marie-Thérèse rolled her eyes, then blew a kiss to Ernestine before gliding out of the room with her retinue.

Ernestine watched as the royal party came together, shimmering in a constellation of precious stones, cheered by every member of the royal household and hundreds of others besides.

Versailles had been swamped with visitors for days, peering into every room, demanding to know where Marie Antoinette was hiding the rumoured pillars of diamonds and walls studded with rubies. Honestly, people seemed to believe anything they were told, no matter how ridiculous. The entire household had been driven to distraction by their leering and prodding.

The Queen's natural joie de vivre had gradually seeped away under the strain. Today, all the sparkling jewels in the world could not disguise the weary resignation in her pale face, as she leaned for support on her dear friend, the Duchesse de Polignac.

Ernestine hastened across the courtyard with a small group of attendants, so as not to miss a moment of the spectacle. They would have a prime viewpoint from the Lesser Stables, overlooking the great gates of the Palace of Versailles. This spot had been specially selected by the King himself for the Dauphin, who had been allowed to leave his sickbed for the day.

A massive crowd had already gathered outside the gates, waiting under fluttering banners for this once in a lifetime event. With the help of a circle of guards, their small group forged a way through the masses, across the wedge of open space that formed the Place d'Armes.

The Dauphin was already seated by a window, his emaciated body almost invisible amongst the pillows and rugs. 'Ernestine, at last. Are they coming?'

'Soon, Monseigneur.' She spoke gently, carefully concealing her shock at how far his condition had deteriorated since she had last seen him. Louis-Joseph, the heir to the throne, was only seven years old and surely not long for this world. It would be another bitter blow to the King and Queen, having lost their infant daughter two years ago.

The Dauphin's valet came to his side. 'Monseigneur, I see the royal party crossing the courtyard.'

The crowd must have seen it too. A roar rose from the street. Some were cheering, but others were chanting, '*Vivant Orléans! Vivant Orléans!*'

Ernestine could only hope that the royal family would be better received at the churches of Notre Dame and Saint-Louis. She tried to dismiss her fears. It was not her place to doubt or ask questions. Her destiny was to serve the royal family, come what may, in return for all they had done for her since her mother's death a year ago. And right now, the young Dauphin was in need of good cheer, not politics.

'Look, Louis-Joseph, here they come.'

The Dauphin tried to sit upright in his chair so his parents would be proud of him. She tucked another pillow behind his hunched back and pushed the chair a little closer to the window, being careful not to cause his withered legs any further pain.

Ernestine stood to the side, while Louis-Joseph leaned forward to see the approaching carriage. 'Why does the crowd chant for the Duc d'Orléans, instead of cheering their sovereigns?'

She had no wish to talk of the King's cousin, the Duc d'Orléans, whose devious schemes had garnered him the support of the people at the expense of the King. 'The duke has chosen not to walk with the Princes of the Blood. Perhaps the people are cheering his support for their cause. I'm sure when they see the King, they will be awestruck.'

'How do my parents look, Ernestine?'

She moved around to his side to distract him from the sounds outside. 'I have never seen the King and Queen look so magnificent,' she said, flinging her arms out with a dramatic flourish, then covering her eyes with both hands. 'Dear sir, I do believe I was blinded when the light caught their glittering diamonds.'

He giggled at her antics. 'Tell me, Ernestine, is my father dressed in gold?'

'Glorious, shimmering gold, wearing a crown with the largest diamond I have ever seen.'

'The Regent Diamond?'

'I believe you are right. His whole costume is strewn with lesser diamonds, from his magnificent sword to his buttons and buckles. I cannot imagine there has ever been another king so majestic.'

The boy smiled and pulled his twisted back straighter. 'And my mother? Does she look beautiful?'

'As beautiful and regal as any queen who ever lived. She is dressed in violet and white, embroidered with silver, covered in diamonds, sparkling like a fairy queen, with a gorgeous yellow diamond in her hair. Look, they are waving to you.'

'I cannot see them very well.' The young prince struggled to rise from the chair but slumped back again. 'I wanted to throw those roses, so my mother would know how well she is loved.'

The sadness in his eyes pricked her heart. 'Shall I throw them for you?'

'It's too late, they have passed.' The Dauphin's cry turned into a cough, sending a spasm through his twisted body.

A glance out the window showed her that he was right. The royal party was already several yards away, followed by a procession of nobility and clergy. The boy coughed again – a hacking cough that seemed to tear through his chest – making her want to weep for his pain.

'Monseigneur, the air is not good for you here.' The Dauphin's valet adjusted the rug across the boy's knees with gentle hands. 'Shall we return to the palace? The chefs have made your favourite cakes for you.'

Louis-Joseph threw the rug off. 'I do not want cake! I want to be part of the parade. Why must I be so unwell? It's not fair.'

His pain was more than Ernestine could bear. 'Please, don't be upset. If I hurry, I could give the flowers to your mother.' Seeing his hopeful smile, she swung her old cloak around her shoulders, grabbed the roses, and ran for the stairs.

The valet dashed after her to the top of the stairs. 'Wait, stop, Mademoiselle Ernestine, you must not go outside alone. It is not safe.'

Ernestine hesitated, but her desire to please the sick boy overcame caution. 'I'll only be a minute or two.'

Outside, the noise and commotion engulfed her. What had seemed like a bustling, cheering crowd from the safety of the window became a seething mass of jeering, jostling, noxious-smelling bodies, towering over her slight figure. To her horror, she realised many of the people around her were chanting foul slogans against the Queen, the exact meaning of which she did not care to fathom.

She tried to move closer to the buildings to avoid the crush but found herself being swept up into the crowd. An elbow hit her nose, a boot stomped on her foot, a reeling drunk lurched backwards and knocked her to the ground. The roses lay scattered, already trampled by muddy feet. Her idea of pleasing Louis-Joseph seemed foolhardy now, as she struggled to rise amidst a forest of ragged trousers and patched skirts.

Once she had forced her way to her feet again, she was still only chest height to the crowd around her, unable to see where she had come from or where she might escape to. She pressed herself into a shallow niche in a brick façade, trying not to let panic overwhelm sense. A drop of blood from her nose dripped onto the pale blue silk of her new dress. Would the Queen be cross with her for spoiling it?

She tried to press her nose with a handkerchief to staunch the flow, but her hand was knocked away by a lump of a man pushing past her, not even noticing her in his excitement.

'The King drinks, the Queen eats, the people cry out,' he yelled, waving his fist at the procession of nobles.

'But not for much longer, my friend,' the man beside him said, slapping his friend on the back and pushing him into Ernestine again.

She tried to push her way through the crowd, but a gnarled hand tugged at her cloak. 'Wassa matter, girl, you lost?'

Another set of grubby fingers plucked at the white sash around her waist. 'Right nice piece of fancy silk.

Hey, Louise, reckon she must be one of them aristo's spawn.'

A third woman crowded her, thrusting close with a dumpling face, pockmarked with disease. 'Well, well. A stray from some rich man's drawing room, I've no doubt. Look, her hands are as soft as a baby's bum.'

'Damn fine bauble on her finger.'

'A silver necklace too. Hey, girl, how about giving it to me, so I can feed my children?'

The hands were coming at her from all directions, poking her flesh and pulling at her jewellery and clothes. She tried to push through them, but dumpling-face slapped her back against the wall. Fear turned to rage as the woman grabbed her silver cross, the only keepsake she had of her mother.

Ernestine latched onto her hand, prising her fingers off the necklace, kicking out with her foot into the tangle of legs, using the leverage of the wall at her back. The woman swore like a trooper as her kick connected with a knee. She dropped the necklace but came back an instant later with a screech and a vicious jab. Ernestine ducked the fist, darting under their arms and cannon balling past their broad hips into the mass of people beyond.

Unfortunately, the crowd had turned towards the scuffle, evidently deciding that the fighting women might provide more amusement than the parade. A man grabbed her arm. Ernestine jerked her arm sharply downward, releasing his grip, but instantly another hand grabbed her, pushing her back to the group of women, while others spurred the women on with drunken chants.

Yet another arm grabbed at her and pulled her backward. Her new assailant pushed her against the wall. With a flash of hope, she recognised him, just as he swung around to face the crowd, fists raised, his back protecting her.

'Leave her alone or you'll be sorry you were born.'

The women started to back off, then realised that the angry voice belonged to a scrawny young lad, who was barely more than a boy. 'Be off, runt. We saw her first.'

The people nearest the edge of the parade suddenly started cheering and chanting, '*Orléans, Orléans.*'

The men watching the scuffle turned to join the excitement of seeing the self-styled hero of the people, the Duc d'Orléans, leaving the two of them against the three women. Something in the lad's stance must have warned them he was not making idle threats. Or perhaps they too wanted to join the fervour of the crowd.

'Come on, ladies, let's leave the whelp to his bitch. Plenty of easier pickings today.'

The lad wasted no time in grabbing her arm again and hustling her up the street to a quieter spot. 'Mademoiselle Ernestine, what are you doing out here? You might have been hurt.'

'Pierre, thank heaven you're here. I've never been so scared in my life.'

Her knees felt so weak, she found it hard to stand. His arm shot out and caught her own, averting her collapse. He tucked her arm through his and set off again. 'Let's get away from here. Where shall I take you?'

Ernestine looked around but she could not recognise the building she had come from. 'Can you take me back to the palace? Better yet, the gardens, so I can collect myself somewhere quiet.'

Pierre Duchamp took a firmer hold on her arm and pushed a path for her through the throng. The crowd was cheering loudly now, as the black-clad mass of the ordinary delegates marched past, carrying with them a promise that the people's voice would be heard for the first time.

Soon, the crowd was behind them, and the tight band constricting her chest faded away. They slipped unnoticed into the gardens of Versailles, heading for their favourite spot in the beautiful semi-wilderness of the Queen's gardens at the Petit Trianon. Ernestine stopped now and then to listen for the steps of guards who patrolled the gardens, who would be sure to march her back to the palace.

A month into spring it might be, but still with a bite to the air. Ernestine pulled her mother's old woollen cloak around her shoulders, thankful for its dull mossy colour, which blended into the surrounding greenery.

She wasn't sure what impulse had made her take the old cloak with her today, instead of the expensive blue velvet one she normally wore. Perhaps she wanted her mother to be present at such a grand moment. Then again, if her mother was still alive, Ernestine might not have been present herself, certainly not in the presence of the Dauphin. How different her life would have been. The woman who attacked her would have paid her no heed if she had been dressed as a servant.

Pierre dipped her handkerchief into a fountain and wiped the blood from her face. 'You're very quiet, Ernestine. Are you feeling faint? I could take you to the palace instead.'

'No. I want to be here in the gardens with you, for a while at least, although I should not linger too long in case I am missed. I'm going to be in a great deal of trouble for leaving my attendants.'

'Please don't look so unhappy. I'm used to seeing you smiling.'

'I was thinking of my mother and how much has changed in the year since she passed away.'

'I'm sorry. I hadn't realised. Was she much like you?'

'Similar in looks, but sweeter in character. She died a few weeks before I met you.'

She pictured her mother in her mind. The blonde curls and blue eyes were easy to recall, as Ernestine saw them every time she looked in a mirror. As time passed, she found it increasingly difficult to remember the exact details of the rest of her face, as if she could only access flashes of memory, rather than a complete picture. The tilt of her mother's head when she listened to her daughter's chatter or the crystal tinkle of her laugh, but not the precise shape of her nose and chin.

They entered a mossy dell, where a jumble of sun-warmed rocks and a ring of trees provided a private nook. The two of them had met here in secret before, on the rare occasions they could dodge their other obligations. Ernestine settled down on her favourite curved-top boulder, her panic retreating under the soothing gurgle of a nearby stream, the rich aroma of the earth and the warmth of the sun on the rock. A swallow flitted over their heads, heedless of their presence.

Exquisite silence, ruffled only by a soughing of the breeze through the branches, was a rare treat. Always, always, always, there were women who attended to their every need and guarded the children against their own wilful desire to run free in the gardens. An armada of under-governesses, dressers, hair stylists, maids, and servers, amidst the swell of tutors, guards, porters, ushers, and dozens of other functionaries, who tended to everything from lighting the candles in the chandeliers, to cleaning the silver, to emptying the chamber pots. Not to mention the endless stream of gawping courtiers and commoners, who watched their every move, as if the Children of France were actors in a play put on for the benefit of all-comers.

Not like Pierre. He was always so easy to be with, always knowing when to speak and when to give her the gift of silence. As usual, he had taken up a piece of wood and was busy stripping off the bark with his knife, his mop of black hair falling forward over his face. She had never seen him without something in his hands, be it wood, a spade or reins. The thought brought a smile back to her face.

As if he had sensed her change in mood, his head flicked up, revealing warm hazel eyes and a dimpled grin. 'What?'

'Just thinking about the first time we met. Only a year ago, but everything seems to have changed since then.'

'For me as well.'

Ernestine studied her friend, seeing him afresh. 'You're a lot taller now and not quite so thin and ragged. Even so, you charmed the Queen that day.'

'I was terrified.'

'How could you be terrified by a party of ladies and children, yet so brave today when faced with those truly scary women? I have never been so grateful to see a friend in all my life.'

'You're teasing me, Ernestine. Can you really doubt that I was frightened out of my wits? A simple country boy, dressed in rags, facing the most powerful woman in France?'

'But we were nice to you, were we not, Pierre?'

'I was amazed by it. The Queen was so gentle and kind, not at all what I expected.'

'She loves to see her children enjoying themselves outside, especially the Dauphin. Although your appearance did cause a few fans to flutter.'

The memory of the outraged expressions on the faces of the ladies-in-waiting brought a smile to her lips. There had been heated discussions afterward about suitable choices for so close an interaction with the Children of France, but the Queen cared not for

110

protocol in the face of her children's happiness. She simply ordered that the boy be made presentable when he was in their presence, and that was that.

'I don't doubt it. The head stableman laid into the groom pretty fiercely afterward for allowing me to appear before Her Majesty in ragged clothes. I remember hiding in the loft, terrified I was going to be whipped or sent away. Then, the next day, I was given a uniform and told to have a bath. I couldn't believe it.'

The next time he had appeared with the ponies, Pierre's scraggly hair was neatly tied back with a black ribbon, and he was wearing the dark blue and red livery worn by the grooms, along with breeches and a waistcoat. For all his sheepish expression, Ernestine thought he held himself a little taller and looked rather dashing in the uniform.

'You looked so smart, none of us recognised you at first.'

Uniform or not, Ernestine had liked Pierre from the moment they met. After that day, they always chatted in a low tone while he led her around on a pony, as long as they were out of sight of the ladies' disapproving eyes.

They both knew it was a completely improper friendship that could never last, but Ernestine was unwilling to give up a friend who did not look down on her, while Pierre seemed equally glad to find someone who treated him kindly. The head gardener was a hard taskmaster, and she gained the strong impression that his Uncle Remy was even worse, especially when he drank too much wine. More than once, she had noticed a black eye or limp, although less often now that Pierre was growing bigger and stronger.

His knife flicked and nipped at the wood, seemingly of its own accord, sending curls of oak in all directions. She wondered if his craft gave him a reason to keep his head down, especially when forced to talk about himself.

'I still feel sick inside every time I come before the Queen. Although I look forward to seeing you, of course.' He glanced up again, shaking black hair out of his eyes as he studied her. 'I've never been quite sure of your place, Ernestine, but thought it would be rude to ask.'

'As you just saved my dignity, if not my life, please ask whatever you want.'

'I just want to understand where you fit in. The Queen seems to treat you like her child, but, well, you're not, are you? Many of the ladies ignore you when the Queen's back is turned.'

'Ah, that's a long story.'

'Can you make it short? Uncle Remy will have me shovelling dung for a week if I don't finish digging the carrot beds this afternoon.' He glanced up at the sun, which was dropping below its zenith. 'Afternoon already. No wonder I'm so hungry.'

'Pierre, you're always hungry. Do all boys have bottomless pits for stomachs?' As soon as she said it, she felt mean for teasing him when he was so poorly fed. 'I'm sorry I didn't bring any pastries with me today.'

'Tell me your story and I'll forgive you. Better yet, bring twice as many pastries next time, or one of those delicious game pies.'

Ernestine wriggled into a more comfortable position and began her fairy tale. 'Once upon a time there was a little girl named Marie-Philippine de Lambriquet. She was no one of consequence, merely the daughter of servants, but for some reason she was chosen as a playmate for the royal daughter, Madame Royale, whom she was allowed to call by her given name, Marie-Thérèse.'

'Marie-Philippine? Is that your real name?'

'Hush, Pierre, do you want to hear my story or not? The Queen changed my name to Ernestine, after a character in a novel.'

'Your parents did not object?'

'They were happy that I was given the opportunity to better myself. Anyway, when my mother died, I was adopted by the King and Queen. They have been the soul of kindness to me ever since, treating me as one of their own in most ways, almost as a true sister to Madame Royale.'

Pierre gaped at her like a stranded fish, his hands still for the first time since they had sat down. 'The Queen adopted the child of servants?'

Ernestine nodded. She was not surprised by his reaction. Everyone else at Court had thought it a bizarre notion that the Queen of France would wish a mere servant girl to be treated as a favoured playmate to her daughter.

'I've heard she wanted to teach her daughter humility, though plenty of people thought it a ridiculous idea for a royal child. They have been as kind to me as true parents, but you're right that others are not so kind.' She could not fail to notice that servants and courtiers alike watched her with a mix of expressions, depending on their own natures, from kindly acceptance to disdain and nasty whispers. 'I'm very lucky. The gifts they lavish on me would amaze you – satin dresses, soft gloves, white plumes and jewels for my hair, even a pianoforte and furniture of my own. Sometimes I think it is all a dream.'

Pierre was still looking stunned. 'You are no relation to them at all? I thought you must be a cousin at the very least. How odd that you and Madame Royale look so much alike.'

'Perhaps that is why I was chosen as a playmate. The Queen takes pleasure in dressing us in the same clothes. You should have seen the whispering and finger-pointing when we attended the theatre together. We amuse ourselves by tricking the newer servants into believing that I am Marie-Thérèse, and she is me.'

'Honestly, Ernestine, it really is like a fairy tale.'

'Well, it's not all pleasurable. It is lovely to have a sister to play with, but there are plenty of times when she'll ignore me for hours at a time or order me around like a servant, whereas I cannot so much as raise my voice to her. She makes me do her schoolwork too, but I don't mind that. I love to learn things. And you would not believe the hours we waste following the rituals of palace etiquette. Getting up, dressing, eating, daily Mass, retiring at night – each and every one at a set time, in a certain way, attended by particular women. And constant changes of clothes, ceremonies, visiting dignitaries, being paraded around like a rare type of exotic creature. Many days, we are too exhausted to play even if we had the time.'

Pierre laughed. 'How tiresome for you, my lady. And to think all I do all day is get up at five in the morning and work for the next twelve hours, shovelling dung, digging the gardens, and tending the animals, all for a couple of bowls of gruel and a few coins.'

Ernestine reached over and punched him gently on the arm. 'All right, I take your point. I'm well aware my life would be the envy of any normal person. I do love having time in the libraries and gardens. Sometimes, the King will let us look through his telescope or at his maps. He is very learned.'

She loved the King dearly. His detractors sneered at his short-sightedness and lack of social graces, but Ernestine knew him as a kind and thoughtful father-figure, who bestowed upon his children the rare gifts of affection and attention, which to them were more precious than material gifts. Most surprising of all, the King included her in his benevolence, perhaps because she was the only one in the household who never tired of his passions for geography and science.

'I envy you, Ernestine. I wish I could look through a telescope and learn about the world.'

'The King showed us once how the water system works. You would love that. The water comes from the Seine and flows uphill to Versailles, to sustain all the fountains and canals.' She was the one who had stayed by his side when he explained the intricate workings of the system, while the other children soon tired of mechanics and raced off to watch the extravagant displays of water being ejected high into the air from the mouths of all nature of men and beasts, from Roman gods to fierce dragons.

But that was all in the past. Now, the King was always busy with the demands of the state.

'You've gone quiet again, Ernestine.'

'Everyone is too busy for picnics in the garden. I hardly see you anymore.'

'Their Majesties will have more important things on their minds right now than picnics. Uncle Remy says the people are fed up with being squeezed by the aristocrats for every sou and grain of wheat they grow.'

Ernestine was more than a little shocked at his implied criticism of the King's rule, but they had long ago agreed that they would treat each other as equals and say exactly what they thought, with none of the intrigues and subterfuges of the Court.

'I don't care for politics. I would rather be out here than inside with a thousand men arguing about the laws of the land.'

Pierre glanced around, but the only sounds were the soft whisperings of nature. Nevertheless, he leaned closer and dropped his voice to a whisper. 'I've heard people say terrible things about the Queen. They even commit their blasphemy to paper. The head groom gave me such a clip around the ears when he found me with one of the *libelles*. I was only going to burn it.'

'You can read?'

'Enough to get by. My family works several acres of land and has hopes to better themselves.'

'I'm sorry if I offended you, Pierre.'

'I don't mind. I'd like to learn to read properly.'

Ernestine leaned closer, afraid that the bushes might have ears. 'What do the *libelles* say about the Queen?'

'Best you do not know. The drawings are the worst part – they show Marie Antoinette doing such disgusting things. I cannot believe people think they are true. They call her Madame Deficit, because of how much she spends.'

'Oh, Pierre, you must not believe all you hear. The Queen may love pretty gowns and grand balls, but she is also very kind and charitable. She has shown me great love, although I am not her child by birth.'

'I hope she does not know what they say about her.'

'The Queen chooses to ignore the lies, but I know she is hurt when people say such terrible things. Besides, her thoughts are mostly with the Dauphin. Did you see how sickly he was at the parade?'

Pierre nodded. 'I haven't seen him since his seventh birthday. We have all been praying that the clean air at Meudon would heal him, but, in truth, he looked very much worse today.'

'He loved the wooden horse you carved for him. His Majesty was most impressed by your method of jointing the legs. We can only hope such moments of happiness will sustain him.'

Pierre beamed at this acknowledgement of his work by the highest of authorities. 'How is the younger brother? Such a sweet-natured boy.'

'Louis-Charles is adorable. We all dote on him, but Marie-Thérèse most of all. She is jealous of how he toddles around after you in the gardens, ever since he demanded you make him a wooden horse of his own.'

'I've seen him outside in the morning, picking flowers for Her Majesty. Perhaps he would be happier as a gardener.'

'We cannot choose our parents, nor our path in life, more's the pity. He will find the time for his passions if he wishes. After all, even the King can find spare hours to go hunting or tinker in his workshop. I do believe he would spend the whole day in there if he could. He has no love for the protocols of the court, nor for the demands of the state.'

'The King has a workshop? For what purpose?'

'He loves to make things. Most of all, he loves to work with locks. You should see his private chambers. They are filled with models and ingenious instruments.'

'I would love to see them, although of course I never will.' Pierre sighed. He was a keen carpenter and tinkerer himself. 'I cannot image the King going about such an ordinary task as lock-making. No one who saw him in all his glory at the parade today could imagine such a thing. A shame that he was born to a position he dislikes, while others crave his power.'

'Shh, Pierre, you must not say such things. It is his God-given right to be King, no matter what the Duc d'Orléans wishes.'

'Why does the King put up with his scheming?'

Ernestine shrugged. 'The Queen loathes him, but he is still the King's cousin. They say he wanted Marie-Thérèse to be pledged to his son, but the Queen refused.'

'My uncle's friends in Paris say the duke's desire for the throne burns like gunpowder. They say he stirs up the rioters and buys the people's devotion with grain. I heard a merchant say he is hoarding flour, to ensure the people are starving and angry.'

'We must not speak of such things. Talk of people starving is only a nasty lie to discredit the King.' Ernestine frowned at his pained grimace. 'Pierre?'

He shuffled closer to her, so his lips were right by her ear. 'The King needs to know the truth, before things get even worse. His people are desperate. Do you not remember how thin I was when I arrived here?'

Ernestine nodded. When she had first set eyes on him, he had been skin stretched over bones. 'I thought you must have been sick.'

'No. I was starving. My family has worked an orchard and farm in the Loire Valley for generations, producing plenty of fruit and vegetables to live on and supply the chateaux. But these last years, despite all of us working night and day, there was never enough left over to feed ourselves after paying all the taxes. Taxes, taxes and yet more taxes, until we were squeezed to the bone.'

She laid a hand on his arm, feeling the rigid tension of the muscles as he let his anger out. 'How bad was it?'

'More than half of what my family earned was taken, to be paid to lords rolling in wealth who paid no taxes of their own. The harsh winter that year, and the floods that followed it, destroyed what was left. That's why I was sent to Uncle Remy – so I could be kept alive and send a few sous back to them to help stave off the debtors' prison.'

Ernestine watched the hard lines of clenched muscles across his still-thin cheeks. 'I'm sorry, Pierre, I didn't realise how hard it had been for you. I can see why you are angry, but you must be cautious about speaking so rashly. After all, what can we do? We are but children.'

Pierre slammed his fist down on the rock, drawing a trickle of blood. 'I ceased to be a child the day my father was whipped half to death for failing to pay what the landowner claimed was due. Though it pains me I can do so little, I will do whatever it takes to help my family survive.'

'Are there others in this situation?'

'Others?' He rounded on her, his cheeks flaring a fiery red. 'Others? Ernestine, after the bitter winter we've just had, the entire country is starving. The harvests failed, and the millponds were too frozen to grind what little grain there was. A single loaf of bread costs as much as a man can make in a day's hard labour. Does the King not know this?'

Ernestine cowered under his fury, shocked by the truth in his eyes. 'His Majesty loves his people. He has given out grain from his own stores. And his sister, Madame Elisabeth, has driven herself into debt to support the poor after the terrible winter we had.' Ernestine paused as she wiped the blood off his hand with her handkerchief. She began again hesitantly, unwilling to believe the situation was quite so dire as he imagined. 'Perhaps the discontent has been overstated. Many people who harbour ill-will towards the King are spreading outrageous rumours.'

Perhaps Pierre realised how distressed she was becoming, because he sank back down and continued in a soft, but compelling, voice. 'No, if anything, it's worse than people dare to whisper. People were rioting in Paris less than two weeks ago over the price of food. Mobs of hungry people attacked Réveillon's wallpaper factory. The guards shot into the crowd and killed over a hundred people. Even the condemnation of the King and the capture of the leaders was not enough to stop them coming back the next day and destroying the factory.'

As if to underscore his fears, a rowdy group of revellers passed by their hiding spot, singing a crude song and trampling the Queen's flowers. Such a thing would never have happened before. Ernestine felt the band around her chest tighten again until her breaths were coming in short gasps.

Pierre stayed close to her until the men had passed. He pressed the piece of wood he had been carving into her hands. 'Hold this whenever you feel frightened. It will keep you safe.'

She opened her fingers, revealing a small but beautifully carved owl. 'Thank you, Pierre. I will treasure it.'

'We should go now. I will walk you back to the palace.'

Ernestine stood up and tucked the owl into her bodice to keep it safe. 'Pierre, is it really true what you said about the riots? How do you know such things?'

'There are always whispers to be heard if you keep your ears open. I help to unload the merchant's carts when they bring in supplies from Paris and I am often called upon to help with the horses when visitors arrive. I am invisible to these people, so they talk freely. And I hear what the courtiers and servants say in the palace, as one of the grooms has a brother who works as a messenger boy. The palace is awash with rumours. Many are making plans to leave if it gets worse.'

'If all this is true, why are you are always so kind and cheerful?'

He shot her a wicked grin. 'Why should I not be cheerful? I have plenty to eat and the comfort of a warm stable to sleep in. And I have you as a friend, my dear Ernestine, to make me laugh and bring me pastries. I will be as round as a prize porker by Christmas.'

'More like a greyhound than a porker, no matter how much I feed you. I promise never to be sad again, as long as you promise to be my friend forever.'

His grin faded, and he strode ahead so fast that she had to run to catch up. When he turned to her again, his face was set in hard lines again. 'I promise I will work hard and make something of myself, so that when you are old enough, I might be allowed to become more than a friend to you. You are not promised to another?'

'Not yet, but they talk of it, as if I am a pawn in a game of chess. I would far rather live with you in a cottage surrounded by gardens than be passed off to some ancient courtier who is owed a favour.' She reached up and kissed his cheek.

Boots scrunched on gravel, heading towards them. Probably only guards on patrol, but not worth the risk. She pulled Pierre down a side path, through a grove of trees. The Palace of Versailles was now directly in front of them, looking as magnificent and unassailable as it always did. But if there really were riots in Paris, would their sanctuary remain safe?

'Pierre, do you think the unrest will get worse?'

'I think the rioting is only just the beginning. Ernestine, you must take care and look out for yourself. They may have adopted you, but they are not your family. You may owe them a measure of loyalty, but not your life.' He touched her hand briefly. 'I will always be here if you need me.'

She smiled and ran a short way up the path, heading for the Orangerie, hoping to sneak in undetected. When she turned to wave, Pierre Duchamp had already disappeared into the shrubbery.

The Girl with the Cameo

Paris, 2019

Sophie stared at the picture on the computer screen, shaking her head to clear her woolly brain. 'Did you just say–'

'Marie-Thérèse-Charlotte, Madame Royale, oldest child of Louis XVI and Marie Antoinette, and the only member of their immediate family to survive the revolution.'

'Well, goodness, I don't know what to say.'

Luc flicked through a few more images, stopping at a younger and happier picture of the same woman as a girl, with golden-blonde curls and a sweet smile. 'The resemblance to Elisabeth's mother is even more striking in this portrait of Marie-Thérèse at about the same age. It's so similar, it might even be by the same artist.'

'Surely, the similarity must be coincidental. Maybe people looked more alike back then, with less mixing of populations? Would they have dyed and styled their hair the same way to look fashionable in the 1700s?'

'Every woman at court slavishly followed the royal family's lead in fashion,' Luc replied. 'If Marie Antoinette wore a new style of gown or hair decoration one day, the rest of the court would be wearing a version of it the next. Pity the poor dressmakers who spent half the night tracking down whatever the day's extravagance was – white swan feathers or exactly the right shade of silk. I expect all the aristocrat's daughters were dressed as replicas of Madame Royale, the royal daughter, just as their mothers mimicked Marie Antoinette.'

'That must be it, then. Do you know anything else about Elisabeth's mother? You did say in your email that she was the child of a servant at Versailles. Perhaps the cameo was gifted to her mother by whomever she served?'

'It would be an exceptionally expensive gift for a servant, unless she did them some extraordinary service.' Luc paused, as if uncertain how much to say. 'There is another possible explanation–'

Before he could finish the sentence, the door buzzer interrupted. 'Damn, I put up a "closed" sign and locked the door. Some tourists just won't take a hint.'

He shut down the webpage, wrapped the portrait up and handed it back to her, and pocketed the cameo, before striding over to check the entry camera. 'Double-damn. What is he doing here?'

He pressed the outer door release and was back across the room in six long strides, flipping a cloth over the items on the workbench.

Sophie didn't have time to ask who it was before the inner door swung open. An athletic man strutted across the room, making a beeline for her, smiling with the self-assurance of a man for whom all others made way. He was perfectly groomed from the top of his slicked-back hair, artfully styled with a dash of grey at the neatly trimmed edges, to the tips of his Italian shoes, via a bespoke suit, silk tie and a Patek Philippe watch that shouted, 'look at me'.

She glanced to Luc for a lead, but her host had not moved a muscle, beyond brushing his rumpled hair back with his fingers and yanking his reading glasses off. From his tight smile, which failed the dimple test, she gathered this man was not a welcome visitor.

Luc snapped out of his trance. '*Bonjour*, Henri. This is a friend of mine, Sophie West. Sophie, Henri Chevalier, one of the foremost private collectors of revolutionary-era items in France.'

'Lucien, you are being too modest on my behalf, as always.' He turned to smile at Sophie as if bestowing a gift. 'I have the very best private collection in the world. And if the government does any more harm to our great nation, I might just have to buy Versailles in its entirety to save them from bankruptcy.'

128

He laughed in a manner clearly intended to be self-deprecating and stepped forward to take her hand. Instead of shaking it, he blindsided her by raising her hand to his lips. Who did that anymore? She tried not to show her surprise, managing a weak smile instead.

'Welcome to Paris, Madame West. I trust you enjoyed your first-class upgrade. Nothing but the best for our mysterious connection to the past.'

Sophie stood with a half-open mouth, as lost for words as a goldfish in a bowl, but suddenly very much aware of her lack of makeup and slept upon hair. In the space of a minute, this stranger had thrown her completely. Luc's mouth had tightened even further into a jaw-clenching grimace.

She collected herself and tried to navigate through the odd currents in the room. 'A pleasure to meet you. I am most grateful for your thoughtfulness, Monsieur Chevalier, although I admit I am completely in the dark as to how you knew about my visit or why you would choose to spend a great deal of money upgrading the airline ticket of a complete stranger.'

Luc stepped forward to stand next to her, so they were both facing him. 'Yes, do tell us, Henri. How did you know Sophie was visiting me and what flight she would be on?'

'Ah Lucien, you know I have my sources, which I never divulge.' He tapped the side of his nose with a manicured nail. 'And Madame West – or Sophie, if I may – you might be a new and most welcome visitor to our city, but your ancestor is a woman of great interest to many people, including myself.'

Henri turned to examine a garishly decorated vase on a nearby shelf. 'Nice piece of Sèvres you have here, Lucien. These early vases are getting as rare as hen's teeth, as you English say. I am lucky to have secured several excellent pieces over the years for my collection.'

He gazed around the room with all the condescension of a potential buyer assessing its value in order to put in an insultingly low bid. The gaze halted at the workbench. 'May I?' he said, strolling over, flipping the cover and picking up the diamond hair ornaments. 'A pretty pair of decorative combs.' His dark eyes swivelled, locking in on her. 'You have brought other items as well?'

'A cute little carved wooden owl and a couple of rings from England. My ancestor travelled to New Zealand by sailing ship, and thus was very limited in what she could bring. I imagine the early immigrants would have prized a stout pair of boots and an axe over pretty trifles.'

His eyebrow rose at her description of the diamond encrusted jewellery as 'pretty trifles'. No doubt the women of his acquaintance would go for jewels over sturdy boots every time.

Henri studied her for as long as it took for her to blink first. 'Did she leave any written documents? Letters, diaries?'

'Only an account of the voyage, Monsieur Chevalier. She didn't write about her past, although she did write amusingly about the wives of the colonials and their disdain for the steerage class. Elisabeth, I'm proud to say, showed strong socialist leanings and made herself useful by teaching the poor children to read.' What was it about him that made Sophie want to mock his snobbery so blatantly?

'How charming. I am eager to hear about her. Sophie, I do hope you will dine with me tonight. I lured my personal chef from one of the best restaurants in Paris, so I can assure you it will be worth your time. And please, call me Henri.'

'How very kind of you, Henri, but I'm afraid I must decline. I have not slept for two days and can scarcely keep my eyes open.'

'But of course, how thoughtless of me. We will dine tomorrow night instead. Here is my card. Send a text with your address to me and I will have my chauffeur pick you up from your hotel lobby at eight o'clock. I have some information about your ancestor, which I guarantee you will find fascinating.'

With that final jaw-dropper, Henri glided out the door in a waft of hair product, before she could say another word. Sophie turned to Luc, but still couldn't think of a thing to say. She hadn't been steamrollered like that since she was knee high to her first-grade teacher.

Luc looked ready to explode. 'I'm so sorry, Sophie. Henri thinks he can do as he wishes, probably because he is so rich that most people let him. He charms women and buys men, although I have to admit, you handled him like a professional.'

He stalked over to the door, checking the camera to ensure Henri Chevalier had left, before shutting the door with enough force to jingle the chandelier.

Sophie sank down onto the sofa, while her host paced up and down the room. 'I can't say I thought him very charming. I would have flat-out refused dinner, but I wasn't sure if he was an important client you didn't wish to offend.'

'Thoughtful of you. I do work for him occasionally, but that should have no bearing on your decision to accept his invitation or not.'

'I'm really not sure I'd like to be alone with him, to be honest, even in a busy restaurant, let alone in his private dining salon. But if Henri has useful information about Elisabeth, I suppose it would be churlish not to go tomorrow night, especially if he paid for my first-class upgrade. Though how he knows so much about me is giving me the creeps.'

The pacing stopped and Luc dropped into the armchair opposite her, leaning forward with his elbows on his knees. 'He didn't hear anything from me, I assure you. I had hoped to keep news of your visit quiet. My older daughter was the only one I told, but she would not have said anything directly to him. She must have told her mother, although I thought she had nothing to do with Chevalier these days.'

He must have seen her confusion, because he added, 'My wife left me for Henri Chevalier several years ago.'

'Oh heavens, Luc, I'm so sorry. What a cheek for him to show up here.'

He shrugged his shoulders a fraction, as if it was of no great importance. 'It is not a problem. We married too young. Once the children were grown, we had nothing left in common to hold us together. Sadly, for Jacqueline, it didn't last long.' Luc glanced at her with all the intensity of his odd green-hazel eyes. 'Henri is always looking for new acquisitions.'

'I will ring him to say I can't join him for dinner. It is you I have come to visit, not him, and I certainly didn't ask him to pay for my flight.'

'I admit he surprised me by knowing which flight you would be on. Though, knowing him, he'll own some high-up official with access to airport arrivals information.'

The whole situation was downright weird. Why would a rich man like Henri Chevalier bother with her at all, let alone go to such an effort to meet her? 'His last comment, about having information on my ancestor, was disconcerting too. How could he know about my connection to Elisabeth? And why on earth is it of any importance to him?'

Luc was on his feet and pacing again, scowling all the way to his eyebrows. 'Henri could have been automatically monitoring the ancestry websites for any mention of her name, the same as I was. But how he knew about her in the first place is a mystery. Much as I hate to say it, I suspect the only way he will tell you is if you agree to dine with him. As long as you feel safe.'

'Don't worry about me. I'll make sure I have my anti-charm spray tucked into my bag next to the pepper spray.'

Luc burst out laughing. 'I wish I could be there to see it. Henri has certainly met his match in you, Sophie, although I warn you, it will only make him more determined. The rarer the object, the more he desires it.'

Sophie flicked her hands up and let out the kind of dismissive 'pifft' sound she'd heard French people make in movies. 'I need some fresh air.'

'Shall we have a stroll around the gardens of the Palais du Luxembourg? It's one of my favourite places in Paris and quite close to here. Then you can check in to the hotel, which is just around the corner.'

'Good plan. If I have a walk and a nap, then I should have a more or less functioning brain again by dinner time, if you are free to meet up. Depending on your other commitments.'

'It would be my pleasure.'

Before leaving, Luc put the jewellery into a modern safe and set a complex arrangement of alarms and deadlocks as they left. 'I pay a fortune to a top-end security company, but it's worth it for the peace of mind. They specialise in museums, so they know what is needed.'

'Wish I'd had the sense to invest in better security. My cottage was burgled just before I left.'

They stepped out into the street, stopping while a trio of scooters zipped past them.

'*Merde*. Did you lose much?'

'Very little, luckily.'

She was about to list the laptop and her mother's antique jewellery box, when it struck her that it was an odd coincidence that the jewellery box had been taken only a day before finding the much older one in the attic. She hadn't made the connection at the time, as she had not known of its existence then. But Henri

Chevalier's unexpected knowledge of her plans and ancestry were enough to put a new and potentially more ominous slant on the burglary.

Luc guided her along a series of streets, pointing out the sights as they strolled. Strange how she had instinctively sided with Luc rather than Henri. Now, as they passed the fabulous buildings of Paris (how good it was to be able to say that!), Sophie realised she had no sound reason to trust one over the other, simply because she had talked to Luc first and had a very distant relationship to him. And her instinctive dislike of self-important men like Henri Chevalier.

Her Aunt Margaret's advice to build trust slowly, before disclosing the existence of the pearl necklace, seemed prescient.

Stepping from the busy streets into the gardens of the Luxembourg Palace was like stepping through a looking glass into another world, from chaos to calm. Long stretches of green grass, and trees and statues aligned to pull the eye over a riot of colourful flowers towards the octagonal pool and on to the graceful façade of the palace. Instead of honking vehicles, the background noises were the cheerful sounds of thwacking tennis balls and squealing children.

Sophie basked in the warmth of a perfect late spring day, a treat after the chilly autumn weather in Wellington. 'I love that they made the park a play area as well as a lovely place to stroll. Last time I was here there was a puppet show. I remember watching it, sitting on the lawn eating crêpes and feeling utterly happy.'

'It's still there, though I doubt there will be a puppet show today. We could come back on Sunday if you wish. They often have musical performances and art displays as well, if you tire of looking at the statues. Did you know they have a collection of statues of famous women?'

'Really? Are they recent additions?'

'Only if you call the mid-1800s recent.'

'In New Zealand, that would be as old as it gets for marble statues.'

Luc didn't seem to mind that she wanted to stroll around the statues of familiar heroines. Despite the silence, Sophie felt comfortable with Luc. With many strangers, silence was a gaping hole begging to be filled with chit-chat. Perhaps, like her, he was an introvert who preferred peace to bustle.

She gestured to an empty park bench in a secluded part of the gardens. 'Before Henri arrived, you were about to tell me about another possible explanation for the portraits of the two girls being similar.'

'I'm hesitant to mention it, as it will seem too incredible to be true, but I think we shouldn't rule it out. Especially given Henri's interest, which suggests he knows that there is something unique and valuable at stake.' Luc settled onto the bench, fiddling with a leafy twig hanging over the back of the seat.

She waited for him to proceed, but the seconds ticked by. 'Just tell me, Luc. Whatever it is, you can't stop now you've piqued my interest.'

'Seeing the portrait of Elisabeth's mother reminded me that you mentioned she was adopted into a wealthy family.'

'Yes…' Was she going to have to get the thumbscrews out?

He flicked the twig back behind the seat and turned to face her. 'I'm not sure if you know much about the household of Louis XVI, but Marie Antoinette was very fond of children and much more charitable than she is usually given credit for. One of her charitable acts was to adopt a girl whose mother had died in her service. The girl was said to look very like Marie-Thérèse and the King.'

'Really? Perhaps the girl was chosen because she looked similar. Like a matching set.'

'Perhaps. The girl's mother was a chambermaid, who died young. I'd have to check the details, but I do recall that the circumstances of the girl's adoption were very unusual and – how shall I put it – open to more than one explanation.'

Was Luc actually blushing? Sophie felt goosebumps on her skin. 'Go on, you've got me utterly hooked.'

'The royal couple was married very young – Marie Antoinette was only fourteen and Louis fifteen – and many years passed with no heir, to everyone's dismay. Eventually, Marie Antoinette's brother came over from Austria to give some forthright marital advice to the King, who evidently had no concept of what to do in the bedroom to ensure the royal bloodline.'

'Seriously?' Sophie choked back a laugh. 'Not a subject most young men need any encouragement on.'

'Indeed. Most of the King's predecessors veered in the opposite direction, gathering a string of royal mistresses, some of whom had more power than the legitimate queen of the day.'

'Like Diane de Poitiers and Catherine de Medici?'

'Exactly. Anyway, Louis XVI apparently wanted to be sure where the fault lay for the lack of an heir, so he used his newly acquired knowledge to bed one of the chambermaids. As chance would have it, both the chambermaid and the Queen became pregnant.'

'Are you saying that this girl they adopted was really the illegitimate daughter of Louis XVI?'

'Nothing is certain, especially as the chambermaid was married. But yes, it's possible. In fact, the evidence is quite strong. The chambermaid's husband was not named on legal documents as the child's father, which is highly unusual. The daughter was adopted by the royal family, renamed Ernestine, and a massive sum of money was settled on her. She grew up alongside the legitimate royal daughter, Marie-Thérèse, and shared the same room, education and luxuries. Suggestive, don't you think?'

Sophie was speechless, so Luc continued, 'And here you are, with a portrait of a young girl who looks very like the King's daughter and a cameo similar to the one worn by her, and who you know was adopted by a wealthy family at Versailles.'

'But … but that would mean …'

'That you and I may be direct descendants of Louis XVI. In fact, our joint ancestor was the only child of Louis XVI to have had children that we know of. Marie-Thérèse was the only other survivor of the revolution, and she had no children.'

'Blimey Luc, you did warn me that it was incredible, but still … it's all a bit much to take in.'

Sophie ran through it in her mind, wondering if she was grasping at a dazzlingly tempting theory, when the Occam's razor principle indicated the simplest explanation was the most likely. But, as Luc had said, the evidence was suggestive, especially given the similarity between the two girls. Could

Elisabeth's mother really have been this girl Ernestine, the daughter of Louis XVI? It seemed preposterous.

'I'd like to see all the evidence, tempting as it is to leap to the most interesting explanation.'

'Rightly so.' Luc nodded sagely, as if confirming she had passed a test. 'What a pleasure it is to deal with someone who values evidence over sensationalism.'

Sophie felt her cheeks go pink at the praise. 'Don't panic. I promise I won't splash it all over social media and the tabloids.' She was startled to see a wave of relief cross his face, although, on reflection, his concern was probably a valid one. After all, he knew as little about her motives as she did about his. 'Tell me more about this girl.'

'Ah, that is not so easy. As far as I recall, Ernestine was separated from the royal family during the revolution and died childless in Paris, at least according to the available sources. The two girls were only children when the revolution started, so Ernestine was more or less invisible to history, with scarcely a word written about her in any of the memoirs from the time.'

'I shudder to think what it must have been like for two young girls, going from the height of luxury into the chaos of the revolution.'

'Not a happy fairy tale ending, for sure. The King was too complacent about the growing unrest, for a while at least, so they probably had little idea of what was about to happen. Louis XVI was famously said to have written the word "*rien*" in his diary for 14 July 1789, the day the Bastille was stormed, which followed two days of rioting in Paris.'

'How is it possible that "nothing" happened during his day, even if he was ignorant of the uprising in Paris?'

'Louis XVI was inordinately fond of hunting and always took the time to record his kills in his diary. "*Rien*" possibly meant he caught nothing that day. Ironic, in the circumstances. He would have been happy if all he had to do each day was hunt or hide himself away in his workshop. He loved to make things, especially mechanical devices and locks. And to be fair, he was probably not himself as he had lost his oldest son and heir only a few weeks before.'

'Maybe the King only used that diary for personal observations. There must have been other, official diaries too, or were they destroyed?'

'We'll never know exactly what was there before the uprising. Some records survived, whereas other documents were destroyed or lost. To be honest, that is one of the fascinations of working with revolutionary-era objects. One never knows what might surface next.' He grinned and nudged her with his elbow. 'Like you. Or rather, your family heirlooms.'

'I'd love to hear more about your work. Never knowing when and where the next find might surface – it must be exciting.'

'In the chaos of the revolution and the purging of anything associated with royalty that followed, our heritage was spread far and wide around Europe and the rest of the world. Much of it was auctioned off for paltry prices.'

Sophie wished she'd had more time to read up on French history. She knew about the storming of the Bastille and the Reign of Terror, but not in any detail. 'The storming of the Bastille must have had ramifications for the King, surely, even if he didn't write about it in his diary.'

'Definitely. There was talk of the royal family leaving Versailles or at least sending Marie Antoinette and the children away, especially given how deeply unpopular the Queen had become. Many other prominent members of the royal household did leave, including the King's siblings.'

'Why didn't they go too?'

'Louis was the King and therefore felt he was untouchable. His place was to rule his people, not desert them. A shame he didn't have more of an inclination for politics, instead of trusting to an unwavering belief that the people loved him, as he loved them, and all would be well when they came to their senses.'

'He sat on his throne, twiddling his thumbs, as rioters tore through Paris?'

'Not at all. In fact, Louis was brave enough to front up to the crowds in Paris and gave in to some of the demands for political change. He tried to negotiate, to placate, but it was never going to be enough. The momentum was already there for change, driven by the desperation of empty stomachs, and whipped up by a group of firebrand leaders who wanted far more power and a proper constitution protecting the rights of every man.'

Sophie sat on the park bench, enjoying the sun and the laughter of small children chasing each other through the trees. So peaceful, so far removed from the horrors of the revolution. 'So, Luc, how do we find out more about this near-invisible child called Ernestine, who shared her life with the royal children and may or may not have been one of them?'

'I need to do some research, so we have all the facts. And you look like you need a rest. Shall we get you checked into your hotel and reconvene in the hotel bar at seven o'clock?'

'We'll have to eat somewhere where Henri Chevalier won't run into us, after I said I was too tired to dine with him tonight.'

'That's easy. Any restaurant without a Michelin star.'

'Just as well, as I didn't think to bring any Michelin-worthy clothes with me. Unless crush-proof travel clothes are suddenly the new little black dress.'

They walked back to Luc's office in thoughtful silence. The hotel was only a few blocks away, a lovely old building with an inviting décor, which was both restful and subtly elegant. Check-in passed in a blur of handing over her passport and letting Luc rattle away in French. By the time she reached her room, Sophie was ready to crash.

But sleep refused to come. Instead, she searched online for information about Marie-Thérèse and Ernestine, finding plenty of articles on the life of the former and almost nothing on the latter, other than what Luc had already told her. Could this girl Ernestine really be the mother of her ancestor, Elisabeth?

She lay back on the stack of luxurious hotel pillows and tried to image two little girls playing at Versailles, as Paris teetered on the brink of a bloody revolution.

Fight or Flight

Ernestine lined up a regiment of tin soldiers for Louis-Charles, while Marie-Thérèse stared at the wall with vacant eyes. The little boy teetered on the edge of interest, before sweeping a pudgy fist through his favourite toys.

'I want my brother!'

Marie-Thérèse took Louis-Charles in her arms and stroked his pretty face and blond ringlets as if he was her own baby. 'Louis-Joseph has gone to heaven to be with our baby sister.'

She must have squeezed too hard, because he squirmed out of her grasp and burst into tears. At four years old, he was too young to understand that his older brother's death the previous month was a permanent loss. His own elevation to the status of heir to the throne of France meant little more to him than the imposition of additional strictures on his life, when he would rather have been playing with his toys.

Ernestine searched for the right words to cheer him, but soothing words were hard to muster when they had every reason to be both sad and worried. Their cosy world was crumbling, slowly but surely.

Even within the palace walls, the god-like respect shown to the royal family was faltering amongst some of the myriad servants. Trifles for the most part – rose petals left to drop on the floor, silver left unpolished, a half-concealed sneer instead of bowing deference – faint echoes of the worsening situation outside the palace walls.

And now the royal family's grief at the Dauphin's death was being compounded by the hasty departure of many of the people closest to them, fleeing France in fear, as the turmoil grew steadily worse.

Ernestine noticed the subtle changes more than anyone, because the servants did not hold their tongues in front of her, as they did with Marie-Thérèse. A few, whom she had known as friends of her mother, treated her as one of their own, but others treated her as if she was one of Marie-Thérèse's beautiful gowns, to be looked after with care, but not attention.

In recent days, as she slipped along the gilded corridors of Versailles, Ernestine had heard dreadful whispers and felt the crackling tension of a thundercloud gathering on the horizon. Only yesterday, hiding behind the draperies to avoid Marie-Thérèse's wrath over a lost ribbon, she heard the chambermaids gossiping openly, as they never would have dared before.

'Rioting in Paris', the more brazen of the girls declared. 'The streets were filled with people openly chanting against the King, crying out for bread and liberty.'

'Quiet your voice, for pity's sake, for I've no desire to lose my place or my head,' the other girl whispered. She gathered soiled linen in silence for a minute, but the temptation to gossip was too strong. 'I heard they stole muskets and cannons enough to supply an army, then attacked the Bastille.'

'What did you hear about it?'

'The crowd was fired upon by soldiers but fought back and won.' Her voice dropped even lower. 'They say dozens of people died.'

The other girl snorted. 'Shows how little you know. I heard it was hundreds, perhaps thousands, killed. The mob cut the heads off anyone who stood in their way, parading them through the streets, cheering and yelling that the Queen would be next.'

'Shh, not so loud. I heard the Duchesse de Polignac and the Comte d'Artois are fleeing the country tomorrow.'

'No! Truly? Good riddance to the hussy and the King's brother. Two fewer distractions in the royal bedchamber, if you ask me.'

'The duchess and the King are lovers?'

'Not that royal bedchamber, imbecile. The Queen will miss the duchess far more than the King will, if you take my meaning. And her brother-in-law too. Not to mention that handsome Count Fersen who follows her around. The Queen is a foreigner, so what can you expect?'

Ernestine had been so shocked by their loose talk that she had stumbled out from her hiding place. The more innocent of the two girls had stared at her with wide eyes for a moment before bursting into sobs and fleeing the room. But the other girl had given Ernestine an impertinent smirk, then swaggered out, banging the door behind her.

Did the King know of the riots in Paris? Ernestine could only imagine that he did, as he had been closeted with a huddle of grim-faced advisers for the past two days. There was talk of leaving Versailles, but naturally the King refused to be forced out by the actions of a small band of radicals. Eager as the Queen was to leave, she adamantly refused to be separated from her husband or children.

While Ernestine's heart hoped the situation had been wildly exaggerated by malicious rumours, she could not help recalling Pierre's words of warning about the mood of the people. She longed to see him, because he would surely know whether it was true that Parisians had seized arms and used them in anger.

Her thoughts were dragged back to the present by the arrival of their governess, the Duchesse de Polignac, who was dabbing at swollen eyes with a lace handkerchief. The governess embraced the children but seemed unable to speak.

'Have you come to give us our lessons, Madame?' asked Louis-Charles, his tantrum over his brother's absence forgotten.

The duchess burst into fresh waves of sobs, so Ernestine answered for her. 'There will be no lessons today. You must be brave and say farewell to our governess, who is leaving us.'

'Why is she going?'

Ernestine was at a loss to know what to say to him. The truth was that the Duchesse de Polignac was fleeing France with her family for her own safety, along with many other aristocrats. Finally, she said, 'She is visiting family abroad. Come now, we must say goodbye, for now at least.'

The children kissed their governess and watched her walk out of their lives. From the window, they saw their mother embrace her dear friend for several minutes, until they were gently separated by the King, who handed the duchess up into the carriage himself. Ernestine had heard that it had been the King's wish that the duchess leave, as she had been the target of vicious scandalmongering and outright threats.

Ernestine retreated to an armchair, while the other two children remained by the window, waving.

Distressing as this farewell was, there was worse to come. A governess could be replaced, but no one could replace their young cousins, with whom they had played all their lives. With numb resignation, the royal family returned to the vast courtyard later that summer's day and bade farewell to the entire family of the Comte d'Artois, one of the King's younger brothers. Tears welled in all eyes, for he was a favourite of the Queen and a stalwart supporter of his brother. His oldest son, the Duc d'Angoulême, was said to be Marie-Thérèse's intended husband, although the boy was only thirteen years old to her ten.

Marie-Thérèse stumbled inside as soon as the carriages had rolled out the grand gates, her grief finally pouring out in a sobbing fit from which Ernestine was unable to revive her. After several failed attempts to calm her sister, Marie-Thérèse erupted.

'Leave me alone, Ernestine.' She swept her arm across a table, flinging a vase to the floor, where it shattered into a thousand shards. 'I want my cousins, not you.'

Ernestine crouched down to pick up the pieces, but Marie-Thérèse overturned the table with her foot, sending the solid mahogany crashing to the floor, missing her head by a whisker. 'Get out!'

Ernestine had enough experience of her adoptive sister's moods to know this one wouldn't end well for her. She raced for the door, hearing it slam closed behind her. She shrugged her shoulders and set off to find something useful to do until such time as Marie-Thérèse had calmed down.

Fortunately, her occasional fits of temper usually burned themselves out after an hour or two. Marie-Thérèse was mostly sweet-tempered with Ernestine, more often venting her ire at her mother's strict standards and the endless protocol of court. She certainly deserved sympathy today after the departure of her beloved cousins.

Meanwhile, Ernestine was free to do as she wished until someone told her otherwise. She was tempted to sneak out to see Pierre, but she knew her greater responsibility lay with her adoptive family in these troubled times. After all the blessings showered upon her by the royal family, perhaps this was her opportunity to repay the debt by giving whatever help or comfort she could.

She went out through the schoolroom, where she had been tutored by the best. Sometimes even the King, who was fond of games and delighted in sharing his enthusiasm for the world, using a gigantic globe that he had commissioned for them.

As Ernestine neared the Queen's suite of rooms, she encountered a trail of servants, gathering up items

152

like ants preparing their nest for winter. From their whispered conversations, she gathered that Marie Antoinette had ordered them to prepare for a hasty departure, should it become necessary.

When Ernestine entered to offer her assistance, she found Madame Campan rifling through the Queen's private papers, ankle deep in a growing pile of letters and documents. Marie Antoinette's Lady-in-Waiting welcomed her help and sat her down by the fire, feeding papers into the leaping flames. As she threw a letter from Austria on the pyre, Ernestine realised the Queen must think the situation very grave indeed, if she had ordered the burning of her personal correspondence.

The desperation of this act thrust home to Ernestine exactly how precarious their position was becoming. A shiver went up her spine, despite the scorching heat from the blaze, at the mere thought – unbelievable as it surely was – that the Queen felt the walls of Versailles might be breached and the very heart of her domain invaded.

The door opened as Ernestine was throwing the last pages into the fire, causing a gust of wind, which scattered flecks of grey ash into her face.

Marie Antoinette hurried in, her face as pale as a wraith. 'Louis insists on going to Paris in person tomorrow to appoint Lafayette as commander.' Her voice was close to breaking. 'Has he no regard for his own safety or that of his family?'

Madame Campan rushed to her side with a silk handkerchief and a kind word. 'No one would dare disrespect His Majesty, Madame. He will return triumphant, as God wills it must be so.'

'You must pack my jewels, for I fear that soon we may no longer be safe even here.' Marie Antoinette turned to survey the room, as if for the last time. 'Ernestine, what are you doing here?'

Madame Campan answered for her. 'She offered to assist me, in order that her loyalty and gratitude to Your Majesty might be expressed in a useful manner.'

'My dear, you are a good girl. But is your sister not in need of your comfort after the loss of her beloved cousins?'

Ernestine rose from the hearth, scattering ashes as she curtseyed. 'Marie-Thérèse wished to spend time alone, to grieve their loss. I will return to her if you wish or stay here to help pack the jewellery.'

'I will go to see her, for I do not wish to be away from my children for long in these dreadful times.' Marie Antoinette turned to her Lady-in-Waiting. 'Would Ernestine be of assistance?'

'Most assuredly, Your Majesty. She is far more careful at packing than some of the ladies, who have not the wit to know how delicate and valuable the pieces are. What do you wish us to take?'

Marie Antoinette went over to the beautiful cabinet that held her jewels and precious stones, opening the tall doors to survey the glittering array. But the effort of deciding what to take appeared to overwhelm her. Or perhaps it was the reminder that the cabinet was a treasured wedding present from the husband, who would be putting his life at risk tomorrow.

'I wish to take it all but I fear we may have to travel with only a modest number of carriages.' The Queen's trembling fingers hovered over the shelves, then dropped to her side. 'You have been by my side for so long, Madame Campan, that you know which are my favourites. I will leave it to your good sense.'

'Might I suggest, Your Majesty, that the items of greatest value are packed separately into a smaller travelling case, so we may be certain to take them even if we are forced to leave urgently in a single carriage.'

The Queen faltered at this dreadful prospect, but recovered quickly. 'Yes, that would be the most sensible plan. You might start with the gifts my husband gave me on my wedding day. So many beautiful diamonds and pearls...' Emotion choked back the words.

'Your Majesty, all will be well. The pearl necklace will be the first item packed, for I know how you treasure it. And of course, I will also pack the emerald and diamond fan and the beautiful diamond watch His Majesty gave you.'

'If we have to leave, I will take the pearl necklace myself, as I could not bear to be apart from it. It can go in the jewellery box gifted to me by Monsieur Riesener when he delivered the wonderful little writing table he made for me.'

Ernestine smiled, for she loved the writing table almost as much as the Queen did. One of her earliest memories was of watching the Queen's pleasure as she demonstrated the clever mechanism that allowed the top to slide back and, at the same time, the main drawer to move forward. The central compartment of the drawer enclosed a velvet-lined writing surface, which popped up to form a bookstand and reversed to show a mirror. If the children had been particularly good, they might be rewarded with a turn at opening up the magical table.

The jewellery box was made in a matching style, with a glowing surface of inlaid wood and edges of gilded bronze, decorated with floral motifs. The Queen herself took her pearl necklace from the cabinet and set it reverently in the nest of royal blue satin inside the jewellery box. She stroked the lustrous pearls, then shut the lid of the Riesener box with a sigh.

Ernestine had only seen the pearl necklace from a distance, because it was too valuable for little fingers to touch. The way the perfectly matched string of pearls glowed against the white skin of the Queen's graceful neck was always much admired at state celebrations. The Queen regarded the necklace as the most important of all the many gifts given to her for her wedding, as it had been handed down the generations to each Dauphine of France since Anne of Austria, who was an ancestor of both the bride and groom.

Marie-Thérèse coveted the necklace for herself, but of course it would go to the future wife of the Dauphin, if God spared him from the illnesses that had taken his older brother and younger sister. The robust health of the two remaining children was a source of great comfort to the King and Queen, having suffered so much with the death of two children.

When they finished the task of packing, which seemed to take hours, Madame Campan sent her back to the other children. Ernestine had had enough of taking orders, so she set off on a long detour via the kitchens, which were so far away that their food often arrived cold at the table.

The servants who had known her when she was the child of a chambermaid let her pass with a nod or a smile, while the newer ones stepped back and lowered their gaze. Not like when she was with her sister, when they practically scraped the floor with their bows and curtseys and averted eyes.

Once she had cadged a slice of crusty bread, fresh from the oven and smothered with creamy cheese by a kindly kitchen maid, she set off to find her father, who was now on the King's staff. Ernestine wove her way at speed through a maze of hidden corridors, which she could have navigated blindfolded. She had not seen her father for several days and was eager to hear what he had heard of events in Paris.

Fortunately, she found him alone. They retreated to a side room, where she flung her arms around him. 'Papa, I've missed you.'

His strong arms hugged her back. 'I've missed you too. I haven't had a minute to spare to talk to you, with all that is happening.'

'I've heard there has been an uprising in Paris.'

'Wherever did you hear that, child?' Her father held her out at arms' length, a heavy frown framing eyelids that drooped with fatigue. His face was as white as the wig on his head and the ruffled cuffs of his shirt. 'Never mind. Come and sit down. It's past time that I had a talk with you.'

They found a corner with a pair of chairs. Her father pulled one around until it was directly opposite her. 'I will not hide the truth from you, dearest child, although no one else dares speak it within these walls.'

'So, it is true? The unrest in Paris is getting worse?'

'My dear, where once there were marches, now there are riots. Even the convent at Saint-Lazare was looted.' He made the sign of the cross at this abomination before continuing. 'A mob besieged the Hôtel des Invalides, taking muskets and cannons, before turning to the Bastille for gunpowder. I've heard reports of many deaths, but everyone tells a different story. Now they are armed, the worst may yet be ahead of us.'

Ernestine tried to hide her shock at this confirmation that the chambermaids' tall tales were true. 'What will happen, Papa? Her Majesty is beset with worry and making preparations to leave Versailles.'

'Then she is wiser than her husband,' he said in a whisper. 'I hope it may come to nothing, but the mood of the common people is turning hostile. Many nobles have fled already, but the King refuses to join them. Very soon, you may have a difficult choice to make, a choice no young girl should have to face.'

'What is it, Papa?' she whispered, feeling as if the air was being squeezed from her lungs.

'If the royal family flees France, you may have to decide between risking your life to stay with them or saving yourself by leaving them.'

'Surely, that is their choice to make, not mine?'

'Not if you plead for mercy. Or if you run away and hide. Your young friend, Pierre, will look after you, if I cannot. Remember, if the situation gets worse, then your life will be at risk as much as theirs. Despite all they have done for you, they cannot ask for that sacrifice.'

'Abandon them?' Ernestine was silent for a few seconds as she took in his words. Finally, she drew her spine straight. 'No, I could never do that after all they have done for me. I may only be their adopted daughter, but they have treated me as one of their own. I will stand by them, come what may.' She looked up at him with pleading eyes. 'You will stay with us too, will you not, Papa?'

Her father returned her gaze, his anguish evident in every furrow of his brow. 'I might not have that choice if they flee Versailles.' He stood up and walked to a small window, not realising she could see his grief in the reflection from the glass. 'If you have pledged your loyalty to them, it is only fair you know the truth, although it pains me beyond measure to tell you.'

When he resumed speaking, his voice had the flat tone of one who was unwilling to speak an unpleasant truth. 'Know that above all else, I love you as a father. But the truth is, you are the daughter of the King. Your mother had no choice but to obey his command and do her duty to France, so that he could prove his ability to sire a child.'

He turned back to her and clasped her hands, beseeching her understanding in the face of this shocking revelation. 'Your mother loved you more than anything else in the world. She knew you would have a far better life than we could dream of. The King rewarded her with a large sum of money, which allowed both her family and mine to rise out of poverty. You have been the saviour of your family – always remember that. And your own future has been guaranteed with a pension of twelve thousand livres from the King.'

Ernestine thought he was about to say more, but he turned away again to hide his distress. She sat in her chair, as immobile and silent as the cushion behind her.

The man she still regarded as her father crouched down beside her and embraced her. 'I am sorry if I have upset you with this news, my dear. I had hoped to wait until you were of age to tell you.'

She reached out to wipe away a tear from his cheek. 'Thank you for telling me, Papa. In truth, it is not such a surprise as you might imagine. I have heard the servants whispering about how extravagantly I am pampered, just like a Child of France. And I see the reflections of my sister and her father every day when

I look in the mirror, as do the many gossips in the palace.'

'You are wise beyond your years, Ernestine. If you suspected, why did you never ask?'

'I did not want to lose you, Papa. I will pray that we can stay together. Pierre too.'

'So will I, although it may depend less on the will of God than the will of the people in the end. Pierre Duchamp will have to make his own decisions about where his loyalties lie.'

A Tourist at Versailles

Paris, 2019

The alarm woke Sophie from a deep sleep. To her surprise, she felt remarkably refreshed, as though her brain and body had given up fighting over the time zone and settled on Paris.

Paris! And not just as a tourist, but right in the thick of the history of the place. No doubt, they would discover that Elisabeth's mother was just a regular girl after all, but right now Sophie was more excited than she had been in years.

After a quick shower, she slipped on her only dress, an old travel favourite in a soft, flowing fabric, which looked like silk, but without the wrinkles. It felt perfect for the warm evening, with a vibrant mix of hues straight from Monet's palette.

She walked into the bar of her hotel on the dot of seven o'clock. Luc was already there, seated in a quiet corner, his gaze flicking between his mobile phone and the door. A slight frown turned to a smile as he put his phone in his pocket and rose to greet her. Maybe she was old-fashioned – or just plain old – but Sophie appreciated punctuality and good manners.

As she walked over, she noticed a man engrossed in a newspaper, seated at the table on the other side of a bushy plant from Luc, with his back to her. He had the same burly physique and swarthy features as the man from the plane, but when she took a second look, she discounted the momentary flash of recognition. This man had a thick mop of black hair, rather than the short brown hair of the man on the plane. After all, Mediterranean features were hardly uncommon here, compared to New Zealand.

'*Bonsoir*, Luc.' She glanced back at the man behind the plant. 'Would you mind if we switched tables to one overlooking the garden?' Better safe than sorry.

Luc stood back and gestured for her to go ahead. The man behind the plant lowered his newspaper for a moment but stayed where he was. A waiter changed direction with them, delivering a bottle of champagne in an ice bucket to their new table.

'A celebration of your arrival in France,' Luc said, as he pulled her chair out for her.

Sophie watched with pleasure as the waiter began the ritual of stripping the gold foil off the ice-misted bottle, popping the cork, and pouring at just the right angle to get the perfect fizz. 'I do love the ritual of champagne, as if it has been perfectly designed to engage all the senses.'

Luc smiled and relaxed back into his chair. 'That proves you must have French blood running through your veins.' He clinked glasses with her, then slid a book across the table – a biography of Marie-Thérèse by Susan Nagel. 'You might like to read this. It sets out what little information there is on Ernestine, which is not much more than I told you earlier today.'

'That's very thoughtful of you, Luc. I'll look forward to reading it as soon as I get a chance.'

The cover shot was the same one he had shown her before, of Marie-Thérèse as a young girl. Sophie was itching to read it but just as keen to hear what else Luc had to say. She took a sip of champagne, closing her eyes to savour the delicate combination of fizzing bubbles, fruity aroma and subtle taste. Bliss.

'You will have to excuse me. I have an unfortunate habit of going straight to business when I'm fascinated by a subject. I should have asked whether you had a good rest.'

Sophie realised she must have closed her eyes for a fraction longer than was normal, a habit she had developed when tasting. 'I'm feeling much livelier, thanks, although it still feels like a dream to be in Paris drinking real French champagne. Absolutely delicious.' Sophie leaned forward and lowered her voice. 'I can't wait to hear more about our ancestors.'

Luc leaned forward too, his slightly mismatched eyes sparkling with excitement. 'I've done a bit of checking, and there are a few other facts supporting the royal link. If your ancestor Elisabeth is really the daughter of this girl Ernestine, then Marie-Thérèse would be her aunt, by adoption or possibly blood. Marie-Thérèse was exiled to England in 1830, which fits the timing of Elisabeth's hasty departure from France carrying some unknown item of value for her aunt.'

Sophie took another long sip of champagne while she worked out how much to say. 'I think it might have been a pearl necklace, based on a comment in Elisabeth's diary.'

'That makes sense. Pearls were as valuable as diamonds in that era. A well-matched set of pearls was coveted as a sign of wealth, and Marie Antoinette was particularly fond of them. Marie-Thérèse would have had one or more sets of valuable pearls.'

Sophie had a short internal battle with herself over whether to tell Luc that her aunt had also gifted the pearls to Elisabeth and they were right at this moment sitting in a safe-deposit box in a bank in Wellington. Her gut told her to trust him, but she had only known him for a few hours. She reminded herself that all the best conmen were experts at appearing genuine.

A slight redirection of topic seemed the best idea. 'I suppose I should consider giving the cameo brooch to a museum here in France.'

'That is a very generous thought, Sophie.' Luc tipped his head to the side and studied her. 'No need to rush into a decision, though. If it was a gift to Elisabeth or her mother, then it is entirely up to you.'

'It seems like the right thing to do.'

'I'm not sure you appreciate just how valuable it is, especially if it can be authenticated as coming from the royal family. Henri Chevalier would pay you a small fortune. He is absolutely obsessed with anything from those last days at Versailles.'

'I'll think about it.' She twirled her glass, watching the bubbles rise as her thoughts drifted back to her ancestor. 'I wonder why Elisabeth never went back to France?'

'That I can answer. The soldiers who were sent to the Duchamp farm were thwarted by Elisabeth and her family, so they burned the farmhouse down and hunted the countryside for anyone who might know where they were hiding. Which rather suggests that the pearl necklace was something very special indeed.'

'They burned the house down? How awful. Was Elisabeth there?'

'No, she had escaped with her aunt's package, presumably the necklace.' Luc paused as the waiter appeared to top up their glasses, not resuming until he was out of earshot. 'We know Elisabeth succeeded in getting to England, which shows she must have been courageous, as she was only eighteen. Elisabeth's parents and brother disappeared and were never seen again. François had to take his family into hiding in another part of France with his mother's family.'

'What a terrible tragedy. How different our lives would be if Elisabeth and François had been born into a normal family.'

'The two of them got on well together, according to François. Elisabeth was born years after her brother, which meant her nephew was not much younger than her. He obviously adored her and his grandparents. Sounds like they had a lot of fun as children, running wild and exploring the countryside, although I expect they had to work from dawn to dusk as well to keep the farm running.'

'Must have been tough losing so many of his family at so young an age.' Sophie had every sympathy for François, having gone through the trauma of her own mother's early death under far less frightening circumstances.

'François had to grow up fast. He came back later and took over the farm again from the neighbour who had been running it for them. It wasn't until the neighbour was dying that he thought to mention that Elisabeth had sent messengers to search for her family.

Unfortunately, the neighbour was illiterate and thought it best to deny any knowledge of the family at the time. Probably a sensible action, given the soldiers' interest, but devastating to François when he found out Elisabeth had tried to contact them.'

'Did he try to find her after that?'

'François wrote to the address on Elisabeth's letter,' Luc said. 'She had already left England, but, by good luck, his letter was forwarded to the Godwin's former housekeeper, who replied that Elisabeth and Anne had gone to Canada. Even with modern methods, I haven't been able to find them. It was as if Elisabeth had vanished into thin air. No emigration or immigration record, no death record – nothing at all after 1841. I thought perhaps she had died at sea.'

'Her diary answers some of those questions. To say she had an eventful voyage would be an understatement. I'm glad she found happiness again in the end.' Sophie opened her handbag and passed him the diary. 'I hope you'll read it to me, so I can get the full story. The combination of the old-fashioned script and being written in French left me guessing at quite a lot. I'll send you the photos of the sketchbook too. It was too fragile to bring with me.'

From the look Luc gave her, he understood how hard it would be to part with the diary. 'You hold on to it for now. I'll translate François' diary for you too. He was quite a storyteller. As a young boy, he swears he overheard a conversation between his grandparents about a stash of family valuables hidden in a cave. It became something of a family legend.'

'I take it there's no truth to it?'

Luc shrugged. 'I've searched the caves on their Loire Valley farm, as he did, but I found nothing. If there was ever any truth to the tale, the valuables must be long gone. Probably it was his overactive imagination or a reference to the items Elisabeth took to England.'

Sophie leaned back, turning over all the new information in her mind. 'What now, Luc?'

'Unfortunately, I have meetings most of tomorrow, which I can't get out of. After that, I've cancelled all my appointments. We can visit the Loire Valley or anywhere you like.'

'I'd really love to visit Versailles.'

'I thought you would. I have arranged for one of their top curators to give you a personal guided tour tomorrow. Her name is Martine Girard and she'll pick you up at nine o'clock tomorrow morning at your hotel, if that suits you.'

'Fantastic! Thanks, Luc. However did you arrange that?'

'Easy. Martine is my daughter. Now, shall we have dinner? There's a little Breton restaurant close by, which is usually pretty quiet and has wonderful seafood but no Michelin stars.'

Within a few minutes, they were sitting in a quiet corner of a cosy restaurant, ordering the house special, an enormous platter of seafood for two from the coast of Brittany, and a glass of crisp white wine to go with it. Luc wanted to know all the details of her story, so Sophie filled him in on her decision to research her family history and how she had found the trunk in the attic.

When she had finished, he said, 'I don't suppose she left a hairbrush with hair still in it?'

'Not that I recall. Why would you want that?'

'I was thinking we might be able to get DNA to match to the Bourbon royal line. Yours might do, but there are a lot of generations of mixed-up genes separating you from Louis XVI.'

She shook her head at this casual comment. 'Honestly, I still can't get my head around the mere possibility of having a drop of blue blood in my veins.'

'After most of the royal family was executed in the revolution, you'd be amazed at the number of people who turned up claiming to be one of them. Especially the Dauphin, Marie-Thérèse's younger brother. He suffered terribly and died in prison, but dozens of young men have come forth claiming to be him.'

Sophie plucked an oyster from its shell. 'Mm, delicious. I can't offer you her hair, but I may have something even better. Elisabeth was stabbed on the voyage and there were traces of a bloodstain on her clothes. I imagine it would be a long shot, even with the wonders of modern DNA technology.'

'Stabbed! I can't wait to read the diary. Elisabeth does seem to have had an inordinately adventurous life. François thought the world of her. He wrote of how she saved her parents from a soldier by jumping on her horse, leaping a fence, and knocking the soldier unconscious before he could swing his sword. François would be delighted to know that we are reuniting the family after all these years.'

'Elisabeth too. Her family was never far from her thoughts.' She contemplated the last langoustine, before pushing the plate in Luc's direction.

'I hope you have space for dessert. The sweet crêpes they make here are divine.'

'I'll explode if–' Sophie's reply was cut off by the arrival of a large group of diners, who packed the small space with noisy, back-slapping bonhomie and alcohol fumes. A small group of musicians appeared from nowhere, filling the air with accordion music. Before long, the place was heaving with massive platters of food, jugs of cider, raucous laughter and folk dancing.

'There goes our chance for quiet conversation.'

The waiter swerved his way through the mob with a tray carrying a carafe of water, just as one of the dancing men threw his arms out. He had the biceps of a sailor, complete with an anchor tattoo, so the carafe was launched into the air, soaking Sophie as she reached out to grab it before it shattered on the tile floor.

The music and babble stopped, leaving an embarrassed silence. As the waiter hurried forward with a cloth and profuse apologies, Sophie waved at the musicians to continue and smiled to show there were no hard feelings. The band started up again tentatively, winding up to full exuberance level within seconds.

The man who had caused the accident came over, apologised in a language that sounded only vaguely like French, and swept Sophie into the small space that had been cleared for a dance floor before she had a chance to refuse. She soon got the hang of the movements, which seemed to involve tapping feet and swinging hands, a little like Scottish dancing. A round woman with a wizened face grabbed Luc before he could resist and pulled him onto the dance floor too.

As the music got faster and faster, the circle of dancers whirled around at ever-increasing speed, until Sophie felt sure she would fall over if let go. Suddenly the music ended and the group broke into loud applause, while her partner scooped her up and whirled her around, laughing, before depositing her back at her seat with an exaggerated bow and a stream of rapid and unintelligible words. Luc replied for her in equally rapid French and shook the man's hand.

He turned back to Sophie with a grin. 'Crêpes?'

'No way. I'm so dizzy I'm struggling to hold down the seafood. Let's get the bill and escape while the coast is clear.'

Luc waved at the man who had bumped the tray. 'Your admirer has insisted on paying the bill for us.' A burly arm with an anchor tattoo briefly emerged from the throng of dancers, sketching a salute, before disappearing again.

Luc was still grinning, so Sophie asked, 'And what else did he say that amused you so?'

'He said I was a lucky man to have a spirited wife with nice legs. I didn't dare tell him we weren't married in case he whisked you off to his Breton fishing village. It would seem you have inherited Elisabeth's nose for adventure.'

'Actually, I think he might have drunk a little much to be a reliable judge. I just wanted to avoid making a fuss over the water. But I have to admit, I had a really fun time tonight.'

'Me too. Let's get out of here.'

The next morning, Martine Girard whisked Sophie to Versailles in a sunflower-yellow 2CV, which perfectly matched Martine's light floral perfume and her soft linen dress in a crisp lemon colour, with a silk scarf in a rich bronze that brought out the highlights in her dark hair. A classic French beauty.

Despite the difference in age, the two of them clicked straight away. Fortunately, Martine spoke English as well as Luc did, having been to school in Cambridge and, later, taking sabbaticals at the British Museum and the Smithsonian.

'Dad was ecstatic when he got your email, Sophie. Honestly, I think he had long given up hope of ever finding out about Elisabeth. Not that he was obsessive, just that it was always in the back of his mind if he came across any new source of information.' Martine tapped at the steering wheel with manicured fingernails, varnished the same shade as her scarf. 'Well, maybe he is a little obsessive at times.'

'It's exciting for me too.' Sophie let out a small squeak as the car took a corner at speed onto the wrong side of the road, only letting go of the door handle again when she remembered that cars drove on the other side of the road here. 'Ten days ago, I only knew of Elisabeth as an ancestor who migrated to New Zealand from England and founded our family.'

'Dad said you found a diary and some jewellery.'

'It was hidden in the attic, so it was a wonderful surprise. You'll have to come by and take a look.'

'Definitely. I'm almost as excited as he is.' She shot across two lanes of honking traffic with all of Luc's nonchalance. 'We'll be at Versailles soon. Was there anything in particular you wanted to see?'

'I'd say all of it, but I know how enormous the palace is. Most of all, I would like to see the rooms where Louis XVI and his family lived, if possible, and the gardens of the Petit Trianon. I can't miss the Hall of Mirrors, of course, and whatever else you'd recommend. But I could take a public tour if you have work to do. I'd hate to get you in trouble.'

'Not at all. The public tour doesn't get to see all the interesting areas.'

'Luc said you are a curator there, Martine.'

'One day I will be. I'm more like an assistant to the assistant curator at the moment. I do whatever is needed, but mostly I help to manage the special displays or hide in my cubicle cataloguing new acquisitions. My boss is still rather old-fashioned about women, which makes it hard to get ahead. Heaven only knows how he'd react if I got pregnant.'

'Do you have any kids?'

'Not yet, but we'd like to start a family. My husband is willing to share the parenting, but it's never easy with two careers to juggle.'

'I know. I only worked part time when we had our two, but some people still felt it was their moral duty to point out that I was a monster to work at all. They implied my kids would end up as emotionally warped delinquents.'

Martine laughed. 'And did they?'

'Heavens no. They begged to spend longer at the playcentre so they could have more time with their friends, and then marched off to school as if they were ready to take on the world. Miracle of miracles, they are now two delightful, well-adjusted human beings, despite their monstrous mother. They even remember my birthday, so I can't have been too awful.'

'Perhaps I should introduce you to my boss after all.' Martine gave her a dimpled smile, which was the very image of her father's.

'It would be terribly hard to give up such a fascinating job. I always get a thrill from seeing objects from a past era, but getting to examine them up close must be even better. It's the everyday things I like the most. Kitchenware, clothes, toys and suchlike, which show how people really lived. And of course, interesting things like books, clocks, doctor's instruments and whatnot.'

'I totally agree, Sophie. Most people only want to see thrones, crowns, huge paintings of battle scenes, and anything made of gold or diamonds. Some people complain that Versailles is not filled with more period items. They don't realise that the palace was stripped of everything during the revolution.'

'What happened to it all?'

'The royal family took some items with them when they were forced to move to Paris in October 1789. Other precious items were destroyed or stolen or "reassigned". All the art was sent to the Louvre in 1792 and everything else was sold at massive auctions in 1793 and 1794, dispersing our priceless heritage around the world for a fraction of its true worth. Furniture, furnishings, even the children's toys and the pots from the kitchens. Much of it is lost to us forever, although many wonderful period pieces have been reacquired over the years. That is where people like my father come in, trying to track down the more important pieces and negotiating to get them back.'

'Luc seems very passionate about his work.'

'Absolutely dedicated. It drove my mother mad. She liked the glittery gala exhibitions and meeting important people, but dad didn't care about that side of it. Give him a dusty storeroom, a magnifying glass, and the chance of finding a hidden treasure, and he's happy.'

'Has Luce always worked independently?'

'No, only the last few years. He worked at museums for most of his life, but the bureaucracy got to him and dad decided he could devote more time to the actual work if he ran his own business. He had the contacts and experience, so it has worked out well for him. Not that he cares about financial rewards. He'd do it for nothing if he had to. Another point of incompatibility with my mother.'

Sophie wondered if she was being too nosy, but Martine seemed happy to talk, so she ploughed on to a more delicate subject. 'Does he work with Henri Chevalier often?'

'Professionally, I believe Henri uses his services occasionally. Privately, they are reluctant colleagues rather than friends. Henri is a major private collector, so their paths cross a great deal, whether or not they like it. Why do you ask?'

'Monsieur Chevalier turned up at Luc's office almost as soon as I arrived and knew all about me. We were wondering how he found out.'

'Not from me. I did mention you in passing to my mother, but she would rather stab herself in the eye with a red-hot poker than speak to Henri Chevalier. Dad probably hasn't told you, but Henri lured my mother away with his glittering lifestyle.'

'Luc must have been very upset.'

'Not as much as you might think,' Martine said, shaking her head emphatically. 'It didn't take a genius to work out they only stayed together for us kids. I suspect dad was relieved when she left. My mother is terrific, but rather high maintenance. If anything, it was her who regretted the split in the end, because the relationship with Henri didn't last long. Sorry, I'm sure you don't want to hear about all this family drama.'

Actually, Sophie was finding it fascinating, but she was tactful enough to change the subject anyway. 'Henri Chevalier manoeuvred me into having dinner with him tonight. He didn't invite Luc, which I thought was rude of him. Now I understand why.'

'Dad knows Henri's ways well enough that it doesn't bother him anymore. At least you'll get a fabulous meal. Henri is renowned for his lavish hospitality.'

'I have to admit, I'm a little intimidated. Simple cafés are more my style. It never occurred to me to pack more than a small selection of comfortable travel clothes.'

'I have a few decent dresses in the back of my wardrobe for opening night galas.' Martine glanced sideways to assess her passenger, causing the car to drift in its lane. The cars around her honked. Martine honked back, barely blinking a mascaraed eyelash. 'Shall I come over with them this evening? We're probably close enough in size to make it work with a few tweaks.'

Sophie started breathing again. 'Really? If you wouldn't mind, that would be fantastic. Thanks, Martine.'

Martine drove into a car parking area and waved her security tag at the automatic gate. When they stopped, she didn't get out. 'I think I had better warn you that my boss, Francis Bonhomme, is not a fan of my father either.'

Sophie was beginning to think she had landed in a minefield of rivalries and feuds. 'You could always introduce me as a friend of yours if we meet him.'

'It's a little more complicated than that. He is friendly with my mother, so he may know why you are here. I'm very sorry that I was so careless as to mention you to her. It's as if my mother goes out of her way to be around men who are part of dad's circle of work colleagues. Not that she can help it, as her work brings her into their circle.'

'What does your mother do?'

'High-powered lawyer. They only use her on critical work, because she's too expensive for routine legal issues. Dad doesn't mind what she does, or he says he doesn't, but Francis feels uncomfortable around him.'

'So, it's just a personal issue?'

'It's more than that. They had a falling-out at work, which is partly why dad set up his own business.'

'But they must both share the same passion for the past. Surely that brings them together?'

Martine snorted. 'You must be kidding. The market for the best royal memorabilia from the revolutionary era is fiercely competitive. Super-rich Asian and American collectors can't get enough of it, so the prices have become hyper-inflated. That, of course, puts museums like Versailles in a difficult position, because they do not have the funds to ensure the return of items that rightly belong here in France. Besides, my boss is deeply suspicious of everyone who is not under his command and most of those who are too.'

'I can see why precious artefacts disappearing overseas would be frustrating.'

'Especially recently. A lot of items have been snapped up before they appear on the open market. Which means someone, or a group of people, are tracking down items under our noses and selling them straight into private collections, which the public never gets to see.'

'Is that illegal?'

'Depends how it's done. My boss is convinced someone is feeding information to this group from within Versailles. Every time we get a lead on an important piece, it has been sold before we can open negotiations. Very few people know enough to do that. And fewer still have the experience to track down missing items discreetly. At a minimum, it's a breach of work ethics, but more likely theft of data. Because it is illegal to sell heritage items overseas without authority, the offenders would also be charged with that and maybe fraud and document forgery. Cultural trafficking is a very serious offence but highly lucrative.'

'Does your boss suspect Luc was involved? I've only known him a few hours, but I find it extremely hard to believe. He said he rarely works with collectors outside of France, because he is determined that precious historical items should stay here in your country's museums.'

'I'm glad he has you on his side, Sophie. I know it's absolutely ridiculous to suspect him. Francis is a normally a reasonable man and should know dad well enough to realise that too. I guess it's just that when there are unknown people stealing French heritage from under our noses, suspicions and frustration run rife. Lately, it's getting worse, with more items being stolen and sold, probably via the dark web.'

'Nobody could suspect Luc of outright theft. It would destroy his reputation.'

'Exactly. My father has old-fashioned values. Honour and reputation mean more to him than wealth. He gets frustrated too, because he wants to track down these criminals as much as anyone. He has a highly developed sense of duty.' Martine glanced at the time and got out of the car, adding, 'I only wish he'd get out more and have fun occasionally.'

If only she could have seen her father dancing like a dervish last night. 'Thanks for telling me, Martine. I had no idea that there would be so many tightropes to walk, but I suppose every workplace has its challenges.'

The main gates were a short walk away, but it was worth it to approach on foot and take in the colossal scale of the palace. Walking down the middle of the grand courtyard, under the imposing gaze of tall windows, every detail of gilding, statuary and filigree served to amaze and intimidate the visitor. 'Wow' didn't even touch the surface of seeing the Palace of Versailles in person.

Martine gathered up visitor brochures and maps for Sophie and guided her out to the terrace, which overlooked formal gardens as far as the eye could see. 'I have a couple of urgent jobs to do this morning, so why don't you enjoy the gardens while the sun is out. We can meet up again here at eleven and tour the interior together.'

'Perfect. Thanks, Martine.'

Sophie would have loved to spend hours strolling through all the different parts of the estate, admiring the water features and statues, and happily losing herself amongst the shrubbery. But her top priority was to see the grounds of the Petit Trianon, where Marie Antoinette went to escape the rigorous etiquette of the palace. Elisabeth's father, Pierre Duchamp, had been a gardener's lad and her parents had met at Versailles, so it was possible that they had spent time together in these very gardens.

It took her a distraction-filled half-hour to make her way across the estate to the Petit Trianon, a delightful walk on a crisp spring day. Even with her best efforts, she couldn't help making frequent stops to admire the absolute precision of the swirls of gravel laid out artfully within manicured lawns and clipped hedging, dotted with ornate fountains and tree-lined avenues.

The precision of the formal gardens was a stark contrast to Marie Antoinette's garden paradise, inspired by Rousseau's pastoral idyll. Wildflowers, trees, rocks, streams, ponds, meadows, even a cave. How the children must have loved to play here.

Finally, Sophie arrived at the replica village, set on another pond, complete with a spiral-staired tower, mill, dairy, dovecote and cottages. Enchanting, if rather idealistic. The millwheel was decorative and ground none of the precious grain the people were so

185

desperate for, while the pristine marble of the dairy was about as far from Sophie's experiences of real dairy sheds as the palace was from her humble cottage. A beautiful folly.

With a start, she realised it was already getting on for half-past ten. Reluctantly, she left the tranquillity enjoyed by her ancestors, the elusive Ernestine and her gardener friend Pierre. She jogged back to the terrace, giving her just enough time to do a quick loop around the *Parterre du Midi* and *Orangerie*, the ornamental gardens the royal children had looked out upon from their rooms in the palace.

Fortunately, Martine was a few minutes late, giving Sophie a chance to catch her breath and take in the stunning view. If Pierre Duchamp had come from a small farm, the first sight of Versailles must have knocked his socks off. It was awe-inspiring even for her, although she had visited before and seen a thousand photos.

'Sorry I'm late, Sophie. Minor crisis over a delayed shipment.'

'Are you sure I can't take a public tour instead?'

'No way. Dad would disown me. Besides, I want to show you around. Let's start with the King's apartments.'

Martine strode across the parquet, already in full flow of a fascinating commentary about life at

186

Versailles. Sophie gasped and gaped at room after room of historical extravagance. Every horizontal surface was dotted with statues, ornate furniture, porcelain, and clocks. Every vertical surface gleamed with gilding, mirrors, tapestries, and magnificent paintings. Every ceiling was festooned with crystal chandeliers and dramatic paintings of heavenly or earthly drama.

After a few rooms, the grandiose décor had her lost for superlatives and feeling just a wee bit queasy. One thing was abundantly clear in the repeated motifs – the Sun King, Louis XIV, was not averse to an overdose of self-aggrandisement. He featured as a central figure in many of the paintings as well, whether as himself or as the face of Zeus or Alexander the Great.

How must young Louis XVI have felt when thrust into the spotlight within these intimidating walls? A pudgy, awkward man, who enjoyed pottering in his workshop with locks or hunting in the woods, who dithered in his decisions and shrunk from the debauched lifestyle of his forefathers, walking every day under the gaze of a royal deity in these very halls.

And how much more difficult must it have been for the teenage Marie Antoinette, who was used to the greater freedoms of her childhood palaces in Austria, as she struggled with the language and customs of this foreign land. Courtiers surrounded her wherever she went, from dining table to marriage bed. Ladies crowded to tend her every need in elaborate rituals until simple matters like dressing for the day became a dramatic production of ridiculous proportions. Loved at one minute, despised the next, vilified and lampooned by those who did not even know her.

As Martine showed her around, she talked about the events that had happened here over the centuries, until the rooms came alive with a sense of drama, rather than simply being beautifully laid-out museum pieces. The stunning Hall of Mirrors became more than Baroque opulence on an epic scale – it was a political statement of French wealth and power to show foreigners exactly who was in charge, right down through time to the signing of the Treaty of Versailles after World War I.

'Come and see the King's private chambers, Sophie. Scientific instruments were very much in vogue during the Age of Enlightenment. There's a fabulous astronomical clock.'

Once again, Sophie was lost for words as she marvelled over the intricate workings of this masterpiece of craftsmanship. The astronomical clock stood like a golden statue, taller than a person, with a glass globe as its head, filled with a miniature solar system of spinning planets. A clock formed its chest, while the gold-embellished belly had a sun moving to the pace of the day.

In the next room, Sophie was drawn to a beautiful roll-top desk, intricately decorated with inlaid wood and edged with gilded bronze. It reminded her of the jewellery box, albeit on a grander scale.

Martine noticed her interest. 'This desk was completed by Marie Antoinette's favourite cabinetmaker, Jean Henri Riesener. He was an incredible craftsman, known for his fine marquetry and for using clever mechanisms. The lid and drawers of this desk open with a single turn of a key. My favourite piece is a desk he made for Marie Antoinette, which had an ingenious mechanism that allowed the top and main drawer to move together, popping up into a writing area and bookstand, which could be flipped to show a mirror on the other side. The royal couple loved anything clever like that, with pivots or levers or secret compartments.'

'I'd love to see her desk,' Sophie said.

'Unfortunately, you're in the wrong country.' Martine brought up a picture from the Met collection on her mobile.

Sophie's pulse hammered as she compared the fine woodwork of the desk to her jewellery box. They must have been made by the same hand, possibly as a matching set, given the similarity of design.

'There's another fabulous piece in the King's library.' Martine led off through the far door into another series of rooms, unaware of her guest's distraction.

Sophie hurried after her in a daze. Her ancestor, Elisabeth, had mentioned the jewellery box several times in her diary, implying that it was important. In fact, she had given the impression that it was a burden she was guarding out of family loyalty. Sophie has assumed she was talking about the contents of the box – the pearl necklace in particular – but if the designer was so famous, then the box itself must be extremely valuable in its own right.

Martine stopped in a fabulous room decorated in white and gold, lined with cabinets full of books. She was standing in front of a large piece of furniture, clearly in the same style as the other Riesener pieces.

'This commode is a great example of what I was talking about earlier – the loss of great works of French culture during the revolution. It was originally here, in the King's library, but it ended up in the hands of a private citizen in 1794, before being on-sold in London about a century later to the Rothschilds in Vienna. After that, it was seized by the Nazis during the war, returned to a museum in Vienna after the war, then returned to the Rothschild family a couple of decades ago. It's only back here now thanks to the generosity of private donors.'

'What an amazing story. The history of the last two centuries tied up in one piece of furniture. I can see why it must be a major challenge to recover these items and prove provenance.'

'Indeed. It's infuriating when are discover something special and it disappears before we can negotiate its return to France.'

Fascinating as it all was, Sophie felt overwhelmed. Her body was back to insisting that it was the middle of the night, even though her eyes were dazzled by the sunlight outside the windows. 'It's a lot to absorb in a few hours. Could we have a look at the Queen's rooms, then have a break?'

'Of course, Sophie. They are opposite here, at the end of the Hall.'

Marie Antoinette's bedchamber was more feminine than the other rooms, although equally bedecked with gold, chandeliers and elaborate decoration. Martine had wandered ahead, but Sophie felt oddly unable to move, as if a heavy weight was pressing down on her.

The next thing she knew, Martine was crouched down beside her. Inexplicably, she was on her knees, with her heart thumping.

'Sophie? Sophie! Are you okay? You're as white as a sheet. I thought you were going to faint.'

Sophie took the offered arm and staggered to her feet. 'Martine, something terrible happened in this room, didn't it?'

The Storm Breaks

Versailles, 5 October 1789

After Paris boiled over in the stifling heat of July, a simmering calm was briefly restored, as the King returned safely from Paris, convinced his people loved him.

But, as the green leaves turned to russet-gold, then deathly brown, so too had bad tidings from Paris piled up in deepening drifts.

Ernestine learned to judge the gravity of news by the speed at which dour-faced advisers scurried to and fro from the King's chambers.

The King and one cohort of advisers favoured relinquishing some control to the populace, while the Queen and other advisers were convinced that no compromise would be enough to satisfy the traitors behind the unrest. Meanwhile, the armies of more nations than France stood ready to advance.

On many days, the children tiptoed around their mother as each new act of disrespect towards the King threw her into rage or despair. Marie Antoinette urged her husband to leave Versailles for the safety of their remaining family, but he insisted on standing firm, and she refused to leave his side, even to save her children.

Meanwhile, the Queen tried to shield her children from distress by cloistering them in their own world of study and play. The one bright note was the new governess, Madame de Tourzel, and her delightful daughter Pauline, whom the children adored.

Nevertheless, they could all feel the tension oozing down the corridors, as each new compromise led to demands for more.

Ernestine failed, as usual, to subdue her curiosity. This unseemly character flaw (as their strictest under-governess, Madame de Soucy, had labelled it on many occasions) drove a need to find out what was happening, because not knowing was even more frightening to her.

She ghosted around the palace making full use of the myriad secret ways and hiding places she had discovered over the years. In truth, hearing news was becoming ever easier because many of the thousands of inhabitants of Versailles cared less and less for discretion, as the level of dissent rose both outside and inside the walls.

On the morning of the fifth of October 1789, life was as near normal as it could be. The King was off hunting, while the Queen was alone to her beloved private residence, the Petit Trianon, where the children joined her for a meal early that afternoon.

They had just finished eating when Madame Elisabeth, the King's youngest sister, was announced. The children perked up. Although Madame Elisabeth was in charge of their religious and moral education, it was her sweet temper and bounteous garden they adored more than her piety.

Madame Elisabeth rushed into the salon with hair askew and skirts rustling, the damp of the day glistening on her cloak. 'Make haste. We must return to the palace immediately. All the women and rabble of Paris are coming, armed and angry, to Versailles.'

Marie Antoinette knocked her chair to the floor as she rose in haste from the table. 'Are you certain?'

'I saw them myself from the terrace of Montreuil. Thousands are marching towards Versailles with muskets and cannons. I came as quickly as I could but the mob cannot be too far behind me. Come quickly, there is a carriage waiting outside.'

Ernestine reached for Marie-Thérèse's hand but her sister had turned to take her brother's hand. She held the boy close by her side, as he was only four years old and already frightened by the alarm in his aunt's voice.

When they reached the palace, the Queen's first thought was for her husband. Word had already reached Versailles and two men had been dispatched to bring the King home. After a nervous wait, the King arrived on horseback, having galloped back at full speed to be with them as soon as he could.

Madame Elisabeth pleaded with her brother to leave Versailles without delay, but the moment was lost to procrastination. Within an hour, it was too late – the crowd of marchers was at the gates, led by a group of fishwives, waving their gutting knives and shouting obscenities. Some in the mob chanted, 'Bread! Bread! Bread!', others called for the Queen's head on a pike.

At this, Madame de Tourzel hurried the children to the safety of an upper storey room, vowing to the Queen that she would stay with the Dauphin, come what may.

'I hate not knowing what is going on,' Ernestine declared. 'Wait here. I'll be back soon.'

She raced along the corridors to a room with a good view over the courtyard and gates. When she peeped cautiously through a window, Ernestine wished she had kept her curiosity at bay. A vast crowd had gathered outside the palace grounds, held back by a contingent of guards. Madame Elisabeth's estimate of many thousands was no exaggeration. Even at this distance, their chanting assailed her ears.

Most of the crowd appeared to be women, who were brandishing every type of household implement imaginable, from cleavers to fire irons. That was frightening enough, but out amongst the sea of discontent, ranks of pikes and muskets waved like victory flags. A few women had breached the fence and were parading around the courtyard as if they owned it, wearing muddy dresses, stained aprons, and the ubiquitous red bonnets of the revolutionaries, sodden from the rain.

The crowd chanted for the King to come out, rattling the great iron gates until they swayed alarmingly. Then, the crowd parted, and a cannon was rolled up. Panic gripped Ernestine at the sight of its black mouth pointing directly at the palace. A volley of muskets fired, killing several soldiers inside the fence. Her nerve broke. She ran from the window, back to the comfort of the familiar.

The children waited for hours while confusion reigned. First, they were to stay in their rooms, then they were told to join their parents, then back to their rooms again. Officials and advisers raced to and fro, forming plans, then rescinding them before they could be acted upon. The children were told to get ready to depart at any moment and watched on as a carriage pulled up near their rooms. Then they were told they were no longer going.

Snippets of news alternated between hope and despair. 'Lafayette has come with the army, we are saved!' said one courtier, while another cried, 'The National Guard has turned against us and fired on our own soldiers'.

And so it went, on and on, until all the girls wanted to do was curl up in a quiet room and shut the insanity out.

Word came that the King was to meet with a small deputation of women. They feared for his safety and waited anxiously for news. What a relief when they were told that the women had been honoured by his presence and had agreed to disburse if they were given bread. His Majesty, stunned at so simple a request, had ordered bread to be distributed to an equally surprised crowd.

Finally, around midnight, the mob tired of their vigil. Whether through fatigue or satisfaction, a fragile peace was restored. The exhausted children were put to bed in Madame de Tourzel's rooms with her daughter Pauline watching over them. There, they eventually fell into a restless sleep.

A loud clamouring outside the window woke Ernestine.

'What's happening?' Marie-Thérèse hissed.

'Shh, listen.'

The noises gradually grew to a crescendo. The crowd was baying like hounds on the scent of a fox, demanding bread and the Queen's head on a pike, with equal fervour.

Piercing screams and the dull thwacking of weapons on bodies signalled that a deadly fight had erupted within the grounds of Versailles. Then they heard yells and shrieks from within the palace. Running feet passed their door but nobody came to get them.

The two girls huddled together, with no idea what was happening. Ernestine had never been so terrified in her life, not even when she had been caught up in the crowd at the parade.

Suddenly, the door burst open. Ernestine heard Marie-Thérèse whimper and clapped a hand over her mouth.

'Quickly, come with me. Don't be afraid, I am here now.'

'Mother? What's happening?'

'Shh. We must go to the King's chambers without delay.'

Marie Antoinette hurried them through the dark corridors and up the hidden stairs to her husband's bedchamber, where they found Louis-Charles and the King waiting for them.

Ernestine went to sit by Madame de Tourzel, while the royal family embraced each other with relief. 'What has happened, Madame?' she whispered.

Their governess was shivering, her face as white as flour. Her voice crackled as she whispered back, 'The mob has broken down the gates, led by that scoundrel the Duc d'Orléans, and forced their way inside the palace. They slaughtered the guards and rampaged through the palace looking for Her Majesty.'

'I heard them outside, chanting for her head. Is she all right?'

'Shocked but unharmed. Her calm in a crisis is extraordinary. Although how she could remain so tranquil, I do not know. Her Majesty escaped her chambers with seconds to spare, after her guards were brutally slain. If she had not had access to the secret passage beside her bed ... well, I shudder to think what would have happened. If I hadn't seen the slashed walls of her bedchamber with my own eyes, I would never have believed it.'

'Rest easy, Madame. Lafayette's army and the palace guards will soon subdue them.'

'I fear not, Ernestine. Many in the army have dishonoured their oath of allegiance to the King. It is impossible to know whom to trust, let alone who will be brave enough to defend us.'

As if to underscore her words, a raucous cheering arose from the courtyard. Ernestine risked a glance out the window, falling back with a shriek when she saw the severed head of a guard being paraded on the end of a pike. The faces of the crowd were crazed with bloodlust as they howled in delight. Madame de Tourzel pulled her away from the window and wrapped her arms around her shaking body.

The family sat silently as others joined them. The entire party wept with relief when Madame Elisabeth finally joined them after a long delay, her slippers red with blood from the corridors.

Meanwhile, the King met with his advisers. Not that it did much good, as there were so many divergent views that no single course of action could be agreed upon, until it was too late to act at all. The crowd, in contrast, was unified in their demand that the King and Queen return with them to Paris. As the hours dragged by, the King became determined to break the impasse by appearing in person before the crowd to assure them of his goodwill.

Naturally, the Queen insisted on going out on the balcony with him. She called for her two children to accompany her. Marie-Thérèse shook with fear but was determined to follow the lead of her mother.

Ernestine thought them incredibly brave to step into the range of dozens of muskets held by bloodthirsty murderers, but perhaps the mob did too, for some in the crowd now cheered their sovereigns. Nevertheless, the demands for the King to go to Paris were unrelenting, until finally he had to agree. Madame de Tourzel took the children back to their rooms to get dressed for the journey.

Marie-Thérèse darted around the room, trying to gather as many of her favourite belongings as she could. 'Ernestine will come with us, won't she, Madame?'

'I'm sorry, Madame Royale, but the carriage will only take six people and we are already eight. I will come with you, as will Madame Elisabeth.' Madame de Tourzel prised the box of treasures from the girl's hands, gently but firmly. 'You must leave these behind. Ernestine will come in one of the other carriages with the rest of the household.'

'Where are we to go?' Marie-Thérèse asked.

'They say we will go to the Tuileries, though I cannot believe it to be true, given the decrepit state of that palace.'

While Madame de Tourzel went to see to the Dauphin, the two girls shared a tearful goodbye, not knowing how long they would be apart.

'Promise me that you will bring all my precious things with you? You're the only one who will know what I want.'

'Of course,' Ernestine replied. 'I'm sure we will be together again before you know it.'

And that was the last she saw of Marie-Thérèse, as the royal party left by way of the back stairs to avoid the worst of the carnage in the corridors.

Outside, the tumult rose to a deafening roar as the royal family took their seats in the carriage. The mob lurched around on unsteady legs, singing vulgar songs, and tripping over the empty flagons of wine and ale that rolled around their dancing feet. Their numbers seemed to have swelled overnight, until there were people as far as the eye could see.

Ernestine could hear feverish activity and running feet, but nobody came for her and she dared not go out by herself. She stood by the window, alone, hidden in the folds of the drapes, with tears coursing down her cheeks. The royal carriage went out through the gates, surrounded by the triumphant mob and protected only by General Lafayette on his white horse at one door, the commander of the guards at the other, along with a handful of faithful guards.

As the carriage disappeared from sight, chants of '*Vive la nation*!' followed, accompanied by erratic blasts of muskets. It would be a miracle if no one was killed by mistake with so many weapons in unskilled hands.

A line of other carriages followed along behind, carrying other members of the royal household, servants and deputies, along with cartloads of supplies. The bulk of the Parisian army brought up the rear.

The strength of will that had held Ernestine together over the past day suddenly evaporated. Watching the mob outside had been terrifying, but it was the near death of the Queen and the destruction wrought by the mob in the very heart of her domain that had her running to the sanctuary of a curtained alcove, not daring to make a sound in case the mob came back.

She went down on her knees and prayed for their safe arrival in Paris, not knowing if she would ever see them again, finishing with a fervent plea for her own life to be spared as well.

The Queen's Bedroom

Paris, 2019

Martine surreptitiously checked her pulse. 'Sophie? Are you okay?'

Sophie hoisted a weak smile to her lips, although her heart still thundered as if she had been under attack. 'I'm fine. Just a momentary dizziness. The sense of history here is so powerful, it's easy to become overwhelmed.'

'You went as white as a ghost, Sophie. Jetlag often catches up with me on the second day back. I imagine it must be doubly hard coming from a time zone ten hours ahead.'

'You're right about that.' Odd, when she had felt so much better this morning. 'Too much strong coffee and too little water hasn't helped.'

'Let's go down to the staff room and get you something to eat and drink.'

'Perhaps we can finish looking at Marie Antoinette's rooms while we are here.'

Martine studied her for a moment, evidently deciding that Sophie was not about to collapse again. 'You asked if something bad happened here, and you were right. Versailles was stormed by an angry mob during the revolution, demanding Marie Antoinette's head. They slaughtered the guards stationed at the foot of the staircase, but two guards managed to get to the Queen's door and warn her, even though they were badly wounded. The Queen escaped via a secret passage to the King's rooms in the nick of time, before the mob broke into this bedroom using axes. You can see the door to the hidden passage over here, by the bed.'

'Terrifying.' The metallic smell of blood lingered in Sophie's nose – an odd after effect of her dizzy spell.

'Best not to dwell on it. Come and have a look at the exquisite jewellery cabinet Louis had made for Marie Antoinette as a wedding gift. It cost as much as a skilled craftsman could hope to make in a lifetime.'

Sophie admired the wardrobe-sized cabinet. Louis had certainly spared no expense to make his present as fabulous as possible. 'I know Marie Antoinette liked her jewels, but even she must have had to work hard to fill this.'

Martine laughed. 'A task she took on with enthusiasm and great success. She spent gargantuan sums on jewellery, not to mention furniture, clothes, accessories, porcelain … you name it, she bought it. She wasn't called Madame Deficit by the people for nothing. Let's have a quick look in her private chambers. There are another couple of exquisite Riesener pieces in there.'

The first of the Queen's private rooms was a small, irregularly shaped room in soothing white and blue, with gold trim, far more restrained in style than the outer room. Serene was the word that sprang to mind.

'Marie Antoinette would rest here during the day. It's called the *Méridienne* room,' Martine explained, before leading her into a maze of other rooms.

Sophie stifled a yawn. Fascinating as Martine's tour was, she was fading fast. The curtained daybed in the *Méridienne* room looked decidedly tempting, although it was still only mid-afternoon. A quick bite to eat and she would call it a day, leaving her time for a brief nap before facing Henri Chevalier for dinner.

Martine must have noticed her distraction, because she guided Sophie quickly through the rest of the rooms, flipping through a few key points with the speed of a normal tour guide running to a tight schedule, albeit without the flock of tourists following along behind.

Normally, Sophie hated being rushed and rarely went to museums with anyone else, in case they got fed up with her reading all the descriptions and examining items in detail. But on this trip, she was a free agent. She could come back another day or even spend an entire week here if she wished. That thought perked her up long enough to follow Martine through a labyrinth of corridors into the staff area.

Her guide stopped abruptly in a doorway and reversed out into Sophie, who was trying to stay close and not get lost.

'*Martine. Attends!*'

Martine rolled her eyes and turned back into the staff room. '*Bonjour, Maman. Comment ça va?*'

An elegant woman rose to greet them, smoothing down a cream suit in the style of Chanel (or possibly a genuine Chanel), which looked fabulous with her dark skin and artfully tied scarf. She was as out of place amongst the Formica tables and utilitarian china as a racehorse in a farmyard.

She leaned forward to air-kiss Martine on both cheeks, being careful not to disturb her perfect makeup. Aside from two symmetrical tendrils of hair curling in front of her diamond-stud earrings, her long black hair was rolled into an immaculate French twist. Sophie would have died happy if she could have achieved such a sleek look with her own wayward hair even once in her lifetime, let alone by mid-afternoon of a workday.

'*Maman*, this is Sophie West. Sophie, my mother, Jacqueline.'

Jacqueline was only a little taller than Sophie, yet she managed to look down on her with the evaluating gaze of an entomologist studying a new species of bug.

'*Bonjour*, Jacqueline, a pleasure to meet you.'

'So, you are the mysterious Sophie West? Martine is showing you around?'

'Your daughter has an amazing knowledge of Versailles. I am lucky to have her as my guide.'

Jacqueline's eyes narrowed. 'Lucien is not here?'

'No. He had work to do.'

'*Vraiment*? I am surprised he has let you out of his sight after so many years of searching for that woman from the past. Has Martine told you of all the vacations we wasted while he searched caves?'

Martine's cheeks turned pink. '*Maman*, this is not necessary. Sophie is our guest.'

A tall man with a nose like a hatchet interrupted them. 'Your visit is most welcome, Madame West.' He shook her hand and kissed Jacqueline. 'I am Francis Bonhomme, specialist in eighteenth-century acquisitions. If you have any items of interest from your ancestor, I would be pleased to give you an expert opinion.'

Sophie wondered just how many people were aware of her visit and had expectations of her. 'The items of most interest to me are my ancestor's diary of her voyage to New Zealand and some lovely jewellery given to her by her English husband. I expect they will be of limited interest to you. There are a couple of minor items from France too, including a charming little wooden owl carved by her father. Luc has them if you wish to see.'

Francis Bonhomme exchanged a glance with Jacqueline, his pursed lips spelling out his disappointment. 'I suggest you be careful where you put your trust, Madame West. As you English say, the apple falls under the tree.'

Instead of expanding on this cryptic comment, he spoke in rapid French to Jacqueline, of which Sophie picked up enough to understand he was apologising for being late. 'You must excuse us. We are due at an exhibition on the far side of Paris. I am hoping to see you again soon.'

With that they were gone, leaving Martine red-faced and Sophie more than a little curious. It was too late for the café lunch, so they got packaged sandwiches and bottles of water from the vending machine.

'I am so sorry, Sophie. My mother got tired of what she called dad's obsession with tracking down relics of the past. My sister and I loved the adventure of searching caves and hearing the old family stories. Honestly, I think dad only kept it up for our sakes.'

Sophie set down the water bottle, already half empty. 'Yet she left him for another collector.'

'True, but Henri Chevalier doesn't enjoy the search as much as the possession. He is rich and well-connected, and loves to go to all the most prestigious events in Paris and sailing on his yacht in the Mediterranean. Whereas dad is happier hiking through forests and clambering through caves, when he is not at work.' Martine levered the plastic pack open and poked dubiously at the wilted salad and unnaturally square slice of cheese. She sighed. 'My parents loved each other once, but they married too young and came to want very different things out of life.'

'It's not uncommon.' Sophie was impressed by Martine's mature attitude and felt some sympathy for Luc. She too preferred the great outdoors to glamorous functions, even it wasn't the norm. 'Their reaction to me was interesting. Monsieur Bonhomme's response I understood – he wants first dibs on anything valuable – although his remark about trust was rather offensive, especially said in front of you. But your mother seemed almost, well, annoyed is the word that comes to mind.'

Martine pushed a discarded crust around the tabletop. 'I think she is upset that dad has finally been proved right – that his efforts to track Elisabeth have not been entirely wasted. She ought to be happy for him, of course, but I suspect she will be furious if the

210

mythical family treasure ever comes to light. Despite appearances, she misses him.' She looked up from the crust and gave Sophie a rueful smile.

'Families, eh? Luc is lucky to have two lovely daughters.'

Martine nodded emphatically. 'Yes, he is, and we don't let him forget it. And now he also has a lovely New Zealand relative, even if it is a very distant link. It would be wonderful to get to know you better, Sophie. We'd love to have you to dinner one evening, depending on what your plans are.'

'That would be lovely. I was originally intending to be in Paris for only a few days. After that, I hope to travel around Britain and Europe, sightseeing and visiting the places my ancestors came from. The trip was rather spur of the moment, so my plans are flexible.'

'Sounds wonderfully adventurous. You are travelling alone?'

'It's more fun than it sounds. I can follow my own whims and meet more locals.' Sophie drained the last drops of water. 'Martine, if you don't mind, I think I might take the train back. My brain is so frazzled, I don't think I can take in any more information. I really need a rest before I face going out for dinner with Henri Chevalier.'

'You don't mind catching the train on your own? I could leave early and drive you back.'

'No need. You have given up enough of your precious time already. I have an app on my phone with maps and timetables and the train goes right to Montparnasse, so it should be easy, as long as I go to the right station. Don't look so worried. I speak enough French to buy a ticket.'

Martine guided her back down a series of corridors to the public area and kissed her on both cheeks. 'I'll drop by around seven o'clock with a selection of dresses.'

As Sophie waved goodbye and headed into the crowd, Martine ran after her and grasped her arm. 'Sophie, no matter what anyone says, you can trust my father.'

She took in Martine's worried frown and patted her hand. 'I don't doubt it, Martine. Thanks again for a fantastic tour.'

Sophie took the elevator up to her fourth-floor room, squeezed into a corner by three large and vocal Germans, who were wearing striped shirts and berets. Her head was still filled with the opulent glory of Versailles, so when the doors opened with a ping and disgorged her into a generic corridor of calming neutrals and unnaturally perky artificial plants, she was disoriented for a moment, until her brain supplied: turn left, around the corner and all the way to the end of the corridor.

As she rounded the corner, Sophie noticed a man slouched against the wall beside the end room – her room – shaking a cigarette out of a blue packet. She only had a glimpse of the side of his face and felt reasonably certain he was a stranger, which was hardly surprising given how few people she knew here. The door to her room opened. She suddenly realised she must have stepped off the elevator on the wrong floor. A simple mistake to make in a crowd.

She was almost back to the elevator when the numbers on the doors registered. They all started with '4', so she had been on the correct floor. Someone had been in her room, or, rather, one person inside and one on watch outside. Any moment now, they would come around the corner and see her. Should she stay and accost them? Or walk as fast as she could in the other direction, so they wouldn't know they'd been seen?

The elevator door pinged again and an elderly Japanese man shuffled out, wearing an 'I love Paris' baseball cap and an Eiffel Tower t-shirt, bulging with a money pouch. He turned in her direction, so she slipped in behind him. Sophie tensed as the two of them rounded the corner, but the corridor was now empty.

The tourist jiggled his entry card in the lock of the second room and disappeared into his room with a weary sigh. Sophie glanced around, puzzled, until she spotted a door to the stairwell halfway down the corridor. No one was visible on the stairs, but the clatter of rapidly descending footsteps echoed up the concrete shaft.

The air outside her room held the faint scent of cigarette smoke that all smokers carry around with them, although this smell was more pungent than the brands of cigarettes sold at home. Her room appeared to be as she had left it, except that the maid had been in to make the bed and clean the bathroom.

Nevertheless, Sophie had a nagging sense that things were not exactly as she had left them. She sniffed. Surely not? Armani cologne again. Either someone was excelling at tracking her or the fragrance was much more common here than in New Zealand.

She scanned the room, stopping at the suitcase, which she was fairly sure she had left partially unzipped as she had hurried out this morning. Perhaps the maid had zipped it as she straightened up the room. A quick inventory showed that everything was present. Her own meagre jewellery was still in the small safe in her room, along with her spare cash, flight tickets and a back-up credit card, although she could have sworn that she had left the tickets under the wallet. Thankfully, Sophie kept her passport and credit card with her at all times and she'd had the foresight to leave Elisabeth's jewellery box in the security of the hotel's safe-deposit facility as soon as she had arrived yesterday.

Was it simply her imagination playing tricks on her? Perhaps the men were hotel staff checking on the standard of service or replacing a light bulb? Or maybe travellers as dazed with jetlag as she was, trying the door and finding it open? Both more likely than an intruder who had broken into the safe but not stolen the cash.

Her mobile broke into her thoughts, blaring out a rousing anthem. *La Marseillaise* – the ringtone she had assigned Luc in a moment of whimsy. '*Bonjour*, Luc.'

'Hi Sophie. I'm calling to see if you are feeling all right. Martine left a message to say you returned by train.'

'I'm fine, thanks. I only came back because I need a break before going out tonight. I had a wonderful time with Martine. What an impressive young woman your daughter is.' She tossed up whether to tell him about the man in her room and decided not to worry him. 'Martine said there is no way Henri Chevalier could know about my visit from her. I met Francis Bonhomme, and he knew too, so the grapevine is obviously running hot.'

'What did Francis say to you?'

Even down the phone, she heard the uncharacteristic sharpness in Luc's voice. 'Only that Francis would like to see anything of Elisabeth's from her life in France. It was only a brief conversation, as they had an appointment, and I told him very little. To be honest, I'm feeling jittery about meeting another complete stranger who knows about me and my ancestry.'

'Oh. There's a reason Francis knows about you–'

'No need to explain – Martine filled me in. It's not how he knows me, it's what he thinks he knows.'

'Sophie? You sound worried.'

'Not worried exactly. Just unsettled by all the odd things that have happened. I think someone searched my hotel room. Possibly the same man who burgled me in New Zealand.'

'What!' Luc's voice boomed through the phone. 'I'll be right over.'

'Wait, Luc, there's no need. I'm okay. If there was a burglar, he hasn't taken anything.'

Silence dragged until she wondered if he was still there. Finally, Luc said, 'I don't think you should meet Chevalier alone.'

It was nice to have someone who was concerned for her, but Sophie needed to assert control over her own decisions. 'It'll be fine. After all, a man as rich as him is hardly likely to mug me for my purse. I'll look forward to catching up with you tomorrow, Luc. *Au revoir*.'

Their conversation reminded her that she had not yet sent the name of her hotel to Henri. Sophie was in no mood for dinner with him but couldn't pass up the chance to find out more about her ancestor. Before she could have second thoughts, she sent the text, receiving his reply within minutes.

The time she had set aside for a power nap was fast disappearing. Should she waste more time changing rooms for safety's sake? She dismissed the idea, partly out of stubbornness and partly because the burglar would not return if he hadn't found anything. And she would feel like a complete idiot if it turned out to be hotel staff checking her room.

In the end, she propped a heavy armchair against the door, set her alarm, and fell into bed.

By the time she had had forty winks, showered, and dried her hair, Martine was at the door with three dresses, all lovely. Sophie ignored the low-cut shimmery one as being too Hollywood-starlet (way too much leg and cleavage at her age, though it would look amazing on Martine). The black dress was the best fit and had a classical elegance that would fit with the Chevalier style. But her eyes kept coming back to the midnight-blue dress, which reminded her of a modern version of Elisabeth's gorgeous gown from the trunk in the attic.

'You have such great taste, Martine. Are you sure you don't mind me borrowing one of these divine dresses?'

'It'll be a pleasure to see them used.' Martine stood back with her hands on her hips, chewing her lip thoughtfully. 'The black dress is terrific, but I do love the blue on you. I bought the silk and had it made in India, but it never quite suited me.' She rummaged in her bag and drew out a sewing kit. Within minutes, she had pinned up a few adjustments, so the bodice was a better shape and the dress was the right length. 'I'll put a few stitches in place while you do your makeup. As long as you don't do any wild dancing, it should hold together.'

The two women kept up a stream of conversation while they went about their tasks. When Sophie had finally run out of superlatives to describe Versailles, Martine gave her a quick rundown of Henri Chevalier's background, while scooping Sophie's hair up into a stylish up-do with no apparent effort.

'His family is old money. Henri took the family's thriving furniture business and turned it into a global powerhouse, specialising in high-end reproductions. He owns loads of property in Paris, a mansion on the Med and who knows how many rich-boy toys. Henri is fabulously wealthy and loves everyone to know it, but he's actually quite sweet when you get to know him. He is generous to good causes, especially to museums and historical research.'

'So, it'll be safe to have dinner with him?'

'Probably. He's known for dating young models, but secretly I think he gets bored with them. Every time I see him really enjoying himself at a function, he's talking to an intelligent woman who doesn't buy into his game. Perhaps he likes the challenge.'

Martine made a last adjustment, then went to answer a knock at the door. A moment later, she was back. 'Dad is here to check up on you. He looks concerned.' Martine gave her a wink. 'I expect you're about to get the "don't stay out too late and no kissing in the backseat" lecture.'

'He's about thirty years too late for that old gem,' Sophie replied, rolling her eyes melodramatically. She took a last glance in the full-length mirror, deciding that Martine would be lucky to ever get this divine creation back again. She came out of the bathroom and did a twirl. 'Great work, thanks Martine.'

'Looks fabulous, don't you think, dad?'

'What do I think?' Luc eyed her critically. 'I think Sophie will need a taser if she's going to wear that in front of Henri Chevalier. What's wrong with a nice pair of trousers and a long-sleeved shirt buttoned to the neck?'

Martine cracked up at his joke, but Luc wasn't smiling. 'Ignore my prehistoric father, Sophie. You look perfect. Henri will be spilling all his secrets before you hit the hors d'oeuvres.'

Luc opened his mouth to speak but the hotel phone interrupted him. Henri Chevalier's chauffeur was waiting in the lobby 'at her convenience'.

'Have fun,' Martine said.

'Take care, Sophie,' Luc said. 'Message me when you're back at the hotel, no matter how late it is. Please.'

Martine gave her a 'what did I tell you?' look, but Sophie agreed to the request with good humour and gathered up her bag and the wrap Martine had lent her. Despite the vague unease she felt about the odd things happening to her since her arrival, it was rather nice to be a traveller in a foreign land and yet still have people who cared about her.

And, she had to admit, as the chauffeur tipped his cap and opened the door of the Mercedes for her, it was an entirely new and thrilling experience to be treated as a VIP.

If only she didn't have to go alone.

Eye of the Storm

Ernestine was alone. Completely and utterly alone.

The last of the carriages had long since departed, swept away by a wave of armed citizens and soldiers, leaving only the fading echo of musket fire and chanting. An eerie silence settled over Versailles – a sensation so unusual that it felt as if her ears were throbbing with the total absence of sound.

Ernestine curled up in an armchair in a corner of the King's library, waiting for someone to come for her. Normally, she loved this room, with its elegant furniture and rows of white cabinets edged in gold, crammed with books, and promising answers to all the mysteries of the world. Today, it seemed cold and bleak, with the fire and candles unlit, and hastily pulled drapes letting in only a slice of dim light.

An hour passed. Two. Nobody came.

Should she search the palace for help? What if the only people here were revolutionaries, searching the empty rooms for prey? Best to stay here, where she had been told to wait.

The churning in her stomach gradually became a growl of hunger. Ernestine stroked the little owl Pierre had made for her, remembering how brave he had been standing up to the group of women who had cornered her at the parade. Standing, holding her fists out in front of her, she squared her shoulders and scowled fiercely at a mirror. The reflection burst into giggles at this foolish waif of a girl, who looked about as scary as a poodle puppy.

If she couldn't be scary, then she would be steadfast in the face of danger. She drew her shoulders up and back, stretching her spine, wiping emotion from her face – chin up, lips pursed, eyes looking down her nose – sending her enemies to their knees with her glare. In a flash of recognition, she saw Marie-Thérèse in the mirror, and finally understood that her sister's famed haughtiness was her defence against the vexations she endured.

This novel feeling of power gave her the strength to take action. She strode into the next room, which was still laid with the long-forgotten breakfast, which none of them had wanted to eat. At the sight of it, Ernestine felt ravenous. She grabbed at food with her bare hands and washed it down with hot chocolate, which had long since gone cold.

The food gave her the energy she needed to take the next step. The state drawing rooms, where anyone might lurk, were a step too far. She retreated into the sanctuary of the King's apartments, passing back through the library and private rooms, and on into her favourite place, the clock room.

How many hours had she spent watching the whirling gears of the marvellous astronomical clock with its golden globe, showing not only the time and date but also everything from the phases of the moon to the movements of the planets around the sun. She reached out to touch its solid familiarity, before moving on into the King's personal chambers.

The continuing silence reassured her that none of the mob had stayed behind to loot the palace. Feeling brave, she stepped out into the Hall of Mirrors. Shafts of late afternoon sunlight shone through the long row of arched windows at a low angle, shimmering off the massive chandeliers and setting fire to the mirrors. Her spirits soared. She danced down the length of the hall, leaping like a ballerina as she passed each of the enormous panels of mirrors, laughing at her daring.

As she skidded to a halt at the far end, a series of loud bangs shocked the fleeting frivolity out of her. The sound became louder as she crept through the state drawing rooms, one by one, under the gaze of gods, kings and mythological creatures.

The noise was coming from below. Halfway down the stairs, she realised the shutters were being closed for the first time in her memory. As the banging came closer, she ran back up the stairs and all the way back to the private chambers.

Ernestine hesitated in the *Oeil-de-Boeuf* antechamber, unsure if she should stay upstairs or go downstairs to the comforts of her own room. Upstairs felt safer, so she went through to the small inner rooms of the Queen's apartments. The *Méridienne* room provided the sanctuary she needed. Small, secluded, decorated in comforting pale blue, white and gold, with a curtained daybed. A room prized by the Queen as a place of calm for her midday rest, and now a perfect retreat from the horrors of the outside world.

The evening passed with no further disturbance. Ernestine lay still but awake as the hours dragged past. A thousand thoughts jostled for space in her mind. Prime amongst them was the question of what she would do now. Hope that everyone would return to Versailles? Wait here until someone came to find her? But what if no one did … or the mob came back to loot the treasures lining the walls of the palace.

Perhaps she should attempt to find some way to join her adopted family at the Tuileries palace. But how would she get to Paris? And what would happen if she could not get to them? She could count the number of visits she had made to the city on a single hand and, even then, she had been safely conveyed there in a carriage surrounded by guards. The realities of life in the world outside these walls were as foreign to her as the customs of the far-away lands depicted in the King's atlases.

And then there was the third option, recommended by her papa. Take the chance to slip away and save herself. At least that was one option she could dismiss immediately. After all, they had done for her, she would not desert her adoptive family in their hour of need.

Finally, Ernestine decided to leave the decision until the morning. With any luck, her papa would find her. If not, she could search the grounds for Pierre. Those thoughts triggered a fresh wave of panic. What might have happened to them? Had the palace servants and gardeners been sent away by the revolutionaries? Or worse, slaughtered by the mob?

At some point in the early hours of the morning, she dropped into a fitful doze.

The next morning, she awoke to silence. Suddenly, the walls seemed to be looming in on her and she felt an urgent need to breathe fresh air. She stumbled out through the hidden door by the Queen's bed.

The Queen's bedchamber was in utter disarray. Shredded bedding lay strewn on the floor, the marks of dozens of filthy boots trampled into the pale silk and linen. The beautiful gilt panels of the room had been slashed and punctured. Ernestine understood now the brutal truth of the words Madame de Tourzel had whispered yesterday. Her Majesty, Marie Antoinette, Queen of France, had indeed been seconds from losing her life to these madmen. Ernestine shuddered to think she had been sleeping so close to the site of this horror.

As she stooped to retrieve the Queen's hastily discarded night attire, a slight breeze tickled the back of her neck. She turned to find it was coming through the splintered door, which had obviously been subjected to a frenzied attack. As she drew closer, Ernestine became aware of an unpleasant smell. She hesitated, half unwilling, half curious to see what lay beyond the broken panels.

As she passed through the antechambers, which also showed signs of a furious attack, the smell grew stronger. When she reached the guardroom, the stench hit her nostrils like a solid entity. Outside the door, on the landing of the marble staircase, a pool of blood spread across the floor. She stepped over it and ventured down the stairs, until she saw a body, savagely hacked and beheaded.

Ernestine added her own vomit to the vile stench, before stumbling back to the Queen's bedchamber, cursing her foolishness. She sank down onto the floor, her whole body shaking so hard that she could not even reach for a handkerchief to wipe her mouth. After a few minutes, the shock subsided enough for her to rinse her face and mouth at the washstand.

The warm bed in the hidden room cried out to her. She would give anything to curl up and retreat into sleep. Instead, she slipped downstairs and through deserted corridors to her own room. The only sounds she heard were the banging of loosely latched shutters and the soft patter of her own steps.

She changed into fresh clothes and headed out onto the terrace and into the Orangerie, not seeing a single living soul. She averted her eyes from the dead bodies scattered here and there, hurrying onward into the gardens, where the fresh air revived her spirits and flushed the panic from her body. As she walked through the trees, taking strength from their solid presence, she went through her options again.

With the mob long departed and Versailles apparently deserted, she would be as safe here as anywhere, especially given her knowledge of hiding places. In contrast, Paris would be both dangerous and unknown. The best course of action was surely to stay here for a few days until someone came for her. And if they didn't, well, she would deal with that when the time came.

Meanwhile, she could make herself useful. The family had left with few of their possessions. The Queen had taken only her most precious jewels, while the King took a few important documents, and the two remaining royal children had not much more than the clothes they were wearing.

In the chaos of their leaving, Ernestine had paid little attention to what was happening around her. From what little Madame de Tourzel had said, the Tuileries palace had not been used for years and was a dank, decrepit place. She hoped someone had had the sense to take essential items, such as clothes, linens, and warm blankets, although she knew even that may not have been possible given the haste of their forced departure.

But what of their most beloved possessions? Here at last was something tangible she could do to help them and keep herself busy. Ernestine would honour her last promise to Marie-Thérèse by gathering their precious belongings and taking them to Paris. Somehow.

With the decision made and a plan of action in front of her, Ernestine realised the roiling dread within her stomach had receded, only to be replaced by a ravenous hunger. She stopped and looked around. The Grand Canal was away to her left, so she was closer to the Petit Trianon than the palace.

In the kitchens, she found the remnants of the meal they had been eating when news came of the march on Versailles. It felt like an eternity ago, although it was less than two days. She helped herself to an odd mixture of savoury and sweet, not really caring what she ate. When she could stuff no more in, she scooped bread, cheese, apples and the rest of the tart into a basket to take back with her.

Her new plan required some means of transport to Versailles, so she continued on in search of the one person she trusted above all others to help her, Pierre Duchamp. She ran to the stable loft, where Pierre slept above the ponies, and called out to him, desperate to know if her friend was alive. No response. She searched the gardens. Nothing. Where else might he be? In desperation, she went to the tiny cottage where his Uncle Remy lived. Before she reached the door, she knew from the raucous, off-key singing that his uncle was the worse for drink.

Through the small window, she could see him slouching on a chair, elbows resting on a cask emblazoned with the crest of Marie Antoinette, taking great gulps from a tankard. It seemed she was not the only one to have taken sustenance without leave. She was about to slink away when he spotted her.

'Ern'stine, tha' you? Come in girl an' join me.'

She opened the door, but did not step across the threshold. 'Monsieur Duchamp, can you tell me where Pierre is?'

'Stupid whelp wen' ta 'elp with the horses. Damn nags frittened by the noise. Shoulda left well alone. Las' I saw 'im, he were jumpin' o'er dead bodies of soldiers, disappearin' into the mob, trying to get to the damn beasts. Never saw 'im again. What'll I tell his folks?'

Ernestine backed out so fast, she fell over a haphazard stack of firewood.

'Come back, girl. Share a drink with your old uncle.'

She ran as if the devil was on her tail, not stopping until she ran out of breath. Through the numbness, she became aware of an ache in one hand and the sting of skinned knees. Blood dripped from splinters in her palm onto the handle of the basket, which, by some miracle, she was still clutching. She pulled the slivers out, ignoring the pain, knowing it was nothing compared to the pain inside, as if her heart had been stabbed through with a sharp wooden stake. Her Pierre, killed by the mob? Please, please, let it not be true.

Hours later, she found herself back in the palace, on her own bed, not knowing how she had got there. She forced herself to sit up. Dried her swollen eyes. Told herself she was not a child anymore, who bawled at the trials of life, but a competent eleven-year-old young woman.

Pierre would still be alive. Was certainly alive, her heart told her.

Ernestine washed her hands and face and began to gather Marie-Thérèse's favourite possessions. Before she had finished picking out favourite books, she heard her name being called.

'Papa!' She ran down the corridor and threw herself into the arms of Jacques Lambriquet. 'You came back for me!'

'Of course I did. I would have come anyway, but once Her Majesty realised you had been left behind, she insisted on it and ordered a horse to be made ready without delay. She was furious with Madame de Soucy, to whom she had entrusted your care.'

'They are safe in Paris, then?'

'Safe enough for the moment, although I fear the violence may flare up again at any time. The Tuileries is a pigsty compared to Versailles. It is an abomination that our sovereigns should be reduced to such conditions. They had to sleep on chairs last night for lack of beds.' He held her by the shoulders, taking in the bandaged hands and torn dress. 'Are you hurt, my dear?'

'No, I am fine. No more than a minor scrape when I tripped over.'

He held her gaze, lines etched deep on his forehead. 'The mob … they didn't … find you?'

'Papa, you know how well I know the hiding places of the palace. I am fine.'

'Thank the Lord for that. Come now, we can rest awhile and exchange news. Tomorrow, you must decide if we are to ride away to the safety of our distant family or return to Paris.'

'You already know my decision, Papa.'

'Then we will talk no more of it today. Let's find something to eat while you tell me what you have been up to.'

Ernestine explained her plan to her father, faltering only when she described her search for Pierre. 'I had hoped he could help me, Papa, by finding a cart and taking me to Paris.' She dropped her face into her hands to cover her anguish. 'But his uncle saw him swallowed by the mob and thinks he is dead.'

'Pierre, dead? Rest easy, my dearest. He is heading to Versailles even now. They needed him to drive a cart to Paris, and now he is returning with it to pick up essential supplies. I came on horseback, and thus arrived first.'

She threw her arms around her father, then danced around the room in an outpouring of joy.

The two of them spent the next couple of hours sorting out what to take to Paris. The King had asked her father to gather additional documents and personal papers, which they added to the pile of personal possessions Ernestine had amassed. Miraculously, the mob had ignored the priceless treasures of Versailles in their frenzied hunt for the Queen.

Jacques Lambriquet stood back, surveying the pile. 'We'll never fit all of it into a single cart. I'll have to leave directions to take additional loads. Arrangements are being made to take enough furnishings to the Tuileries to make the place habitable.'

'We might be able to take more things if we had something to pack them into.'

'Trunks perhaps. Although, I suspect the brigands who infest the road to Paris would take one look at the royal insignia and rob us. I don't fancy ending my days lying in a ditch with a slashed throat. Why didn't I think to arrange for some soldiers to accompany us?'

'I might have an idea.'

Ernestine whirled at the sound of the voice behind her. 'Pierre!' She ran over and threw her arms around him. 'I'm so happy to see you alive.'

He hugged her back. 'I could say the same of you.'

'When you two have finished squeezing the life out of one another,' Jacques Lambriquet interjected, with a chuckle, 'I'd like to hear your idea, Pierre.'

'Coffins.'

'Coffins?'

'Before I left, the estate carpenter told me the King had ordered him to make coffins, so the bodies of the dead soldiers and servants could be given a decent burial. I'd wager there's a pile of them ready, as the carpenter is as quick with his hands as he is slow with his words.'

'Brilliant idea. The brigands will have no interest in stealing dead bodies, at least not those in plain coffins. Pierre, why don't you head down to the stables and see to the horses, then visit the carpenter. We'll leave at first light tomorrow.'

'Wait.' Ernestine went over to the table and retrieved the basket of food. 'You must be starving.'

'You know me, Ernestine. I'm always hungry.' He took the basket from her, lifted the cloth, and licked his lips. 'I'll be back in time for supper.'

By suppertime, they had filled eight coffins with the treasured personal effects of the royal family. Ernestine had found black clothes for all of them to wear. Nothing too ostentatious, just respectable clothes, such as might be worn by the grieving families of dead servants.

When all the work was done, Ernestine lit a candle and took Pierre on a tour of the palace. It was late in the evening when they returned, as he had gasped and gaped in awe at every magnificent room, statue, painting and chandelier.

His favourite rooms were the clock room and the workshop, where he gathered up a selection of maps, tools and instruments for the King. He looked straight at her and said, 'A man needs his favourite things around him, Ernestine.'

She felt herself blush. Suddenly, the world seemed a much brighter place.

The next morning, they loaded up the cart and headed to Paris.

Dinner for Two

Paris, 2019

Henri Chevalier's apartment was only a few kilometres away in distance but a world away in prestige.

The area in which Luc lived was steeped in a delightful combination of grand Parisian architecture and bustling everyday life, yet it seemed almost ordinary compared to the ancient churches, classic buildings and narrow streets they were driving through now. At ground level, the shops glittered with luxury name-brand boutiques, fancy restaurants, art galleries, and bijou delicatessens and wine bars. The cars were not the Citroëns and Renaults (or, heaven forbid, Toyotas and Fords) of outer Paris, but a mix of Mercedes, Audi and BMW.

Sophie leaned forward to ask the chauffeur what area they were passing through, or as close to that question as she could muster in French.

He replied in excellent, if heavily accented, English. 'Saint-Germain-des-Prés, madame, one of the most historic areas of Paris.' He turned into a narrow street lined with galleries and antique shops, before gliding to a stop outside a building with a discreet brass plaque saying '*Institut Chevalier*'.

Henri Chevalier was waiting to open her door and help her out of the car. 'Madame West – Sophie – what a pleasure to see you again. I must apologise for not escorting you myself.' He waved a hand towards the plaque. 'Urgent business. But now, I am all yours. Welcome.'

The ground floor of the building was a combined gallery and workplace. Everyone had gone home for the night, except for one light in an office at the far end, but the dozens of desks indicated a substantial staff. Henri took her up in the lift, for which she was grateful, given her borrowed high heels.

'May I say you look beautiful tonight? Your lovely blue dress is the perfect complement to your eyes.'

'Thank you, Monsieur Chevalier. It was kind of you to invite me.'

'Call me Henri, please.'

Sophie couldn't help but gape as they walked down a corridor lined with art. The grand living room, furnished with period furniture and older paintings, could have been a room at Versailles. Nevertheless, it was warm and inviting, with armchairs and a sofa arranged in an intimate cluster in front of the enormous fireplace.

'You have a beautiful home, Henri.'

Henri waved a hand dismissively. 'This is only my city residence. I will take you to my house in Saint-Cloud if you have time, to see the bulk of my collection.'

He guided her to a chair and took her wrap. She held onto her bag, out of a traveller's long ingrained habit of never being separated from her passport and valuables.

'May I offer you a drink, Sophie? I have champagne, in honour of your visit, if it pleases you.'

Never one to turn down a glass of bubbles, let alone the genuine stuff, she nodded. Sophie would have loved to have asked him how he knew about her, but he was being so charming that it seemed rude to pepper him with questions straight away. Instead, she nodded to the uniformed waiter, who had arrived silently with a silver ice bucket, to pour her champagne into a delicate crystal coupe.

Henri settled himself in an armchair, set at an angle to hers. 'Do you care for art, Sophie?'

'I know little about art. My inclination is more towards the colours and light of the impressionists, rather than the heavy realism of the older masters, but I am looking forward to visiting the Louvre to improve my knowledge.'

'For impressionists, you must visit the Musée d'Orsay, not far from here.' He raised his glass to hers and added, casually, 'I have a Monet in my collection, if you would care to see it.'

She was tempted to say, *'only the one?',* but she would never have been able to pull off the necessary nonchalance. Instead, she replied, 'Yes please, I'd love to see it,' and bounced out of her chair, ready to go. At that point, she realised he probably meant after they had had a leisurely drink.

His eyes twinkled with amusement. 'Always delightful to share with an enthusiast.' He led her down the corridor to a door with a security panel, shielding her view as he punched in the key code.

And no wonder, because when the lights came on Sophie saw the vault had more works of French art than were probably housed in the whole of New Zealand. On one wall, she admired the Monet, a Degas and a Renoir, along with other artists she had vaguely heard of. The other walls held older works, which were no doubt worth as much or more, if not so pleasing to her taste.

She went slowly along the line, taking in each painting. 'A stunning collection.'

'I cannot take the credit. My parents and grandparents were avid collectors too.' Henri placed the palm of his hand on her back and guided her out of the vault. 'My grandparents met Monet once. Quite an amusing story, actually.'

She never got to hear the story, because a man in a suit, who was exiting the apartment at the far end of the corridor, turned and said something in French to Henri, which she translated roughly as 'I've left the documents on your desk.'

Henri waved a hand in his direction and used the other on her back to guide her into the living room. When they were seated again, he said, 'I must apologise if I sounded arrogant at Duchamp's office yesterday. We are old adversaries. He is so very earnest. It brings out the worst in me, I'm afraid.'

He said it with a laugh, but she got the distinct impression that Henri was in some way intimidated by Luc. Henri was charming, amusing, and ostentatiously wealthy. Why would he feel such a rivalry with a man he considered his inferior? 'I do not know Luc well, of course, but I find him very pleasant. We did wonder how you knew about my arrival, Henri.'

'I have known about your ancestor, Elisabeth, for many years and I am as eager to find out about her as Lucien is,' he replied, without answering her question. 'I too monitor many sources of information, such as the ancestry site you used, in the hope of finding someone who knows what happened to her. And here you are, the answer to our prayers.'

At that moment, to Sophie's annoyance, the waiter appeared again to announce that dinner was ready. Henri led her into a small dining room set for two and pulled out her chair. She certainly couldn't fault the manners of the Frenchmen she had met so far.

The plate of food the waiter set before her was so artistically arranged it felt wrong to disturb it. 'Scallops with white alba truffle foam, madame.'

Henri plunged his fork in as if this was everyday fare, so Sophie followed his lead. The tastes melded in her mouth to perfection. Heavenly. She must have sighed aloud, because Henri smiled and began a witty account of the history of French cuisine.

They chatted easily about France and New Zealand, food and art, favourite travel destinations and world affairs. The courses came and went – the saddle of venison in a port reduction was divine – accompanied by a series of matched wines. It crossed her mind that Henri was softening her up for the interrogation to come, but she was enjoying herself so much that she no longer cared. The evening was turning out to be much more fun than she had anticipated.

When Sophie had scooped up the last mouthful of a blissful chocolate souffle, drizzled with berry coulis, she wondered if the other women he entertained slurped up every morsel so enthusiastically or whether

241

they graciously declined after the first mouthful to preserve their figures.

'What a pleasure it is to dine with someone who has such an enjoyment of fine cuisine,' Henri said, as if he had read her mind. 'You have a very refined palette. I had no idea that New Zealand was a nation of culinary experts, like my own nation.'

Sophie decided not to tell him that most Kiwis probably preferred fish and chips over truffle foam, not that there was a lot of the latter to be had. 'That really was a fabulous dinner, Henri. I'm no culinary expert, but I know deliciousness when I taste it.'

'Shall we return to the comfort of the armchairs? I have a very special cognac that I keep for visitors who can appreciate quality.'

'Sounds lovely, but I really feel I have had enough to drink.' In fact, the rich food, more wine than she was used to, and tiredness were combining to make her feel decidedly light-headed.

Henri poured a short measure into an enormous brandy balloon. 'You must have a taste.'

The vapours in the glass rose to her nose enticingly. Sophie took a sip and sighed. 'Incredible.' Even if she left with no information, the evening was one she would remember for a long, long time. 'Shall we talk about Elisabeth? I fear I might embarrass myself by falling asleep if I stay much longer.'

'Tell me, Sophie, what do you know of your ancestor?'

'Very little, I'm afraid. I only found her diary a few days ago in an old shipping trunk, which had been hidden in an attic since the 1880s. I know Elisabeth was widowed at a young age and came to New Zealand in 1841, where she married again and lived happily ever after. The voyage and her life in New Zealand are documented, but I could not find out anything about her origins. Hence my query on the ancestry site.'

'And Lucien Duchamp? What has he told you?'

'He believes she is Elisabeth Duchamp, who left her family farm in France in 1830 to deliver something to her aunt in England. Luc lost track of her when she left England in 1841, presumably as her name never appeared on the passenger list of the ship.'

Henri slanted his head to the side and pursed his lips. 'And this is all he told you?'

'As far as I know, that is all Luc knows for certain, other than that Elisabeth's young nephew thought she was carrying something of great value. The nephew thought there might be other items hidden somewhere, but there is no evidence to support the notion.'

'From what I saw at Lucien's office, your ancestor had two valuable diamond hair ornaments in her possession. A little unexpected for a farm girl, don't you think?'

'Luc believes – but does not know for certain – that Elisabeth's parents were servants at Versailles when the revolution broke out. It would appear that Elisabeth's parents shared nothing about their past with either of their children, hence the uncertainty. Luc thought it possible that they "liberated" some valuable items in the chaos. I suppose the temptation for servants to take advantage of their master's downfall must have been too great to resist.'

Henri's lips curved into a smirk. 'Well, it seems my sources of information are far superior to his.'

So that was it. He envied Luc's intellectual talents. 'Are you willing to share your knowledge?'

'Under certain conditions.'

Here it comes, she thought. There's always a price when dealing with a man like Henri. 'And those conditions are?'

'If we are to pursue this together, then is it not unreasonable that I take a share of whatever is found, if anything, and first refusal on whatever you wish to sell from your share. And credit for my contribution, naturally.' Henri put his cognac glass down and leaned towards her. 'I have access to resources that Duchamp could only dream of.'

'By "together", I'm assuming you mean with me and Luc. I cannot make any promises without consulting him, but I can tell you for certain that both

Luc and I would prefer to see to see any important cultural items go into a public museum in France, rather than a private collection.'

His smile remained fixed, but his eyes failed to join the party. 'Of course, my dear. But perhaps there may be items that could be displayed elsewhere? Or documents that my staff could study?'

'To be honest, Henri, this is all hypothetical, since we have no evidence that there is anything to find beyond the wishful thinking of a young lad who overheard a conversation. Luc has spent his life searching around the family farm with no success.'

'Indeed. I have followed his attempts with interest over the years. Unlike Luc, I am in the position of knowing for certain that valuable items were hidden on behalf of Louis XVI and his family. Unfortunately, I do not know *where* they might be hidden. This is the information that I hoped your ancestor's account would provide.'

On this question, Sophie had no need to play cat and mouse. 'I'm truly sorry, Henri. Elisabeth left no indication whatsoever that could help us. Her diary is almost entirely about her voyage to New Zealand, with only the barest of hints she ever lived in France. There is not a single mention of any supposed hoard of valuables.'

A flash of irritation crossed his face. 'I must admit, I am disappointed to hear that.' Henri picked up his cognac again and sipped. 'Do you know why Elisabeth left France?'

'Only that she was delivering something valuable to England, which I assume she did.'

'That's where you are wrong. She tried to make the delivery but was intercepted at the handover. The woman she was with threw the package into a lake, where it was lost forever.'

'How on earth do you know that?'

'My document collection is very extensive. I purchased many items, including correspondence, from the estate of the Duc d'Orléans, who became King Louis-Philippe in 1830. He was convinced that the daughter of Louis XVI, Marie-Thérèse, was in possession of several priceless family heirlooms. Getting his hands on them became something of an obsession for him.'

Henri obviously had access to a great deal of useful information about the past, making it hard for her to keep her excitement in check. 'Fascinating. I know that there was an enmity between the branches of the royal family. Do you think the duke was speculating, or did he have proof?'

'There's no doubt about it.' Her host failed to suppress the triumph in his voice. 'Marie-Thérèse was searched before the new king allowed her to go into exile. He found several letters between her and a woman she called her sister. As there was no other survivor from her family, I presume she meant the girl who was adopted into the royal family. Marie Antoinette apparently had an odd whim that her daughter should be taught humility. It speaks to the desperation of Marie-Thérèse that she entrusted this mere servant with one item in particular and perhaps more.'

Sophie ignored the implied slur to her family. Just how much did Henri know? She put on her best poker face. 'Do you know what it was?'

'A pearl necklace, which Marie-Thérèse referred to as her most precious piece of jewellery.' Henri was watching her closely as he said it but must have been disappointed in her lack of response, as he pursed his lips and carried on. 'It must have been a magnificent piece, because Louis-Philippe was absolutely determined to have it for himself. He sent soldiers to retrieve the necklace and the valuable jewellery box it was in. He was furious when he heard that your ancestor, Elisabeth, had escaped with it to England and was absolutely enraged when Marie-Thérèse threw it in a lake rather than give it to her enemy.'

'Goodness, what an extraordinary tale. But why do you have an ongoing interest in Elisabeth if the necklace was lost?'

'The two soldiers who were present at the lake swore the necklace was lost, but an odd thing happened ten years later. A man named Cloutier sent a message to the King, asking for funds to pursue Elisabeth, indicating that the necklace was not lost after all.'

With all this new information, Sophie became completely caught up in the story. It had a ring of truth about it, as Elisabeth had definitely been pursued and, of course, Sophie knew for a fact that the pearl necklace had come with her to New Zealand. Not a fact she cared to share with anyone right now, given the enormous value of the necklace and the trouble it had caused over the centuries. She needed to do some serious reflection before she decided who to trust.

'This Cloutier was a trustworthy fellow?'

Henri grunted. 'Far from it. He was a violent, greedy brute of a man. What is that word the English use? Thug? Yes, that's it. Cloutier was a thug. He had a personal vendetta against Elisabeth, as she had escaped him before. It is possible that he sent the message as a way to make easy money, but he must have known he was taking a tremendous risk if he was lying.'

'What happened to him?'

'Cloutier disappeared, just like Elisabeth.'

'Intriguing. Much as I'd like to believe it, isn't it rather more likely that the necklace was lost, as the two soldiers reported? Even if it wasn't, surely Marie-Thérèse would have kept it, if it meant so much to her.'

Henri shrugged. 'You may well be right. But to return to the main point, the letters between the two women indicated that the adopted sister had also hidden many valuable items from Versailles for the royal family during the revolution. Letters between a former under-governess, Madame de Soucy, and Marie-Thérèse hint the same. In fact, she later blackmailed Marie-Thérèse over it, threatening to tell the new king.'

'So, all very vague, but also extremely tantalising.'

'Exactly. If there is even the remotest chance of a priceless treasure hidden somewhere … well, you can see why many people have a great interest in finding out what happened to Elisabeth and particularly whether she kept any diaries or letters.'

'I'm sorry to disappoint you, especially after your generosity in paying for my first-class airfare and sharing this wonderful meal tonight.'

Henri's face softened as he leaned forward and put his hand on hers. 'I am sharing this information with you because I would very much like to read her diary for myself, on the chance that you have missed something. A few odd words, a drawing, anything that might hint at a location to someone who knows what to look for. And, of course, I would love to see any other items you have from Elisabeth.'

She smiled politely and picked up her glass, thereby removing her hand from under his. 'I have promised that Luc can read the diary first. I expect he will wish to read it soon, so you may not have to wait long.'

Henri opened his mouth to say something but closed it again. He tapped his fingers on the armrest, before deciding to speak his mind after all. 'Sophie, I'm not sure how to say this without alarming you, but I urge you to be extremely cautious in your dealings with Lucien Duchamp. He may seem harmless, but there are things you do not know.'

Sophie crossed her arms and looked him right in the eye. 'Such as?'

Henri was not the least bit put off by her defensive reaction. 'Lucien was fired from his last position. Francis Bonhomme, his former boss, refused to say why, but I heard on good authority that he was implicated as the "inside man" in a group trafficking cultural objects. Despite being fired, Luc miraculously had enough funds to purchase his current premises and start a lucrative business.'

Luc Duchamp, a criminal? Sophie would have scoffed if Henri hadn't looked so darn serious. In fact, she could have sworn that Henri believed it. 'Do you know for sure that he was selling information or whatever it was he was supposed to have done? If so, why was Luc not charged with a crime?'

'My sources say that nothing could be proved. But had Luc been innocent, I have to wonder why he was fired.'

'No smoke without fire, as the saying goes?' Someone was certainly blowing a lot of smoke in Luc's direction, but did it mean that he was guilty? Either way, it was very disturbing, especially after what Bonhomme had said.

'Perhaps you think I say this out of personal enmity, because of his wife. But it is Luc who holds a grudge against me, not the other way around. I became friendly with his wife only after she left him. She never trusted him after the truth came out about his father's dishonourable behaviour. The English, you know, they value money over honour.'

This gob-smacking slur floored her. Suddenly, she felt overwhelmed with exhaustion and the bizarre events that had stacked one upon another since her arrival. Was it only yesterday? 'I must apologise and excuse myself, Henri. I'm too tired to think straight. This news about Luc really is the last straw, especially after finding two people searching my hotel room this afternoon.'

Henri seemed genuinely shocked. 'No, that's terrible. Did you recognise them?'

'I only saw one, and he was a stranger. Hardly surprising, as I know so few people in Paris.'

'Who knew where you were staying, Sophie?'

Reluctantly, she admitted the truth, which hadn't occurred to her before. 'Only Luc and his daughter, Martine.' Martine might have mentioned her arrival to her mother, but Sophie doubted she would not have told her mother which hotel she was staying in.

Henri raised an enquiring eyebrow. She didn't have to be a mind reader to work out what he was thinking – are you sure the second man in the hotel room was not the only man who knows which hotel you are in, Luc Duchamp? And he was dead right, she wasn't sure. Luc not only knew where she was staying, but also that she was supposed to be miles away at Versailles for the day.

'Sophie, I am concerned for you. I have a small apartment for visitors. I would like you to stay there tonight. In fact, stay there for as long as you wish. It has a keypad entry, so you can set your own entry code. Lucien need never know you are here.'

Sophie tried to work out what to do, but she'd had too much wine, too much rich food, and far too much drama. All she could think was, how could I have been so wrong in trusting Luc? But was she any better off staying here with another man she barely knew? She felt more comfortable with Luc than Henri, despite his charming and considerate behaviour tonight.

On the other hand, she felt weary to the bone. The thought of falling into a bed here, probably with a zillion thread-count sheets, was very tempting. 'That's very thoughtful of you, Henri. Can I have a moment to get my thoughts straight? I need to use your bathroom.'

He rose politely as she got up and directed her to the bathroom. When she came back, he was standing by her chair, holding her bag out to her. 'Follow me and I will take you to your room.'

She took her bag off him rather more briskly than intended. 'Thank you for your kind offer, Henri, but I have decided that I feel safe going back to my hotel.'

He looked as if he was about to argue, then nodded. 'If you insist.'

'Thank you for the marvellous dinner, and for so generously sharing your knowledge of my ancestor, Elisabeth. I will be in touch when I decide how to proceed.'

'It was my pleasure. A pleasure I hope to repeat soon. I'll call my chauffeur.'

He took her arm and guided her out, which she was grateful for, as she was feeling quite light-headed.

Sophie spent the short drive back to the hotel turning the situation over in her mind. Henri Chevalier had been charming and informative but had also been open about his motive – fame and fortune. And Luc? Her instinct was to trust him, but then she had trusted her husband and failed to see his deceit. If she had known Mike for thirty years and failed to judge him correctly, how could she trust Luc after not much more than thirty hours? Both Chevalier and Bonhomme had warned her off him. More to the point, Henri was right. Only Luc had known where she was staying.

By the time Sophie walked across the lobby of her hotel, she had made one decision. She would be naïve to forget how vulnerable she was, alone in a foreign country, thousands of miles away from family and friends. Changing hotels was the least she should do to ensure her safety.

The night manager tried to dissuade her from leaving the hotel, by offering her another room, an upgrade on the one she had. She reassured him that she would not make a formal complaint or write a bad review, but, for her own peace of mind, she was determined to leave tonight. The manager gave in, promising to retrieve the jewellery box from the hotel safe and to check the security camera footage to see if the intruders could be identified. Unlikely, but worth checking.

It took Sophie less than half an hour to change, pack her belongings, and book an anonymous international hotel a few blocks away. Within the hour, she was tucked up in bed in a room so bland it might have been anywhere in the world. The one concession to France was a Monet print in a plain white frame. Water lilies, of course.

Her fingers hovered over her phone. Should she text Luc, as promised? He'd worry if she didn't, so she sent: 'Safely back, amazing souffle.'

His reply came back in seconds. 'Thanks for letting me know. Souffle? Full of hot air, just like Henri!'

Sophie turned off the light, hoping that a good sleep would give her greater clarity in the morning. After churning past and present events over in her mind for hours, she finally sent herself to sleep by chanting her new mantra: 'You can walk away at any time.'

Fury Unleashed

Tuileries Palace, Paris, 18 June 1791

The sounds of chanting and clashes of steel outside had become as familiar to Ernestine as the bustle of servants inside the Tuileries. Almost two years had passed since she had returned to her adoptive family and not a month of that had gone by without outbreaks of violence.

Once the dilapidated palace had been properly aired, scrubbed, repaired and furnished, it was habitable, although the foul odour from the Seine was ever-present. It seemed as if the entirety of the city's sewage and refuse from its slaughterhouses ended up in the river, drifting past them every minute of the day. How she longed for the sweet scent of the gardens at Versailles.

At first, they were not locked in, although the continual gawping of people peering through their windows made them feel as if they were confined inside a menagerie. The routines of daily life, study and religious devotion were reinstated, interspersed with needlework, reading and card games, to give their lives a sense of structure and normality. Occasionally, the children were allowed to go on outings to the Bois de Boulogne, while the King still enjoyed the pleasures of hunting.

But the powers of the King and the respect shown to his family gradually eroded as the weeks passed until they were effectively prisoners in the palace. Every day, it seemed there would be some new intrusion by so-called officials from whichever faction was currently claiming power, bearing a new edict about what they must or must not do. It was becoming intolerable.

Over recent months, a restless undercurrent had swelled beneath the surface routine. While His Majesty held his official meetings, the Queen had her own stream of furtive visitors. The sense of impending crisis had increased over the past few days, as disused trunks were pulled out, filled with clothes and hidden again. Faithful friends, loyal servants, and even the Queen's personal hairdresser, Léonard, had been sent away with letters, packages, and boxes discreetly tucked under skirts and cloaks.

On the morning of the eighteenth of June 1891, Marie Antoinette had Ernestine brought to her room. As she entered, she noticed one of the Queen's most trusted ladies hastily shutting the doors to a jewellery cabinet, which appeared to be almost bare. Ernestine knew the Crown Jewels, including the magnificent diamonds and pearl necklace adored by Her Majesty, had already been surrendered into the hands of the

National Assembly. But what had become of the Queen's extensive collection of personal jewellery?

'You may leave us now,' Marie Antoinette told her ladies. When they had departed, she turned to Ernestine with a kindly smile, belied by the tight lines around her eyes. 'You have been a devoted and loyal daughter to me, Ernestine. I know the constrained life we now lead cannot be pleasant for a lively girl like you, so I have arranged for you to go into the country with your father for a time. I wish that all of us might go, but that, of course, would never be allowed.'

Ernestine hesitated for a fraction of a second, wondering whether she should ask why. Something in the intensity of the Queen's gaze – was it a plea? – cut her question off before it reached her lips. 'As you wish, Your Majesty. When am I to leave?'

'As soon as may be. I have left clothes for you behind the screen. Once you have changed, you will leave by the servant's entrance, where your father awaits you.'

'May I say farewell to Marie-Thérèse?'

The Queen gathered Ernestine into her arms and planted a kiss as soft as a butterfly's wings on her forehead. 'I am sorry, truly sorry. For reasons I cannot explain, I do not wish anyone to know you are leaving, not even your sister.'

Ernestine stepped back and curtseyed, taking the Queen's hand to her lips. 'I will remain your faithful servant wherever I am.'

She spun around and headed for the screen, so that she would not see the pain glistening in her adoptive mother's eyes, nor expose the Queen to her own.

The garment behind the screen was a simple dress, as might be worn by a scullery maid, complete with an apron and bonnet. By no means new, but clean and a good fit, although far inferior to the pretty muslin dress with a silk sash that she was wearing.

When Ernestine had made the transformation, she returned to face the Queen, masking her emotions behind a smile. 'I wish you and your family well, Your Majesty.' With a final curtsey, she headed for the door.

'Wait, Ernestine…' The Queen seemed uncertain about whether to proceed. 'Before you go, there is one last favour I wish to ask. You may refuse if it alarms you.'

'There is little that can scare me now,' she replied with more bravado than she felt.

'I see that in your eyes, child. When I look at you, I have to remind myself that you are not yet thirteen years old. Far too young for me to be asking this favour.'

'With the greatest of respect, Your Majesty, at that age you braved a journey to a far-off country to wed a powerful stranger who did not even speak the same language.'

At that, the dark cloud lifted from the Queen's brow and she laughed. 'You are such a clever girl, Ernestine. I often think it a pity that women may not be diplomats and leaders.'

What pleasure to hear her laugh again after so long. 'I will do whatever you wish of me.'

The Queen opened a safe, hidden behind a secret panel in a wardrobe. She lifted out a box that Ernestine had seen before, the beautiful jewellery box crafted by Monsieur Riesener.

'You recognise this, Ernestine?' The Queen opened the box, revealing the prized pearl necklace nestled in folds of royal blue satin.

Ernestine gasped. 'Is it not the necklace given to you on your wedding day? I thought the men from the Assembly had taken it with the Crown Jewels.'

'Where did you hear that?'

She blushed at the sharpness of the question, but forged ahead with the truth. 'I overheard Madame Campan saying so. She was very angry that it was taken from you, especially as the commissioner who came for the Crown Jewels had agreed that the necklace was yours to do with as you pleased.'

'That is true, but I feared that others in the National Assembly would not have agreed with him. Greed and envy are powerful emotions.'

'Then…'

'They may be covetous, but they are also ignorant. I doubt they will notice that the pearl necklace I handed over is not the famed necklace handed down from Anne of Austria to each new Dauphine, and now mine by right of my position. I found I could not bear to part with it. However, I fear it will not be safe in my possession. I doubt it has escaped your keen notice that sentiment in Paris is not on my side. The next few days will be perilous, hence your departure.'

'You wish *me* to take the pearl necklace? But… I…' Ernestine paused to collect her scattered wits, before dropping to a curtsey. 'What I mean to say is that I am honoured by your trust in me.'

'Only for a few days, until we see you again. But are you sure, my dear? It might be dangerous for you and your father if the necklace is discovered in your possession.'

Ernestine conjured her face into an expression of sweet innocence. 'I am merely a lowly scullery maid, begging a lift with a stranger, that I might see my dying mother one last time. Who would think I carried anything worth stealing?'

The Queen's lips twitched up into a smile again. 'I have written a note ordering you to carry these on my behalf. I would not have you accused of theft.'

A note? From the hand of Marie Antoinette? The naivety of it astounded Ernestine. She might be severely punished as a thief, but a far worse fate would await her if she was known to be a courier for the Queen.

'I see your concern, my dear. Let me show you the cleverness of the craftsman who made this box.' She showed Ernestine how to press firmly on certain parts of the decoration on the lower half of the jewellery box, releasing a hidden compartment in the base. 'With the note in here, no one will ever see it unless you choose to show them.'

Ernestine walked out of the room two minutes later in a daze, with a linen bag full of humble clothes and essentials in one hand and an old sack containing bread, cheese, fruit, and a priceless heirloom wrapped in an apron in the other. She slipped unseen down the narrow servant's stairs and out into the courtyard, where her papa, Jacques Lambriquet, waited in a shabby cart.

He helped her up, took up the reins, and flicked the whip above the horse's back. Without a word, they were off, rattling over the cobbles with a cartload of old wine barrels.

An hour later, safely clear of the heart of Paris, Ernestine broke the silence. 'I don't understand, Papa. Why am I going away with so little notice?'

'No questions now, my dear. A few days in the fresh air of the countryside will do you good. We are to return these wine barrels to a vineyard owned by your mother's family. Your birth mother, I mean.'

This was welcome news, for her mother had died before Ernestine had met her family. She held back the torrent of questions bubbling up inside her, sure that her father would tell all when the time was right.

He said no more of it as they drove out of the city and on to the east, stopping now and then to rest the horse and take some food. At night, they tethered the horse on a long rein in a grassy glade, out of sight of the road. They dined simply and slept under the stars.

The next two days were a repeat of the first. When they weren't chatting about everyday things, Ernestine simply sat and watched the miles of countryside roll by – an endless tapestry of harvest-ready wheat, ripening grapes and grassy meadows, dotted with smallholdings and villages. Farm workers went about their chores, giving them a friendly nod if they passed close by.

A skylark trilled, filling the air with joyous song. Ernestine shaded her eyes with her hand, catching sight of him halfway to heaven. 'Out here, Paris seems as far away as the Orient.'

Beside her, her father flicked the reins lightly onto the horse's rump to remind him of his task on this sultry day. 'Let us hope we are not the only ones who feel that way.'

'Their Majesties are going to attempt to escape from Paris, are they not, Papa?'

Jacques Lambriquet replied in a whisper, although they were completely alone apart from a few cows chewing their cuds in the field beside the road. 'If all has gone to plan, they will leave tonight and speed towards the safety of the eastern border, where armies wait to protect them. The Queen has been planning this for months.'

'How do you know all this?'

'Such planning cannot be done without the help of many people. The new carriage, the false identities, the fresh horses standing ready at staging points. Too complex a plan, if you ask me. Too many people know.'

Ernestine tried not to think of what was happening to Marie-Thérèse, instead imagining what Pierre was doing right now. All she knew was that the King had rewarded him well for his loyalty at Versailles, especially for bringing him his beloved tools and locks from the workshop. Pierre had ridden off on a newly purchased horse to see what had become of his family in the Loire Valley.

He would be almost fourteen by now, not much younger than Marie Antoinette was when she married. And he would be strong, healthy, charming and in possession of enough gold coins to make him a desirable catch to the pretty country lasses. Ernestine sighed. Fate had driven them apart and there was nothing she could do about it, other than resign herself to never seeing him again. Or so she tried to tell herself.

'Whatever is on your mind, my dear, there is no sense brooding on it. Let me tell you about your mother's family. They will be very pleased to meet you, as the money the King paid to your mother went into buying the piece of land they now work. I have never been there myself, but I understand they have prospered and created a vineyard of some renown.'

When they reached the family vineyard on the evening of the fourth day, they were given the promised warm welcome. Ernestine was feted and embraced by uncles, aunts, cousins, and grandparents she had never met before. They saw to the exhausted horse, stored the wine barrels in an empty cellar, then joined the family at a long table under a vine-covered trellis for a celebratory feast.

The next few days were equally joyful. Indeed, Ernestine felt as if she could be happy here forever, were it not for the growing disquiet in her father.

After several days of watching him pace by the window, she could stand it no more. 'What is wrong, Papa?'

He took her out into the vineyard where no one would overhear them. 'God willing, the royal family has escaped Paris. They were to pass not far to the south of here and send word when they reached their destination.'

'To what purpose?'

'You remember Pierre's ruse with the coffins?'

'The wine barrels! You are delivering their treasured possessions, as we did before?'

'That was the plan, but they are long overdue.'

At that moment, they spotted a horse cantering up the track to the house. Her father ran to greet the messenger, but it was only his brother-in-law, Armand, returned from business in town.

'I must talk with you, Jacques. The news is not good.'

'We both want to hear whatever it is,' Ernestine said.

'Well, then, prepare yourselves for a shock, my dear. The royal family was captured at Varennes and forced to return to Paris. They are alive and well, as far as I know, but their flight has not helped their cause at all. The mood of the people is dark indeed.'

Tuileries Palace, Paris, 10 August 1792
A sense of déjà vu gripped Ernestine as she stood at a window of the Tuileries watching the frenzied crowd swarm outside the gates like bees around a disturbed hive. Discontent had ebbed and flowed over the past year, but with a growing undercurrent of ferocity, matching the escalating fanaticism amongst the successive leaders of the ever-changing revolutionary regime.

Ernestine had returned to the palace after hearing of the failure of the escape plan, against the fervent pleas of the man she still loved as a father and her own better judgement. Leaving the joyful normality of the vineyard behind was one of the hardest things she had ever done. Now she saw that her loyalty would come at a heavy price.

The dreaded cries of 'death to the tyrants' rang out over the din, yet again. Revolution was rapidly turning into anarchy. The circle of guards, who kept the chanting mobs out and the royal household in, was a fragile deterrent against such fury.

Fear stalked alongside them every minute of the day and night. The sound of guns firing had kept them awake last night, fearing some new incursion into their domain, while the morning light brought more bad tidings. The mob had swelled in number and anger, joined by many of the National Guard soldiers. Only the Swiss Guards could be trusted now.

The commander pleaded with the King to remove his family to the safety of the National Assembly, as too few loyal guards remained here to ensure their security. At last, he was persuaded, against the wishes of the Queen, who spent the day going back and forth between the negotiations and her children.

Ernestine embraced Marie-Thérèse as they prepared to be separated again. Both girls were terrified at what lay ahead. Madame de Tourzel lifted the Dauphin into her arms and followed Marie-Thérèse, Madame Elisabeth, and Madame de Lambelle out of the room where they had huddled for safety.

The Queen lingered a moment longer, defeat written in the slope of her shoulders. 'His Majesty thinks everyone else will be safe once we have departed. Nevertheless, I have asked Madame de Soucy to take you away from here. Once again, I must take my leave of you, dearest Ernestine.'

The words 'perhaps for the last time' remained unsaid, although they hung in the air as the Queen turned away. At the door, Marie Antoinette straightened her spine, pulled her shoulders back, lifted her chin, and exited with regal assurance.

Ernestine could not muster any words. She stood with the dumb resignation of a weary carthorse waiting for its next burden, forgetting even to wave farewell.

Not long after her family left, the cannons and muskets roared anew. She dragged her body over to a window, staying to the side and peering out with due caution. The sight that met her eyes sickened her to the core. The mob was attempting to besiege the palace and the Swiss Guards were firing pell-mell into the masses.

Far from subduing the crowd, the shots magnified the rage. Before her eyes, she saw the gates give way and the masses swarm into the courtyard, screaming out their frenzy, hacking at the Swiss Guards with terrifying bloodlust, until the bricks of the courtyard were covered with red coats, awash in a sea of scarlet blood. She saw hundreds slaughtered, beheaded, eviscerated, as waves of bellowing drunks went berserk, swamping the guards, killing friend and foe alike. As she stood rooted to the spot in utter terror, four heads were mounted on pikes and paraded outside the window.

A blaze of cannon fire and musketry rang out, sending projectiles through the windows and into the walls. Ernestine turned and ran for her life, even as the sound of the outer doors being smashed echoed through the corridors. She reached the doorway at the same moment as Madame de Soucy appeared outside it.

'There you are, girl. Come, there is not a moment to lose.'

By the time they reached the bottom of the stairs, they were having to step over mutilated bodies. Outside, in the courtyard, the scene was even worse than the initial slaughter she had witnessed. Tendrils of smoke rose from within the palace, adding the smell of burning to the stench of blood, gore and gunpowder, but she dared not stop to retch.

By a miracle from heaven, they cheated death and emerged onto a side street unscathed. Madame de Soucy grabbed at her sleeve and urged her on. She obeyed, running as fast as she could, despite the fear and exhaustion that were close to claiming her.

When they reached the Carousel, Ernestine gasped out, 'Please, a moment's rest, or I shall collapse.'

Beside her, the ribs of her companion were heaving every bit as hard as her own. Madame de Soucy's pale face was an unhealthy shade of puce, tinged with green. She turned and vomited into a gutter. A timely act, as the stench drove away a small group of ragtag men coming to prey on two well-dressed women on their own. They lurched off down the street, singing loudly and stumbling over dead bodies.

'I will find a carriage, if I can. Wait here and scream if you need help.'

Madame de Soucy disappeared. Long minutes crept by as Ernestine crouched in the meagre shelter of a tumble-down wall. Eventually, she decided her guardian had deserted her, which did not come as a surprise as there was little love between the strict under-governess and her charges. There was no option left, other than to make her own way through the deadly streets.

But where? Ernestine knew no one here. Perhaps she could beg refuge in a church or convent? With this in mind, she stepped out from behind the wall and ran to the corner, where there appeared to be a few shops. A shopkeeper would know where to direct her.

When she rounded the corner, the smell of burning flesh almost knocked her flat. The street was scattered with entrails, blood and bodies, some of which had been set alight.

One of the drunken men who had passed her was slouching nearby, his brutish body propped up by the wall. His bloodshot eyes swivelled towards her. 'Oy, slut, come 'ere.'

He lunged at her, but his reactions were slowed by wine. Ernestine side-stepped and turned to run, but another man was standing behind her, carrying a cudgel as big as his ferret-face. This one was not as drunk, nor as large, but far more dangerous.

'Holy Mother of God, it's the Austrian bitch's daughter. Whassername, Princess Thérèse.' He jabbed the cudgel into her shoulder, trapping her against the wall. 'I seen your face going by in a carriage once, looking down on us like I was no better than the dung under your pretty silk slippers. Mark my words, princess, your head will look better on a pike.'

The cudgel swung back behind his shoulder, sweeping up and down in a deadly arc. This is it, she thought. This is how I am going to die.

An Issue of Trust

Paris, 2019

Sophie woke up feeling queasy and edgy, probably due the combination of rich food, too much wine, and a sleepless night. She had lain awake, stewing over Luc Duchamp. The worst of it was, she had really liked him, right from the start. Could she have been so wrong? The information Henri Chevalier had provided was disturbing, to say the least. Fired for leaking information? It seemed the opposite of what Luc stood for … or what he claimed to stand for.

She stretched out on the giant bed, realising she was not as tired as she expected to be. A quick glance at her phone told her why – it was after ten o'clock. The décor might be fifty shades of beige, but she couldn't fault the hotel on the quietness of the room or the thickness of the light-blocking drapes.

Fifteen missed calls and messages! Beginning with a calm 'what time will I see you?' from Luc, escalating through increasingly concerned queries to 'Where are you?? The hotel says you checked out late last night!', followed by messages from Henri and Martine asking if she was okay.

With a sigh, she texted Henri and Martine back, telling them she was fine and thanking Henri again for dinner. Luc was a more difficult problem. In the end, she had no choice. He still had Elisabeth's smaller pieces of jewellery in his safe. And he had the right to tell his side of the story. She sent him a text message as well: 'Sorry, overslept. Phone on mute. I'll be at your office soon.'

Reluctantly, she rolled out of bed, did some stretches to unkink her knotted muscles and glugged down a bottle of water. Oh, to be twenty again and able to leap out of bed in prime condition after just a few hours' sleep. After a shower and a change of clothes, Sophie went in search of caffeine.

The sky was ominously dark, matching her mood, but it was not actually raining. She lingered in the lobby a moment, trying to decide whether to go back for a coat, but decided to risk it. A block later, she caught sight of an attractive café across the road. When she came out, feeling better for an industrial strength espresso, she smelled a distinctive reek of tobacco. The man lounging against the wall outside, under the canopy roof, was smoking the same brand of cigarettes as the man who had been standing outside her hotel door.

'*Excusez-moi, Monsieur, quel type est votre cigarette?*' A rather odd question to ask a stranger, but she was beyond worrying about trivial matters of etiquette.

The man gave her a sultry appraisal, from head to toe. He pulled a blue packet out of his pocket, emblazoned with the Gauloises logo, and offered her a cigarette. He leaned forward to place his hand on her lower back and whisper in her ear.

She may not have understood the exact words but his intent was clear, especially as his hand moved downward to her bottom. She gave him her best 'over your dead body' look, pushed past him, and walked away as fast as she could manage while still maintaining her dignity. In what sane universe does a man asked a simple question by a middle-aged tourist in the late morning interpret it as a sexual invitation?

By the time she reached Luc's office, she was not only seething inside but steaming damp from the light drizzle. After a few deep, calming breaths, she pushed open the door.

A stranger was seated at the computer, with Luc standing behind him, obviously sharing a joke. Luc glanced up and waved. The man looked around the edge of the computer monitor to see who was there.

Time stood still as she took in his facial features, unable – or unwilling – to believe that this was the man last seen outside her hotel room, shaking a cigarette out of a blue packet, while his partner searched her

275

room. She'd only glimpsed him in profile outside her room, but the tilt of his head as he'd turned was exactly the same today and a blue packet poked out of his shirt pocket. Her hammering heart told her it was the same man.

Luc spoke to the man in rapid French, then turned towards the door. 'Sophie, come in.'

She stood in the doorway a moment longer, hovering between flight and fight, before the instinct to flee took over. Sophie raced back down the steps, two at a time, and up the street. She was halfway to the corner when she heard the door slam and Luc's voice yelling.

'Sophie! Wait!'

Glancing back over her shoulder, she saw that he had started to run after her, at a speed more reminiscent of a track-team sprinter than a desk-bound academic. She slowed a little, torn between trusting her gut and feeling foolish for panicking.

Out of the corner of her eye, she saw a blur of motion – another man on the opposite side of the street running towards her. Not just a man, but a tattooed human tank, clad in black. That clinched it. She sprinted for the corner, disregarding grace in favour of speed. At the corner, she slid to a halt, lungs heaving, spotting a line of taxis down the street. She risked a glance back, seeing the human tank yelling abuse at

Luc in a stream of high-octane French, flailing his arms as if he was on the verge of thumping him.

Suddenly, she realised the stranger must have stepped in to help her, presumably having seen her fright and thinking that Luc was trying to attack her. The thought of her host getting pounded by a well-meaning tough guy was too much guilt to bear. With a last wistful glance at the taxi, she turned and ran back to the two men.

To her surprise, Luc had twisted his attacker's arms behind his back and was calmly reassuring him that Sophie was in no danger. Her self-defence instructor, all those years ago, had tried to convince her that cleverly applied leverage could beat brute strength, but she'd never been so happy to see it in action.

With a mix of simple French and soothing gestures, she intervened, thanking the tank for helping, but assuring him that all was well. The placated hero shook Luc's hand and strolled off down the street with a merry wave, his good deed for the day done.

Luc stood in the middle of the pavement, feet splayed and palms upturned, with the same heartfelt look of injured innocence used by footballers disputing a red card. 'All's well, is it? Then would you care to explain why the heck you ran out of my office like the devil was after you?'

Sophie took a step back, wishing she hadn't sent the tank away.

Luc must have seen the alarm in her eyes, because his exasperation drained away in an instant. 'I'm sorry if I upset you. Sophie, what is going on?'

'I wish I could answer that.' She turned the options over in her mind, opting for a compromise. 'Luc, can you go back to your office and give the man there some excuse for why I had to leave urgently. Forgotten appointment or whatever. In fact, send him away, if you can.' She could see he was about to ask why. 'Please, just trust me.'

He hesitated. 'Will you stay here while I talk to Paul?'

Damp clothes and draining adrenalin were sending goosebumps up her arms. 'Can we meet in a nice warm café instead?'

Luc hesitated again, then pointed to the end of the street. 'Turn right, next block, under the red awning. I'll be there as soon as I can.' He turned and jogged back towards the office.

Sophie ordered two bowls of soup at the café before heading for the bathroom. An ancient man, whose face appeared to be made of wrinkled parchment over protruding bones, watched her with interest, then pointed to a narrow corridor hidden by a curtain. She smiled her thanks, and he touched the brim of his cloth cap, which had surely not been fashionable since the Great War.

The mirror reflected a pale, mascara-smeared face under a bedraggled mop of damp hair, perfect for an extra role in a zombie movie. No wonder the tough guy had come to her rescue. Fortunately, she carried tissues and a small emergency repair kit in her bag. With those, and the help of the hand drier, she re-emerged from the bathroom in a more or less dry and respectable state.

The ancient man gave her an approving nod as she passed, raising arthritis-bent fingers to salute her with his cloudy yellow drink. The leather seat was indented in his shape, making her wonder if the old man was a permanent fixture in the cafe. She smiled back and took a seat in one of the high-backed booths, perfect for the meeting she was dreading.

Had she overreacted in Luc's office? Possibly, but more likely not, as she was sure she had identified the man correctly. No matter how she turned the facts over, the man who had helped to search her room was well-known to Luc. And Luc was a man obsessed with tracking her ancestor down, obsessed with whatever it was he thought she had.

The pearl necklace and jewellery box were clearly extremely valuable. Should she turn them over to an appropriate museum in France and get the hell out of here? But who could she trust to take them, if Martine was right about the criminals having insider help in stealing heritage pieces?

Meanwhile, Luc still had the items she had shown him in his safe and she was reluctant to abandon them, especially as her gut persisted in telling her that he was no criminal, despite the warnings.

Sophie looked up the next available Eurostar train, which departed in two hours. Her finger hovered over the 'Book now' button, but Luc chose that moment to come through the door, a wave of relief crossing his face when he saw her. She put the phone down, as he dropped into the seat opposite her.

'Sophie, thank heavens you're here. I've been beside myself with worry. What the hell did Chevalier tell you last night that had you changing hotels in the middle of the night?' His hands hovered, tentatively reaching out, before being jerked back to his side of the table.

The waiter arrived with two steaming bowls of soup and a basket wafting the yeasty aroma of fresh baguette. She'd only ordered to ensure they had the table for as long as they needed it, but now the food was in front of her, she realised she was hungry after all, having skipped breakfast.

'I'm sorry I ran out on you earlier, Luc. There's some weird stuff happening to me and it all got too much. I need some answers from you or I'm taking the first train out of Paris.'

'Weird stuff?' His bewilderment seemed genuine.

Sophie took a spoonful of soup, allowing the warmth to sink in as she gathered her composure. 'First my house was burgled by someone who followed me here on the plane, then my hotel room was searched, perhaps by the same man.'

'What? That's the first I've heard of you being followed here. Who was this man?'

'I don't know who he was. I simply had a hunch that one of the men on the plane might have been the burglar, because he was wearing the same distinctive Armani cologne as I smelled at my house. It sounds crazy, I know, but there was also an Armani man in the hotel bar who had the same features. That man had different hair and a beard, but those are fairly easy to disguise. And now the same smell in my hotel room after it was searched.'

The waiter returned with a carafe of water. Sophie reached for it but found to her horror that her hands were shaking too much to pour.

Luc took the carafe from her. 'That's very worrying. I wish you had told me earlier. But why did you run away from me when you came into the office?'

'Because the man standing guard outside my hotel room while it was searched was the same man who was laughing with you when I walked in. Can you explain that?' She spoke far louder than she had intended, spilling the water as she picked the glass up. 'Why is it that each time I tell you something, someone turns up to burgle or harass me? In short, I need you to tell me what the heck is going on.'

'Sophie, slow down. I can see you're upset, with good reason.' He tore off a piece of bread and buttered it, giving her a chance to deflate.

'The man in my office was Paul Tomas, who looks after my computer system and security. He is an employee of a reputable company called AntiqGarde, which specialises in security for museums and private collections. Henri Chevalier uses them. In fact, I think he owns a share of the company. Or possibly all of it, knowing him.'

'So why was this Paul Tomas outside my hotel room?'

'You're absolutely sure it was Paul?' Luc brought up the AntiqGarde website to show her a picture.

'Yes, that's definitely him.'

'That is extremely disturbing.' Luc tapped his fingers on the table in a staccato beat. 'I can't think of a single reason Paul would burgle you, but I assure you he didn't do so on my behalf.' He stopped tapping and frowned at her. 'How would he have known where you were staying?'

Damn the man for being so calm and rational. If Luc was involved, this was the one question he wouldn't want asked. 'Exactly. You were the only one who knew where I was staying and that I would be out for the day.'

Luc didn't blink under the force of her glare. 'I'm grateful you gave me the chance to explain after what you've been through.'

Sophie scanned his face for signs of deceit, bluster, defensiveness – any of the emotions he would likely show if he was one of the bad guys. All she saw was concern and sincerity, unless he was a terrific actor. 'Now that I know Paul Tomas is your IT guy, I can see there is another explanation. Presumably he has access to all the information on your computer system?'

He nodded mechanically, drumming his fingers faster and faster as his frown-lines deepened. She could almost hear his brain whirling at maximum revs. 'If he wanted to, Paul could access every online contact I have had with you, every booking I made, and everything I do in my business.'

Luc got up and started pacing, realised he was in a café, and sat down again. 'What's more, he has access to everything in my office. Including all the files of information I have gathered on disappearing cultural artefacts, not to mention my research on potential acquisitions. Damnation, I really have handed it to him on a plate.'

'Not just you, Luc. Potentially all the museums and collectors who use AntiqGarde.'

Luc dropped his head into his hands with a groan, as the magnitude of the potential crisis sunk in.

Sophie reached out a tentative hand, touching his shoulder gently. 'I expect you'd like to leave now, to get your systems checked for spyware as soon as possible.'

'Yes, but I don't want to leave you until I've answered whatever questions you have. May I just make a quick phone call?'

His frown gradually relaxed during the high-speed conversation in French. 'Martine's husband is meeting me as soon as he can in my office. Hugo is one of the smartest tech guys in Paris. I wish I'd used his services, but AntiqGarde was becoming the industry standard, so I used them instead.'

'Why don't you go and we can finish our conversation later? Unless you'd like to have some soup. It's very good.'

Luc looked at the soup as if he hadn't even noticed it was there. He hesitated, perhaps out of politeness, so she said, 'Go. This is your business and reputation we're talking about. Not to mention my safety.'

'Thanks, Sophie.' He got up and shuffled out of the booth. 'Please promise me you won't leave Paris until we've talked. I'm not sure how long I'll be, but I promise to bring your things from my safe when I come back.'

'Text me when you've finished.' She hesitated for a second, then scribbled down her new hotel and room number on a napkin and handed it over.

He paid for their lunch by throwing a handful of euros to the cashier, then hurried out of the café, with a quick backward glance at her. Sophie called the waiter over and asked if the old man in the corner might like the untouched soup.

Ten minutes later, feeling fuller and calmer, she went for a walk, while waiting for Luc to text. Fortunately, the rain had stopped, and the sun was working hard to find a gap in the clouds.

Three hours later, Luc arrived at her hotel, with a scowl as grim as a toddler with a toothache.

'Bad news?' Sophie pulled up a second chair for him.

'The worst. My entire system has been compromised.' He ignored the chair and paced the room, although it was no more than five long strides in each direction. 'Paul Tomas has loaded some type of spy software that means he has access to everything remotely. Hugo swept my office and apartment for bugs, which I thought was over the top, but it turns out I've been bugged as well as hacked. I've changed all my security passwords and safe codes and Hugo has promised to do what he can to purge my systems. He's coming over later to check your things, if that's okay.'

'I guess so.'

He sat down beside her and leaned forward. 'Sophie, you must be very upset by all this. I wouldn't blame you for a second if you decided to walk away.'

'Believe me, I've considered it. The fact is, if these people have the resources and determination to send someone to burgle my house in New Zealand as soon as we contacted each other by email, where will I be safe? What I don't understand is why they would do it. Why go to all that bother and huge expense, especially when they knew I was coming to France in a few days' time?'

Luc thought about it for a few moments. 'They must have wanted to get their hands on whatever they think you have first, which suggests something of great value. My guess is that they didn't want to risk you and I meeting, which suggests … I'm not sure what, to be honest.'

'That we each have pieces of the puzzle? Or you would recognise the significance of what I have?'

'Perhaps. We need a safe place to think and talk this through. One positive. If I was one of them, it would have made more sense to wait until you arrived in France.'

'I see what you mean, Luc. Why would you send someone to New Zealand, when I was about to put myself into your evil clutches?'

'Not quite how I would put it, but yes. Sophie, I want to know that you trust me, despite everything. If you feel you can't, you are free to leave.'

She hesitated. It would be so easy to get on a train and disappear. But the truth was, she was fascinated by the mystery surrounding her ancestors. Curiosity won out over caution. 'My gut reaction is to trust you. But I need some answers. Two people have warned me away from you, Luc. Francis Bonhomme was pretty cryptic, saying the apple does not fall far from the tree. Henri Chevalier said you were fired from your job for leaking information.'

'I must say, this is a new low, even for Francis. I wonder if he meant my mother, who is English and therefore not to be trusted in his eyes. Or my father, who is French, but also one of those arrogant banker types who almost destroyed the world economy in the Global Financial Crisis. I don't know how it was in New Zealand, but in Europe, admitting to being a banker back then was like painting a target on your back.'

'It was your father's behaviour Francis was referring to, not your mother's unfortunate choice of birth country. I take it you are not much like your father?'

Luc shrugged. 'He cut me out of his life when I chose to study history instead of something useful, such as law or economics. Rather ironic, considering how close he came to being charged with financial crimes.'

'Your father must be proud of what you have achieved, even if you didn't choose to become a banker. Can't he see what a tremendous success you have made of your career?'

Luc let out a snort. 'You obviously don't know my father. If you're not making a fortune by screwing the system, then you're a pathetic loser. He already despaired of me, for being the quiet kid who preferred reading books in the library to facing up to bullies and pummelling them with my bare knuckles. It wasn't easy being half-French in a British boys' school.'

'And your mother?'

'Quietly enrolled me for a few judo lessons and gave me a pair of running shoes. Which tells you everything you need to know about their personalities and who I took after.'

The anecdote was obviously designed to reassure her of his character, and she had to admit it carried a ring of truth, especially given his handling of the tank-man today. 'Oh, for a world without bullies, corporate raiders and financial manipulators.'

'Peace, harmony and fluffy pink unicorns?'

'Exactly.' Sophie smiled, applauding the sentiment and happy they were back on bantering terms. And now she was about to ruin it again. 'Luc, I'm sorry, but I have to ask. Were you fired from your job for leaking information?'

'Francis again. That man really has it in for me, although I don't know why.' Luc sighed. 'He likes to think he fired me, but actually, I resigned. We worked for an institution that specialised in tracking down lost items from the revolutionary era. Because we worked on behalf of several museums, I was the first person to see the pattern of objects disappearing under dubious circumstances. I compiled a file of all the information and took it to Francis, but he refused to take it any further.' Luc shook his head. 'He thought it would not reflect well on us as an institution if we were the ones to blow the whistle.'

'What happened?'

'I went over his head to the director. Francis got angry and tried to fire me, but I had already decided my position was impossible and resigned. I've never been happier since I set up my own business and certainly never regretted doing what I did. Francis left not long after that to take up a position at Versailles.'

'Did the director do anything about your information?'

'Straight away. He convened a meeting of all the museums. When we all collaborated, it became obvious that we had an even bigger problem than anyone realised. A specialist unit of the police has been following it up, with no success so far. I've been giving them whatever help I can.'

'Forgive me for asking so many personal questions, but Henri was also suspicious of where you got the money to start your new business.'

'A convenient side-effect of my disagreement with Francis. My ex-wife was angry when she found out what he had done. She is a high-powered lawyer, so the mere mention of the words "constructive dismissal" was enough that the institute were falling over themselves to arrange a termination payment. I didn't know she'd done it until the payment arrived in my bank account, but I wasn't about to argue. Not that I needed it. I live a fairly frugal life, with enough savings to do as I wish.'

'Okay, that all sounds reasonable. Anything else I should know?'

'I don't want you to get the wrong impression. Sure, there are the usual professional rivalries and personality clashes, but most of my colleagues are decent people. It's just that everyone is on edge over this problem of trafficking in cultural objects. A multi-million-euro criminal enterprise operating in our midst breeds distrust.'

'Martine told me about the black-market activity in museum-quality pieces and how every time they tracked down a possible acquisition, it disappeared under their noses. And now it seems valuable pieces are being stolen to order as well.'

'Nobody knows who is behind it – at least until now. Part of the problem is that many museums and collectors are having the same problem and therefore it's hard to pin down who is to blame. But, if all these people used AntiqGarde, the random pattern starts to make sense. It seems so obvious in retrospect.'

Now it was Sophie's turn to pace the room. It seemed to her that Luc could be in a whole lot of trouble, and she had just made it ten times worse. 'You need to be careful, Luc. If the crooks have infiltrated your systems, then they must know you are investigating their illegal activities. They would have every reason to spread rumours hinting at your involvement in trafficking to deflect blame. Who knows how far they would go if they thought you posed a risk to them? Or if they believe we are on the cusp of finding something of immense value.'

Luc thought it through. 'I suppose the first thing to do is to take everything we know to the police officer who is dealing with this matter at the Cultural Trafficking Unit. He should be able to find out what Paul Tomas is up to.'

'I wish we had more to go on. It's not a crime to loiter outside a hotel room and I have no evidence that he was inside or that he took anything. Can you prove it was Paul Tomas who tampered with your computer system?'

His grimace was answer enough. 'If other AntiqGarde clients are affected, we might have a case. Henri Chevalier will be livid. If he owns the company, then he is Paul's boss, and therefore under suspicion.'

'Surely Henri is wealthy enough to buy whatever he wants without resorting to illegal or underhand means.'

'True. But he is also a man obsessed with having the best of everything. There is no telling how far he would go to get the objects he wants for his own collection. I'm willing to bet he tried to overwhelm you with charm last night, hoping to win you over.' Luc raised an eyebrow, making it a question.

'Henri is certainly an entertaining host. But I'm also too long in the tooth to be won over by charm alone, let alone by conspicuous displays of wealth. And if we are talking about obsession, I'd have to say that word has been used several times about your determination to track down Elisabeth and whatever she was carrying.'

She expected anger, or at least denial, but Luc laughed. 'Sounds like you've been talking to Jacqueline. And she is right. Elisabeth's disappearance has always fascinated me. But it's always been a dead end until you showed up in my life.' His expression turned serious again. He got up and came over to where she was leaning against the window frame. 'It's been wonderful to meet you, Sophie, but now all I can think of is how worried I am about your safety. I'm sorry you got dragged into this.'

This would have been the perfect moment to agree with him and take the next train out, but somehow that's not what came out of her mouth. 'Tell me, Luc, what would you do if I did have something of great significance to French history? For example, if the cameo turns out to have belonged to the daughter of Louis XVI.'

'What would I do?'

'Would you want to sell it to the highest bidder, keep it, what?'

'That wouldn't be my decision to make, if it was something you have. If it was me, I'd arrange to have it put in an appropriate museum.' He paused for thought. 'Well, I suppose if I'm honest, I would probably make them sign a deal in which I got to publish the research on it.'

She smiled at the utter guilelessness of his reply, compared to Henri Chevalier's desire to keep anything valuable for himself.

'Sophie, you've been through a lot already. I'm sorry you have been exposed to all this – I honestly didn't see it coming. If you don't trust me, I would completely understand. I'll walk out of here right now if you want me to. Though I'd have to admit, it would break my heart not to read Elisabeth's diary.'

That clinched it for Sophie. She had mentioned the possibility of having something of value and he had gone back to wanting to see the diary rather than grilling her about what she had. 'Relax, Luc, you can read the diary.'

Luc's phone rang, and he took the call out in the corridor. It occurred to Sophie that he probably hadn't had lunch, so she ordered from the room service menu while he was talking. His call took a good twenty minutes, allowing her time to think through all she had learned.

'That was Hugo. He'll be over soon.' Before Luc had crossed the room, there was a knock at the door. 'That was quick.'

Sophie opened the door to a waiter wheeling a trolley carrying a pot of tea and an enormous silver tray with a domed lid. She was an experienced enough traveller to know the presentation was always far flashier than whatever lay under the dome. Sure enough, the mixed platter of small savouries, cheese, crackers, and fruit looked reasonably appetising without being lavish.

She tipped the waiter and closed the door. 'You missed lunch, Luc. Dig in. The tea is English Breakfast, or I have a bottle of water if you'd prefer.'

'Thank you. Now you mention it, I am rather hungry.' Luc sat down and loaded up a plate.

'While you're eating, I'd like to share the story Henri told me last night. Then we can decide what to do.' She poured two cups of tea and pushed one across the small table.

'Henri confirmed Elisabeth is the daughter of the girl adopted by the royal family, Ernestine. He has correspondence between Ernestine and the surviving legitimate daughter, Marie-Thérèse. When Elisabeth left France in 1830, it was to return a valuable pearl necklace to her aunt, Marie-Thérèse.'

'How is it that no one had heard of these documents?' Luc demanded, emphasising his annoyance with the point of the cheese knife. He looked sheepishly at the knife before putting it down with a clatter. 'Sorry. What I mean is, why aren't such important documents archived for research purposes?'

She smiled into her teacup at his question. 'Most people would have asked about the valuable necklace rather than the documents.'

'I do want to hear about the necklace too, of course.'

'Unfortunately, Elisabeth's meeting with Marie-Thérèse was ambushed. Rather than give up her family heirloom to her enemy, Marie-Thérèse threw it into a lake, where it was lost forever. Henri seems to think it was the pearl necklace given to Marie Antoinette as a wedding present. He got the documents from the collection of the man who became king in 1830, whose name I forget. It seems the man felt that the necklace rightfully belonged to him.'

Luc leaned forward with a look of intense concentration. '*Mon dieu*. The pearls Louis XVI gifted to Marie Antoinette on their marriage were handed down from Anne of Austria and worn by several generations of the wives of the heirs to the throne of France. I thought the necklace was now in America. If they are the true Anne of Austria pearls, they would be priceless.'

Sophie clattered the teacup into the saucer before she had a heart attack and spilled tea everywhere. 'Wow, no wonder everyone is so intent on finding them.'

'Even if they are another set of pearls belonging to Marie Antoinette, they would be enormously valuable. But if they were lost, why is Henri so interested in Elisabeth?'

'He thinks there might be more to the story than the official version. There was a note from a decade later, written by a man called Cloutier, to say he had a lead on both Elisabeth and the necklace. But that was the last mention of it, as Cloutier and Elisabeth both disappeared.'

'If the pearl necklace can be found, it would be a sensation.'

'That's not the half of it, Luc. Henri has evidence to suggest the necklace was part of a larger hoard, rescued from Versailles during the revolution by Ernestine and hidden until the royal family could retrieve it. His eyes were practically on fire when he talked about it.'

'Which agrees with what François thought. But I have searched everywhere in the vicinity of their home, with not a single hint of anything like that. I assume Henri does not know where the treasures were hidden either?'

'Correct. That's why he is so keen to read Elisabeth's diary. By the way, did you know Henri was keeping tabs on your research?'

'I suppose that shouldn't surprise me. Between Henri spying on me and his security company hacking my system, I'm beginning to feel like a complete dupe.'

A knock on the door startled them both. But it was only Hugo, bearing two new, anonymous phones.

Hugo kissed her on both cheeks. 'Pleasure to meet you, Sophie. Martine enjoyed your visit yesterday.'

He returned to French, explaining technical details to Luc with the enthusiasm of a man delighted at the prospect of some interesting computer bugs to exterminate. Before he left, Hugo swept her luggage, coming up with two tiny bugs – one in her handbag and one in her suitcase. He handed them to her with the cheerful look of a man in his element, little realising the shock she felt at this invasion of her privacy.

When he'd finished, Hugo kissed Sophie again, reiterating his wife's invitation to dinner. Luc went with him to the hotel lobby, leaving Sophie perched on the overstuffed hotel chair, staring at the tiny electronic devices (now smashed) that had been planted in her luggage. What she needed right now was a deckchair out in a garden. A nice safe garden well away from here, where the only bugs were the aphids on the roses.

Luc shut the door and snibbed the lock and chain. 'Hugo says we should assume they know our mobile phone numbers and can track them. He suggested we only make calls and use the internet on these new phones. If we only give the numbers to people we trust absolutely, we should be safe.'

Sophie shook her head in horror. 'My life is on my mobile. All my contacts, photos, calendar, everything.'

'No problem. Hugo says we can use the old mobiles in flight mode as long as we also turn off GPS.'

'So, what now, Luc? I feel like I'm caught in a vise, which is being steadily wound tighter. The sophistication of their operation worries me – planting bugs, hacking computers, tracking phones, flying around the world at the drop of an email.'

'I know what you mean. I'd like to get out of here. Hit the reset button, and hopefully turn the tables on these villains, now we know what they're up to.'

'I agree. We need to talk. If there is a key to this mystery, I'd like to think we are in the best position to solve it.'

'I'm heartened by your use of "we". Does this mean you'll work with me, Sophie?'

'It means I want to go somewhere safe, so I can read François' diary and have you read Elisabeth's diary. If there are any clues to this mythical hoard, I can't think where else we will find them. I wish we had access to Henri's documents as well.'

Luc raised an eyebrow. 'You wish to invite Henri to join us?'

She looked up to see if he was joking, but his expression had an endearingly earnest look about it, which suggested he would bow to her wishes if he had to. 'Henri does have an excellent cook and very comfortable armchairs, not to mention a fabulous view. On the other hand, the only time I was separated from my handbag was at his place last night. How else could my handbag have been bugged?'

'Added to the fact that Henri owns the security company.'

'And the fact that I wouldn't trust him not to put his own interests first.' Not to mention the drama of having two conflicting personalities on the same team.

'Excellent, just us then.' Luc was obviously relieved, but instead of gloating, he switched to practical mode. 'I suggest we use our old phones to let everyone know we are going to the Loire Valley for a few days of sightseeing. As it was always the plan, it will be believable, and it will give us some breathing space. Meanwhile, we go somewhere nobody will look for us.'

'You have somewhere in mind?'

'I do. Comfortable, secure, comes with a passable chef.' He was relaxed again, a distinct improvement.

'I could get used to this lifestyle, preferably without the bad guys. So where is this place?'

'Remember I said I was looking after the car for a friend? He left me the keys to his apartment, too. He doesn't know many people in Paris and I hadn't seen him in ages before he arrived a few months ago, so it's unlikely anyone will make the link.'

'Do you have the address? I'll let my children, auntie and a couple of friends know where I am.'

Luc set up both of the new phones and messaged the address to her. 'I'll need to go back to work and sort a few things. Maybe make some calls to other AntiqGarde clients and the police to get the investigation underway. Couple of hours should do it.'

He disappeared, leaving her to pack – again – and ponder what in heaven's name she was doing – again. And, more specifically, when was she going to tell him she had the pearl necklace and jewellery box. Play it by ear, was the best strategy she could think of. As soon as he read the diary, he would know that Elisabeth had the necklace, so she couldn't put it off for long. She shrugged and headed out to get some extra cash and a few groceries, before retrieving the jewellery box from the hotel's safe.

It was closer to three hours by the time Luc got back. 'Sorry. Escaping is never as simple as it sounds. I've still got a couple of calls to make, if you don't mind.'

She could pick up enough of his rapid French to make sense of his side of the conversation, more or less. The owner of the apartment was happy for them to stay. The second call was more fractious, judging from the scowl and the rapid flailing of hands. Luc mentioned her name several times. He was talking to Francis Bonhomme and saying he would get her to call the next time he saw her. Then there was a rapid exchange about the security company – the reply on the other end was explosive enough for Sophie to hear across the room – before Luc scribbled down a name on the hotel notepad and said goodbye.

'Francis Bonhomme, who is now Martine's boss at Versailles,' Luc said, unnecessarily.

'Yes, I met him yesterday.'

'Right, I forgot. He wants to invite you to dinner, not wishing to be outdone by me and Henri Chevalier, and especially not wanting to miss out on any juicy information you might have. I told him we were about to leave for a trip to the Loire Valley.'

'Why do I feel like I'm being hunted down by a pack of wolves?' Her unthinking use of this phrase jarred her memory. What was it Elisabeth had written

302

in her letter? *Tragedy has tailed my family like a hungry wolf.* Sophie shivered and turned her attention back to the phone call. 'What was that about the security company?'

'They upgraded their computer system in the acquisitions department at Versailles about a year ago. Francis was not pleased when I told him to have it checked for spy software.'

'I gathered. I could hear him from the far side of the room, so your eardrum must be ruptured.'

'Francis is known for his dynamic leadership rather than his calm hand on the tiller.'

'A prima donna with a temper, in other words.'

'I never said that, exactly,' Luc protested, but the twitch of a smile confirmed her impression. 'He's putting the blame squarely on the man who was head of IT at the time, Edgar Joubert, who recommended the new system. He's not there anymore, but Francis gave me his contact number. The interesting thing is that a couple of other museums I rang also mentioned they had upgraded their systems after talking to Joubert. Suspicious, but possibly just a reflection of his expertise in the area.'

'Does Joubert use Armani cologne?'

'I've absolutely no idea. I don't even know what I use. Something one of my daughters gave me for my birthday, probably.' Luc rubbed a palm over his face and sniffed. 'Hope it doesn't offend your sensitive nose.'

'No, your daughter has chosen wisely.'

Luc raised an eyebrow. 'Eau de ancient parchment with a top note of dust?'

'Citrus trees on a summer's day with a hint of cedar.' Lovely.

That gained her a double eyebrow raise.

Sophie shrugged. 'We all have our strengths. If it had been you on the plane, you'd probably have noticed the man was wearing a signet ring bearing the crest of Roderick the Great, or Egbert the Incontinent, or something like that.'

'Roderick the Great? Welsh? Ninth century? Not sure I know any Incontinent Egberts, though, unless the first king of England had urinary issues.'

'My point exactly. I plucked a name from the air as a joke, because I know so little about history, but you didn't even have to think about it.' Sophie was glad the tension between them had eased, but she still had more questions. 'Getting back to Edgar Joubert – do you know what organisation he works for now?'

'I don't. I've never had much to do with him. Let's check.' Luc tapped rapidly on the phone keys. 'Well, well, that is interesting.'

He turned the screen around so she could see Joubert's Linked-In profile. 'Note that his current position is listed as head of IT and security at Chevalier Enterprises.'

'Joubert looks vaguely familiar. I think he might have been at Henri's place when I went for dinner. I saw him down the end of a dim corridor, so I can't be sure. It was just after Henri had showed me his Monet, so I was a little distracted.'

Luc rolled his eyes. 'Could Joubert have accessed your handbag while you were engrossed in Henri's collection?'

'No, I don't think so, unless....' Sophie paused to visualise whether she had taken her bag with her to see the paintings. No, she had been so eager to go, she'd left her bag by the chair. 'Actually, yes, he could have. So, Joubert is an IT and security expert who works for Henri. Henri owns AntiqGarde. Paul Tomas works for AntiqGarde. You don't have to be a genius to see the pattern.'

Luc nodded. 'It's easy to see now how they know so much. I've always been in two minds about Henri Chevalier. There's no doubt he has the funds to buy whatever he likes, but he also seems to have an uncanny knack of getting his hands on the very pieces he wants. Having said that, I have to say I thought he would be too honourable to be mixed up in anything illegal. Why bother when he's already on the rich list?'

'I agree. But the history of villainy is littered with likable fraudsters for whom no amount of wealth is too much. Let's not take any risks.'

Luc scrolled through a series of page searches, stopping at a Facebook photo. Henri Chevalier, Edgar Joubert and Paul Tomas at a formal event, looking very cosy. 'I'll make a quick call to Martine to give her my new number. And to my police contact, Marc Vincent, to tell him about our trio of suspects. Vincent is the only person with the resources to gather the evidence needed for prosecution of frauds of this scale. Then we can leave.'

'Good. My head is spinning with all this information. I need a safe space to process it all. I'm sorry if I'm overreacting, but my gut instinct is giving a full tsunami alert.'

'Absolutely. I feel as if I'm under attack too.'

Storm Debris

Paris, 18 June 1791

Ernestine lunged sideways as the cudgel arced downward, feeling the wind from it swish by her head. Her attacker bellowed as the weapon smashed into the wall, the power of it shuddering down his right arm. She turned to run, but he grabbed her around the neck with his left hand.

'*Putain!* I'll see you burn in hell.'

'Let the girl go, you filthy sewer-rat, or you'll be going home with one arm.'

Ernestine flicked her gaze sideways, seeing a wizened man wearing a shopkeeper's apron, brandishing an ancient sword in the face of her would-be murderer.

'Step aside, old man. This is the Austrian bitch's daughter, trying to escape the will of the people.'

'Ridiculous. She's no more a princess than I'm a duchess.'

The attacker looked as if he was about to argue, but the shopkeeper swished the sword under his nose, a whisker away from the tip. After several long seconds, he released his grip on her neck and spat on the ground. 'Plenty more whores where that one came from.' He picked up his cudgel with a sneer and sauntered off, stopping at the corner to get in the last word. 'She's probably got the pox, anyway.'

Ernestine sank back against the wall, her whole body as limp as a silk thread. Suddenly, the shopkeeper lunged towards her and thrust her away. She had a fleeting moment to register shock, then a large object hit the wall where she had been standing. To her horror, she saw it was the burning body of a Swiss Guard.

The drunken man laughed uproariously, before staggering off down the street. She sank to the ground, her whole body shaking, trying to hold back the nausea rising in her throat.

The shopkeeper propped his sword against the wall and crouched down beside her. 'Come inside, mademoiselle. No decent person is safe on the street today. Rest assured that lout will wake up tomorrow with a vile pain in the head and blistered hands.'

She took his offered hand and allowed herself to be pulled to her feet, keeping one hand on the wall to steady herself. 'Thank you, sir. I thought I was about to die. Indeed, I would have, without your courage.'

'It's a bad business, indeed it is, Madame Royale. What are you doing out here?'

'I beg your pardon, sir, but I am not the princess.'

'If you say so, Your Highness, though you look mighty like the girl I saw in the royal carriage once.'

'An unfortunate coincidence, I assure you. I'm sorry, I have no money to reward your service to me. Perhaps you would like this silver pin?'

The shopkeeper bowed low and came up smiling. 'Whoever you are, I am honoured to assist you. I need no reward to do what God would want of any good Christian.'

'Ernestine!'

She turned to see a carriage approaching, with Madame de Soucy waving frantically from the window. 'Sir, I will pray for you tonight.'

'And I will pray for an end to this tyranny and for the return of the King. I wish you well, mademoiselle.'

Ernestine used her last ounce of energy getting into the carriage, collapsing onto the hard leather seat as the carriage moved off again at a sharp pace. 'They thought I was Marie-Thérèse. I would have died if that brave shopkeeper hadn't rescued me.'

'Now then, calm yourself, Ernestine.' Madame de Soucy patted her shoulder and passed over a handkerchief. 'I'm sorry I was so long. Carriages were not to be had at any price. We're safe now, thank the Lord.'

'Thank you for coming back for me, Madame. Where will we go?'

'My mother has acquaintances in the city. They will help us travel onward to the safety of my family. I promised Her Majesty I would look after you.'

'I hope your mother is safe. Madame Mackau was always kind to me.'

Madame de Soucy turned her head away. 'I do not know what has happened to my mother, nor to any of the other members of the household.'

Ernestine placed her fingers lightly on her guardian's hand. They pulled the blinds over the windows and lapsed into silence for the rest of the journey, for there was nothing they wanted to see, and nothing left to say.

Mackau house, early September 1792
Ernestine was chafing at her enforced solitude. Grateful as she was for the generosity of Madame de Soucy and her family, every day that passed was filled with the frustration of not knowing what was happening in Paris. Not that she could complain. She was safe, well fed, and comfortable. The air was fresh with the scent of gardens and the only noises were the soothing sounds of birds and flowing water. A far cry from the horrors of Paris.

No one knew quite how to treat her, as she was neither royalty nor servant. In the end, they fell into a compromise, whereby Ernestine was always polite and helpful, but nothing was demanded of her beyond what she chose to do. Except that they would not let her leave the house or even show her face at the window.

Messengers and visitors arrived at the house sporadically, but none of their news was passed on to her. In the end, she regressed to her childhood trick of hiding and listening. Not very dignified, but how else would she hear the news? Often, she wished she had remained ignorant, as the news was all dire.

Soon after they arrived, she learned that the royal family had been imprisoned in the tower of the ancient Temple of the Knights Templar. From the gasps of dismay that greeted this news, she gathered it must be as grim a place as it sounded. The entire household was in shock for a week at the unspeakable effrontery of putting the royal family behind bars in such a vile place.

The shock deepened soon after, when word came that the rest of the household had been separated and taken to the dreadful La Force prison. Madame Mackau, Madame and Pauline de Tourzel, the Princesse de Lamballe, and many other noble names languishing in that hellhole – it was an outrage, most especially in the case of the elderly and venerable Madame Mackau.

Madame de Soucy slipped into a state if despair and kept to her room. Ernestine prayed long and hard for Marie-Thérèse and all the other prisoners. She thought even longer and harder about what she might do to help them, but to little avail.

Today, she was so deep in thought that she didn't hear the carriage wheels on the gravel until it had passed right under her window. Too late to find a place to overhear the news. But, to her surprise, she was called downstairs by a familiar voice.

She raced down the stairs, almost tripping over the hem of her dress in haste, and launched herself into waiting arms. 'Pauline, is it really you?' Turning, she saw Pauline's mother taking off her travelling cloak. 'Madame de Tourzel, how wonderful to see you and your daughter.'

Across the room, Madame de Soucy was looking happier than Ernestine had ever seen her, as she assisted her elderly mother to the most comfortable armchair in the room, next to the fire.

'Madame Mackau! How wonderful to know you too are safe.'

Ernestine reached for the bell to call for refreshments, but the maid was already coming through the door with a laden tray, her eyes glistening and her hands shaking with emotion. The maid went straight to Madame Mackau and settled her more comfortably with a cushion, before pouring her coffee and selecting the tastiest treats for her from the tray.

The old lady was evidently as much revered in her own household as she had been at Versailles.

The distraction allowed Ernestine to take Pauline aside, eager to hear their news. 'We had word that you were all in La Force prison. I do hope it was a false rumour.'

Pauline settled into an armchair with a sigh. 'A comfortable chair and the smell of coffee – how I have yearned for such simple pleasures. La Force is not fit for the rats that swarm every surface. It is no place for ladies of noble birth.'

'May I ask what happened?'

'The short of it is that we were all arrested. I escaped La Force through the kindness of a benefactor, but the others were only released after being pardoned by the court. We reunited in the home of a relative, who warned us to leave Paris immediately. I would not wish to tell you any more about it and beg you not to ask, for it was a dreadful time.'

The maid came over and served them with coffee. Pauline reached for the cup with shaking hands, spilling a little over the rim. Prison had aged her far beyond her years.

'And you, Ernestine? How did you get here?'

'Madame de Soucy helped me to escape from the Tuileries. Oh Pauline, it was a massacre. I will never forget the savagery on their faces.'

Pauline closed her eyes and shivered, despite the warmth of the room. 'Her Majesty was most insistent that my mother should find you and ensure you were safe. I am very glad to find it so. Have you heard how the royal family fares?'

'No. Only that they are imprisoned in the tower of the Temple. Madame de Soucy does not wish me to be alarmed, and thus does not share any news she receives.'

'The Queen must be devastated at the loss of her beloved friend.'

Ernestine leaned forward. 'Which friend?'

'Then you have not heard? A mob stormed the prison. Hundreds were killed in the most brutal way imaginable, including our dear friend, the Princesse de Lambelle, whose sweet nature was admired by all.'

'Oh,' was all Ernestine could say. The situation was dire indeed if even the prisons could be besieged. After some moments of reflection, she took Pauline's hand. 'Will you help me get back to Paris? I know there is little I can do, but I need to be nearby in case I can be of service to my family.'

'No, Ernestine, it is impossible. You would be in great danger there. You cannot imagine how terrible the situation is. No person, whether of high or low birth, is safe anymore.' At this, Pauline bowed her head and clutched at a cross around her neck, her lips whispering a few words of prayer.

'But I am no use here. I am nothing more than an unwanted burden on this household. Her Majesty has always treated me as one of her own children. I owe it to her to do what I can.'

Madame de Tourzel came up behind her and patted her shoulder. 'Your loyalty is admirable, Ernestine, but there is nothing you can do. Her Majesty took great care to ensure you escaped to safety. Do you not owe it to her to stay away from danger? We were advised in the strongest of terms to leave Paris. You would be most welcome to come with us, if you do not wish to stay here.'

Ernestine weighed up her options quickly, deciding she would be better placed with Madame de Tourzel and more likely to hear the latest news. 'Thank you, Madame. You have always shown me great kindness.'

'Why don't you pack while I talk to Madame de Soucy. We need to leave as soon as possible, so we can arrive before nightfall.'

Packing took no time at all, as Ernestine had few possessions and an eagerness to depart. She took her leave of Madame de Soucy with more emotion than she expected, giving thanks for her courage in rescuing and hiding her. Before the mantlepiece clock chimed the next half-hour, she was in the carriage, heading to wherever their destination might be.

'May I ask where we are going, Madame?'

'Our kind saviour, Monsieur Hardy, offered us rooms in Vincennes. I do not even know the man, yet he helped secure releases for both of us, and then was the means of reuniting us again when I was frantic with worry. Even so far from Paris, he has cautioned us to stay inside and not show our faces at the window.'

Pauline squeezed her mother's hand. 'Mother was staying with an elderly relative in Paris, Madame de Lège, who has shown us nothing but kindness. I doubt my mother would have been persuaded to leave her, as she lives alone with only a few servants, had it not been necessary for me to leave Paris. I escaped La Force prison without being officially pardoned, which means I will be arrested if found.'

Ernestine felt the glimmer of a plan forming. 'You must be concerned about the welfare of Madame de Lège.'

'Perhaps so, although I doubt they would dare to touch a woman of such advanced years, who is so well respected.'

'May I offer a suggestion to ease all our concerns? If I return to Paris after the carriage has taken you to Vincennes, I could offer my services to your relative and let you know she is well. If the situation in Paris gets worse, I could assist her to travel to you at Vincennes.'

Madame de Tourzel glanced sideways at her. 'I know you too well to fall for such a gambit, my dear Ernestine. I stand by my decision – you will not be safe in Paris.'

To Ernestine's surprise, it was Pauline who spoke up on her behalf. 'Mother, you would not leave Paris if I was still in prison, nor would I leave you. Do you not understand how Ernestine must feel?'

'Perhaps, but the Queen would wish her to be safe.'

'What if Ernestine could return to Paris, yet still be safe?'

'How so, my dear?'

'Madame de Lège might be pleased to have a companion. If Ernestine was to wear simple clothes and tuck her hair under a bonnet, she might be passed off as a poor country cousin of little consequence, especially if she stayed indoors.'

Madame de Tourzel's lips remained pursed, but Ernestine could tell by the way her head nodded ever so slightly that she was considering the suggestion.

'I expect we will never hear the end of it if she is not allowed to follow her chosen path.'

At that, Madame de Tourzel rolled her eyes, just as she always had when she discovered the children in

317

some prank or other. 'I shall not hear the end of it either way. You're getting too clever for your own good, young Ernestine. You used to be the only one who obeyed me without question.'

Ernestine felt her smile widen. 'Is it so surprising that my childhood nature has been altered by events?'

'Perhaps not, but you'd be a fool to be happy with this choice. Let me be absolutely clear, so you know what you are about to face. The day I was released, I saw bodies strewn about the streets in great piles, slaughtered in the most heinous manner. They say thousands died in those few days. There is no limit to their depravity, even ransacking monasteries and degrading nuns in their convents.' Here she took Ernestine's hands between her own and squeezed them to the point of pain. 'The Princesse de Lamballe was butchered, and her head paraded on a pike through the streets to the Temple. Can you face such horrors as this?'

Ernestine forced down the nausea threatening to rise in her throat and answered with no more than a slight quaver in her voice. 'Madame, I saw such things during the massacre at the Tuileries. I am not a child anymore to run away when I get scared. I have only one concern – that I do not place Madame de Lège at risk.'

Madame de Tourzel wiped her eyes with a lace handkerchief, managing a weak smile. 'She's a tough old lady. In truth, I think anyone who crosses swords with her would come off the worse for it. She willingly took us in, despite the risk, and considers it her duty to help others like us. You will be well placed there.'

Pauline took Ernestine into her arms and embraced her tightly. 'Brave Ernestine, you will find many others like yourself in Paris. Madame Cléry has proved to be a heroine for the cause. She has taken rooms opposite the Temple and manages the activities of a group of loyalists.'

'I am delighted to hear it. What has she been doing?'

'She arranges criers to shout the news outside the prison, so Their Majesties know what is happening, and plays music when they walk in the gardens to uplift their spirits. But most of all, she is the best source of information, as she is one of the very few who is allowed inside their prison, although only to visit her husband. Did you know that Monsieur Cléry was brave enough to present himself at the gates and offer his services to the King and Dauphin, when he might have gone free? They have few servants to help them in there and fewer still with his devotion and loyalty.'

'I always thought Monsieur Cléry was a good and loyal man, but now his courage inspires me. How might I find Madame Cléry?'

'You should not approach her, as that would put her schemes in danger. She has a band of messengers who pass word amongst the faithful, including Madame de Lège. Rest assured, you will know what is happening.'

These were glad tidings indeed. Ernestine sat back and spent the rest of the journey plotting how she might persuade Madame Cléry to take a message into the Temple. How low the prisoners' spirits must be, especially after the loss of dear friends in so shocking a manner.

Two days later, the carriage deposited a travel-worn Ernestine at the Paris house of the Marquise de Lège in the receding glow of twilight. The footman handed her down and took her to a side door. His fourth knock was answered by a harried middle-aged woman, her sweating forehead, rotund figure, and flour-dotted apron identifying her as the cook.

'Come in, mademoiselle, come in.' The cook turned and shouted, 'Jeanne, where are you girl?', before turning back to Ernestine with a shake of her head. 'We've few enough to help in the house without a maid whose head is always in the clouds.'

A slim, lively girl with a sparkle in her eye appeared in the hall. 'All right, cook, don't get your apron in a twist. I was busy settling Madame with her evening apéritif.' She turned to Ernestine with a precisely judged bob of the knees – just low enough to be courteous to a welcome visitor, but not so low as she might for a guest entering through the front door. 'Welcome, mademoiselle. Madame de Tourzel sent a messenger ahead, so we were expecting you. Please, follow me upstairs. I will show you your room.'

Jeanne took her meagre bag of belongings and headed upstairs, stopping at a modest, but comfortable, room two flights up. 'You'll find water in the ewer, if you wish to refresh yourself. Shall I return in ten minutes to take you to Madame?'

'Thank you, Jeanne.' Ernestine slipped off her hooded cloak.

Jeanne's mouth forming a delicate 'O' as she registered Ernestine's face and wavy blonde hair. A slight frown followed, as Jeanne's eyes flicked down to the simple dress, which looked little different to her own. She said nothing, but the deeper curtsey she immediately dropped into said what words did not.

Ernestine had her story prepared but was disconcerted at having to use it so soon. 'No need to treat me as a guest, Jeanne. Pease call me Emily. My parents were servants in Madame de Tourzel's household some years ago. I am grateful for her kindness in offering me a place to stay for a few days, while I find a suitable position in Paris.'

Intelligent eyes appraised her once again. 'Well then, "Emily", it is.' Jeanne turned to go, but hesitated. 'I may be a bit of a handful on occasion, as I'm sure my mother will tell you – she's the cook, by the way – but I know how to keep my mouth shut when it counts.'

Ten minutes later, Jeanne returned and led her down to an elegant, but cosy, sitting room. The woman in the armchair by the blazing fire appeared to be asleep. Despite the deep wrinkles and white hair of advanced age, her back was as straight as the chair behind it, even at rest. When the two girls crept closer, her eyelids opened and Ernestine found herself transfixed by two ice-blue eyes, which had the hard sparkle of diamonds in the firelight.

'Mademoiselle Emily–' Jeanne's introduction faltered for want of a full name.

Ernestine came to her rescue. 'Emily Noiret. I am pleased to make your acquaintance, Madame de Lège. You are most kind to take a stranger into your house.'

'That will be all, Jeanne.' The old lady waved a frail hand at the door, her thin fingers weighed down by several rings bearing precious stones larger than her knuckles. 'We will take supper early. Mademoiselle Noiret must be hungry after her journey.'

When Jeanne's footsteps could no longer be heard on the stairs, the old lady turned her penetrating gaze on Ernestine again. 'Not entirely a stranger, I think, Mademoiselle Noiret. When I was younger, I visited Versailles occasionally.' Her eyes flicked up to the portrait of Louis XVI above the fireplace, then back to Ernestine. 'You are most welcome to stay here, as long as you please.'

'I am not–'

'I know exactly who you are, and I can guess why you wish to be in Paris, when everyone else yearns to be anywhere but here. You will find I am old, but no fool, young lady. Come now, don't look so despondent. We will have some interesting conversation, I think. Gossip is all I have left, now that I cannot travel further than the few rooms of this house.'

'I would be honoured to act as your eyes and ears about Paris, or to serve you in any other way.' Ernestine couldn't help but smile. Even in this brief meeting, she knew she had found a great ally and a diverting companion in this shrewd grande dame.

Within days, she felt at home here. At first, she remained inside, assisting Madame de Lège in her daily routine and reading to her in the evening. While Madame had her afternoon doze in front of the fire, Ernestine went downstairs to help with the chores, as she felt guilty that she had taken over most of the light work of a lady's maid, leaving Jeanne with the less pleasant tasks.

The two girls were of similar age and soon fell into an easy friendship. Jeanne was bright and cheerful and seemed pleased to have the company. As they sat mending, she chatted with Ernestine about what was happening in Paris, with much emphasis on the various attractive messenger boys who came to the house. One in particular had caught her eye.

'He's not the most handsome of them, but not so stupid as most of them either. I like the way his smile lights up his eyes.'

'Does he have a special smile just for you then, Jeanne?' Ernestine teased.

'I would like to think so, but he shows me no particular favour, no matter how hard I flutter my eyelashes. Polite, but disinterested. Perhaps he has a girl already.'

After a week had passed without incident, Ernestine was allowed to accompany Jeanne on a trip to the market, on the promise of keeping her head down and not lingering any longer than necessary. Jeanne had found her a tatty shawl and apron left behind by a long-vanished scullery maid, along with a worn bonnet she trimmed with ribbons of red, white and blue, so that her allegiance to the revolution would go unquestioned. The final touch was a few smears of grime on her hands and face to disguise her unblemished skin, and a dusting of soot in her pale eyebrows.

The streets were busy with people, mostly going about their everyday business, albeit with prominent displays of revolutionary colours. Ernestine saw no dead bodies this time, but many wounded and disabled soldiers. The criers shouted out the latest news, which seemed to be dominated as much by battles at the borders as political intrigues within Paris.

It appeared the combined Prussian and Austrian armies had crossed into France, but hopes were high that they would be defeated. Of course, the blame for the war was laid squarely at the feet of the King and Queen, who would prefer France to be overwhelmed by foreign armies than to lose their place on the throne, according to the criers and the people handing out pamphlets to passers-by. Ernestine glanced at one and was about to drop it into a gutter running with filth, when Jeanne grabbed it from her hand.

'Don't do that,' she whispered fiercely. 'Never, ever, show disrespect for the regime. There are spies everywhere who love nothing more than to denounce others for the most trivial act of disloyalty to the cause.'

They hurried on to the market. At a vegetable stall, the stallholder was talking in a low voice with another woman, who smelled of sour wine. Jeanne stepped forward to get their attention, but Ernestine held her back. Instead, she sidled closer, examining the leeks and onions with feigned interest.

'I tell you it's true. Thieves broke into the State Treasury last night and stole sack-loads of royal jewels from right under the noses of the guards.'

'And how would they do that, pray tell?'

'Climbed up through the first-floor window, while the guards stayed by the front door.'

'Sounds stupid enough to be true, but how do you know?'

'My man overheard them bragging about it in our tavern when he served them their ale. They plan to go back tonight to get more loot, and he reckons he'll leave me to look after the Fat Hog, while he goes along to see what he can pick up.'

'Wonder what they are like, those jewels?'

'I seen them myself not three months ago, when they was still letting us lowly folks in to gawk at what them royals used to have. Crowns and other royal whatnots, made of gold and studded with whopping great stones – diamonds and rubies and suchlike. You could never imagine such a heap of treasure all in one place. The guard said they was worth more than twenty million livres.'

'Lord preserve us! Can you imagine how much bread we could buy with that!'

'Might see if I can get me a bloody great diamond for my bonnet.' The women who smelled of wine snorted out a laugh and slapped the other woman on

326

the back. 'Or better yet, sell that stinking tavern and go home to Bayeux, where the air smells of the sea not the puking piggery.'

'How about yer man picks up a ruby or two for me? I'd fancy a trip to the seaside.' As the stallholder doubled over with laughter, she noticed the two girls lurking and waved a fist at them. 'What are you smirking at? Be off with you.'

Ernestine and Jeanne hurried away to fill their baskets elsewhere. Back at the house, Ernestine shared the news with Madame de Lège.

'Can't say I'm surprised, given the depths of madness all of Paris seems to have descended into. But a dreadful day, to think that centuries of France's accumulated glory should disappear in such a ridiculous manner. No doubt the criminals will sell the entire collection of Crown Jewels for a fraction of their value, and they will be lost forever.'

'Unbelievable as it seems, Madame, the woman said the thieves are going back for a second time tonight. Presumably, there was too much to be carried away in one go. Her husband is going to see if he can steal some jewels for himself.'

'Probably half of Paris will be there if his wife is spreading the news in the market. Still, it gives me an idea. Have Jeanne send for a messenger. Tell her to ask for the clever dark-haired one. She'll know who I mean.'

Three hours later, Jeanne knocked on the drawing-room door. 'The messenger has arrived, Madame. Do you have a letter for him?'

From the blush on her cheeks, Ernestine felt sure this was the young man Jeanne fancied. She was eager to see him for herself.

'Bring the lad up here, girl. Emily, you may stay.'

Ernestine retreated to the corner, where she covered her hair and took up a piece of embroidery. When the door opened, she got such a shock that she stuck the needle into her finger and gasped.

The young man looked in her direction, his hazel eyes widening under a thatch of black hair. Three years had passed. He was much taller and broader now, a man instead of the boy she had known. Regardless, she would have known him anywhere.

Ernestine could see he was about to say her name, so she ran the five paces separating them. 'Pierre Duchamp, if I'm not mistaken. I'm Emily Noiret. Do you recall when we met some years ago?'

Pierre clasped her hands, his beaming smile telling her all she needed to know. Suddenly, he realised he was the centre of attention. He dropped her hands as if they had scalded him and took a step backwards under the cover of a sweeping bow. 'Mademoiselle Noiret, how delightful to meet you again after so long.'

Jeanne looked from one flushed face to the other, her own cheeks as red as theirs.

'Coffee please, Jeanne,' Madame de Lège ordered. When the door banged shut, she added, 'You two know each other already, I perceive.'

'We are the oldest and best of friends, Madame. Pierre was a great favourite with the–' She had been about to say with the Dauphin, but she caught herself in time. 'A great favourite with the children. And a great help to the family since, in ways which would meet your approval.'

'I see.'

No doubt she saw far more than she let on, but Ernestine could not keep her delight in check.

'Well, take a seat, you two. I can see you wish to renew an old acquaintance, so I shall hold my tongue until the coffee arrives.'

Pierre took her hand again and guided her to the chaise longue. 'Ernes … Emily, I came back to Paris to look for you, but they would not let me into the Tuileries. After the palace was attacked, you vanished without a trace. People said you must be dead, but my heart told me it could not be true.'

'You came back? Oh, Pierre, I thought I might never see you again. What luck to meet you here.'

'Not luck, really. There are not so many houses in Paris where loyalists may be assured of safety.'

'Loyalists? I had thought your sentiments were in favour of change.' How quickly they had dropped back into the gentle teasing and easy conversation of the past.

'Change yes. A sharing of power and wealth and bread with the people, without question. But this … this anarchy and slaughter? No, that was never what I wanted. The only way to save France now is to get the King released. I believe he was in favour of improving the lot of his people and will have the power to set things right.' Pierre glanced over at his hostess. 'In my humble opinion, for what little it's worth.'

Jeanne appeared again. She set a tray on the table with a thump, spilling coffee from the jug, before leaving without a word. Ernestine served Madame first, before pouring a cup for Pierre.

Pierre accepted the porcelain cup as if unsure what to do with so delicate a thing. 'I am honoured, Madame.'

The Marquise fluttered a hand, as if it was a trifling matter to have a messenger lad to afternoon tea in her private drawing room. 'Emily, would you like to tell this young man what you heard in the market.'

When she had finished, Pierre shook his head. 'The entire collection of Crown Jewels – guarded only at the street door? Are you sure the woman wasn't spinning a tale?'

'Possibly, but I'd say her eyes were alight with greed rather than jest.'

Pierre turned to his hostess. 'Madame, I take it you would like me to pay a visit to the State Treasury tonight and do what I can to track down the criminals?'

'Exactly. This is a far more dangerous mission than carrying messages, so if you do not wish to go, please say so now.' Madame de Lège's eyes glittered in the candlelight, as her gaze fixed on Pierre.

He didn't so much as blink. 'Madame, I do believe you are enjoying this as much as I am.'

Ernestine was a little taken aback by his forthright manner. Her friend was a far different person from the boy who had been frightened of the Queen a few years before. While she wanted him to say no to this crazy plan, she held her tongue.

Madame de Lège merely chuckled. 'One does what one can for King and country. Which is little enough stuck in this chair. I will arrange a plain carriage to take you tonight, with a footman, in case you need assistance.'

'That is unnecessary, Madame. I will be less obvious on my own. Besides, I want to see if I can find out what tavern the men were drinking in. Might be easier to follow them home if they've drunk too much.'

'The Fat Hog.' Ernestine said. 'It's near a piggery and probably reasonably close to the market we visited this morning.' She clasped his hand tightly. 'Pierre, please … be careful.'

'You must promise me you will simply observe and follow the robbers if you can do so safely, and not put yourself at risk,' Madame added. 'I want you to come back here as soon as you can, no matter what the time, as neither I nor Mademoiselle Emily will get any sleep until you do. Once we know where the rogues are hiding, we can arrange a surprise visit to liberate the jewels.'

When Pierre had gone, the piercing eyes turned on Ernestine. 'He's a fine young man. I am sorry to put him in harm's way. I confess I know little about him, other than his character.'

'May I tell you his story another time, Madame? If you permit, I would like to go upstairs to rest, as I fear it will be a long night of waiting.' She gathered up the coffee cups and untouched plate of cake. 'I'll take supper in my room.'

'If you wish. As long as you don't take it into your head to follow him. I will station the footman at the door to ensure it.'

The coffee cups rattled as she jerked the tray. 'You believe me to be that reckless?'

'I see plenty of loyalty and courage in you, *Ernestine*, and cleverness too. If you had been born male, you would have been a finer leader than many others of the blood. Don't look at me like a startled rabbit, girl. As I've told you before, I may be old, but I am not stupid. You will be safe here as Emily Noiret.'

'Thank you, Madame. Perhaps this catastrophe would never have happened if women such as yourself were in control of France.' She closed the door on cackling laughter and thanked her lucky stars to have found herself in this refuge.

Jeanne managed a weak smile when she entered the kitchen. 'I see now why Pierre showed no interest in me and why he always seemed so sad. I'm glad he is happy again, truly.'

'I'm sorry, Jeanne. If I had known before who he was, I would have said something. Pierre and I have known each other for many years.'

Ernestine gathered a platter of food for her supper. If she couldn't follow Pierre tonight, as she had planned, then she might as well rest up before he returned to the house.

As the hours dragged by, her head grew heavier. Come back soon, she prayed, allowing her eyelids to close for just a moment.

A noise from downstairs jolted her awake. A door slamming, footsteps pelting up the stairs, voices in the drawing room. She unwrapped herself from an awkward position in the chair, not having intended to sleep at all, and ran downstairs, just as a loud banging rattled the front door.

Pierre stood in the drawing room next to Madame de Lège, who hadn't moved from her chair by the fire. His chest was heaving, and he was dripping with sweat. 'I was spotted. They think I am one of the thieves. Is there another way out?'

Downstairs, she could hear the door being opened and the sound of a booming voice demanding entry. 'Too late. We'll have to hide you. Madame?'

'I can't think of anywhere safe. They will tear my home apart if they think he has the Crown Jewels.'

Downstairs, the clash of pots and slamming of doors told them that the rooms were being searched. The house was not large. They had two or three minutes at most. Too late to go up to the attic, as they might be seen on the stairs.

'May I put him in your bed and pretend he is sick?'

The old lady rallied. 'Put my nightcap and gown on him. My granddaughter often comes to stay, so I can pretend it is her.'

Ernestine pulled Pierre into the adjoining bedchamber, throwing the nightgown over his own clothes, as there was no time to lose. The frilled collar and lilac embroidery were not going to fool anyone for more than a moment, not with that masculine face and black hair. She could hear footsteps on the stairs now, a light tread from above and a stomp from below.

'I don't care whose authority you are acting on. You may not disturb my mistress in the middle of the night.' It was the footman's voice.

There was a short scuffle before the stomping resumed. Ernestine whirled around desperately, catching sight of Madame's dressing table. As Pierre tucked his hair under the nightcap, she attacked him with powder and rouge, sending him into a convincing fit of coughing.

Out in the corridor, the booming voice said, 'Stand aside, girl. A fugitive was seen running down this street and I have the authority to search every house.'

'This is an outrage. My mistress is a lady of impeccable reputation. You are wasting precious time searching for a criminal in this house.'

Jeanne's stand at the door to the drawing room gave Ernestine the time she needed to tuck Pierre under the covers. She shoved a basin at him. 'Can you make yourself throw up?'

With a squeak of protest from Jeanne, the drawing room door burst open, at the same moment as

Ernestine came through the door to the adjoining bedchamber.

Madame de Lège glared at the intruder. 'What is all this commotion? My poor granddaughter is extremely ill and must not be disturbed.'

The man took a step backwards under the force of her imperious tone. 'I apologise for the intrusion, Madame, but I must search the whole house. May I ask you to leave this room while I do so?'

'I most certainly will not.' She waved her stick under his nose. 'I am an old lady. Standing up causes me great pain. My lady's maid will show you my room, if you insist. The parlour maid will accompany you upstairs. If you are not out of my house in ten minutes, I shall complain to Robespierre himself.'

The soldier blanched and took another step backwards. From inside the bedchamber came the sound of vomiting and groaning, followed by more coughing.

'It's a terrible disease, sir.' Ernestine hunched over, making herself look as timid as possible. 'I pray the fever ain't catching. Never seen such nasty red blotches as on that poor child's face.'

The soldier wrinkled his nose, but still he went into the bedchamber and glanced around. 'I'll have a quick look upstairs, before leaving you to your vigil.'

He looked back at the figure under the bedclothes, shuddered, then left the room in a hurry.

A few minutes later, the front door slammed shut, and they all breathed again. Jeanne popped in briefly to see if they needed anything, before going back upstairs. When the house was quiet, Pierre emerged, still looking comical with red spots on a white face, albeit not quite so comical as when he'd been wearing Madame's nightclothes.

'Don't laugh at me, Ernestine.'

'Honestly, I'm far too petrified to laugh at anything right now. Let me get you a basin of water to wash in.'

She gathered up the sick-bowl and left the room to get warm water and soap. When she got back to the door, she could hear a whispered conversation, but the talking stopped as soon as she entered the room. Although she felt annoyed at being left out of the discussion, on the whole she was relieved she didn't have to hear what new danger Pierre was going to be thrust into.

She seated Pierre on the chaise longue and sat down beside him, gently swabbing the powder out of his eyes. 'What will you do now, Pierre?'

Madame de Lège answered for him. 'He must leave the city immediately and stay away until the furore dies down.'

The two young people glanced at each other and shuffled a little closer together without being aware of it.

'You two will have to be patient, content in the knowledge that you are both alive and well. Emily, Pierre has shown courage for our cause, but now he is in danger. Would you have him risk his life by staying in Paris?'

'I would have him safe, above all else, Madame. Might I have a few more minutes to talk to him before he leaves? I have not seen him in such a long time.'

Madame de Lège appraised them for several long seconds. 'Very well. It would be better if he left around dawn, anyway. It is long past the hour of my bedtime. No more than a few minutes' talk, or your young man won't be able to stay awake on his horse tomorrow. Perhaps you could prepare him some food to take, Emily.'

Ernestine helped her up and into the bedchamber. 'Sleep well, Madame. You were very brave tonight.' She reached down and placed a gentle kiss on the old lady's forehead, getting a wink in return.

When they were seated in the kitchen with a bowl of the thick broth that simmered night and day above the embers of the fire, Pierre caught up her hands. 'It took me so long to find you, Ernestine. I have no wish to leave again.'

'If you weren't in danger, I would feel the same. Will you return to your family's home in the Loire Valley?'

'There is an urgent need for a messenger to travel to the border, where the King's brother waits with an army. That is what Madame was asking me to do when you left the room. Don't look so stricken, Ernestine. It will be far safer than staying in Paris, but I'll still be doing something useful.'

'They must have great faith in you, my dearest friend. I know I cannot dissuade you, so I will only wish you Godspeed and ask that you take as few risks as possible.'

'And you, Ernestine. Promise me you will stay well hidden.'

She smiled but offered no promise. 'I haven't heard what happened tonight. Tell me, Pierre, while I put together a parcel of food for your journey.'

'And another plate of broth?'

'Some things never change.' She pushed over her untouched bowl and sliced more bread.

'It started well. I found the tavern. More than one group was talking about the theft of the Crown Jewels, but nobody seemed to be sure who the thieves were. Or rather, everyone thought they knew, but a dozen different names were whispered. Once I got to the State Treasury, I realised why, as there must have been more than a dozen men climbing up to the first floor and coming down again with loaded sacks. By the time I climbed up, the inside was a mess of discarded items with all the large jewels prised out.'

Ernestine froze with her knife halfway through a round of cheese. 'You went inside? You were only supposed to be watching!'

Pierre shrugged. 'No point coming back with half the tale. Anyway, four of the men got into an argument with the others, accusing them of barging in on their crime and stealing their loot. At that point, a pair of soldiers appeared and gave chase. The soldiers followed the larger group, so I went after two of the original thieves, trailing them right back to their lodgings near the tavern.'

'How did the soldier end up chasing you?'

'I waited until the thieves left, assuming they would go to the tavern to celebrate. Then I broke in and searched their lodgings. I'm guessing, but probably the soldiers chased all the other men back to the same tavern, as none of them seemed very clever, and arrested them all. No doubt the original thieves were pointed out. Next thing I knew, a group of soldiers arrived with the two thieves in tow. I was out the window and running for my life.'

'A close call, Pierre. No wonder you need to leave Paris. At least the authorities have got some of the

Crown Jewels back, although it's a shame you didn't find their hiding place first.'

They were both silent for a time, as Pierre tucked into the broth and Ernestine found apples and more bread to add to the cheese.

'You should get some sleep. You have a long journey ahead.' She pushed the food parcel across the table, not wanting to meet his gaze in case she burst into tears. Instead, she gathered up the bowls, wrapped the cheese, wiped up breadcrumbs, twisted her apron strings.

'Don't look so sad, Ernestine. I will come back, I promise.'

'I hope so, but we both know in times such as these, it's not always possible to keep promises.' She sat down beside him again and rested her head on his shoulder, savouring the feel of his fingers stroking through her hair. 'I need to ask you for another favour, Pierre.'

'Anything.'

'Do you recall when we rescued those items from Versailles to take to the Tuileries?'

'How could I forget? How young and naïve we were then.'

'My father and I did the same again when the royal family escaped last year. I have heard nothing more from Papa since. Just in case something happens to me, it is vital that someone else knows where we hid their possessions, so they can be returned to the royal family when they are released from prison. One item is particular is treasured by the Queen, a pearl necklace in a beautiful marquetry jewellery box.'

'I pray nothing will happen to you.' His hands tightened on hers. 'But, of course, I promise to do what I can to return their valuables if necessary.'

Ernestine pulled out a scrap of parchment, on which she had sketched a crude map of the location. She explained to Pierre how he would find the hiding place. 'The property belongs to my mother's family.'

'I never met your mother, Ernestine. What is their name?'

'Noiret. They should be easy to find, as they have a thriving vineyard. If fate takes you there, promise me you will raise a glass of champagne to my memory.'

'On the contrary. I promise we will visit together and raise two glasses to our future happiness.'

'I like the sound of that.' She hugged him close and felt his lips on her forehead.

'You could come with me,' he whispered.

The temptation to walk away was so powerful it seemed like a physical force binding her to this man. Why did their lives have to be so complicated, when all it would take is two people walking out the door to a new life together, away from all this madness?

'Pierre, I... I don't know what to say. My heart is torn between what I want and what I must do.' She unclipped the silver chain from around her neck and held it out to him. 'It belonged to my mother. I pray it will keep you safe.'

He kissed the silver cross and tucked the necklace into his coat. 'Our time will come, my love. I wish I had a token to give you.'

She drew out the little carved owl, which had travelled next to her heart since that long ago day at Versailles.

He reached out a finger and touched the owl with a tender smile. '*Au revoir*, Ernestine. I promise to come back for you as soon as I can.'

The Jewellery Box

Paris, 2019

Sophie recognised the first section of the journey as they retraced their route to the airport. Somewhere to the north of Paris, they disappeared into a part of the city she didn't know at all. Within minutes, they arrived at an apartment block, which looked not unlike the one Luc lived in.

The interior was a stark contrast to his apartment, with cutting-edge modern décor, white-on-steel surfaces, gorgeous blown-glass vases and avant-garde paintings. An enormous television took up much of one wall in the lounge, while the open-plan kitchen overflowed with shiny chrome gadgets. Clearly, Luc's friend had masses of money and no small children or pets in his life.

Luc must have read her mind. 'He's a history graduate who somehow lost his way and became a very successful investment banker. This is what my father would have wanted for me.' He stacked two bags of groceries on the kitchen counter and loaded the fridge with food and wine, with the efficiency of someone familiar with the layout. 'Make yourself at home. Take the larger bedroom. If you lean out over

344

the balcony far enough, you can see the edge of Saint-Denis.'

Sophie went out into the lobby first and retrieved Luc's bag and the last of the groceries. Starvation was not on the agenda. Of the two bedrooms, the largest room was the most luxurious, but it did not appeal. The designer brief must have been 'make it modern and masculine – don't hold back on the sharp edges, black paintwork and chrome fittings'. The smaller room was more to her taste, albeit generically neutral.

An hour later, she was lying back in the most comfortable recliner chair it had ever been her pleasure to indulge in, a crisp white wine in one hand, nibbling on flatbread loaded with tapenade.

Luc flopped down on the sofa. 'Not quite up to Chevalier standards.'

'Are you kidding? I live alone in a small cottage with squeaky floorboards and thirty-year-old furniture. This is heaven.' She reached out to clink glasses. 'When does the chef arrive?'

'I'm here. No Michelin stars, but I'm an expert at opening packets and tossing salad.'

'That's an offer I can't refuse. Before we eat, would you like to see the photos I took of the sketchbook of Elisabeth's voyage? I didn't want to bring it with me as it's too delicate and precious.' She moved over to the sofa, opened up the gallery of photos on her mobile, and passed it to him.

'What a magnificent find!' Luc flipped through the photos slowly, studying each one. 'The artist had a rare skill at capturing the moment. I'd love to see the originals. Even in the photos, I feel like I could reach out and touch the ship.'

Sophie reached over to tap the screen. 'I think this one is a picture of Elisabeth.'

Luc glanced between her and the picture. 'A definite family resemblance. Amazing after so many generations.'

They took a break for dinner, before starting on the translation of Elisabeth's diary. Luc's talents in the kitchen went far beyond opening a packet, so it was Sophie who tossed the salad, while Luc rustled up *coq au vin*.

Which explained her intense sense of post-dinner contentment as she adjusted the recliner into semi-recline and listened to Luc reading the diary to her in that lovely caramel voice of his. She felt a smile creep across her face and realised that, despite all the stresses of the last few days, she was actually enjoying herself again. Was it only a week ago she was ruing the lack of excitement in her life?

'Sophie, are you awake?'

'Mm. Just letting the words wash over me.'

'Why the smile? You find Elisabeth's plight amusing?'

'Heavens, no. I have every sympathy for a woman who was badly treated and forced to travel to the ends of the earth. But don't you think she rises to the challenge admirably? I rather think she enjoyed the adventure, despite the awful things that happened to her.'

Luc lowered the diary and studied her over the top of his reading glasses. 'Are you talking about Elisabeth or yourself?'

'Am I that transparent? It has been a crazy couple of weeks, but now we are safe, I couldn't be happier. A delicious meal, a comfortable chair and a puzzle to solve – what could be better? Perhaps Elisabeth felt the same. Although I must apologise again for dragging you into it.'

'Are you kidding? I've searched for Elisabeth all my life and now here you are, bringing her voice to life. Not to mention that you've cracked the problem of who is stealing my data and France's heritage from under my nose.' He took up the diary and pushed his glasses back up his nose. 'Can't wait to find out what happens next.'

Luc read on and Sophie lay back, absorbing the fluent translation of Elisabeth's diary. She had gotten the main gist of it from her own reading but picked up more of the fascinating detail this time. Suddenly, she realised he hadn't spoken for several seconds. When she opened her eyes, she nearly closed them again at the force of Luc's glare.

'Quite a voyage, wasn't it?'

'Oh, yes. And I know exactly what you are thinking right now. Why didn't I tell you that I already knew Elisabeth had the pearl necklace with her on the ship?'

'I assumed you did not realise until I translated the diary.' His intonation was carefully flat, but the raised eyebrow made it a question.

'*Mea culpa.* My French is not that bad, and I did know.'

He was looking over the glasses again with the penetrating gaze of a headmaster sizing up an errant pupil. 'Perhaps the necklace was sold, so Elisabeth and the ship's doctor could make a new life in New Zealand?'

Sophie adjusted the recliner so she was upright and looking directly at him, as she slowly allowed her smile to widen.

'*Mon dieu*, you have it!'

'It's locked away safely in New Zealand. I'm sorry I didn't tell you before, but with so much happening so quickly … well, it was hard to know who to trust. The fact that so many people are willing to go to such lengths to track it down had me on edge.'

'I suppose I would have done the same. You didn't tell Henri Chevalier or Francis Bonhomme?'

'Heavens, no. The only other person in the world who knows is my eighty-year-old aunt, and she's not about to spill the beans. She was the one who knew enough to judge that a string of pearls of such size and perfection would be worth a fortune.'

'More than a mere fortune, Sophie. With the diaries and the documents Henri has, it's possible we have a chance of establishing the provenance of the pearls. If they were a wedding gift from Louis XVI to Marie Antoinette, they would be a sensation. Every collector in the world would be beating on your door. It will be a career highlight for me just to see them, if you will allow it.'

'Luc, I thought you might know me better by now.'

'I've known you three days. Although, I grant you, it feels like far longer.'

'Is it really only three days? Even so, you should realise that I have no intention of claiming the pearl necklace for myself or selling it to the highest bidder, whatever the price. I'll donate it to a museum in France, where it belongs for all to see.'

Luc jumped up and kissed Sophie on both cheeks, his eyes glistening with emotion. 'I am lost for words at your generosity. We should celebrate. Champagne?'

'You may want to wait until I finish my confession.'

'There's more?' Luc flopped back down with a groan. 'Should I give you my cardiologist's phone number before you hit me with another shocker?'

'No need, I have a first-aid resuscitation badge from my college swimming days.'

'Very comforting. Tell me, Sophie.'

'I also have the jewellery box Elisabeth mentioned several times in her diary. I had the strong sense that it meant almost as much to her as the pearls, which didn't make sense to me until I visited Versailles yesterday. Based on the items I saw there, I'm fairly sure the jewellery box was made by the Marie Antoinette's favourite cabinetmaker, Riesener.'

Luc let out a long whistling breath. 'I wish I could see it.'

Sophie picked up her bag and pulled out the padded package, which she handed to Luc. 'If I had known it was so valuable, I would have left it at home too. At least I had the sense to put it in the hotel safe, rather than leaving it in the room safe. The intruder had no problem cracking that lock. Fortunately, he had the decency to leave my spare cash alone.'

Luc was staring at the package as if it contained a bomb. 'I should be wearing gloves.'

'Luc, it has been passed from hand to hand for hundreds of years, survived a dangerous voyage on a sailing ship and a return trip by plane, not to mention the inside of my bag, albeit well-wrapped. I think you might take a peek.'

He didn't need any more persuasion, although he did treat it with due reverence, turning the jewellery box over in his fingers, as if it was made of fragile crystal rather than wood.

'Say something, Luc. I can't stand the suspense.'

'I'm speechless. You'll think me foolish, but I feel a sense of its history when I touch it, like a little buzz of electricity.'

'On the contrary, I know exactly what you mean. I get the same feeling with all of Elisabeth's possessions. In fact, there was a moment in Marie Antoinette's bedchamber at Versailles … I don't know how to explain it. It was as if I was sensing the past rather than the present, if that doesn't sound too mad.'

Luc placed his hand on top of hers for a moment. 'You have the gift too. Not uncommon amongst the more obsessive in my profession. Most of us refer to it in general company as a good intuition, but it's more than that. I always thought it was years of experience acting instantly and subconsciously, recognising an object for what it is, well before our conscious brain can tick off the features and come to a conclusion.'

'But I have no such experience, so it must be my good imagination. Reading too many mystery novels, I expect.'

'Whatever it is, this jewellery box is very special indeed and almost certainly made by Riesener.' Luc put the box down on the coffee table in front of them, where they could both admire it. 'He was a master craftsman.'

'Martine showed me some of his pieces at Versailles. All stunning. She also told me about the day the royal family was forced by a mob to go from Versailles to Paris. It sounds as if Versailles was simply abandoned that day. Perhaps a prime opportunity for our girl Ernestine to gather treasures important to the royal family and hide them away? We know for certain that Elisabeth's mother hid items for the royals during the revolution and was rewarded for her loyalty. With the chaos at Versailles that day, what better chance would there have been?'

'That would suggest Ernestine was left behind on her own. She wasn't even a teenager by then, as I recall.'

'True, but she might have had help. Her father – or rather her mother's husband – was a servant there. Ernestine was not listed as being one of the people in the royal carriage, so it's not clear when she left Versailles for Paris.'

'If they were already friends,' Luc added, 'she might also have had help from our other ancestor, Pierre Duchamp. He worked as a stable boy and gardener, which means he had access to transport.'

'Were there other opportunities for her to have hidden the family valuables? When the royal family tried to escape, perhaps? We know Ernestine ended up at the Tuileries palace, then left again before the royals mounted their disastrous escape plan.'

Luc sighed. 'Whenever it happened, it doesn't help us with a location for the hiding place. Pierre might have suggested taking everything back to his home, where he could guard it, but it would have been easier to hide items close to Versailles or Paris. Impossible to know, especially as we don't know if we're looking for a small box or a cartload or a room-sized stash.'

'Ernestine disappeared after escaping from the Tuileries, didn't she? I can't find any further mention of her.'

'Other than the supposedly official records, which suggest she married and died childless in 1815. But we know that can't be true, as Elisabeth and François would never have been born, and we would not exist.'

Further speculation seemed pointless until they got further clues. 'I'm shattered. Shall we call it a night?'

Despite his yawn of agreement, Sophie noticed Luc gathered up the diary and took it into his room. She felt the same – exhausted, but too excited to sleep. She went to her own room and slipped under the duvet, opening up the biography of Madame Royale and reading about the terrifying downward spiral of the royal family, ever closer to the guillotine.

Sophie woke to the sound of activity in the kitchen and the smell of brewing coffee. She threw a sweater over her nightwear, brushed her hair, and went to see if a shot of caffeine might be had.

Luc was standing by the hob with headphones on, tapping his bare feet and humming, 'I Can't Get No Satisfaction'. The omelette pan was wafting a delicious aroma, mingled with the steam coming out of the espresso machine. A perfect start to the day.

Sophie leaned against the doorframe, enjoying the performance. 'So, this is where Mick Jagger hangs out when he's not on tour.'

Luc spun around and ripped the headphones off. 'Oh no, was I singing out loud? I'm so sorry if I woke you.'

'Morning person?'

'Guilty as charged. Jacqueline used to hate it when I was cheerful before ten o'clock in the morning, hence the headphones.'

'No need to hide the sharp knives. Singing isn't really my forte, but I enjoy a good dose of cheerfulness in the morning, as long as it comes with a nice strong cup of coffee.'

'Hint taken.' Luc folded the omelette and divided it between two plates, while Sophie hunted out cups and cutlery.

They sat down at the table and clinked coffee cups.

'To discovering beautiful things,' Luc said.

'And finding long-lost relatives,' Sophie added.

'I've been thinking,' they both said simultaneously. Each gestured the other to go first, before speaking again at the same time.

With a laugh, Sophie said, 'You go first, while I do justice to this breakfast. It's such a treat being cooked for.'

When they had devoured the omelette, Luc poured more coffee, while Sophie gathered up the plates. He rocked back on his chair and said, 'I've been thinking about the jewellery box. Did Martine tell you much about the Riesener pieces at Versailles?'

'She showed me several wonderful pieces, and I had a look at more online. I especially liked the clever way he incorporated mechanical levers to raise up parts of a desk or open everything out in one smooth action with a single push of a button, like Marie Antoinette's writing desk.'

'Riesener was famous for it. Both Marie Antoinette and Louis XVI loved clever craftsmanship, especially pieces with levers, locks … or secret compartments.'

Luc's emphasis on the last two words hung in the air as the implications sunk in. Sophie let out a quiet 'Oh', wiped her hands, and went back to her room for the jewellery box. She cleared the coffee cups off the table, gave it a good wipe and dried it with a clean towel, before putting the box in front of Luc's place, as he arrived with glasses, gloves, a magnifier, and a kit of what looked like jeweller's tools.

Luc lifted the box to examine it closely under the built-in light of the magnifier. 'What a fine piece of design. It's scarcely visible, even under magnification, but I believe there might be a hidden drawer at the bottom.'

Sophie forgot to breathe as she watched Luc testing the panels with the finesse of a neurosurgeon. Finally, with fingers splayed across two points of particularly detailed marquetry, a slim drawer slid open. She clapped a hand over her mouth to stifle a squeal.

Three very thin sheets of paper were nestled inside, as if untouched in the intervening centuries. Luc laid a pristine sheet of acid-free paper on the table and used a special set of implements to lift the pages out, one by one, laying them down and teasing the first one open in slow-motion. He looked at her with sparkling eyes and let out a long breath.

'The suspense is killing me. What does it say?' Sophie couldn't stand the delay as he read, so she moved around to look over his shoulder. The first thing that struck her was the signature, which was instantly recognisable.

'The first is a letter from Marie Antoinette to "my daughter Ernestine", to confirm the jewellery box and pearl necklace had been entrusted to her for safekeeping until such time as they could be returned to her. I expect she felt Ernestine might need to prove she had not stolen them, whereas she was probably putting Ernestine's life in danger by linking her to the royal family so blatantly.'

'Still, it shows the regard the Queen felt for her adopted daughter. How wonderful.' Wonderful felt like a ridiculous understatement of the excitement that was geysering up inside her.

'Wonderful for sure, but also extremely helpful in establishing provenance. She makes it clear they were the pearls handed down to the royal wives.' Luc carefully folded the letter along the original folds and picked up the second letter.

He took forever to read it, or so it seemed to Sophie, who was gripping the back of his chair with white knuckles. 'What is it?'

'A letter from Marie-Thérèse to Elisabeth Duchamp, who she calls 'my niece', congratulating her on her engagement to John Godwin and formally gifting her the pearl necklace and jewellery box. Written in 1830 and addressed to the Godwin household in London. No wonder Elisabeth was chased halfway around the globe. A royal heirloom as valuable as that necklace would be a prize desired by every legitimate family member, who would be outraged that it was given to the child of an illegitimate daughter and a gardener.'

'How can you remain so calm after reading these letters?'

Luc glanced over his shoulder, allowing a weak smile to penetrate his concentration. 'You wouldn't say that if you were taking my pulse right now. I'm terrified I'll damage them if I allow my excitement to boil over.' He reached out and squeezed her hand. 'You realise what this means? With this proof that the items were gifted, nobody can deny they belong to your family.'

'Wouldn't there have been other surviving family members who would have contested such a lavish gift? Didn't the brothers and sisters of Louis XVI flee in the first few months of the revolution, except for Elisabeth, the King's youngest sister?'

'Poor devoted Elisabeth, who suffered the ultimate price for her loyalty to her brother. Perhaps she was the woman for whom our Elisabeth was named.'

'Who was in line to inherit the necklace?' Sophie asked.

'In fact, Marie-Thérèse had a good claim on it. When she was finally released from prison, she married her cousin, the oldest son of the King's brother. Her husband came within an inch of becoming the king in 1830, when his father abdicated, which would have made Marie-Thérèse the Queen of France, like her mother before her. Arguably, she was the rightful owner of the pearl necklace by descent, as well as by position, when she gave the necklace to Elisabeth.'

'What happened?'

'The Duc d'Orléans seized the throne as King Louis Philippe I, after a devious piece of trickery. Thus, he had a case for claiming the pearl necklace was his – or his wife's – by right of position.'

'King Louis Philippe I? That's the name Henri Chevalier mentioned. Henri purchased the documents implicating Ernestine from his estate.'

'With the new King's determination to have the pearls, his enormous power, and the mutual hatred between the two branches of the family, it's a miracle that Elisabeth and Marie-Thérèse made it to safety. If Henri is right, Louis Philippe also knew the Duchamp family were hiding other items for Marie-Thérèse.'

Sophie now understood the compelling reasons for Elisabeth's hasty escapes from two countries. 'Now I see why the jewellery box needed to be protected. Louis Philippe wouldn't have wanted those letters to see the light of day.'

'Our Elisabeth must have been an extraordinary woman to evade his men. And her mother Ernestine too.' Luc went back to reading the letter. 'Listen to this. Marie-Thérèse's letter says that Elisabeth's courage and loyalty were matched only by that of her mother, who "*willingly sacrificed herself to save me, when all hope was lost*". It certainly sounds like Ernestine did more for her adoptive sister than saving priceless family heirlooms.'

'Ah, well, I've had some thoughts about that.'

'Have you indeed? I can't wait to hear what other surprises you have in store for me, Sophie.'

'Let's see what's on the final piece of paper first.'

Luc folded the second letter and took up the third, which was no more than a scrap of faded parchment. He sat back, allowing her to see better. 'What do you make of it?'

If the scrap was a note, it was so faded that only a few random squiggles could be discerned. She twisted her head around to see if it made sense in any other orientation. 'Hard to make much sense of it. I suppose it could be a crude map. Or a sketch of something?'

Luc peered at the paper, turning it back and forth with the tips of his tweezers. 'There's not much to go on if it is a map. No obvious rivers as far as I can see, which might mean François was wrong in assuming his parents hid valuables near their home in the Loire Valley. Unless it's a very small-scale map of a local area.'

'Nothing seems to be labelled. How could anyone have made sense of it?'

'Presumably whoever made it left more explicit instructions elsewhere.'

'Which isn't much help to us, if we don't know where to start, especially with all the changes that might have happened since. It could be under a city or motorway by now.' Sophie leaned closer. 'Luc, could you hold it up to the lamp?' In the brighter light, faint lines could be seen. 'Maybe it was labelled, but the writing has faded. This bit looks as if it was shaded and written over.'

Luc angled it this way and that. 'Maybe R-something?'

Sophie reached over and took his hand, angling it so she could see more clearly. 'Possibly R. Could be Pr. I can't make out anything else, except that it is a short name or an abbreviation. How many towns in France start with R?'

Luc put the paper down with a sigh. 'Dozens. Not to mention cities, villages, cross-roads, monasteries, chateaux and rivers. Hundreds, maybe thousands.'

Sophie let out a groan. The shock of their discovery had left her too excited to think clearly. What they needed was time to process the fresh revelations, so their subconscious could work to join the dots of all the information. 'How about a stroll in the fresh air to refresh our little grey cells?'

'Are you okay, Sophie? You look a little pale.'

'Is it any wonder? I feel weak at the knees at the thought that I've casually carried the jewellery box around for days, with no idea of its value.' Saying it out loud made her realise that she quite literally felt weak at the knees. She sank into her chair and prodded the box gently, as if it might spring open and reveal more secrets. 'It's a bit like those Antiques Roadshow episodes where the person discovers they have been using a rare £100,000 Ming vase as an umbrella stand.'

'£100,000 doesn't even come close to the value of what you have here.'

Luc took photos of the papers and box, including several of Sophie holding them. He flicked back through the shots, showing her one of her holding the box gingerly with a look of intense concentration on her face.

'You look like you're holding a grenade.' He kept flicking. 'Can you hold the paper up to the light again, so I can get the best possible shot of the potential map?' When he was done, he slid the papers back into the hidden compartment with delicate precision.

'Luc, given the events of the last few days, I think these items should be put somewhere secure. I don't want to be responsible for carrying them around. I would suggest depositing them straight into a museum collection, but–'

'–who can we trust? I know there is a high-spec safe in this apartment, which I'm sure my friend will let us use. But I would prefer you decided.' He looked away, a faint blush rising on his cheeks, as he took another couple of photos of the jewellery box. 'I realise you may still feel uncertain about where my loyalties lie. I want you to know that you can walk out of here, alone, and put everything in a safe-deposit box at a bank of your choice.'

Sophie felt a strong urge to hug him for his thoughtfulness at allowing her to be in control, especially when this was a career-defining find for him. She pushed the box towards him. 'The safe here sounds good to me, especially as no one knows where we are. Then you can take me on a walk around of the neighbourhood, if there is anything worth seeing, so we can take some time to think through our next step.'

After a moment of silence, he gave her a solemn nod. 'There's a very special place nearby that I'd love to take you to. We can go via the local market, to give you a proper taste of Paris.' He rummaged in the kitchen cupboard for a couple of carrier bags. 'May as well stock up while we're there.'

'Perfect. Not that we need any more food, but I think we could both do with the distraction.'

The Marché de Saint-Denis was so close that a wall of odours hit her nose as soon as they left the apartment. A weird mix of flowers, raw fish, fresh bread, decomposing rubbish and a thousand other smells. And no wonder, as Sophie saw when they walked into what looked like a large, red-brick train station, which was packed with people and food.

'Fascinating,' she said, over the shouts of vendors, after they'd strolled down an aisle of raw meat, pigs' heads and offal. 'But do you think we might go somewhere a little quieter, with fresher air?'

Luc took her arm and steered her across to the aisles packed with cheeses, bread, gateaux, and delectable chocolates.

'Oh, my lord, I've died and gone to heaven!' Sophie stopped in front of a tall cabinet stacked with massive rounds of cheese, under a countertop with small samples of each type. Luscious scents filled her nostrils, sending a surge of saliva into her mouth.

Luc launched into a rapid discussion with the woman behind the counter, of which she caught enough words ('visitor', 'New Zealand', 'cheese', 'organic') to get the gist. He turned to Sophie. 'Madame Durand will be delighted to show you her specialities. She speaks a little English and comes from Normandy. I'll get some bread and salad while you're indulging your cheese fetish.'

'Don't hurry back,' Sophie said over her shoulder, as Madame Durand handed her a sample of the creamiest Camembert she had ever tasted.

When Luc returned fifteen minutes later, Sophie was chatting happily to the cheese lady, who was packing a bag with wedges of cheese and bottles of Normandy cider and Calvados. 'I may have got a little carried away,' she admitted, 'but everything was delicious and the vendor so charming – how could I resist? Shall we go?'

Luc guided her out a side exit and down a couple of streets, popping out at a paved square, with an enormous cathedral at the far end. They stopped at a brasserie with an unimpeded view of a tall bell-tower, perched atop a grand façade of arched doors and windows, which dwarfed the few humans milling around attempting to take selfies.

'The Basilica of Saint-Denis,' Luc said proudly, as if introducing a favourite child. 'As you can see, a masterpiece of early gothic architecture. It is also the burial site of almost all our kings and queens since King Dagobert, who died in 639. The site has Roman ruins under it and has been used as an abbey or church ever since Rome retreated.'

'The depth of history here always takes my breath away. In 639, New Zealand was still a deserted cluster of isolated islands. You can see why Kiwis love visiting Europe.'

'Saint-Denis has a special significance for us, as the final resting place of the presumed remains of King Louis XVI. He never made it out of prison. To the shock of almost everyone, he was put on trial and guillotined in early 1793.'

Sophie felt goosebumps on her arms, bringing to mind the old cliché – as if someone had walked over her grave.

Tower of Terror

Over four months had passed since Pierre had left her on his mission to the border. Ernestine knew she was lucky to be living in comfort with good people, but her heart still felt hollow.

Her days were busy, while her nights were plagued by nightmares. Reports from within the Temple painted a bleak picture of the conditions endured by the prisoners. All the plotting and scheming of the loyalists, all the urgent messages to powerful contacts outside of France – in the end, nothing made a whit of difference. Not only did each plea to release the royal family meet with an adamant refusal, but the level of hostility to them grew steadily worse.

As autumn passed to winter, the unthinkable happened – the King was put on trial for his life. The year ended in despair. His Royal Highness, Louis XVI, who began his life worshipped as one anointed by God, was to meet his end by guillotine on the twenty-first day of January 1793.

The day of the King's execution, Ernestine put a pillow over her head to drown out the sounds of the bells ringing, the drums beating, the crowd chanting, and the pounding of thousands of soldiers' boots upon the streets. She stayed in bed all day, shutting out the raucous celebrations, weeping for the man who had fathered her, even if his paternity had never been openly acknowledged. She knew it to be true, not only by their looks, but by their shared interests, and the tenderness with which she had been treated by him.

The next day, she rose before dawn after a sleepless night, put on her shabbiest clothes, and set herself to scrubbing floors. The servants were horrified, but Madame told them to leave her be. She scrubbed and scoured, cursing all those who had voted to take her father's life, especially the traitorous Duc d'Orléans, the King's cousin. When Jeanne finally lifted her to her feet at the end of the day, her arms were dead weights and her knees were raw from kneeling, but she had worked out her rage and devised a plan of sorts.

Ernestine was desperate to visit the prison. It was said that the Queen was so weakened by the loss of her husband that she could scarcely rise from her bed. Marie-Thérèse and Louis-Charles were rumoured to be desperately ill, although no doctor was allowed in to see them.

Madame de Lège was as kind as a grandmother to her, nodding sympathetically as Ernestine unburdened her heart and calming her with memories of happier times. But nothing roused her spirits enough to get her to eat. By the end of January, she was gaunt and pale. Then, the miracle she had prayed for happened.

Madame de Tourzel arrived, bringing with her one of her women, Mademoiselle Pion, who had received permission to enter the Temple prison to make mourning clothes for Marie Antoinette. She would be the first visitor allowed to see the Queen in months. Being both brave and honourable, she had agreed to carry a message of hope to rally the prisoners' spirits.

Ernestine ignored the churning in her belly and waited for the right moment to speak. When the plan had been discussed and talk returned to mundane matters of family health and the difficulty of procuring bread, she stood up and stated her request, clearly and firmly.

'I want to go with Mademoiselle Pion. She will need an assistant to help with measuring and fitting. I feel I have the right to see how the royal family fares and do whatever is in my power to bring them comfort. More than a right – it is my duty.'

Madame de Tourzel was the first to react. 'Absolutely not. It would be far too dangerous for you to be seen anywhere near the prison.'

'Even you would not recognise me, Madame, if I went in disguise.'

Mademoiselle Pion looked to her mistress. 'Madame, she would put me at great risk. None of us knows what questions and searches I will undergo before they allow me in. Carrying a message to Her Majesty is surely risk enough.'

To Ernestine's surprise, it was Madame de Lège who supported her plan.

'Emily's a courageous girl and rather good at disguise. And she makes a fair point. An assistant would be required if the dressmaker is to fit all the family for mourning clothes.'

Both the other women stared at her in alarm, but she carried on. 'Perhaps Mademoiselle Pion could go alone the first day, so she can see what security measures the guards take. After that, we can decide whether Emily should join her for the final fitting.'

She could see the other women were wavering. 'Is it not our duty to bring whatever comfort is in our power to our grieving Queen? Think of the joy it will bring to Her Majesty and the children to see so well-loved a visitor.'

When Ernestine had their reluctant agreement to the plan, the dressmaker was sent out to secure the fabric and prepare her sewing kit. Madame de Lège turned back to Ernestine, fixing her with a diamond-hard glare. 'You're sure of this, my dear? Mademoiselle Pion could claim, with full justification, that she had no knowledge of who you are. But, if you are caught, it would not go well for you. Temple prison is not fit for a pig, let alone a girl used to comforts.'

Ernestine was in too great a turmoil to do anything but nod. As those sharp eyes held hers, she had the strong feeling that Madame knew exactly what she had planned. If she could find the courage within herself to go through with it.

Three days later, Ernestine scuttled along beside the dressmaker, darting between the puddles of freezing slush on this dismal winter's day. She kept her eyes down, hidden behind the wide brim of her bonnet and the bulky parcel of mourning clothes in her arms.

She told herself, over and over, that nobody would recognise her in the black wig and borrowed clothes. The broad patch of puckered red skin disfiguring her face would, she hoped, be the only thing anyone would notice. Ernestine and Jeanne had worked through the night to create this piece of repulsive cosmetic artistry.

Not once did she look up. Not even when the rabble in the street jostled her, still drunk from celebrating the death of their rightful king. The dressmaker glanced back at her now and then, as if hoping Ernestine might have taken fright and run away. Each time her hopes were dashed, the furrows on her forehead grew a little deeper.

The poor woman was terrified, yet she kept moving forward. It was a small comfort to know that Madame de Tourzel had a carriage waiting nearby, to whisk them far away from Paris as soon as their task was done. If they made it out of prison.

When the pace of her companion slowed and her steps became hesitant, Ernestine knew they must be approaching the prison. Mademoiselle Pion stopped in front of her without warning, her whole body as tightly drawn as a bowstring.

Ernestine raised her eyes for an instant and wished she hadn't. The blackened-brick walls of the Tower of the Temple loomed over her, even more terrifying than the sight of the sneering guards, leaning on their pikes, guzzling wine. For humans – even at their very worst – might somehow be appealed to – their humanity leaving some tiny chink in their scorn for royalty. But this monstrous structure in front of her offered no possible hope. A brave raven might perch on the black turrets or swoop down the five storeys of impenetrable wall at its whim, but no person, save those with a key, could escape this soaring tower. Even its shuttered black windows were meanly scattered, as if to proclaim that not even sunlight might pass into this place of despair.

They moved forward again to the entrance, their noses wrinkling at the smell. The guards ignored them, remaining huddled around a brazier, hunched in their greatcoats. Eventually, a guard pounded on the door with the end of his pike.

The man who appeared reminded Ernestine of the monkeys in the Royal Menagerie. A small, stooped figure, with a hairy body, wearing one of the despised red caps of the revolutionaries. From his simian hands dangled a set of keys as large as the man's head.

He assessed them with a leer, running his eyes over them from top to bottom. 'And what brings you two citizenesses to our door?'

'Delivering the Widow Capet her mourning clothes, as you well know.'

'Why the box and the girl?'

'My sewing kit, to make the final adjustments, for which I need my assistant.'

'No need for that. They can take 'em as they come.' He turned to the slouching guard. 'Have you searched them?'

'Don't mind if I do. The woman looks to have plenty of warm flesh to hide things in. And the young one is as ripe as a mid-summer cherry.'

Before the guard could complete his drunken lunge in their direction, the red-hatted monkey pursed his lips and pulled Ernestine towards the door. If she thought for an instant that he was sympathetic, the thought was a fleeting one.

'Never you mind. Time I had myself a little reward after looking after those arrogant scum for weeks on end.'

Ernestine tripped on the top step, but the man was holding her arm tightly and jerked her upright and into the antechamber before she could fall. He thrust his paw under Ernestine's chin, lifting her head to his eye-level, instantly jerking it away again at the sight of her hideous disfigurement, only partially covered by a thin strip of bandage.

'By the Almighty Lord, you're an ugly wench. Ain't touching that festering face again for a hundred sou.'

The dressmaker's eyes went wide, and her hand clamped on her mouth, shutting down a startled cry and turning it into a high-pitched cough. Ernestine hung her head again, so the bonnet covered her face.

With admirable presence of mind, the dressmaker came to her aid. 'Now, citizen, how about we get these clothes delivered, so a hard-working seamstress can get back to her husband. He works for the Convention, so don't you be giving us no problem.'

The leering eyes focused on the dressmaker for several seconds, but the man didn't push his luck. With a sharp nod, he gave them both a cursory search, paying more attention to the sewing kit and the parcel of clothes than to themselves. Evidently, he felt he had struck sufficient terror into the dressmaker on the previous visit to dissuade her from trying to smuggle contraband into the prison. The search completed, he turned without a word and walked up the stone steps, leaving them to follow as best they could in the dim light.

They trudged up three flights within one of the tourelles at the corner of the larger tower, stopping in front of a door made of heart oak, thick as a man's fist and studded with iron. The monkey-man shared a few coarse words with the guard, who was slouching in a chair with his feet up on a stool. Beside him hung a large, framed copy of the Declaration of the Rights of Man.

Three doors led off the antechamber. The jailer strode up to the centre-most door and pounded on it briefly, before barging in without pausing to give the prisoners time to collect themselves.

The three women in the room said not a word at this insolent behaviour, although Ernestine saw a tight grimace cross the Queen's face, while her sister-in-law Elisabeth resumed her embroidery with jabbing stitches. Marie-Thérèse appeared not to even notice them.

Nor did the man bow in their presence. 'Widow Capet, your mourning clothes are here.' In a voice hovering between indifference and spite, he added, 'If it were up to me, you'd not have been granted the favour of mourning that tyrant.'

The Queen looked up at the two women with red-rimmed eyes, which appeared devoid of all life. Ernestine had braced herself for the worst, but still found it almost impossible to believe that this haggard, white-haired figure was the merry, vivacious Marie Antoinette. She followed the dressmaker's lead, bending her knees only slightly in front of the assembled group, rather than dropping low as proper etiquette would dictate.

Marie-Thérèse did not look up, but remained slumped in her chair, her whole demeanour one of utter despondence. Her sister's sickly pallor and rasping breath tore at Ernestine's heart. She had made the right decision.

Little Louis-Charles gave them a disinterested glance before returning his focus to a solitary toy soldier. His presence was yet another barrier to the success of her plan. Would he recognise her and give the game away? The only surviving royal son – now the rightful king, Louis XVII – was not yet eight years old and had always been more inclined to mischief than common sense. What changes had been wrought upon him by his imprisonment and his father's horrible death?

The jailer turned to the dressmaker. 'Make it quick, I don't want to spend all day breathing this foul air.'

Surely the man would not stay while the Queen dressed. She caught the dressmaker's wide-eyed glance at her. No doubt the woman was rightly terrified at what might befall her should Ernestine be discovered passing a note to the royal family. For that, she felt a thud of guilt, but she had no choice but to continue.

Mademoiselle Pion stiffened her spine and advanced on the jailer with hands on hips. 'The women must be allowed to divest their garments in privacy, citizen.'

The monkey-man shrugged his shoulders and settled his skinny rear end more firmly on the stool. 'I have my orders. You are not to be left alone with them. No more than ten minutes to get the job done, then you'll be searched again on the way out, so don't try nothing clever.'

Madame Elisabeth solved the problem by taking a flimsy screen from between the beds and setting it up across the far corner of the room. 'Come Antoinette, your dressmaker awaits you.'

The calm demeanour of the King's youngest sister brought dignity and command back to their side. Ernestine moved forward to put the package of clothes on a plain cherry-wood table beside the bed. As Marie Antoinette moved behind the screen, Ernestine busied herself with undoing the package and laying out the mourning clothes on the bed.

Madame Elisabeth had moved back to allow the dressmaker access to the corner and set herself to the role of entertaining Louis-Charles, engaging him in a lively game, which had the dual effect of distracting the boy and the jailer.

God bless Madame Elisabeth, Ernestine thought, as she lifted her head to face her adoptive mother, placing a warning finger on her lips. She lifted the edge of the wig, to show her blonde hair, but the Queen's eyes were boggling at the ugly red patch disfiguring her face.

Ernestine gently eased the fake skin off her face so as not to disturb the red-tinted wax. 'Our visit to Madame Tussaud's Salon of Waxworks was most instructive, was it not, Mother?'

The Queen peered more closely. 'Ernestine, is that really you?'

'Yes, Mother. Forgive my brusqueness, but we have little time. You must let the dressmaker tend to you and not say a word. I will attend Marie-Thérèse.'

'Oh, my dearest girl, how lovely it is to see you. You should not have come, though it brings joy to my heart to see you alive.' She pulled Ernestine into a tight embrace, squashing her cheek against the large medallion she wore around her neck, a cameo of the faces of the two royal children. 'I pray you have brought good news.'

'There is little time to talk now.' Ernestine turned to the dressmaker, who seemed rooted to the spot. 'Mademoiselle Pion, please attend to Her Majesty. We must make haste.'

The dressmaker, with commendable pluck, snapped to attention and began undoing the fastenings of the Queen's plain dress, while Ernestine laid out her black cloak, black taffeta dress, white lace fichu, bonnet and gloves. The fateful moment had come for Ernestine. While the prison terrified her, she could not ignore the plight of her sister.

'Mother, it is time for me to repay the kindness you have shown me. I am to take the place of Marie-Thérèse, so that she might go free. God willing, you will see her again soon, but meanwhile, I hope your heart will rest easy knowing one Child of France is safe. Please call Marie-Thérèse over.'

Marie Antoinette stared at her, shock overlaid with a spark of hope. Yet she made no move to call her daughter over, merely shaking her head sadly, as if a cast die could not be taken back for another throw.

'There is no other choice, Your Majesty,' Ernestine hissed. 'Recent events have proved that there is no limit to how low these fanatics will sink. The royal line must endure, and this is our only chance.'

Her voice softened again at the sight of the Queen's stricken expression. 'Our only chance at the moment, I mean. Of course, everything is being done to secure the release of you all. But Marie-Thérèse can go now and be assured of the best care. Recall how often we were mistaken for each other. Call her, please, I beg you.'

Marie Antoinette, with tears flowing down her pallid cheeks, called to her daughter. 'Come, my daughter, you must be fitted for your mourning gown.'

When Marie-Thérèse was shielded behind the screen, her mother whispered in her ear. The girl's head whipped around to Ernestine, a low squeal erupting from her at the sight of the black wig coming off and Ernestine's clothes falling to the floor.

The Queen clamped a hand across her daughter's mouth. Out loud, she said, 'Now dearest, don't fuss. Please put these clothes on. The girl will help you.'

Marie-Thérèse lunged at Ernestine and enveloped her in a fierce embrace.

Ernestine hugged her back equally fiercely for a few seconds, whispering in her ear, 'Dearest sister. You must hurry and not say a word. You are to leave today. Madame de Tourzel awaits you outside the prison walls. She will keep you safe.'

Marie-Thérèse pulled away from her, the familiar stubborn expression replacing her joy in an instant. 'I cannot leave my family.'

'You are not well. Think how much relief you would give your poor mother, knowing you were free.' Even while she was whispering these words, Ernestine finished stripping off her own clothes, before turning to undo her sister's dress.

The Queen leaned over. 'Please, my dear, I beg you to do as she says.'

Ernestine flinched when she saw her sister's body, which was swollen and seeping from large boils. No wonder she had appeared so deathly ill. Still, she kept working as quickly as she could, as if it were merely another day at the palace. 'Arms up, dearest.'

Marie-Thérèse relented, allowing Ernestine to pull the worn dress over her head, replacing it with her own. When the dress was on, Marie-Thérèse turned to her mother and whispered, 'I will rally my uncles and our Austrian family to rescue you. I promise I will not rest until you are free, Mother dearest.'

Ernestine gathered her sister's hair into a net and set the black wig and bonnet on her head. She had a moment of terror when the fake skin, slippery with her sweat, refused to stick, no matter how hard she pressed at its edges. She wiped it frantically.

'How long does it take to put on a dress?' Their jailer's voice was cranky and accompanied by the sound of the legs of the stool scrapping on the floor.

The dressmaker was too terrified to say a word. Ernestine could hear the jailer's footsteps crossing the room. Still the patch would not stick.

Lighter footsteps and a quiet, assertive voice came to their rescue. 'You will not remove that screen until I am satisfied that Her Majesty is ready.'

Madame Elisabeth appeared at the side of the screen, her mouth gaping at the sight of Ernestine near-naked and Marie-Thérèse dressed in her old clothes.

Finally, Ernestine had the patch on, largely held in place by the thin bandage. With a final adjustment of the wig, she stepped back and nodded. The girls were alike enough that only those who knew them well would have noticed the switch, even without the disguise. With the distraction of her disfigured face, only the closest of confidants would have spotted the switch – or so she hoped. Ernestine squeezed her sister's hand between her own hands, the only farewell she would get.

'Enough fussing. Get that screen down.'

Showing impressive reactions, Madame Elisabeth seized the black cloak off the bed and threw it around Ernestine's bare shoulders. She pushed her into a chair, reached for a silver-backed brush, and stroked the bristles through Ernestine's dishevelled hair.

The monkey-man yanked the screen aside to find a tableau as ordinary as any lady's chamber. 'You'll have to finish dressing in your own time.' He turned to the dressmaker. 'Come on, time's up.'

The poor dressmaker was pale and trembling but held herself together. 'Believe me, I've no wish to linger in this foul place. Come on, girl.'

She bustled Marie-Thérèse towards the door, before the girl could do anything stupid, such as burst into tears or try to farewell her family. Fortunately, the shock of events had rendered Marie-Thérèse speechless. She slunk towards the door like a bewildered puppy unsure of where the master's boot would land next.

'Now, just you hold on,' the guard barked. 'Stand still while I search you.'

'You already searched me. I brought nothing in.'

'Yeah, but you might be taking a message out.' He ran a hand over her, pinching the dressmaker's ample rear with a smirk. He did the same for the dressmaker's assistant, raising her head as he had before.

Ernestine watched him out of the corner of her eye, her heart thudding fit to burst. Would this be the moment her wild plan came apart and destroyed them both?

The monkey-man spat a glob of saliva onto the floor. 'God Almighty, how can your family stand the sight of you?' He turned and went out, followed by the dressmaker and her dazed assistant.

The door slammed shut and a heavy key scrapped in the lock, leaving Ernestine inside, her present and future irretrievably locked in place, but as yet unknowable.

Wild Speculation

Paris, 2019

Sophie gazed up at the soaring walls of the Basilica of Saint-Denis, as Luc's words sunk in. 'What do you mean by this being the resting place of the *presumed* remains of Louis XVI?'

'In fact, not only the King, but his wife Marie Antoinette, and his sister Madame Elisabeth as well. Their bodies were not treated with much respect after their executions during the revolution. The remains were dug up from a pile of bodies in 1815, after the Bourbon restoration, and buried here in a new crypt. Their youngest son is also here, or rather, his heart is. His is a grim story even by the abysmal standards of the time.'

'I've been reading the biography of Marie-Thérèse you gave me. The son's treatment in prison made me feel sick.' Sophie shuddered, despite the warmth of the day. 'How anyone could abuse a young child so callously is beyond belief.'

Luc closed his eyes and shook his head. 'There is no excuse for what happened to any of them, or indeed to the thousands of ordinary citizens who were tortured and slaughtered.'

'I understand why resentment boiled over, of course. The excesses of royalty must have seemed intolerable when people were starving.'

'Not only royalty. The nobility and clergy were just as bad, living a life of luxury, while the entire burden of work and taxes rested on the shoulders of the working class, leaving them with little to spare. Ironically, few people desired the removal of the king even then – they asked only for a greater say and a modicum of fairness. But it got out of control, like a wildfire. Sparked by a few firebrands, stoked by spiralling brutality and retribution, consuming the innocent and the guilty alike.'

Sophie gestured to the solid stone building dominating the foreground. 'I read that many churches, monasteries and convents were pillaged or destroyed. It's a miracle Saint-Denis still stands. As a burial place of kings, I'd have thought it would have been a prime target.'

'Oh, it was. The medieval abbey was destroyed, the tombs were desecrated, and the royal bodies were thrown into a mass grave. The church survived, but it was deconsecrated, then restored in the 1800s.' Luc's voice dropped to a whisper, visibly wincing as he added, 'Everything of value was stripped, aside from a few items that the clergy were able to hide. Even the lead off the roof was melted down.'

'What was lost?'

'The usual items of value any church would have – crosses, chalices and so forth. But Saint-Denis also held a unique position as the place where the royal regalia were kept. All the symbols of royal power used for the coronation of kings were removed, destroyed, stolen, lost, or melted down, as were many priceless artefacts of immense historical and religious significance, presumably to pre-empt any attempt to crown a future king. It was so chaotic at the time that it's difficult to determine exactly what happened to individual items, although some were saved and are now in the Louvre. I can hardly bear thinking of the loss of our French heritage that happened inside the walls of that cathedral.'

'History so often seems to come down to this. Each "civilisation" doing their darndest to wipe out the predecessor.'

'Tragically, yes. This was not the only loss of huge significance, of course. One of the most bizarre episodes was a break-in at the State Treasury in Paris in 1792, a few weeks after the royal family was thrown in Temple prison. The Treasury was being used to store the Crown Jewels, which had been confiscated, but it was so poorly guarded that the thieves casually returned several nights in a row, helping themselves to the entire collection. One of the thieves commented that it was as easy as breaking into an ordinary house.'

'No! How is that possible?'

'Either by incompetence or treachery, only the doors were guarded, not the inside of the room, which allowed the thieves to enter via the upper storey windows. They got away with priceless jewels, some of which are still coming to light. Have you heard of the Hope Diamond?'

'Vaguely. Hasn't it got something to do with that famous kidnapping case in America?'

'Right. It has been owned by several wealthy Americans who are said to have suffered bad luck and tragedy. One of them pawned it to raise money for the ransom on the Lindbergh baby, but it was paid to a con man rather than the real kidnappers. The Hope Diamond is in the Smithsonian in Washington DC now.'

'Are you saying the Hope Diamond was stolen from the State Treasury in France?'

'The Royal French Blue Diamond certainly was. Scientific analysis indicates it was recut into the Hope Diamond.'

'Incredible. What a loss for France! What else did the thieves get away with?'

'They literally had access to the entire collection of Crown Jewels. Imagine breaking into the Tower of

London and helping yourself to whatever took your fancy.'

He paused to let the thought sink in. Sophie had visited the Tower of London and, like all other visitors, had been awed at the collection of crowns, sceptres, and enormous jewels. The thought of tucking a royal crown into her handbag was mind-boggling. 'I'm having a vision of wearing the Koh-i-Noor diamond next time I go out to a posh dinner.'

'That's exactly the kind of thing they stole. The Regent Diamond, which is now worth tens of millions of euros and makes the Koh-i-Noor look like a modest bauble. The beautiful, pale yellow Sancy Diamond, which ended up in Russia. A massive sapphire. Thousands of gemstones and other valuables were stored there, worth a colossal fortune.'

'Unbelievable. Did they catch the men?'

'Most of them. A lot was recovered, only to be sold off at auction a few years later. Other priceless pieces simply disappeared. It's difficult to know what happened to many of the important pieces, as many of those involved had reason to suppress the truth.'

Sophie started to laugh, then covered her mouth with her hand. 'Sorry, I know it's not funny, but I'm picturing a band of robbers coming back night after night, helping themselves to the Crown Jewels. It sounds as crazy as the slapstick antics of those old black and white movies like The Keystone Cops.'

'An apt analogy. Not a proud moment in French history.' Luc pushed away his cup and stood up. 'Come on, you're obviously in need of a dose of serious contemplation of the glories of my country. Despite my gloom and doom, many amazing treasures were saved by a few brave souls. The stained glass here is incredible too. Then we can say hello to Ernestine's putative father.'

Not another word was said as Sophie roamed in awestruck wonder around the vast interior of Saint-Denis Basilica, cricking her neck by staring at the vaulted roof and magnificent rows of stained-glass windows. Oddly, for all its soaring grandeur, the cathedral retained a pleasing simplicity of design, as if the glory of the building was being allowed to assert itself without needless frippery.

They paid their respects to the rows of kings and queens, or rather the remaining tombs. Luc walked beside her, providing centuries of turbulent history in a low murmur, as befitted the sombre surroundings. Even the infamous Catherine de Medici had her place.

A statue of Marie Antoinette, another queen with a tarnished reputation, knelt in prayer alongside her husband, their stone effigies projecting a noble and pious serenity, at odds with the violence that ended their lives. 'Say hello to our ancestor, Louis XVI,' Luc said. 'Can't say I see much of a resemblance, except for the nose. Lucky you, missing out on that genetic gem.'

'It's very … regal.'

'If you say so. Seen enough? There's a pleasant park nearby, for the long-promised dose of fresh air you asked for.'

The park was relatively quiet and a beautiful mix of flower gardens and trees. As they strolled through the bright display of purple and yellow irises, Sophie rewound the cathedral through her memory. 'I take it the kings were crowned at Saint-Denis, since all the regalia were stored there.'

'Actually, no. The coronation ceremony was traditionally held at Reims Cathedral.'

'Reims? I haven't been there.'

'It's less than two hours' drive to the north-east of Paris in the Champagne region.'

'In that case, I'll add it to the top of my must-see list. But only because we're looking for cities starting with R, nothing to do with champagne, honestly.'

'Ha, likely story. Shall we head back and plot our next move?'

Luc was silent on the short walk back to the apartment and for the following half-hour, until Sophie put a late lunch in front of him, assembled from their market purchases. 'You're miles away,' she said. 'Penny for your thoughts?'

Luc picked up the salad servers and waved them in the air. 'When François wrote in his diary that he thought his parents had hidden something valuable near their home in the Loire Valley, he specifically mentions caves used for the storage of wine. But what if he overheard his grandparents talking about wine storage caves and just assumed they meant the local caves? Because, logically, that is where he would think of first.'

'Are there other places with caves used to store wine?' She took the servers from him and dished out salad, ham and bread onto his plate, watching in amusement as he began to eat automatically, apparently without being aware of it.

'There are caves all over the country. They are perfect for storage because they maintain a stable, cool temperature. But I think it's fair to assume we're looking for somewhere within a few days' ride of Paris. Probably not much more than one or two hundred kilometres, depending on the state of the roads and the transport options available. Perhaps further, if there were only a few small items that could be transported by a person on a horse, rather than a cart.'

'Pierre and Ernestine were only in their early teens. Wouldn't it have been difficult for them to travel far?

'Young people took on adult responsibilities at a younger age back then. Remember Pierre worked in the gardens and stables, so he would have been strong and resourceful, and able to get his hands on a horse and cart if he needed it. The real question is, where would they go?'

'I remember reading that Ernestine was sent away before the royal family's attempted escape, the so-called flight to Varennes. One of the memoirs I read said she was sent to "her father in the country". I wonder where Ernestine's birth family came from originally?'

'I don't know.' Luc pondered for a moment. 'If we're looking for places starting with "R", Rouen springs to mind. And Reims, for that matter, if we assume R is a town rather than a small village or something else entirely.'

'Tell me about Reims.'

'Points in its favour include the strong royal connection and the fact that it is in the right direction for fleeing the country, unless by sea. In fact, the route taken by the royal family, when they escaped in 1791, took them close to Reims.'

'Caves?'

'Absolutely. Reims is world famous for its champagne, including big names like Taittinger. Many estates store their champagne in underground caverns, carved out of old chalk mines originally dug as far back as Roman times.'

'Wow, I'd love to see them. Would they have used these chalk mines for champagne in 1789?'

'We can find out.' Luc tapped away on his mobile. 'Listen to this. Ruinart was established in 1729, making it France's first champagne house, after Louis XV allowed wine to be transported in bottles. That makes sense – there would be much more money in champagne if it could be carried around the country in bottles. No doubt other types of wine date from much earlier, as it could be transported in barrels.'

Sophie looked over his shoulder. 'This vineyard looks nice, tucked up near Montagne de Reims Regional Natural Park, south of Reims. I can't wait to travel around France once we have this little puzzle sorted out.'

'Hardly a little puzzle. More likely a lifetime of fruitless searching.' Luc glanced down at his plate, looking mildly surprised it was empty. 'Meanwhile, I have a few loose ends of business to sort out. Do you mind?'

'Not at all. That'll give me a chance to put some things through the wash and finish the biography of

Marie-Thérèse. Could I have a look at François' diary too?'

Despite her good intentions, her mind drifted back to the champagne caves and the thrill of being a few hours away from so many fabulous places to visit. The boutique vineyard to the south of Reims looked especially tempting.

As she flicked through the history page of their website, a name caught her eye. 'Making champagne since 1779, when founder Armand Noiret gave up his job as a cooper and bought the land still used to grow some of the best champagne ...' Why did she know that name?

Sophie went in search of Luc, but he was hunched over his laptop, typing at speed with the intense focus she had come to know well. Instead, she finished reading the Marie-Thérèse biography, so she could have all the facts to hand about Ernestine and the events the two girls experienced during the revolution.

After reading for some time, a twinge from her subconscious told her there was something she was missing. She checked her notes on Ernestine and there it was: daughter of Jacques Lambriquet and Philippine Noiret, born 1778, settled with an extremely large pension later in the same year.

Was it a coincidence that a vineyard was bought by a local barrel-maker named Noiret the following year, founding a champagne house that still existed today? Possibly. But her hand was shaking as she found the photo of the scrap of map and tried to match it up to a modern-day map. It simply wasn't possible to match them up, as the rolling hills did not seem to have any standout features, despite being near a natural park with 'mountain' in its name.

Thwarted, she put the map to the back of her mind and finished the book, jotting down more notes, testing out a series of increasingly wild theories about what her ancestors might have been up to. Easy enough to think up, far harder to prove. Luc came by with a glass of water in each hand, just as she was finishing up.

'Thanks, Luc. Shall I cook tonight?'

'You're on holiday, Sophie. We could go out.'

'I've got some ideas I'd like to run by you, which would be better done in private.'

'By the gleam in your eyes, it's something good. Care to tell me now?'

He took a seat on the sofa and made himself comfortable, while Sophie opened up the website of the Noiret vineyard to the history page and slid her notes on Ernestine in front of him. The moment he saw the connection was like watching dawn break.

'Incredible. Nice detective work, Sophie.'

'Might be a coincidence–'

'–but worth checking out–'

'–worst-case scenario, a lovely drive in the country followed by a glass or two of champagne.'

Luc glanced at his watch, which made her smile. 'I didn't mean we had to leave right away.'

'Why wait? We've got a couple of hours of daylight left if we get away soon. That'll give us a full day tomorrow to visit the Noiret champagne house.'

Sophie gave the nonchalant French-style shrug she'd been perfecting in front of the mirror, though her heart was beating in quick time. 'I'm game. Give me quarter of an hour.'

They met at the door in fourteen minutes exactly. Sophie had repacked her bag when her clothes were washed and dried, so most of that time had been tidying the apartment and throwing some food into a grocery bag. She figured she could attend to minor details like makeup and hair when they arrived.

'Jewellery box?'

'Already in the safe.'

'Excellent. Let's go while there's still light to enjoy the trip.'

Down in the basement garage, Luc got into a Lexus, which was parked beside the distinctive Peugeot. 'Less obvious,' he said.

'Your friend appears to be extremely trusting.'

'We shared a house throughout university. I got him out of a few scrapes and vice versa. And he got his start in banking working for my father.'

'I'd love to meet him. Reckon he must have a few good stories to share.'

'Not a chance, Sophie. Old university pals take a blood oath never to tell tales.' Luc negotiated the tangle of motorways out of Paris without batting an eyelid and soon they were flying along the N3.

'Last time I came to France, we puttered along in an ancient van, which needed a push start on cold mornings. I spent half the trip with my head in a map. No online maps back then, of course.'

'At least you didn't have to put up with those dreadful GPS devices, which demand you turn right at the next intersection, even though it's a one-way street going in the wrong direction.'

'Then they tell you off like a naughty schoolkid for overshooting the route and insist you do a U-turn in the middle of a motorway. So much easier travelling with a local human.'

Luc set the cruise control once they were on the broad sweep of highway, letting the Lexus purr along quietly at high speed. 'New Zealanders seem to love travelling. Wherever I go, there's always one nearby, propping up the bar or heaving around a backpack.

Last cycling trip I did, I swear I met more Kiwis than French people.'

'When we were planning our trip to Europe, before Mike died, cycling and canal boating were at the top of our very long list of things to do.'

'I'm sorry you never got to have your trip with him. But for you, it is still possible, no?' Perhaps he saw her smile fade, because he was quick to change the topic. 'Do you have any more brilliant ideas about what our ancestors got up to?'

'Brilliant, no. Crazy, off-the-wall ideas, absolutely. But you have to promise not to laugh.'

'As if I would. Your crazy ideas have a disturbing habit of hitting the bullseye. So, tell me.'

'I stayed up late reading the biography of Marie-Thérèse. It got me wondering about exactly what it was that Ernestine did for her to create such a strong bond between them. Especially now we have seen Marie-Thérèse's comment in the letter about Ernestine saving her life.'

'Yes, I've been wondering about that too. *"Willingly sacrificed herself to save me, when all hope was lost"* gives a strong impression of a heroic act. I wondered if Marie-Thérèse was threatened by the mob when they entered Versailles in 1789, and Ernestine saved her. But that seems unlikely, as there are written accounts of the events that would surely have mentioned such an incident. From what we know, Marie Antoinette fetched the children and kept them safe.'

'For all we know, Ernestine might have rescued her during childhood. A runaway horse, a nasty fall, or something like that. But would that count as all hope being lost?'

'My thoughts exactly.' Luc glanced over. 'Such an expression seems better suited to the revolutionary era. Over the 1792 to 1795 period, her family and their friends were being killed one by one. Marie-Thérèse must have lived in terror that her turn was next.'

'You must have read my mind. Being imprisoned in the Temple must have been a frightening experience for a young woman to go through, especially at the age of only fourteen. Even looking at a picture of it gave me the shivers. How awful to be locked inside such a bleak tower, never knowing what would happen, and who would be dragged away to the guillotine next.'

'You think Ernestine was involved in arranging Marie-Thérèse's release from prison? The insistence that Ernestine be included in the party to take Marie-Thérèse to safety in Austria does strike me as being significant.'

'But would you call it a sacrifice on Ernestine's part?'

'Maybe, if she had to come out of hiding to do it. But no, not really.'

Sophie was on the home straight of her theory now and not wanting to be perceived as too crazy. 'You know of the various switch theories?'

'That Marie-Thérèse was so destroyed by her time in prison, she swapped identities with Ernestine after she left prison, living a reclusive life in Germany as the so-called "Dark Countess". You know the theory has been disproved, or at least shown to be unlikely?'

'And anyway, our own family history disproves it. Marie-Thérèse's release from prison was in December 1795, and we know Ernestine and Pierre Duchamp married soon after. Do you recall the make-up of the party that took Marie-Thérèse to Vienna?'

'I remember there were a couple of people whose presence was a mystery. Didn't the woman who accompanied them bring along a boy who was listed as her son, but who couldn't have been her own son? People speculated it was Ernestine in disguise, as I recall.'

'The boy's name was Pierre, and he was the right age for our Pierre Duchamp. There was also a young maid, who I think a more likely candidate as our girl. Did you know that the woman who went with them was no friend to Marie-Thérèse and later blackmailed her for increasingly large sums of money? Kind of interesting, no? Her name was Madame de Soucy, and she knew both girls well, as she had been an undergoverness to the children. Marie-Thérèse must have had something to hide to give in to blackmail. Henri has letters suggesting it was to do with the hidden valuables, but I wonder if there was more to it.'

'Interesting.' Luc glanced sideways. 'So, you're saying that both Ernestine and Pierre went with Marie-Thérèse when she was released from the Temple and allowed to go to Austria. That seems perfectly reasonable. Why do I get the feeling you're about to spring a giant-sized, jaw-dropping, gut-punching surprise on me?'

Sophie laughed. 'You are starting to know me too well. It's no fun when you're expecting it.'

'Spit it out. Can't be any crazier than some of the wild conspiracy theories I've heard.'

Sophie ticked off the points on her fingers. 'First, we know the girls grew up doing everything together and were sufficiently alike that they were mistaken for each other. Second, we know enough of Ernestine's loyalty to the royal family that she would do anything to help them, especially when she could see her sister enduring the horrors of prison.'

'Agreed. Especially after the execution of the King in early 1793, when they must have fallen into a deep despair.'

'And yet, point three, Marie-Thérèse arrived in Vienna in remarkably good shape for someone who spent over three years in prison in severe emotional and physical deprivation.'

'Hmm. Do you recall the portrait I showed you on the day you arrived, Sophie? It was painted in Vienna soon after her release. She did look remarkably well, though that might have been artistic license.'

'And also, when she was to be released, Ernestine was proposed to accompany her, but could not be found, at least not where she was supposed to be.'

'Sophie, what exactly are you saying?'

'What if Ernestine and Marie-Thérèse switched places *during* her time in prison, rather than *after*, as has been proposed by others? Ernestine literally sacrificing herself to save her sister, knowing she would likely die in prison or on the guillotine.'

The car veered wildly as Luc swung his head in her direction. He swore aloud as he straightened up and grimaced as a car overtook at speed with its horn blaring. 'Sorry, I wasn't expecting anything quite that startling. How on earth could they have switched places in prison?'

'There must have been servants to bring food and do washing. And they did have some outsiders coming in. For example, when Louis was executed, a seamstress came in to make mourning clothes for the ladies. One of Madame de Tourzel's women, in fact, who was a devoted follower of the royal family.'

'Certainly, they must have been desperate enough by then to try anything. Can you imagine what it must have been like for Marie Antoinette? After years of faithful belief that all would be well in the end, suddenly the unthinkable had happened – the King was executed. She must have given up hope at that point.'

'And her two children were dying before her eyes. Constantly sick, covered in boils, shut away from everything civilised. Would she have refused a chance to save one of them? To maintain the Bourbon line she had given birth to?'

'When you put it like that, it seems almost sensible. But … but there must be a whole load of buts. For one thing, Marie-Thérèse wrote a memoir in the final days of her time in prison.'

'Part of it was written at the very end of her time in prison, the rest later. And it was later amended to cover up discrepancies. Whoever wrote it certainly had intimate knowledge of what happened in prison, but was it Marie-Thérèse?'

'Wasn't the handwriting in the memoir later determined to be the same as that of Marie-Thérèse?'

'Luc, the girls grew up together. I'll bet they knew exactly how to imitate each other's handwriting to the last loop. My friend and I did exactly the same at school, so we could cover for each other.'

'Okay, that's feasible, I suppose.'

'And don't you think it is a little strange that Ernestine is so rarely mentioned? Marie-Thérèse mentions her only in passing in her memoir.' Sophie rifled through her notes. 'Here, when Ernestine is sent away into the country before the royal family's escape attempt, she calls her "*a young girl who was usually with me*". Hardly an effusive way to talk about someone with whom she had grown up and shared her life.'

'But why would Ernestine have written a memoir, when she might have risked giving herself away?'

'Have you read the memoir? I thought it seemed rather unemotional, given the circumstances, as if it was intended only to share the facts of her incarceration. If it was Ernestine in there, she would have had to write something exactly like that, so Marie-Thérèse could pull off the subterfuge that she had been in prison all along. As you know, Marie-Thérèse used it as propaganda for years. "Poor orphan in the Temple" sympathy was strongly in her favour. It helped her family regain power.'

'You seem to have an answer for everything, Sophie. Presumably, Marie-Thérèse would have been in hiding, recovering from her ordeal and maybe even lobbying her relatives to act. Where would she have stayed?'

'There were still people who remained faithful to the royal family, right to the end. If I was a betting person, my money would be on Madame de Tourzel and her daughter Pauline, who seemed to have been unwaveringly devoted to Marie Antoinette and her children. There were still many royal supporters who would have proudly taken the secret to their graves.'

'So, you think Marie-Thérèse swapped back with Ernestine after she was released from prison, on the journey to Austria?'

'Leaving the legitimate Bourbon daughter to arrive triumphant in Vienna in 1795, while Ernestine and her devoted Pierre quietly slipped back to France, where they married and lived happily ever after on the generous reward for her bravery.'

'It would explain why Marie-Thérèse was so grateful to Ernestine and how they paid off the debt on the Duchamp farm in the Loire Valley.' Luc was staring at her, positively glowing.

Sophie struggled to keep a lid on her own excitement. 'It's only a theory. Or perhaps wild speculation is a better way of putting it. But it does at least explain some facts that don't fit otherwise. Not that we have a hope in hell of proving it.'

'What a reunion it must have been when the three of them got back together. The girls would have been about seventeen years old by then.'

'Pierre must have been beside himself to see her again after so long.' Sophie sighed. 'None of which helps us locate this mysterious hoard of treasure, which may or may not exist. I wonder why the items weren't returned to Marie-Thérèse when she finally came back to France?'

'Perhaps they were. Or she might have been waiting until she became queen, so she could triumphantly present the long-lost treasure to a grateful nation. Damn–' Luc braked hard and swung onto an off-ramp. 'Sorry about that. I need to concentrate on driving rather than history or we'll end up in Germany.' They looped around and joined up with a wide highway, flashing past a sign to Reims. 'We'll be there in under an hour. Could you sort out a hotel?'

Sophie got out her mobile. 'Any preferences?'

'As long it has beds and a shower, I'm happy. Preferably somewhere tranquil where I can process the bombshells you keep dropping. Cracker of a theory, by the way.'

'Sometimes, seeing a problem from the perspective of an ignorant outsider can be helpful. No knowledge equals no assumptions.'

'Don't underrate yourself, Sophie. I'd take you on in a flash if you ever wanted a change of career. Fancy a full partnership in the business?'

'A foreigner who doesn't speak French and has no qualifications? I'm sure your clients would be as delighted about that as the French revolutionaries were about welcoming an Austrian princess to the throne.'

'Not quite that bad, Sophie. I doubt my clients would call for your head on a pike.'

She smiled and scrolled through the accommodation options, stopping at one with jolt of glee. A few clicks and it was sorted. 'Travel in the internet age is almost too easy.'

'You'd rather go back to the old days, when you had to lug around piles of guidebooks filled with out-of-date information?'

'But where is the spontaneity?'

Luc let out a bellow of laughter. 'Do you really, honestly, feel your life lacks spontaneity? Wasn't it only a couple of weeks ago that you had a vague plan of travelling and nothing in your attic but junk?'

Sophie's grin widened. Whatever rut she had been in at home, she had well and truly been flung out of it.

Behind Locked Doors

The three women scarcely breathed in the long minutes that followed the slamming of the prison door. They heard no yells, no screams, no sounds that would tell them the switch had been revealed. Only the cries of the newspaper sellers in the street outside and the occasional clatter of boots or weapons on the cobblestones below.

Ernestine sat in the plain wicker chair, her eyes closed, not daring to move. Madame Elisabeth continued to brush her hair with long soothing strokes. Marie Antoinette stood still, her gaze fixed on nothing, for all the world like a marble statue, except that her fingers picked nervously at the black lace of her mourning dress.

Eventually, Madame Elisabeth put the brush down and sank to her knees, murmuring a quiet prayer. The other two joined her, holding hands and pleading with God to keep Marie-Thérèse safe. When the prayer was finished, both ladies embraced Ernestine with a fierceness that squeezed the breath from her lungs.

'God gave me a miracle in sending you to us, dearest Ernestine. My daughter was so ill, I feared for

410

her life.' Marie Antoinette's voice was so choked with emotion, her words were barely audible.

Louis-Charles decided he had been ignored for long enough. The little boy ran over to their huddle and forced himself into the centre. Only then did he realise the third woman in the room was not Marie-Thérèse.

'Ernestine? What are you doing here? Where is my sister?'

'Hello, dearest. I have come to keep you company while your sister is unwell. Would you like me to play games and read to you like I used to?'

It said a lot about what the boy had been through that he merely nodded his head, accepting yet another unfathomable change in his young life.

Madame Elisabeth took the boy's hands between her own. 'Darling nephew, you must promise us, on your honour as King of France, that you will pretend that Ernestine is Marie-Thérèse. On no account, call her by any other name or tell anyone else who she is. Swear to it.'

The boy looked up at his mother, who nodded solemnly. 'All right. I swear I shall do as you say. But where has my sister gone?'

'She will stay with Madame de Tourzel.'

'Will she be with Pauline?' the boy whined. 'Mother, I want to go too.'

Marie Antoinette's eyes lit up. 'Are my friends safe? What a joy to hear, when I feared they too might be lost. But, my dear son, only your sister can visit them right now. You must stay here with me for a while yet. Your turn will come.'

Louis-Charles stomped off to a corner and resumed his game, quickly becoming absorbed into a happier imaginary world, where he was in control and the toy soldier bowed before him.

The three women retreated to the far corner, eager to catch up on news. Ernestine told them how Pauline had escaped, while Madame de Tourzel and Madame Mackau had been released from La Force to everyone's surprise and delight. She did not mention others who had been executed or slaughtered by the mob, especially beloved members of the Queen's retinue, such as the Princesse de Lamballe.

The Queen was eager to hear every morsel of news. 'What of my husband's brothers and my family in Austria? What plans do they have?'

'I can only say what I have heard from others. Many parties are working tirelessly on your behalf. I fear the chaos devouring Paris is matched by the chaos caused by competing factions on our own side. Some favour outright war to restore order to France, others seek a negotiated release of your family in exchange for French prisoners.' Realising she sounded defeatist, she added, 'But we have high hopes that they will soon succeed, and you will be set free.'

Later that evening, when the Queen had fallen into an exhausted slumber, Ernestine curled up next to Madame Elisabeth. 'Tell me, how is Her Majesty coping with the tragedy of the King's death?'

Madame Elisabeth shook her head sadly. 'She has not eaten enough to keep a sparrow alive since they were separated. She cannot even bear to take air, as to walk outside would mean passing his door.' A tear rolled down her cheek, which she quickly wiped away. 'To be honest, Ernestine, I think she no longer has any hope left in her heart.'

'Please, Madame, you must not call me Ernestine, even when we are alone.'

'Of course, my dear niece, Marie-Thérèse. And you must call me Aunt, or simply Elisabeth. Ceremonial titles seem very much out of place between these grim walls.'

'I hope the Queen might take some pleasure in knowing her daughter is safe.'

'I haven't seen her smile since my brother was taken away, until you came to us. What you have done is the bravest act of self-sacrifice I have ever witnessed, my dearest niece.'

'No braver than your own actions, Aunt,' Ernestine replied, though her heart swelled at this praise from a woman she much admired. 'You stayed beside the King when others fled.'

'I did my duty, out of love for my family and France, little knowing the consequences. But you came here knowing exactly what the consequences to yourself would be, which is a far braver act. Shall we say a prayer together?'

'I should like that. I will need all your strength to see me through this, because I am not as brave as you think.' In truth, Ernestine was terrified, but also determined to do what she could to bring cheer to a cheerless situation.

Over the next few weeks, Ernestine settled into her new life as Marie-Thérèse. She hid her face and never talked when outsiders were present, knowing her voice was unlike her sister's. When forced to face her jailer or other officials, she adopted a haughty expression and never responded to their jibes. Each time they walked away without answers to their questions, she felt a tiny surge of power, that her body might be in prison, but her spirit was flying as free as the birds.

Not that there were many visitors to worry about and none who would know her in the dim light from the barred window. Within days, her own voice was reduced to an unrecognisable rasping, because of the freezing damp of the stone walls and the unwholesome vapours given off from the centuries-old filth surrounding them. Firewood was always in short supply, even now, when winter still had her claws out.

Servants brought adequate amounts of food. By no means the gourmet delights of Versailles, but better than many endured outside of these four walls. The regular visits from municipal officers became less and less frequent, leaving them to converse without supervision.

The Queen's mood was very low, as expected after the brutal death of her husband. Ernestine set herself the task of serving the Queen, ensuring that every morning she was washed, coiffed, fed and feted. She read aloud from the few books they had until her voice was hoarse, or devised games to play, knowing how the Queen had enjoyed such pastimes in the past.

Every smile was a hard-won victory, but gradually a little light came back into Marie Antoinette's eyes, especially when she watched on as her son played with Ernestine or sat enthralled as she spun stories.

Sometimes, they were allowed a stroll in the garden or on the upper floor, some hundred and fifty feet from the ground. Ernestine pointed out the rooms hired by Madame Cléry, from which that devoted lady had played music for the captives as they had walked in the gardens, until the authorities banned it.

Before long, blinds were placed between the battlements to prevent them from seeing and being seen by the well-wishers and assorted rabble who crowded the streets around the Tower and waved from the balconies across the street.

Now and then they received messages of hope (or otherwise) from the outside, through the goodwill of faithful servants, such as M. Turgy, who had served the King in the past and had now secured employment in the Tower's kitchen. He and Monsieur Cléry had devised a system of hand signs, with which to keep the royal captives informed. If the Austrians were fighting on the Belgian frontier, he was to place the forefinger of his right hand on his right eye. If they entered France, on the right ear, and so on. Other messages would be written in lemon juice on fragments of paper or conveyed wrapped in linen.

Rumours grew that they might soon be released. Perhaps this explained why their guards treated them a little better and they were left to themselves. And yet, the weeks crawled by, and nothing happened.

Outside the walls, the tocsin was rung with increasing frequency, signalling fresh horrors, of which they were relieved to remain ignorant. Being shut away from the mob in the streets was one of the few positives of their incarceration, although they could hear them when their revolutionary fervour ran high.

Ernestine lay on her bed for hours at a time, wondering what was happening outside the walls. Was Marie-Thérèse safely recovering from her illness? Would Pierre be back from Austria with news that a rescue had been negotiated? If so, would he ever forgive her rash act of self-sacrifice? She wondered if she would have made the same choice if she had known how appalling life in prison would be. But there was no use dwelling on things she could not change.

In the long, dark nights, she took her wooden owl from its hiding place and ran her fingers over it, until the carved feathers became smooth with wear. She tried to remember every detail of the times they had had together. All the little things Pierre had done for her – the pilfered strawberries from the glasshouse, perfect roses still wet with dew, his dimpled smile when she made a joke, his calming hand on the leading rein. How the horses had loved him. Even the goats who pulled the Dauphin's miniature carriage had behaved themselves in his gentle hands.

Odd moments of joy were savoured. A faithful servant, Monsieur Cléry, had been entrusted with the King's gold wedding ring and a parcel containing locks of his family's hair, so precious to him that the King had preserved them with great care in a silver seal. Cléry had sent them a message but had been refused permission to visit. Finally, two months after the King's execution, a kind official named Toulon slipped the Queen those precious gifts from her husband. She had a wistful tenderness about her for days afterward. Her smile vanished again when they heard Toulon had been executed for his act of kindness.

By then, conditions in the prison were becoming steadily worse again. The more sympathetic warders were accused of overindulging the royal prisoners and dismissed. None dared go against the increasingly brutal and punitive regime, fearing their own necks would end up on the guillotine, like so many before them.

Even their nights were disturbed occasionally, as sudden night-time searches were instigated. The searches uncovered nothing more incriminating than embroidery needles and prayer books, even though the guards searched right down to the mattresses on the beds, while the ladies stood shivering in their nightwear. By daytime, their puny freedoms were further restricted, until even the sight of daylight became a rare pleasure. Outside walks in the garden and the opening of shutters were forbidden.

Marie Antoinette was barely functioning. It was the stoicism and kindness of Elisabeth that got Ernestine through those never-ending days and nights. They told each other stories, both real and imagined, during the long, dark evenings. Elisabeth spoke at length of her beloved estate, Montreuil, where the children had loved to play. They laughed softly as they closed their eyes and imagined the floating drifts of orange blossom and the juicy delights of the harvest.

On darker days, Elisabeth would talk about events that Ernestine had not been a party to, such as their escape and recapture at Varennes and their early days of imprisonment in the Temple. On those days, it was Ernestine who brought them back to the light, by telling stories from her childhood, until Elisabeth dissolved into fits of giggles.

'Honestly, I cannot believe you two girls were so naughty and no one knew it. The cooks swore they never left the door to the kitchens open. Nobody believed them, for how else could a dozen hens get in and cause havoc.'

'I do feel a little guilty about that little escapade. Mostly we were just having harmless fun, like sneaking out on hot summer evenings to play in the fountains, or swapping clothes to confuse visitors. Although, I admit I was worried we'd get into serious trouble when Marie-Thérèse rode her pony down the corridors and around the salon of the Petit Trianon. No one ever did figure out how those marks got on the floor.'

As their chuckles subsided, Elisabeth became sombre again. 'It all feels so long ago now. You've been such a great support to us, Ernestine. I forget you are still only fifteen years old.'

'Most days, I feel like an old woman. I don't think I could survive in here without your kindness, Madame Elisabeth. I only wish I could do more to thank you.'

'Perhaps you could name your first daughter after me,' Elisabeth said wistfully. 'Nothing would make me happier than to hold a baby girl in my arms and know she had a bright future.'

Although Ernestine knew the words were meaningless in their current situation, she was touched by the thought. She put her hand over Elisabeth's. 'I promise. I hope my Elisabeth will be as brave and kind as you.'

Weeks merged into months as their situation grew steadily worse. Just when it seemed she could endure no more, either physically or mentally, further blows fell, one after another. Louis-Charles fell ill again, his fever raging for days and wearing him thin, before a doctor was allowed to see him. Ernestine herself suffered from the agonising boils of the type she had seen on her sister's legs, bred in, and exacerbated by, the filthy conditions in which they lived.

One fateful day, guards stomped in and read a decree ordering the young king to be held separately within the Tower. Louis-Charles ran to his mother and wrapped his arms around her, sobbing.

The Queen clung to him, shifting her own body between her son and the guards. 'You will not take my son. I forbid it.'

The ice-hard anguish in her voice did nothing to touch their hearts. They argued for an hour, with increasing threats, until Marie Antoinette was undone by their final ultimatum – the guards would either take him or kill him on the spot. The cruel set of the guard's face left no doubt that he would enjoy skewering the boy in front of his family.

The Queen collapsed, so it was Ernestine who had to gently prise the weeping boy away from his mother. Though her heart was heavier than the stones surrounding them, she knew the guards would get their way, with or without bloodshed.

'Come, my little darling, let me help you into your clothes. Whatever happens, always remember you are the King of France and loved by all who matter.' She dried his eyes and helped him dress.

The boy did as he was told. Although he was too frightened to help with dressing, beyond lifting his arm or leg when ordered, he attempted to be stoic, as befitted a king.

She kissed his cheek. 'Give your mother a kiss and say goodbye for now.'

Seeing him being dragged away by those beasts was perhaps the hardest burden of all they had endured. Or so she thought. As the days passed, there was worse agony to bear. Louis-Charles could be heard in his cell, wailing and screaming. Then the beatings would begin again, making him cry out even more pitiably.

As the days passed, the torments became ever more degrading. The boy's jailer, a particularly vicious man named Simon, could be heard teaching the young boy foul language, forcing him to drink alcohol, frightening him with the guillotine, even loudly boasting about using prostitutes to infect the poor boy with diseases.

They prayed it wasn't true, but the harsh reality was that nothing was too foul for these evil monsters. Locked away from their beloved boy, they suffered their own torment as the moans and screams drifted up to their cell and stabbed at their hearts. The Queen spent her days alternating between sitting hunched in a corner with her hands over her ears and standing by the window on the chance of seeing her son.

Less than a month later, the guards dragged Marie Antoinette away in the dead of night. She was no more than a shell of her former self, a lifeless body with a gaunt face, white hair, and a tortured soul. Ernestine pleaded to be taken with her, or instead of her, but they showed no mercy. The guards forced her arms away from around the Queen's narrow waist and kicked her to the floor.

The Queen pulled her up and embraced her. 'My dear daughter, you have the courage of a Bourbon. Do not let it fail you now. Trust in yourself and your Aunt Elisabeth.'

As she left, the Queen hit her head on the lintel of the door.

'Mother, are you hurt?'

The Queen looked at her with vacant eyes. 'No. Nothing can hurt me now.'

The modest cell seemed cavernous with only two of them left. Madame Elisabeth tried to maintain their routine of study and prayer, while Ernestine did her best to keep her spirits up, outwardly at least. But inside, constant anxiety ate away at her core, made worse by bouts of fever brought on by the cold, damp conditions.

The municipals made their regular visits, each one causing a flash of panic at the prospect of being the next to be dragged away. Scraps of news still reached them by way of the few decent people remaining. A whispered word or a concealed note to tell them that Louis-Charles and Marie Antoinette were still alive was worth more than any material comfort.

Still, the tidings were grim. The Queen faced outrageous accusations of betraying the people of

France and continuing to conspire against the new regime from within the prison walls. Elisabeth made haste to gather every piece of writing secreted within the room, to prevent innocent words being used as further ammunition against her sister-in-law. She even cast the remaining few stubs of pencils into the fire. Such a trivial loss, yet Ernestine stared into the feeble flames long after the stubs were reduced to glowing embers.

A few days later, the room was searched again and all the pieces of tapestry they had been working on to pass the hours were taken away. The reason? The tapestry might contain secret messages. Ernestine could only shake her head in disbelief at their delusions.

As weeks passed, the indignities and restrictions mounted. They were reduced to a single room, with no one to serve them and only basic necessities allowed. Candles, china, sheets, extra blankets were all removed. Even the armchair Elisabeth liked to sit in. Worse still, they no longer had any means of hearing the news.

Time ceased to have meaning. Some days, Ernestine felt that the quick flash of a guillotine blade would be preferable to the torment of uncertainty, but she did not voice her thoughts, either to Elisabeth or to God.

She never saw the Queen again, but she was taken to see Louis-Charles once, months later, when the outside air was fresh with an autumn chill and the smell of fallen leaves. The instant the door to her brother's cell was opened, Ernestine gagged at the foulness of the odour spilling from the room.

None of the horrifying scenes she had witnessed in her short life had sickened her stomach as much as entering that cell and witnessing the pitiful state of the young king. She scarcely recognised the pallid, frail creature lying motionless in his own excrement, covered with fleas and bugs. His emaciated body was scarred with boils and his stomach bloated with sickness. The window was locked and clearly never opened.

She forced back rising vomit and rushed to his side. '*Chou d'amour, chou d'amour,*' she whispered, hoping the Queen's pet name for her son would rouse him. Tears flooded down her cheeks. How could any decent person allow an eight-year-old to be treated so cruelly?

He did not have the strength to hold his head up to look at her. He did not even blink an eyelid at her voice. Had it not been for a bout of coughing, which spasmed through his whole body, she would not have known he was alive.

'For pity's sake, bring me soap and water,' she begged. 'My brother must have clean clothes and bedding at once.'

His tormenter smirked at her with hooded eyes and crossed arms, looking her up and down as if assessing a price.

She hastened to the door, where her guard stood at a distance with averted eyes, pinching his nostrils closed. 'Please,' she begged. 'We must do something for him. May I not open the shutters for a little sunlight? Anything to bring this wretched child some tiny comfort.'

'You are not here for his comfort,' he mumbled, before forcing her back to her cell, leaving her heaving with despair.

Soon afterwards, the guards burst in again, before Elisabeth was even dressed, dragging Ernestine away to the bowels of the Tower. There, an ordinary-looking man with foul breath gestured for her to sit in a rickety chair in the corner, hard up against a wall of black stone. He began peppering her with absurd questions, relentlessly demanding the answers that he wanted, regardless of the truth.

What treachery had the King been planning before his death? Who was conspiring with him? Where had the Queen hidden her vast piles of jewels? When would the Austrian army march on Paris? How were they getting messages to the loyalists?

Perhaps the visit to Louis-Charles had been intended to break her spirit. If so, it failed. The memory of her brother's appalling state only hardened her will to iron. Though she trembled inside as she faced this inquisition alone in the dank cell, she held her head up high and steeled herself to give them nothing but disdain.

The interrogator was incensed, standing over her, spitting increasingly insane questions at her, slapping a baton into his gloved palm, inches from her head. Question after question, with scarcely time to think, let alone respond. No slander was too outrageous. Why had the King deliberately withheld food from the people? What debauched sins had the Queen committed with men, women, children, animals? Had the Queen defiled her own son?

Ernestine seethed at the repulsive accusations, but held her ground as the hours passed, giving only the minimum of uninformative answers, allowing no emotion other than scorn to cross her face, and absolutely refusing to say a word against anyone dear to her. She would be slaughtered anyway, so it was better to die with honour than be broken.

When she was finally returned to her cell, she crawled into her bed, too exhausted, too battered, too overwhelmed, to do more than curl up in a tight ball and pray for a quick death.

Elisabeth tried to go to her, but she was dragged away to face her own interrogation.

Death did not come that day, nor any of the following. Of Marie Antoinette, Queen of France, they still heard nothing. The only news they gleaned now was from the muffled cries of newspaper sellers in the streets outside. Nothing but death and destruction.

Almost nine months had passed since Ernestine switched places with Marie-Thérèse, while Elisabeth had suffered fourteen months of imprisonment. It would be another seven months of mind-numbing endurance before the next major test of her fortitude, when Madame Elisabeth was ripped from her arms one evening. Although she had sworn to herself that she would never let the two of them be separated, it happened so fast, she had no time to react. As her protector was dragged from the cell, she implored Ernestine not to lose her faith in God.

Ernestine screamed and banged on the door until her fists were bloody and her throat raw. Faith in God? How was it even possible to believe in a benevolent God, when loved ones were ripped from her arms, one by one? She slammed her meagre possessions against the walls, cracking a stool, upending her bed, kicking the toilet bucket, until finally she slumped on the floor, exhausted.

The silence was absolute. She was truly, utterly alone.

The guards refused to tell her the fate of her adoptive family. In her mind, she created visions of their escape from France, though in her heart she feared they were all dead, or soon would be. The only question was, when would her own time come? She prayed it would be soon – better the quick slice of the guillotine than a slow slide into madness.

Each time the door of her cell opened, she braced herself for imminent death. As more months dragged by, a succession of officials came to observe her and talk to her. She fixed her gaze on a spot on the wall and said as little as possible, beyond repeatedly asking for news of her family. All she learned in return was that the regime was in constant upheaval, based on the ever-changing nature of the questions she was subjected to.

At times, the changes were positive, even if only in the smallest of ways. A man named Laurent was assigned to the children and spoke the first gentle words Ernestine had heard in months, bringing her to closer to breaking point than harsh words had achieved.

He took a bed from her room to give to Louis-Charles, whose own bed was mired in filth and vermin. Thus, she knew at least one member of the family still lived, although the man refused to confirm the fate of the others. He did bring her some candles, a precious gift to banish the endless hours of darkness, but nothing to banish the freezing cold seeping through the damp stonework.

Other officials made promises they did not keep, not that she expected them to. What efforts were being made beyond these walls for their release, she did not know. Her life was diminished to an endless daily routine: rise, dress, comb hair, clean the room, read from Elisabeth's book of prayers, eat, pray, sleep. She sang, recited poetry, invented stories, counted numbers into the thousands, enacted scenes remembered from the theatre.

Ernestine told herself these solitary entertainments would keep her sane, although she wondered if they merely proved she was already insane.

Almost a year and a half after her incarceration, when she was nearing her seventeenth birthday, the unthinkable happened – her situation took a turn for the better. She was given a companion, a sweet and educated woman, Renée de Chanterenne. With her, this angel of mercy brought books, clothes, and materials for drawing, writing and sewing. With adequate supplies of firewood and pleasant company, her life was filled with inner and outer warmth.

Ernestine had not spoken for so long that her voice was scratchy and quavering. Renée refused to tell her any news, though the grim look on her face at Ernestine's questions made her fear the worst.

She was overcome with longing to have this kind woman as a friend, after so long in solitude, regardless of whether or not the woman was a spy for the regime. They settled into a comfortable pattern of lessons, chatting about books, reading aloud or just sitting, enjoying the company of a compassionate woman after so long cut off from every hint of humanity.

One wonderful day, she was allowed to go out into the prison garden again – her first chance to breathe fresh air in months. A red bundle of hair and sinew raced towards her as she rounded a corner.

'Coco!' Ernestine hugged the dog tightly, unable to believe her brother's spaniel was still alive.

'Madame Royale,' said Renée, 'I do believe that is the first smile I have seen from you. I hope it is not the last.

Her words were prophetic, for as the days went by, further joys lit up her life. Amongst the crowds of onlookers up on the balconies of the nearby buildings, she spotted a friend or two from the past or heard them call out to her. Occasionally, the sound of songs from her childhood drifted to her on the breeze. The loyalists not only played music, but signalled to her, giving her hope.

On the next walk, she searched the balcony eagerly for familiar figures and was rewarded with the happiest sight of all. A slim figure with tousled black hair, waving manically. Pierre!

She waved back with as much energy as her debilitated body could muster, her soul afire with delight that he had survived. She began to believe that perhaps she had a future after all – a future that might not end by the bloody blade of the guillotine. A few weeks ago, joy was a tiny candle flame or a few sticks of kindling. Now, she was overwhelmed with pleasures.

Her friendship with Renée grew stronger, until finally she told Ernestine the news she most wanted, yet dreaded, to hear. Alas, the Queen and Elisabeth had been executed, as she had feared.

Louis-Charles would greet his loved ones in heaven soon. Despite the improved treatment, he grew weaker every day. On the ninth day of June 1795, word was passed to her that her brother, Louis XVII, King of France, had died. She grieved silently for the sweet boy whose only memories were of years of misery and abuse.

His death brought one tiny ray of light. Public sympathy for the 'Orphans in the Tower', which Renée said had been building in recent months as news of their hardships had been made public, now reached a crescendo, tipping the balance in favour of clemency for the sole surviving child, especially when word spread of her fortitude under the atrocious conditions she had suffered in prison.

Ernestine was told negotiations were underway for her release to Marie Antoinette's family in Austria, although each side had so many conditions that any release might yet be months away. She set herself the task of making a record of her time in prison, so the real Marie-Thérèse would know enough to convince the world that she had been in prison all along.

Her heart was glad to know that some sympathy remained for the royal family. She prayed Marie-Thérèse was still alive, that she might benefit from it. She refused to think of the possibility her sister was no longer alive or the ramifications that awful situation would hold for her.

After the harsh years in prison, she knew that even her closest relations would not recognise her by sight. But surely, the switch would not stand the greater scrutiny of conversation with Marie-Thérèse's relatives, unless she claimed complete memory loss. Besides, she wanted nothing more than to be reunited with Pierre and leave this nightmare behind.

With the novelty of having pen and paper, she was eager to set her story down, even if it took an age, as her hand was unsteady after so long without writing a word. At least that would disguise any slight differences between her handwriting and that of

Marie-Thérèse. Such a small thing, their copying of each other's handwriting as children, but now their futures might rest upon it. She began her narrative with the storming of the Tuileries Palace, filling in the gaps when she had not been present with the stories she had been told by Elisabeth.

Each time her cell door opened, the sputtering candle flickered to one side and her own spark of hope flared, that today might finally be the day she would be free from these four oppressive walls of stone.

She had almost given up hope, when the door opened and Madame Mackau, Madame de Tourzel and Pauline entered. She flung herself into their waiting arms and heard the longed-for words from their lips, that they held great hopes of accompanying her when she was released and sent to Austria.

Champagne

Reims, 2019

The sun was on its downward arc towards the hills as they reached their destination. To Luc's surprise, Sophie directed him to bypass Reims to the south, but his frown lifted as they made their way down a minor road through quaint villages, with grapevines stretching in verdant rows as far as a horizon of forested hills.

His smile widened as they pulled through the old stone gates of the vineyard, with a brass plaque of grand proportions announcing their arrival at 'Champagne Noiret'. The driveway passed under a vine-covered arch, which led to an ancient house made of pale time-smoothed stone that seemed to have grown organically out of the ground it sat on. The sensation of blending with nature was heightened by the heady scent of early season climbing roses, in the palest of pink hues, which enveloped a trellis running the length of the veranda.

Sophie stepped out of the car and closed her eyes as she breathed in the fragrance, sharpened by the cool of the early evening air after a hot day. When she opened her eyes again, Luc was already at the door to the reception area, holding it open for her.

He smiled as she hurried through. 'I'm never going to get you away from here again, am I?'

Sophie laughed. 'Not a chance.'

They were still smiling at each other when a man of about sixty entered via a door behind the reception desk. His hair was a wiry grey and his face was furrowed with lines, but his solid physique and rosy cheeks radiated the robust good health of a lifelong farmer.

Sophie noticed Luc eyeing up a display of historic photos of the vineyard. 'Go on. I'll sort out the booking.' She went to the reception desk, handing over her passport and credit card with a smile. '*Bonsoir, Monsieur. J'ai une réservation.* Sophie West.'

'Madame West, *bienvenue.*' He switched to English as he flicked open her passport. 'New Zealand? You are far from home, madame. You are enjoying a romantic tour of France with your husband, yes?'

Before she could answer, Luc's mobile rang. 'It's Martine. I'll take it outside.'

He tossed his passport to her, and she put it on the counter beside hers. 'Monsieur Duchamp and I are only recent friends. We are very much looking forward to seeing your famous chalk cellars.'

'And tasting our champagne, I hope? Noiret is one of the oldest and very best champagne houses.'

'Absolutely. I adore champagne. Would we be able to book a tour and a tasting session for tomorrow?'

'Of course, madame.' He punched at the computer keyboard with chunky fingers, staring at the screen with a frown. 'Excuse me, the wife of my son usually does the cottage bookings, but they are away.' He entered Sophie's name, then flicked open Luc's passport.

A minivan skidded to a halt outside, disgorging half a dozen brawny lads, who filled the reception area with raucous English, football jerseys, and testosterone. Armand ushered them into another room and shut the door firmly behind them.

'My apologies for the interruption. They will not be here for long, if you wish to have a quiet dinner at our award-winning restaurant.'

'Perfect.' Sophie gestured to the bookshelf behind the desk. 'I notice you have a book on the history of the vineyard. May I buy a copy of that as well please? My friend and I share an interest in history.'

Armand took down a copy of the book, which had an old photo of grape harvesting on the glossy cover.

'I would be pleased to answer any questions you wish to ask. I am Armand Noiret, named after the man who founded our vineyard in 1779.' His eyes twinkled with the pride and pleasure of sharing his passion.

'An honour to meet you, Monsieur Noiret. How wonderful to hear that your family has made champagne here for so long.' Luc came back in at that moment, so Sophie turned to him. 'Luc, this is Armand Noiret, who is descended from the original owner.' She raised one eyebrow enquiringly and got a fractional nod in return.

'Monsieur Noiret, a pleasure to meet you. I'm not sure how much Sophie has told you, but we are very interested in the founding of your vineyard. It is possible we are distantly related to each other. I'm sure you will find it a fascinating story.'

Armand looked from one to the other. 'I enjoy a good story from the past. Perhaps you would join me for dinner tonight? Eight o'clock?' He handed over a key. 'Your cottage is further along the road, the second one on the right. There is a walking path through the vineyard, if you prefer.'

'*Merci*, Monsieur Noiret, we will look forward to dinner.'

Sophie couldn't resist the chance for a walk through the vineyard in the freshness of the early evening air. When she got to the cottage, after a stop at a stone seat with a gorgeous view over the valley, Luc was already looking very much at home on the rose-twined veranda, relaxing on a swing-seat with his feet on the railing, a tall glass of water in one hand and the history book in the other.

'I was about to send out a search party, but decided I was far too content here to bother.' He shuffled over on the seat to make room for her to sit down. 'Martine says she's had many phone calls from Henri and others, so I've told her to tell everyone we're having a delightful holiday in the Loire Valley and don't want to be disturbed.'

'Close enough to the truth.' Sophie took the other glass of water from the table. 'Marvellous, isn't it? I wonder if Pierre or Ernestine once sat in this valley, enjoying the tranquillity after a long ride from Paris?'

'I was just wondering the same thing.' He waved his hand at the table. 'Cheese?'

Sophie gazed longingly at the platter of market cheeses Luc had assembled, before pushing it aside. Tempting as the pungent yellow Livarot was, she rather suspected dinner at the vineyard would be worth the wait. 'Luc, assuming for a wildly optimistic moment the mythical treasure hoard is here, who would own it?'

'The first presumption of French law is that the landowners hold the rights to anything found on their property, although the finder may also establish the right to a share. Where it gets tricky is if the original ownership of the find can be established or the items found have an archaeological or heritage value of national significance, which they would have in this case.'

'So, a pile of gold coins with no documented original owner would go to the current landowner, but a painting stolen from the Louvre would not?'

'More or less. We need to proceed with caution and sound out the views of Armand Noiret. Let's hope he isn't a profit-driven materialist.'

'I doubt it. Armand seems charming and very proud of his family history. After we've talked to him, I'll leave it to your judgement whether we take him into our confidence.'

After unpacking and changing, they walked back to the main house. Despite being close to eight o'clock, it was still light enough to see.

Armand greeted Sophie with a double kiss to the cheeks, squashing her up against a woolly jacket that smelling of grapes, garlic and human warmth. His greeting made her feel as if she was part of the family already – a feeling only enhanced by the welcoming, rustic-grandeur of the sitting room he ushered them into. Outside the french doors, the garden-ringed patio glowed in the soft light of the setting sun, highlighting a profusion of flowers and whimsical marble statues.

'What a beautiful home you have, Monsieur Noiret.'

'Thank you. Call me Armand, please. I am looking forward to hearing your story. But first, I must feed you and tempt you with our vintage champagne.' Armand took her arm and steered her towards another room, from which delicious aromas were wafting. 'Only the best for special guests, not like the cheap wine we gave to those stupid boys. They drink it with no care.' He wrinkled his nose disdainfully and mimed a drink being chugged down in a single gulp. 'One of them, he asked for beer. *Mon dieu!* I'm glad they did not stay for dinner.' He puffed out his chest in righteous indignation. 'We do not serve hamburgers and chips here.'

Over dinner, which was most assuredly not even in the same food universe as hamburgers, Armand explained, with the help of Luc's translation, that they had diversified the business to smooth out the vagaries of grape harvests and make best use of the talents of his two sons and their wives. The tourist side of the operation – six cottages, an award-winning restaurant and underground cellar tours – were run by one family, while the vineyard operations were run by the other, with Armand in a supervising role and running the champagne tastings. Or, as Armand was quick to correct her, Champagne with a capital C.

'The only true Champagne in the world comes from this region. We are almost at the limit of grape-growing, but it is the very coolness of our climate which produces the finest Champagne, due to the acidity of the grapes. The soils are chalk, which provides good drainage, and here we are perfectly placed to grow the very best pinot noir grapes. The great kings of France recognised the excellence of Reims wine as early as the Middle Ages. It is said that Louis XIV drank nothing but Champagne, for the good of his health, until those scoundrels from Burgundy lured him away.'

No doubt, Armand had said these words a thousand times to rapt audiences, but his voice still rang with passion.

'The Noiret vineyard was established in 1779, I believe,' Luc said. 'Did you supply champagne to Louis XVI?'

'Of course. Only the best for Louis and Marie Antoinette. The road to Paris was a well-travelled path for the winemakers of Reims. Family legend has it that Louis XVI was the source of the money that allowed my forebear to switch from making barrels to filling them, though it seems an unlikely tale to me. Probably just our founder exaggerating a minor royal connection. The original vineyard made other varieties of wine as well, but soon the quality of our Champagne eclipsed all else.'

Luc and Sophie exchanged glances. Sophie raised her champagne flute to her host. 'Long may it remain so. Thank you for sharing this delectable Champagne with us.'

The meal passed in a thoroughly pleasant blur of conversation about winemaking, food and French culture. Sophie mounted a spirited defence of the wines of New Zealand, many of which had won prestigious international awards, but her fellow diners only flared their nostrils in polite disbelief, sure of their own country's age-old superiority in viticulture. In the end, she had to be satisfied that they both agreed to try a pinot noir from Martinborough, if such a thing could be found in Reims.

After dinner, Sophie sank into the comfort of a plump sofa in the sitting room, basking in the happy glow of excellent company, and fine food and wine. The two men wandered away to examine an old earthenware jug and some Roman coins, which had been dug up on the estate. Her eyelids drifted shut as she mused on the impossibility of refusing a dessert of crème brûlée, artfully decorated with a delicate tornado of spun sugar, despite having an extra serving of the divine duck confit.

Did life get any better? Of course, by the end of this trip, she'd be doomed to elastic-waisted trousers and hardened arteries, but it was worth it. She hardly stirred from her gourmand reverie when Luc slid into the seat beside her, so close she could feel the warmth of his body.

Luc leaned down and whispered, 'What do you think, Sophie? Do we trust him?'

She sat up with a start, feeling flustered by his warm breath on her ear. 'Definitely.'

Armand took the armchair opposite them and laid out a trio of brandy balloons and a bottle of XO Cognac. 'So, you have a story to share, my friends?'

'It will seem like a fairy tale, but we believe it is based on the truth.' Sophie swirled the liquid, inhaling the fumes like a glue addict. 'Wow, this is amazing.' Much more of this lifestyle and she'd never leave. 'Luc, perhaps you could explain in French, so there is no misunderstanding.'

She leaned back and watched the two men, as their words and gestures flowed thick and fast. Rather like watching a French movie, she could pick up the tone from the hand flicks and facial expressions, while she caught enough of the meaning to know Luc was telling the full story, from the birth of Ernestine to the escapades of Elisabeth.

As she sank back into the soft cushions, the movie seemed to be playing at high speed, and she realised she was more than a little tipsy. Despite that – or perhaps because of it – the words became easier to follow, as she let them flow over her rather than trying to concentrate on individual words.

When Luc finished talking, Armand switched to English for her benefit. 'So, you think the money to buy this vineyard might have come from Philippine Noiret, whose "service to the King" resulted in a child called Ernestine. This young girl is thought to have hidden valuable items for the royal family during the revolution with the help of a gardener's boy, Pierre Duchamp. And you believe they may have left those items here.' He said the words with casual calmness, but one fluffy grey eyebrow was raised so high it disappeared into his wavy thatch of grey hair.

'Exactly. I did say it would sound unbelievable.' When laid out so starkly, it sounded ludicrous to anyone who hadn't seen the trail of evidence.

'My dear Sophie, your story is no stranger than a thousand other crazy things that happened during the revolution. Of course, I would love to believe it, but...' His words trailed off into a full body shrug.

'I think none of us will believe it until we see it with our own eyes,' she agreed, 'if indeed there is anything to find.'

'But the possibility is too intriguing to ignore,' Luc added. 'We wondered if you had an archive of old documents that might shed some light on it, despite the passage of centuries.'

'We do. I would be delighted to do anything I can to assist you. At worst, I have gained two rather amusing relatives and a tale that the Noiret family will tell for generations to come. If we discover any hint of a royal connection – well, I do not need to tell you it would be very good for our business.'

'And if we found something valuable on your land?' Luc said the words casually, but Sophie could feel the tension in his body.

Armand looked at them both appraisingly. 'Sophie, what would you do if anything was found?'

'Scream and dance with excitement for a couple of days, then donate it to a museum for public display. After taking a zillion photos to prove to doubters that our ridiculous tale was actually true.'

'Luc?'

'The same, except I would probably plead my case to be included as one of the specialists studying whatever items were found. I would not wish to see the find sold, but it is true it might be worth a colossal sum of money.'

'Ah, money. The world cannot get enough of it, no?' Armand continued contemplating them for a long time, during which Luc's hand reached down to grip hers with a bone-crushing grip. 'We have built a solid business here, thanks to those who passed before us. Not every season is good, but I am proud to say we have had enough fine vintages to stand with the best champagne houses. I agree with both of you – anything found on our land belonging to the royal family must be returned to state care for all to enjoy.'

He hesitated a moment before adding a rider. 'I will need to consult my family, as it is their business and future too. I know they will agree, but perhaps they might request that one or two items be retained for display here? And we would want the right to promote the vineyard using the story.'

Luc released Sophie's hand and thrust out his hand for their host to shake. 'Thank you, Armand.'

'It is getting late, and I have to be up early. By the time your tour finishes tomorrow, our archivist will be back from his pétanque tournament in Reims, hopefully not too hung over.'

'Perfect.' Luc rose and held out his hand to hoist Sophie out of the soft embrace of the sofa.

'Sophie, Luc, it has been a delight to meet you.'

'Thank you for a wonderful evening, Armand. We'll look forward to seeing you tomorrow at ten.'

Armand took Sophie's hands between both of his and kissed her cheeks. 'I hope you will stay awhile with us. I look forward to knowing you better.'

They walked back to the cottage, bathed in moonlight, in air that felt as smooth as velvet. When the cottage was visible as a glow of white, Luc said, 'We are fortunate the vineyard owner is a man with such a respect for the past. Armand seemed to take an instant liking to you, Sophie.'

'I'm sure he was just being polite. I must admit that I find it hard to read the context in a culture where kissing is so common, especially after so much champagne.'

He stopped so suddenly that she bumped into him. 'People do not kiss in New Zealand?'

'Yes, of course. But, apart from lovers, we mostly kiss old friends and close relatives, not casual acquaintances. You must understand, having spent time in England.'

'You're right there. The most affection my English grandfather ever showed to his wife was an occasional pat on the hand, in company at least. They had five children, so it can't have been quite so restrained behind closed doors.'

He chuckled and strode off down the lane towards the cottage before she could reply. She caught up with him at the gate, where the scent of roses was an almost tangible presence in the still night air.

Despite the long day, Sophie didn't want to go inside on such a heavenly night. 'I think I'll sit out on the veranda for a while. I need to drink some water or I'll feel like a slug tomorrow.'

'Mind if I join you?'

They sat in silence, the darkness accentuating the tiny noises around them – a slight rustling of a small mammal amongst the leaf litter, an owl in the distance, the soft squeak of the swing-seat as it rocked gently back and forth in a hypnotic rhythm.

Finally, Luc broke the silence. 'Armand was right about one thing – it is a romantic spot. You must be sad that you cannot share it with your husband.'

To her horror, she felt tears prickling under her eyelids. She should have agreed with him and left it at that. But sitting in darkness, so very far from home, with a near stranger who nevertheless seemed so in tune with her, must have loosened something inside. Perhaps it was long past time she stopped hiding within her shell.

'I'm not sure that I would ever have had the chance to visit, if he had lived,' Sophie said softly. 'It's complicated, as these things often are. I thought I had a good marriage, but after his death I found out he had been having affairs.'

The seat swung back and forth half a dozen times before Luc replied. 'Betrayal is something I know all too well. No matter how hard you try to put a brave face on it and move forward with life, it manages to sneak back in at unguarded moments and stab you in the heart all over again. It makes it hard to trust other people.'

'Yes, exactly. If he'd been honest and said our relationship wasn't enough for him, I could have coped. People change. I get that. But to sneak around behind my back … it made me feel as if I was not even worth the effort of telling the truth.'

Luc gently lifted her chin and looked her straight in the eyes. 'Sophie, I think it was completely the opposite. Your husband must have thought your relationship was worth keeping, or he'd have walked out. He was a greedy fool, wanting more when he already had everything – a loving, intelligent, beautiful wife, a home, children.'

She considered it for a while, swiping away the unwanted tears with the back of her hand. 'Thank you, Luc. I've never thought of it that way before. I don't regret marrying him, because he gave me two wonderful kids. We had a lot of fun too.'

'If it's any consolation, it gets easier as time goes by, until one day, you find it really doesn't matter anymore, compared to the good things you have in your life.'

'Like travelling to an exotic land of champagne and historical marvels?' Sophie took a deep breath of rose-scented air and focussed on relishing the moment.

'I honestly can't remember the last time I enjoyed a day so much.'

'Congratulations. You have just passed your first lesson in French culture – make the most of every moment of joy.' He got up from the seat and bent down to kiss her on both cheeks. 'Lesson two: special people deserve a kiss, whether you have known them for a day or a lifetime. Good night, Sophie.'

Lesson two left her more flustered than ever. It was obviously meant as a reminder to celebrate friendship, so why was her heart doing the samba?

The next morning, Sophie woke up to sunlight pouring around the edges of the roman blinds. The clink of crockery and the smell of coffee told her Luc was in the kitchen. A few minutes later, there was a soft knock on the door.

'Come in if you're the bearer of an extremely strong coffee.'

The tray Luc had prepared bore not only coffee, but a large glass of water, poached eggs, toast, a few strawberries, and a perfect rose. 'Thought you might need something to settle your stomach.'

'You're an angel of mercy. What time is it?'

'You've got about an hour until we're due to take the cellar tour. If you feel up to it.'

Sophie grimaced. 'Never felt better.'

Fifty-five minutes later, they arrived at the main house to find a cluster of about two dozen people hanging around outside, next to a tour bus, chatting in at least four different languages. Their tour started right on time in the wine-making area, where the grapes would be gently pressed and processed at harvest time, as they had been for centuries.

But it was the descent into a deep cellar, carved from the chalk rock, which piqued her imagination the most. Thousands of the distinctive dark Noiret bottles lined the walls in racks, resting for a decade to produce the finest vintage in the perfect underground microclimate.

Another member of the tour party asked the inevitable question – how much is all this worth? The guide gave what was obviously a well-rehearsed answer about the differing price depending on the vintage, but with top prices of more than a thousand euros per bottle.

As they walked through a series of underground tunnels and caverns, Sophie couldn't help but peer into corners and dark side rooms, wondering if Ernestine and Pierre had been here before her. Might they have carved their names in the soft rock? Or dragged a sack of Versailles' treasures into one of these abandoned tunnels?

An hour later, they returned to the house, amidst a babble of excited tourists, both their own group and another tour, which had arrived for the next tasting session. Armand gathered everyone into a covered courtyard, where champagne bottles were lined up along a long oak table. He opened the first bottle with a satisfying 'pop' and poured samples for the enthusiastic crowd, providing a commentary on each vintage as he worked.

When everyone had a sample in their champagne flutes, he came over to them. 'My father is back from his pétanque tournament. Why don't you examine the archives while he's still awake. I promise there will be more Champagne later.'

Monsieur Noiret senior must have been getting on for ninety, with a face as wrinkled as a raisin, but he rose to greet them with no more than a slight crackling of hip joints. He rattled off a string of sentences at far too fast a pace for Sophie to understand.

Luc translated. 'Monsieur Noiret says the records go back to the founding of the vineyard in 1779. The original Armand Noiret was a barrel-maker and obviously something of an entrepreneur, but the interesting thing is that the records hint that the money to buy the land came from the original Armand's sister, who worked at Versailles.'

A bolt of excitement shot through Sophie, as the evidence fell into place. 'Philippine Noiret, our

Ernestine's mother? Paid off by Louis XVI for her services?'

'It would be amazing to have proof. I can't wait to see exactly what is documented.'

The elderly Monsieur Noiret led them downstairs at a snail's pace, into a room underneath the main house, keeping up a stream of rapid French. He entered a code into a modern keypad and swung the metal door open, revealing a room stacked with hundreds of journals.

'He says they are aware of the value of such a long-standing archive of documents. The vault is secured and climate controlled. It appears the Noiret family is as terrific at keeping records as they are at making bubbles, thank heavens.'

'Fantastic. But how the heck are we going to get through all these documents?'

Luc conferred with Monsieur Noiret, then they both put on gloves. 'It's all in date order. We can start with key dates.' He followed along behind Monsieur Noiret, as he carefully slid volumes off the shelves and handed them to Luc. 'I know I should start at the beginning, but I have a strong feeling that we need to find out as fast as possible if anything valuable was brought here, before anyone works out where we have gone.'

'Surely, we're safe. Nobody knows where we are except Martine.'

Luc piled the journals onto a central table, which had all the accoutrements of an archivist laid out – a reading lamp, document stand, pens and paper, magnifier. 'These crooks know far too much for my liking. They've tracked our every step so far, so I don't want to make any assumptions.'

'What can I do?'

Luc pulled another pair of gloves out of his pocket and tossed them over to Sophie. 'Let's lay out the journals in date order. Can you go through and find the pages for key dates, especially October 1789 when the royal family was forced to leave Versailles, June 1791 when they fled Paris, August 1792 when they were imprisoned, and December 1795 when Marie-Thérèse was released from prison. If that doesn't yield any results, we can widen the timeframe.'

Each of them took up one journal. As luck would have it, Sophie was the first to find a clue. '22 June 1791. I'm pretty sure this says, "Jacques and Marie-Philippine Lambriquet". That's Ernestine's birth name, isn't it? And her father?'

Luc's eyes sparkled as he leaned over her shoulder, translating. 'Jacques and Marie-Philippine Lambriquet arrived from Paris with a delivery of wine barrels.' He scanned through the next couple of pages.

'It seems they stayed for several days, before heading back to Paris. Presumably after they received news of the failure of the royal family's escape plan.'

He turned to the archivist with a question. After an animated discussion, he turned back to Sophie. 'This notation here indicates where the barrels were moved into storage, but he says it makes no sense. There is no such location.'

After another brief flurry of words, Monsieur Noiret went to search the shelves. He shook his head and fired off an instruction to Luc.

'He needs time to check while we get some lunch.' Luc glanced at his watch. 'A very late lunch. I asked him whether he needed a break too, but he reckons he only needs his daily fix of champagne to keep him in top form.'

Monsieur Noiret senior joined them as the *tarte tartine* was served. Sophie inhaled the appley deliciousness with regret, pushing her portion in front of the old man. He pushed it back with a tut-tut and signalled the waiter. Moments later, as if they had been awaiting his arrival, plates of pâté and apple tart and a glass of champagne were set down in front of him. Predictably, he began with a lip-smacking sip of the champagne, while Luc fidgeted in his chair, like a schoolboy waiting for the final bell.

'*Patience, jeune homme.*'

Sophie needed no help to translate that as 'patience, young man', but she was as antsy as Luc, desperate to find out what he'd learned. In slow motion, the ancient archivist set the glass down and spread pâté on toast. Only after dispatching it in two bites, with a click of loose dentures, did he begin to speak. By that time, the lunch crowd had long dispersed, and Armand had joined their table.

Luc translated as Monsieur Noiret senior attended to the rest of his meal. 'He said the storage notation made no sense until he wondered if it belonged to one of the cellars of the original small vineyard that was here before the Noiret's ownership. The original vineyard was abandoned when the present house was built. Apparently, the old cellars were prone to cave-ins. He thinks there might be an old map in one of the earliest volumes of records.'

'I have detailed modern maps if that would help,' Armand added.

Sophie licked the last flakes of pastry off her lips. 'Compliments to the chef again, Armand. Shall we have a look at those maps now?'

'I have another tour group soon, but I can show you quickly, then leave the maps with you.'

Armand returned with the maps within a couple of minutes. He unrolled the geological map on the table, pinning the corners down with clean spoons. 'Here

457

you can see the band of ancient chalk, which underlies the entire region and gives us our special Champagne terroir. Chalk is a very soft rock, which is useful for carving out cellars, as you saw this morning.'

Sophie waited until Luc had finished translating the more technical details, then said, 'Our tour guide said there are hundreds of kilometres of underground tunnels and caverns around Reims, some dating back to Roman times.'

'That's right. Chalk has been mined for building and agriculture for centuries. The countryside is dotted with old pits and mines, many only discovered when they cave in after heavy rain. And, of course, vineyards have dug their own storage caverns in more recent times, since about the fourteenth century.'

'People sheltered in the underground caverns of Reims during the war,' Luc added. 'We'll have to visit some of the more interesting sites while we are here.'

Armand unrolled the topographic map. 'We are here. The original vineyard was further up the hill, here.' He drew a wide circle around the old vineyard. 'This part we have left to return to nature, as the terroir is not as good for grapes as our current location. As you see, it is close to the Montagne de Reims Natural Park.'

Luc leaned over for a better look. 'When was the old vineyard abandoned?'

'A generation or two after the Noiret family bought all the surrounding land, I think.' Armand peered closely, then tapped the map. 'The chalk layer comes to the surface here and forms an open face behind the old vineyard. There is a tunnel cut into it, leading to the original storage chambers. All long since emptied, of course.'

'Are there deep underground chambers, like we saw this morning?' Sophie asked.

'The original vineyard was never large or productive, so the cellars are not so big.' Armand tapped the map with the end of the pencil as he thought. 'There is evidence of ancient chalk mining on the other side of the hill, but only a few short shafts as far as I know.' He drew a light circle with a pencil. 'Maybe around here. The ground is rough and not close enough to the vineyard to be of use for storage. Probably abandoned for the easier terrain closer to Reims.'

'Has anybody inspected the area thoroughly?'

'We've had a good look around over the years, of course, but I wouldn't say we've checked every inch of ground, by any means. No one else should be up there, as it is private property and not easy to find. We like to keep it that way, as it is dangerous.'

'Dangerous?'

'The old tunnels are unstable and there are many natural holes and man-made pits hidden by plants, as well as deep ponds that are hard to see amongst the trees. A boy disappeared there years ago, and they never found him. Many people fear the forest too, because of the trees, which are said to look like tortured souls.' His mime of a body twisted in agony made the meaning clear without Luc's translation.

'Sounds lovely,' Luc said. 'Are you willing to let Sophie and I have a look around tomorrow?'

'Of course. Now that I have heard your story, I would love to join you. Unfortunately, at this time of year, we have so many tourists that I can't spare the time.'

'If we find anything, you will be the first to know.'

Armand tapped the map again. 'This road up to the old vineyard is very rough. With an ordinary car, you can go to about here, then take this track on foot through the forest.'

Sophie took the pencil and marked the spot. 'We'll head off at first light tomorrow. Luc, do you want to see what else you can find in the archives, while I head back to the cottage to get our gear together?'

'Good plan.' Luc strode off across the room, eager to get back to the treasure trove of old documents.

Sophie turned to Armand. 'Can I make a copy of the map and borrow a few things from you? Torches, maybe a few tools? We'd better swap phone numbers too.'

Armand made a quick call on his phone. 'Call in to the maintenance building on your way back. I've told my foreman to give you whatever you need. It's the big green building on your left. Do come over for dinner again tonight, Sophie. And now, I really must go.'

Back at the cottage, Sophie hummed happily as she packed two large daypacks with essentials for the next day. There was no better feeling than packing for an adventure., and this was the biggest adventure of her life.

She twirled around the cottage in time to the beat in her head, pirouetting madly, until she caught sight of the clock. Time to change and head back to the main house. She felt she ought to take something, but what can you bring for a host who has his own restaurant and vineyard? After a quick look around, she decided on a bottle of the Calvados from Normandy, hoping Armand wouldn't be offended by an offering from another region.

When she arrived, Armand wrapped her in a bear hug, kissed her on both cheeks exuberantly, and said he was delighted with the Calvados. Luc swept in with an apology at getting carried away with his research in the archives and losing track of time, following

461

Armand's lead by kissing both her cheeks. Clearly, they were determined to ensure her cultural education.

The meal was great fun, with increasingly unbelievable anecdotes of past adventures, as the champagne flowed and each of them tried to outdo the others. To her delight, Sophie realised she was understanding enough of their French to catch most of the conversation, except when they got over-excited and talked too fast.

Sophie and Luc walked back to the cottage in silence, taking a seat on the veranda automatically, as if they did this every night. Eventually, Sophie broke the silence. 'This time tomorrow, our quest might be over, except for the months of work you'll face documenting whatever we find, if anything.'

'Whatever happens, the trip was well worth it, if only for the riches of the Noiret's document archive. And getting to know my delightful distant relations, of course. As for the rest, I think we need to be prepared for disappointment. In all likelihood, anything valuable was retrieved long ago.'

'Honestly, Luc, I don't mind either way. I've had an amazing time. I think we should be proud of ourselves for getting this far on a mystery that hasn't been solved in two hundred and thirty years.'

'We make a good team.' Luc pushed the seat into a gentle swing. 'Life is going to be unbearably dull without you, Sophie. What are your plans after this?'

'I haven't forgotten your offer to take me to the Loire Valley, and I'd definitely like to see more of France and the rest of Europe. After that, I don't know. As you said, life is going to feel pretty tame after all this excitement.' She shivered in the cool night air. Or was it because she didn't want to think about the future just yet?

Luc suddenly put his foot down to stop the swinging. 'I almost forgot to tell you what else I found in the archives. How on earth could it have slipped my mind?'

'The old map?'

'Yes, showing the location of the original vineyard and cellars, as well as a notation indicating an old chalk mine on the other side of the hill. I've taken a copy, so the original stays safe.'

'May I see it?'

Luc went back inside, returning with the map and his mobile phone. By the light of the phone's torch, Sophie examined the crude map of the original vineyard. Seeing the area without all the detail of the modern topographic map triggered something in her memory.

'Luc, does this remind you of the drawing on the scrap of parchment we found in the jewellery box?'

He leaned over her shoulder. '*Merde alors!* I think you're right. Let's lay all the maps out on the table and compare them.'

Sophie's pulse was racing as they confirmed the similarities. From the way Luc's hands were shaking, he must have been feeling overwhelmed, which was hardly surprising, after a lifetime of searching. 'So, maybe not a wild goose chase after all?'

'Definitely not. That's not all I found in the archives.'

The intensity of his voice made her turn to him. Any minute now, he would start emitting sparks. 'Out with it. What else did you find that has you so wound up?'

'Pierre Duchamp was here in September 1792 without Ernestine. Whoever recorded his visit seemed suspicious when he arrived – presumably because they didn't know him – but the following day's journal entry was in a completely different tone, as if they were excited, even honoured, by his visit.'

'How exciting.' Sophie gripped his arm so tightly she left dents in his skin. 'Sorry. Go on.'

'Clearly, Pierre had convinced the Noirets that he had come on behalf of Ernestine on important business. He had a map drawn by her, which may be the one we now have, and presumably a letter of introduction. What's more, he brought more items for storage. He obviously impressed them.'

'Items?' Her voice came out as a squeak. How thrilling it would be to find something – anything – from the past. 'Do you know what he brought?'

'Unspecified. He came on a horse, so something fairly small. Pierre arrived only a few weeks after the royal family was taken from the Tuileries palace and imprisoned in the Temple.'

'Intriguing. When Ernestine escaped from the Tuileries, perhaps she was able to save some items of value? Given the haste of their escape, it would have been something easily carried.'

'That's not all. Pierre was here again just before Marie-Thérèse was released from prison in 1795. Unfortunately, on the return visit, he took items away, again unspecified. Hopefully, we'll find out if there is anything still there tomorrow.' He glanced at his watch. 'Make that later today. It's midnight. Time to get some sleep, if we can.'

Freedom

Paris, 19 December 1795

At the stroke of midnight, Ernestine stepped through the gates of the Temple prison. She had no desire to glance back at the place that had robbed her of almost three of her seventeen years. Indeed, she had to restrain her legs from breaking into a run to hasten her escape. Keep calm, walk away, draw no attention – for freedom came with a new set of dangers.

The journey to Austria was to be conducted in utmost secrecy, as neither side wanted the royal princess to be slaughtered by an over-zealous soldier or an angry mob. So, she slipped through the dark streets with a single escort to a nondescript carriage, which would take her to the post-chaise that would take her onwards to freedom. If everything went to plan.

Her meagre bag of possessions from the prison, and a lavish collection of new gowns provided by the regime, had been sent ahead. The gowns were intended to demonstrate how well she had been treated, so that she might arrive as a princess should, in all splendour. A ridiculous notion, given what she had lived through. She vowed she would never wear them.

Two carriages were waiting in a quiet alley not far away. Ernestine had hoped to see Madame de Tourzel or one of the other ladies she had asked for. Instead, as they switched carriages in the dark, the barely visible face looming above her as she got into the post-chaise was that of Madame de Soucy, former under-governess to the royal children and her rescuer from the Tuileries palace. A soldier and a guard made up the rest of their party.

'Hurry, we must leave as soon as possible,' Madame de Soucy said, as she shuffled over to make room. She tucked a soft blanket around Ernestine and drew the blinds down, plunging them further into darkness. 'I cannot tell you how relieved I am to see you, Madame Royale. You will be travelling under the pseudonym "Sophie". I will refer to you as such until we reach Vienna.' She rapped on the partition.

As the carriage rattled off, Ernestine felt a surge of delight. 'Madame, the pleasure is all mine. I fear I shall wake up from this dream and find myself still in prison.'

Madame de Soucy made no response. No doubt she was thinking that their escape had only just begun and may yet become another nightmare. Better to wait until they were beyond the French border before

467

celebrating. 'May I ask who is travelling in the other carriage?'

'Only a few faithful servants. They would not allow us to have a large party. Monsieur Hüe, my maid, another servant and cook, and my son. Oh, and your brother's dog.'

Ernestine was annoyed, but not surprised, to learn that Madame de Soucy was bringing her own maid, while she herself had no attendants. Adding her son to the party instead of bringing someone to be with Ernestine seemed an even more blatant snub. No matter. God willing, Marie-Thérèse would be waiting for her in Vienna and her own life would resume. What her life would be was an open question, but all she cared about right now was to get safely away from that cursed tower.

Thus, instead of complaining, she merely said, 'Can Coco not travel with me? It would be such a comfort to us both.'

'You might be recognised. The little dog has become quite well known. I suggest you try to rest. It will be a long journey.'

Ernestine made herself as comfortable as possible in a nest of cushions and blankets. The length of the journey was not the main hazard they faced by any means, but neither woman wanted to voice the other risks that lay ahead. It would be a miracle if they made it to the border.

Despite her excitement and the jerking progress of the wheels over cobblestones, the dark interior of the carriage and the late hour lulled Ernestine into a deep sleep. She woke briefly when they were stopped at a town, but a bribe to the local officials soon saw them on their way again.

She did not wake up again until they stopped to break their fast. The next six days became a test of her nerves, as they spent long hours bouncing around on rough roads, stopping only for checkpoints or for food and fresh horses. Despite being recognised at one point by an officer, and thereafter finding every town crowded with onlookers, their journey was marked by the support of cheering crowds, instead of the expected mobs hissing with anger and derision.

They reached the French border on Christmas Eve, stopping for a last night on French soil at the Hotel du Corbeau. Ernestine shivered as she walked under the swinging sign of the raven, which looked more ominous than welcoming. All she cared about right at that moment was being shown to a bed that didn't rock and roll underneath her tired body, in a room without bars on the windows.

The maid who showed her upstairs to her room mentioned that the other carriage in their party had arrived before them, but Ernestine only had eyes for the clean, comfortable bed. All she wanted to do was sink into it and sleep for a week. Thus, the knock on the door was most unwelcome.

'Who is it?'

'Madame de Soucy's maid, Mademoiselle Sophie. She sent me to attend to you.'

'I wish to rest,' she replied, but the door opened anyway.

Ernestine was about to shoo her away when something about the girl's walk made her look up sharply. The girl approached her, twitching the veil from her face and putting her index finger to her smiling lips. Marie-Thérèse! Thank heavens that years of training in prison had taught her how to suppress any reaction.

'Madame, I am Catherine de Verenne. How wonderful it is to see you free at last.'

Ernestine answered with a grin as wide as a platter. She caught up her sister's hand and clasped it between her own. 'How kind of you to attend to me, Mademoiselle Catherine.'

'I desire only to see the King's daughter safe, Madame Royale.' Marie-Thérèse winked. She closed and latched the door behind her and rushed into Ernestine's embrace. 'Dearest sister, how can I thank you? I would not have survived another week in

470

prison. But here you are, alive and free. I feared I would never see this day.'

'Let us not speak of it now. I long to be Ernestine again and to see you in your rightful place. Shall we exchange clothes, before you decide you'd rather be me forever?'

The girls stripped with joyful abandon, flinging bonnets, gloves, shawls, fichus, and gowns in all directions. The spark disappeared from Marie-Thérèse's eyes when she saw the many scars of healed sores on her sister's skeletal body. She dabbed her eyes with a handkerchief, but made no comment, instead using this time alone to tell Ernestine about her time in hiding with Madame de Tourzel and how they had arranged her release.

When they had switched clothes – and lives – Ernestine twirled joyfully, then embraced her sister again. 'I cannot recall the last time I felt so utterly, blissfully happy.'

Marie-Thérèse shot her a cheeky grin. 'I think I might know how to put an even wider smile on your lips. Wait here.'

A couple of minutes later, Marie-Thérèse returned to the room, taking her sister by the shoulders and turning her towards the door. 'I believe you have not yet had the pleasure of meeting Madame de Soucy's "son", Pierre.'

At that, Pierre Duchamp entered the room, now several inches taller and broader, but with the same twinkling hazel eyes and dimples. Ernestine took a sharp intake of breath and stood rooted to the spot, noting the uncertainty beneath his smile. So much time had passed since they had seen each other, so much had happened. She had no right to expect that their friendship would continue as before.

Neither could think of what to say, so she drew out the carved owl from her bodice and held it out on the flat of her palm.

He stared at it, perhaps not recognising the small lump of wood, which had been worn completely smooth by nervous hands. Then his eyes lit up. He pulled out the silver cross from around his neck, then rushed forward, scooping her into his arms.

'Oh Pierre, I thought I might never see you again. To see you safe is a dream come true.'

'I was never the one in danger, my brave Ernestine. Although I may never forgive you for leaving me, I truly hope I'll have the rest of my life to make sure you never stray again.'

'I promise,' she whispered, as she held him so tight that she could hear his heart thumping under his coat.

The bell rang to call them for dinner. The three young survivors of the revolution wanted only to be together and hear each other's stories, but Marie-Thérèse, ever the one in charge, was quick to see that the charade must go on.

'Let's eat first, then talk. We'll go downstairs, act our roles, and say as little as possible. And Ernestine, dearest, please try to keep your rapture under control. Remember, you are supposed to be a poor, put-upon maid who has been dragged across the breadth of the country by your surly mistress, not a young woman madly in love.'

Ernestine tried to compose her face, but the bloom just wouldn't be reined in, especially with Pierre still looking at her with such tenderness.

Marie-Thérèse rolled her eyes, sent Pierre off to the dining room, and adjusted a veil over Ernestine's blushes. 'Perhaps it will help your performance if you think about sleeping in an uncomfortable cot in a draughty attic tonight, while I enjoy this delightful bed.'

Ernestine shot a regretful glance at the soft quilt and followed Madame Royale out the door.

Marie-Thérèse walked straight-backed to the central table in the room and seated herself with regal grace on the chair pulled out by Monsieur Hüe, completely ignoring the slight figure of the maid who slipped into the room unnoticed behind her.

The talk of their table that night was all about how they might achieve the next stage of their journey. Scouts had left messages at the hotel telling of envoys lying in wait to divert Marie-Thérèse to her various relatives. The seventeen-year-old princess was now the only surviving child of Louis XVI, and therefore a great prize. Now she was free, she would be a fly in the web of political intrigue, as both her French and Austrian family wanted to bolster their claims to power by marrying her into their ranks.

Marie-Thérèse herself had no doubts. Her parents had wished her to marry her cousin, the Duc d'Angoulême, son of the King's younger brother and thus second in line to the throne of France. She would respect their wishes, for in marrying him, she would become Queen of France one day, God willing.

The new maid, Ernestine, hid behind her veil at a corner table, watching Madame de Soucy watch Marie-Thérèse through narrowed eyes. She was the person to be feared the most.

Madame de Tourzel had worked together with other loyalists, including the faithful Monsieur Hüe, to shelter the real Marie-Thérèse and then to bring about the reverse switch, so that Madame Royale would arrive in triumph in Austria. They had insisted Madame de Soucy agree to the two extra members of the party, who were travelling as her maid and son.

474

Madame de Soucy had given in to the demand only after securing a substantial payment for her troubles.

Given her suspicious looks now, Ernestine thought it likely that more funds would be required to buy her continued silence. She was one of the few remaining people who knew Marie-Thérèse and Ernestine well enough to tell them apart, and the only one of that select group who might cause trouble. Ernestine could only hope that the changes wrought by their time in prison would serve to confuse her.

The soup arrived, a mouth-wateringly thick broth with chunks of meat and vegetables, but her uneasiness robbed her of her appetite, so she pushed the bowl away. As she watched Marie-Thérèse sipping daintily, it dawned on Ernestine that it was no longer her problem. With a joyful lightness of spirit, she realised that tomorrow she would be truly free, and no one would care where, or with whom, she went or what she did. She reached for the spoon, suddenly ravenous.

By the time the party retreated to their rooms, Ernestine was ready to drop with fatigue. Nevertheless, when Marie-Thérèse commanded her to come to her room to prepare her for bed, she rose immediately and followed her up the stairs.

'I know you must be exhausted, Ernestine, but tonight is the last chance we will have to talk. I have arranged a carriage to take you and Pierre back to his home, leaving early tomorrow morning.'

'But how did you know he would want me to go with him?'

Marie-Thérèse looked at her as if she was a half-wit. 'You wouldn't be asking such a question if you knew how angry he was when he returned to look for you and found me instead. I swear, he would have marched me right back into prison, if Madame de Tourzel hadn't calmed him down. Ever since, he has dedicated himself to getting you released. I hate to think how many hundreds of miles he must have ridden, carrying messages to and from all the negotiating parties.'

'I owe him my life, then. And all the others who helped to free both you and me.'

'As I owe you my life, dearest Ernestine. I fear my mother's kind intentions in adopting you have brought you far more pain than pleasure.'

'Then let us promise to remember only the good times we had, when we were blessed with a happy life. Will I see you again, Marie-Thérèse?'

'I hope so, but who knows what will happen. I should be sad indeed if I never set foot in France again. You could always come and visit me in Austria. I would much prefer it if you stayed with me, but I can see it would not be sensible.'

Ernestine imagined the peaceful life she would lead with Pierre on his farm. She certainly had not a single ounce of envy for the life Marie-Thérèse would now be facing. 'Yes, it would be best if we stayed apart. You must return to your rightful place on the throne, by building on the sympathy the people feel for your status as the Orphan in the Tower. No one must ever know my role in it.'

'It feels wrong that you cannot receive the acclaim you deserve, but I see the sense of it. You must tell me everything that took place after I escaped.'

Now it was Ernestine's turn to rummage in her bags. 'I can do better than that, since I have written an account of it. I implore you to wait until you are safe and alone before you read it, as it will be extremely distressing.'

As the memoir passed from one girl to the other, Marie-Thérèse's back stiffened, while Ernestine felt so light that she might float away. The switch was complete.

'And tomorrow, I will disappear and cease to exist as Ernestine.'

'Will you go back to your birth name, Marie-Philippine Lambriquet?'

'No, I think I need a new name entirely if I am to stay in France, in case my role in your escape becomes known. Besides, I have a cousin who shares the same name.' With any luck, if someone tried to track her down, they would find only the innocent cousin, who could prove she had lived quietly through troubled times.

'You could continue using the name Sophie. I chose it in honour of my baby sister. If she had lived, I would have wished her to grow up like you.'

'Then I will gladly use Sophie as my new name.'

'I would like that.' The fleeting look of pain at the thought of her sister dissolved into an impish grin. 'I think I can guess how you will leave your surname behind. I look forward to the day when I can visit Pierre and Sophie Duchamp in your rural paradise in the Loire Valley.'

Ernestine felt a blush flaring on her cheeks. 'Pierre has not asked me to marry him. At least, not since I was ten years old.'

'He will. Pierre is rather an extraordinary young man. How many gardener's lads would put their own life at risk for a cause he did not follow? Especially when he had every opportunity to flee with enough money to create a prosperous life.'

'Pierre always holds himself to the highest standards. He never saw himself defined by his position.'

'It's true he has always showed great loyalty, but you must know that his loyalty has been entirely for you, my dear sister, despite your unfortunate relations and reckless behaviour. I fear he still detests me for putting your life at risk. Although most people think us alike, Pierre told me once that he considered us dissimilar in almost every way.' She laughed. 'And he certainly did not mean it as a compliment to me.'

'I hope he will forgive both of us.' How mature her sister had become, laughing at implied insults from a young man of no status, rather than being angry, as she might have been in the past.

'He knows the switch was not my choice. I still feel ashamed that I was not strong enough to refuse you.'

'Even if you had not been so ill, I think it would have been impossible to refuse your mother when she saw a chance to save you. Her children were everything to her.'

They shared a long moment of silence, neither wanting to talk about the pain of losing a family.

'How much has changed,' Marie-Thérèse murmured, her voice raw with emotion. 'I look back at the little girl I was when we left Versailles and do not recognise her. I'm ashamed of how badly I treated you then. My mother insisted that adopting you as a sister would teach me humility, but at first, I only saw the daughter of servants being given the privilege of sharing everything that was mine.'

Ernestine wondered if Marie-Thérèse had guessed they shared the same father, but now was not the time for such revelations. 'Your family gave me every advantage a girl could desire. I know it was hard for you.'

'Actually, I loved having a sister, although I would never admit it to my mother. I learned a lot from you. Certainly, I would not be alive today if I had stayed in that squalid cell, watching my family being taken away, one by one. Oh, Ernestine, how can I ever repay you for your sacrifice?'

'You have no debt to repay. Besides, you have brought Pierre back to me. What more could I ask?'

'Just as well, as I having nothing to reward you with until I reach Austria.'

The two young women embraced each other tightly, each counting their blessings, so the evils they had witnessed might be pushed a little farther down the dark corridor of memory.

'I envy you, marrying for love. Are you sure you wish to swap places?'

Ernestine let out a laugh of pure joy. 'I wouldn't swap back for all the diamonds and gold in the world.'

'Well then, let us say farewell. Your carriage will leave before first light tomorrow.' Marie-Thérèse sighed. 'As for me, I have many hours ahead of me, composing letters to appease my warring relations. Please don't wake me before you go, or I might decide to join you after all.'

'*Au revoir*, sister.'

'*Au revoir*, sister.'

Ernestine reached for the door at the same instant as a soft knock sounded on the other side. She opened the door a crack, wondering who could be calling so late at night. To her surprise, it was Pierre. She pulled him in, checking the corridor quickly before shutting the door again.

'My apologies for disturbing you at such a late hour, Madame Royale.'

Marie-Thérèse pointed to the sole chair in the room, while the two girls sat on the bed, wrapped in the quilt. 'No need to be formal, Pierre. We are old acquaintances, are we not? What is it you wish to ask?'

'Monsieur Hüe tells me you have arranged a carriage tomorrow to take me home.'

'You and Ernestine. It is safer if we are not seen together in Vienna.'

Hazel eyes turned on Ernestine. 'You wish to come with me?'

'Nothing would make me happier, Pierre, if that is what you want.'

'Of course. You are all I ever wanted.'

Marie-Thérèse looked from one to the other. 'Do stop gazing into each other's eyes like a couple of cooing doves. I have a kingdom to regain and no time to lose.'

'Before we go, I have something to give you, Madame Royale.' Pierre opened the canvas sack he had been carrying, pulling out a package wrapped in linen and a bag that clinked when he handed it over. 'I thought you might need some gold to get you out of France, Madame, and to give you some independence when you reach Austria.'

Marie-Thérèse tipped a handful of gold coins out of the bag into her hand with a gasp. 'I thank you, for your loyalty and your forethought. I wish there were more like you in France, Pierre Duchamp.' Marie-Thérèse unwrapped the linen bundle, revealing the Riesener jewellery box. Ernestine watched as the other girl lifted the lid, heard her intake of breath as she saw the beautiful pearl necklace, surrounded by smaller pieces of exquisite jewellery, and two miniature portraits of the King and Queen.

Marie-Thérèse held the miniatures with trembling fingers, kissing each one and holding them to her heart, her eyes tightly shut. With a sigh, she returned them to the box and stroked the pearls in their bed of satin. When she had recovered enough to speak, her voice was choked with emotion. 'You have brought me the most precious of gifts, Pierre Duchamp. I would have chosen these above all the treasures of Versailles.'

'Ernestine told me how much the pearl necklace meant to you and the Queen.'

'I can't thank you enough. Where did you get these things?'

'Thank Ernestine more than me. She carried the jewellery box to safety for the Queen before your family escaped from Paris.'

Ernestine took up the story. 'Her Majesty gave most of her jewellery to other people to take out of France, aside from what she took herself. But this most precious piece, she entrusted to me, along with the personal items we retrieved from Versailles.'

'My mother thought you were extremely brave to have gathered all the possessions most precious to our family. And clever, to have found a way to bring them to us from Versailles, with the able assistance of Pierre and your father. What happened to our treasures that dreadful day, when we fled the Tuileries?'

'The plan was to rendezvous south of Reims. When our hopes for your escape were dashed, I hid everything at the vineyard owned by my mother's family, hoping to return them to you one day. I had no idea that Pierre had even been there, let alone had the brilliant idea of bringing your favourite pieces here.'

'You are not the only one with a secret or two, my dearest Ernestine. Do you remember the night when the State Treasury was robbed?'

'How could I forget? I chuckle every time I see a nightdress with frills.'

'Very amusing. You assumed I had escaped from the thieves without finding anything, and I thought it was safer if you did not know the truth.'

'What in heaven are you two talking about?' Marie-Thérèse interrupted.

'While you were in prison, thieves broke into the State Treasury and stole the Crown Jewels. As stupid as the guards were to let it happen, the thieves were no cleverer. I followed them back to their lodgings and liberated their stash, or at least what few items I could find. There were so many thieves by then that the rest of the jewels must be scattered far and wide by now.'

'But, Pierre, I entered the drawing room seconds after you arrived back at the house. You had no bag and the soldier's search found nothing.'

Pierre laughed. 'Did you not wonder at how still Madame de Lège sat, refusing to stand even when threatened by the soldier?'

'I did remark on it. I commended her on her bravery.' Light dawned as Ernestine replayed the scene in her mind. 'Madame winked at me! She had the jewels stashed—'

'— under her skirts. She couldn't move a hair in case they jingled in the sack. You told me the location of your family vineyard that night—'

'— and you were heading to the eastern border—'

'– it seemed a sensible idea to hide everything together.' He stood up and bowed to Marie-Thérèse. 'When Madame Royale becomes Dauphine and later Queen, she will have jewels to wear, safely stored away in a cave at the Noiret vineyard until needed. Ernestine's map of the precise location is in the hidden compartment of the jewellery box, so you may retrieve them whenever you wish.'

The two girls looked at one another with open mouths, then burst out laughing simultaneously.

'I am speechless' Marie-Thérèse replied. 'How can I thank you?'

'All I ask is that you use your fortune wisely, putting the needs of your people above all else. I want our children to live in peace and prosperity.'

Marie-Thérèse flushed at his impertinence, but she nodded, nevertheless. She opened the bag and gave Pierre a handful of gold coins, then opened the jewellery box and took out a pair of hair decorations, twinkling with tiny diamonds. 'I would like you to take these as a token of my gratitude, Ernestine. When my fortune is restored, I will reward you properly.'

Ernestine twirled them in her fingers, her thoughts lost in the sparkle of the diamonds in the candlelight. 'Thank you, I shall treasure these. There is no need for further reward.' She smiled at the man beside her. 'Pierre and I have everything we need.'

Early the following morning, two slim figures slipped out the back door of the inn into the stable yard, where a plain carriage was waiting to take them home. Marie-Thérèse's prediction proved correct. As soon as the town was behind them, Pierre went down on one knee and asked her to be his wife.

The future Sophie Duchamp thought she had never been so happy as she was on the long journey home, when the hours passed with talk of orchards and farming, children and love. He even promised to carve her a new owl.

In the Dark

Reims, 2019

The alarm woke Sophie from a deep sleep in what seemed like the middle of the night. After a moment of confusion, she remembered the plan to go up to the original vineyard early, so they would have the whole day to search. She prised herself out of bed and shuffled into the kitchen to make coffee and breakfast, clattering the pans loudly enough to wake Luc.

He emerged with rumpled hair and a yawn, but already dressed in clothes and boots suitable for hiking.

Sophie handed him a coffee. 'You eat while I finish packing lunch.'

By the time she had finished her second coffee, Luc was eager to go. 'I can see you've been busy preparing for a major expedition,' he said, nodding his head at the two bulging packs by the door. 'Is there anything else I need to bring?'

'A strong back. I thought we might need a few tools, so I borrowed some from Armand, plus torches, batteries, warm clothes, water, food, maps, compass, kitchen sink – just the essentials.'

Luc lifted the two packs onto his shoulders with an exaggerated groan and headed out the door. 'Maybe next time we could leave the kitchen sink behind?'

At the parking spot where the road curved around the hillside, a gravelled track disappeared into a pocket of forest. They shouldered their packs and walked through a thin layer of undergrowth into a world of stately oaks, interspersed with open meadows, and still dark ponds.

Even at its thickest, it was more woodland than forest, at least compared to the almost impenetrable forests in New Zealand that Sophie was used to. Here they might call it a 'mountain park', but it was not much more than a rolling hillside compared to the jagged peaks of her home country.

She breathed in the fresh, humus-scented air, happy to be outdoors after so much time inside. Luc was strolling along, whistling a jaunty tune, and clearly enjoying himself as much as she was. When they reach a stand of twisted beeches, Sophie realised how apt Armand's mime of tortured trees had been. The track narrowed and headed up a rise, amidst a jumble of rocks and gnarled roots.

It was so pleasant to be surrounded by nature that Sophie was almost sorry when they reached the old vineyard. It wasn't much more than a tumble of blocks and decaying oak beams, but there was a four-wheel-drive track, which looked as if it was rarely used.

They sat down on a beam, enjoying the tranquillity. Sophie passed Luc a water bottle, their fingers touching for a moment, until Luc took it from her. He glanced at her, then busied himself with spreading the map out between them.

The obvious place to start was the low chalk cliff, about two hundred metres beyond the dilapidated building. Here, they found a narrow, arched tunnel, carved a long time ago using hand-tools, heading into the chalk layer.

Unfortunately, not far from the entrance, an old iron gate blocked their way. As if that wasn't enough of a hint, a dust-covered sign hung in the middle of the gate, bearing a skull and crossbones symbol in a red triangle.

Luc rattled the gate, but it was locked and solid. 'Armand did warn me it would be here. I hoped it might have rusted through.'

Sophie opened Luc's pack and got out the bag of tools, handing him a crowbar. 'Would you care to do the honours?'

He looked at the crowbar as if it was about to bite him. 'At the risk of sounding like a pedant, can we try to do as little damage as possible? This may be preserved as a historic site one day.'

'Apologies.' She hid her smile and rummaged through the bag. 'Screwdriver? Wire?'

Luc pulled an ancient key out of his pocket. 'I rather thought I might try this key Armand gave me.'

Sophie rolled her eyes. 'Where's the challenge in that?'

He grinned and slotted the key into the lock. The grin faded to a grimace, as the key refused to turn. Sophie pushed the crowbar fractionally towards him with a toe, but Luc delved into his pack and brought out a can of spray-on lubricant, which he sprayed liberally into the lock. 'Shall we go outside and have a quick break while this stuff works its magic?'

They exited out into the sunshine, blinking with the suddenness and intensity of the glare. While Sophie hunted for food in her pack, Luc stretched out on his back on a flat rock, with his hands cushioning his head, looking very relaxed and happy.

She turned to hand him an apple. 'I thought you'd be impatient to get behind the locked gate.'

'Whatever is there has been there for hundreds of years, so there's no rush.' As he sat up to take the apple, he froze. 'Sounds like a vehicle.'

He pulled a pair of compact binoculars out of his pack, and they walked up to an outcrop of rock, where they could see down to the old vineyard building. A chunky, black four-wheel-drive was bumping up the last stretch of track. The vehicle parked and a man got out.

Luc trained the binoculars on him. 'It's Marc Vincent, the special investigations officer I told you about. When Martine rang yesterday, she said he was desperate to get hold of me. Being a police officer, she thought it was safe to tell him where we're staying.'

'It must be important if he's come all this way, rather than phoning. How did he know we were at the old vineyard, I wonder?'

'Maybe the police can track my mobile.'

'All the way up here?' She pulled her phone out of her zip pocket and was surprised to find four bars showing. 'Actually, cell coverage is good.'

'Or he might have stopped at the vineyard to ask Armand where we are.'

Sophie tucked her phone away and turned to Luc. 'Do you trust Vincent?'

'Sophie, I don't trust anyone completely anymore, except you, of course. I'm not very impressed by the lack of progress he's made on the case, but he is a police officer, so that must be high on the trust scale, surely.'

She snorted. 'You never heard of corrupt cops? Call me paranoid, but it strikes me a man in his position would be ideally placed to make some money on the side, based on his knowledge of how to access and sell stolen goods. And he could get access to airline passenger lists and other information.'

'Point taken. We're in a tricky position, as he must know I am here. How about I go down and see what he wants, while you stay out of sight?'

'Vincent will know I'm here too, so there is no point in me hiding. Two against one are better odds, anyway.'

As Marc Vincent turned to take something out of the car, his profile triggered a memory. 'Luc, hand me the binoculars.' With the extra magnification, she was in no doubt. She grabbed Luc's hand. 'Run. Vincent is the man from the plane – the burglar.'

They sprinted into the scrubby bushes in the opposite direction to where the vehicle was parked. Behind them, two doors slammed, and voices shouted. Damn, Vincent was not alone, and they had been spotted. Sophie glanced back, seeing three men running in their direction.

'Duchamp! Stop or we'll shoot.'

Luc dropped her hand and pushed her towards a patch of thicker vegetation higher up the slope of the hill. 'More chance if we separate. Run like hell.' He lunged downhill, yelling 'Come on Sophie, this way,' and lashing through the undergrowth to make his direction visible.

Sophie sprinted as fast as the rough ground would allow, spurred on by the sound of heavy boots behind her. She plunged on through the tangle of vegetation, past a jumble of boulders, until, suddenly, the ground vanished under her feet.

She stifled a shriek as she plunged into a dark void, managing to twist and land on her pack, rather than her skull. Boots stomped rapidly towards the rocks outside, as she lay winded and unmoving, like a turtle on its back.

When her pursuer had passed and the sound of his boots faded, she extracted herself from the straps of the pack with a wriggle. She brushed chalk dust off her trousers, ignoring a rip in the shoulder of her shirt and the ache in the muscle under it.

In the light of her mobile phone, she could see she was in an old shaft dug into the chalk layer. Cautiously, she poked her head back through the thick curtain of creepers, which had screened the mouth of the shaft from her and the man behind her. Voices were yelling further down the hill, but she couldn't make out what they were saying.

Only when she climbed to the top of a nearby outcrop of rock could she see what was happening. Vincent and another man were standing at the base of the low hill. They were too far away to hear, but it was evidently an animated discussion, with fingers being pointed in her direction.

As she watched, two other men appeared, Luc and Paul Tomas. Tomas forced Luc to his knees, holding a pistol to his head. Luc knelt awkwardly, with his hands fastened behind his back, his helpless state shaking Sophie to her core.

Vincent stepped away from the group and shouted with the full force of his impressive lungs, 'Sophie West. We know you are here. Come out or we will shoot Duchamp.'

Luc jerked his head up and screamed, 'No,' earning him a vicious kick.

Her brain whirled through her limited options. Logic told her to go for help, but she could not abandon Luc. 'I'm coming,' she yelled. 'Give me a minute. I'm tangled in some brambles.' Anything for a few extra seconds to do what little she could. Her face and arms were covered with slashes and punctures from all the prickly plants and sharp branches she'd run through, so it was not too far from the truth. The blood oozing through the cut in her shirt helped.

One of the men ran up the hill towards the sound of her voice. Before he got there, she stood up and limped down the hill. As he got closer, she realised he looked vaguely familiar, then her memory kicked in. Joubert, the man who had been in Henri's apartment. He might be a security expert now, but his bearing and fitness suggested a more active past. Military perhaps.

He reached her and grabbed her roughly, spinning her around and pulling her hands behind her back with leather-gloved hands. In heavily accented English, he said. 'Move and I break your arm.'

Cold metal clicked around her wrists. Handcuffs. These men were no amateurs.

The man jerked her around again to face him, holding a pistol in her face. 'Don't be stupid. I will shoot.'

Her heartbeat seemed to slow down as she stared, mesmerised, at the black hole at the end of the barrel.

He pushed her unexpectedly, sending her stumbling backwards to the ground. A classic schoolyard bully, who couldn't resist tormenting his victim, even when she was beaten. He jerked her upright again, wrenching her arms to the edge of their sockets. 'Walk.'

When she reached the rest of the group, Luc looked up at her with anguish in his eyes and blood on his face. Paul Tomas was still holding a pistol to Luc's head, apparently not caring that he had shared a joke with him only a few days before.

A whiff of Armani cologne drifted to her nostrils as Vincent came up beside her. He grabbed her by the chin and forced her to look at him. His gaze swept slowly down her body, as if he owned it. Not a man you'd like to meet in an interrogation cell.

'Sophie West. Delighted to meet you at last.' His eyes drifted back up, until they were staring into hers with cold determination. 'Show us where the valuables are hidden, or your boyfriend will lose his not so pretty face.'

Luc shook his head slightly, but Sophie knew they had lost this fight. Even if she didn't show them, Vincent would find the entrance to the cellars and see their packs outside. 'Follow me.'

Vincent took one look at the tunnel and sent Tomas back to the vehicle for a torch, while he dispatched the old lock with a couple of vicious blows from the crowbar. When Tomas returned, Vincent took the powerful police-issue torch for himself and handed the other torches to his men, leaving Luc and Sophie to carry the backpacks.

Beyond the gate, the tunnel angled downward in a straight line into the chalk hillside, growing steadily darker. As the buzz of insects died away behind them, the warmth of the sun faded to a uniform coolness, stopping drops of sweat in their tracks. The air smelled of dry stone rather than damp, a promising sign.

The tunnel ended in an underground chamber, not unlike the ones they had seen yesterday at the Noiret vineyard, although more roughly carved. Here, the ceiling formed a shallow dome of time-darkened chalk, descending in graceful arcs to regular lines of pillars. Stout as the pillars were, it seemed to Sophie as if they were far too insubstantial to hold up the weight of rock above them.

In the past, this vaulted chamber must have held hundreds of barrels of wine, but now it only held five people and the echoes of their voices. Vincent left Joubert on guard duty, while he and Tomas conducted a thorough search of the cellar.

'You don't have to do this, Joubert,' Luc said. 'If you let us go now, you won't spend the rest of your life in prison for kidnapping.'

In response, Joubert thrust the end of the pistol against Sophie's forehead, while keeping the torch beam on her, so Luc could see exactly what his plea would achieve. She shut her eyes and tried to ignore the cold metal digging into her skin. Seconds ticked by in silence.

The other two men came back and the entire group moved on down a short tunnel. The second cellar was much the same as the first, except that, here and there, the light of the torches picked out a slab of chalk or a pile of rubble, where part of the structure had given in to gravity and time.

Nobody said a word, but the frequency with which the torches shone on the ceiling indicated their captors were thinking the same thing as Sophie was – just how unstable was this place? The skull and crossbones symbol on the gate had seemed excessive in the muted daylight at the entrance, but it was clear that Armand had not exaggerated his warning.

Disregarding the danger, they pressed on into a third cellar, which was worse, and a fourth, which they could only access by squeezing past a heap of rubble. Once inside, they could go no further, as the final cellar had partially collapsed on the far side. If there had ever been another exit, it was now blocked by a massive pile of rock. Fortunately, two solid pillars had held up the ceiling at each side of the cave-in, preventing a total collapse.

'*Merde,*' Vincent muttered, as he examined the rockfall. He swung the brilliant torch beam on Luc and rattled off a question in rapid French.

Judging by the way he pointed the pistol at her, Sophie gathered he was demanding to know where the jewels were hidden, or he would take great pleasure in shooting her.

Luc stepped in front of her. 'I know no more than you. We don't know for sure if there was ever anything hidden here. If there was, it was probably taken away years ago.'

The standoff was interrupted by Tomas, who had completed his search of the cellar at the other side of the pillar from the rockfall. 'Vincent, *ici*.'

Tucked in an alcove, with the other three sides protected by the pillar, the wall, and the rockfall, was a mound that seemed too regularly shaped to be a pile of rubble. As they watched, Tomas cleared the surface of a thick layer of chalk dust and debris from the cave-in, revealing the edge of a barrel. With a grunt of satisfaction, Joubert went to join him, working at speed, until six wine barrels were visible.

Sophie could see the exultation in their faces as they turned to Vincent. Beside her, Luc's shoulders slumped. She felt desperately sorry for him, after all the years of effort he had put into tracking this find, only to have his success ripped away by these crooks at the last moment. Her hands were still cuffed, so she leaned forward until her chin touched his shoulder, feeling his muscles relax as he leaned back into her.

Vincent barked out a command. The two men stepped back to guard Sophie and Luc, while Vincent went forward, the crowbar swinging in one gloved hand, throwing menacing shadows on the wall in the torchlight.

Luc winced as Vincent forced off the top of the first barrel, heedless of any historic value it might have. Four pairs of eyes watched intently as the top of the barrel fell to the ground. Four pairs of ears listened to Vincent's intake of breath.

He reached down into the barrel and pulled out handfuls of straw, shaking each one carefully in the torch beam before dropping it to the floor. By the time he had his head inside the barrel, scraping around at the bottom, it was clear to all that there was nothing to find. Vincent pulled his head out, let out a string of curses, and lashed out at the barrel with steel-capped boots, sending it crashing into the side of the pillar in a puff of chalk dust.

Vincent started on the second barrel, ripping its lid off violently. He gave a shout of triumph. Luc stepped forward without thinking, but stopped at the click of the safety catch on the pistol. Slowly, Luc retreated, putting himself between the gunman and Sophie, pushing her against the wall.

Very gallant, but galling that now she couldn't see what Vincent had found. She leaned to the side in time to see Vincent pulling clothes out of the barrel, checking each item over as he went. The bright beam picked out cloaks, dresses, shoes, coats and culottes – everything a royal family from the 1780s would need for everyday wear. No doubt worth a considerable sum to collectors, but apparently devoid of jewels, judging from Vincent's profanities.

Leaving the clothes dumped on the floor, Vincent set to work on the remaining barrels, but each was as disappointing as the first. At one point, he let out an 'ah-ha' and plucked a couple of small items out of the bottom of a barrel. He examined each under the torch, holding them with the tips of his fingers, before putting them in his pocket.

When the last barrel was dragged out of the alcove and flung on its side with a thrust of his boot, he turned on them. '*Rien*. A couple of tiny diamonds and some old clothes.'

Vincent advanced on Luc and punched him in the stomach with the full force of his heavily muscled arm. Luc reacted quickly enough to avoid the worst of it, but it must still have been a sickening blow. He crumpled backwards into Sophie, who was powerless to help, aside from providing him with a soft landing.

They slid down the wall to the ground in a tangle of limbs. Luc groaned and curled into a ball, gagging. Vincent lashed out with his foot, missing them by a whisker, as Sophie rolled them both sideways.

Luc raised his head and gasped out, 'Marc, get a grip. You must know it was always a long shot. People don't just leave valuables around uncollected.'

'Then why did you keep looking all these years?'

'The thrill of the chase? Academic interest? Obsession? The very slim chance that something might still be hidden away?'

Vincent swung the torch beam onto Sophie. 'And the pearl necklace your ancestor stole?'

She scrambled to her feet awkwardly, blocking the route between Vincent's boot and Luc's head. 'I know you have seen Chevalier's files. It was thrown into a lake two centuries ago. The soldiers who saw it disappear into the water swore an oath before their king. Whoever this Cloutier man was, who pretended it still existed, must have been lying, probably hoping for a reward.'

Vincent pushed her aside and dragged Luc to his feet, holding him by the hair in front of Sophie, the pistol to his temple. 'Would you swear on Duchamp's life that the necklace is not in your possession? Or secured somewhere in Paris? I warn you, I will know if you are lying.'

Sophie tried to focus on Vincent's face, not Luc's or the blinding beam of torchlight. 'I swear by his life, my life, the bible, anything you want – I do not have the necklace in my possession and it is not in a safe in Paris. You should know – you've burgled me, followed me, searched my bags, set Henri Chevalier on to me.'

She breathed in and out as normally as she could manage, praying that he believed her. Technically, it was not a lie, as the necklace was not in her possession, but stored in a bank's safe-deposit box back in New Zealand, out of harm's way.

'Chevalier? That pompous fool knows nothing. He's going to find himself in prison for a long time all the same. He is so busy parading his own importance, he never bothers to observe what is happening under his nose.'

'And us?'

Vincent grunted. 'What do you think? I can't let you live to tell tales, can I? By the time your bodies are recovered, I'll be relaxing beside my new pool in a country without an extradition treaty. It would have been nice to have one last gigantic payday, but I've amassed enough of a fortune to live on without it.'

'You'd shoot us in cold blood?'

'Not at all. The tunnel will tragically collapse, trapping you two in here until you run out of oxygen … unless the whole cellar system collapses and crushes you to death. What a terrible accident.' He turned his mouth down in mock-sadness. 'We checked at the vineyard, but unfortunately everyone was busy with tourists, so nobody will rush to your aid. Especially when I remove your car and text them on your phone. "Urgent business in Paris, so sorry we didn't have time to say goodbye." Which reminds me – I need your keys and phones.'

Neither of them moved.

Vincent turned to his men. 'Search them.'

It took Tomas all of three seconds to find Luc's phone and keys in his pocket. Joubert patted down Sophie's pockets and ran his hands over her torso and down her legs, with all the gentleness of a butcher manhandling a side of beef.

He held the torch a hand's breadth from her face. 'Where is it?'

She closed her eyes against the bright light. 'I don't have it with me.'

He turned to Vincent. 'Shall I strip-search her?'

'No need. We can send the message on Duchamp's phone. If she has hers, it won't do her any good. No cell reception underground.' He turned to Luc, holding up his phone. 'Passcode?'

When Luc told him, Vincent checked he could unlock the phone, then left Joubert to guard them, while he and Tomas went back through the cellar. Time crawled by with agonising slowness, but eventually Vincent returned alone. He took their handcuffs off, then both men retreated without another word, leaving them in pitch darkness.

Sophie rubbed her wrists. 'Shall we try to make a run for it?'

'Too dangerous. If they are about to blow the entrance, we can't risk being under it.' Luc grabbed her arm. 'Get into that alcove where the barrels were. If they trigger an explosion inside the tunnel, the blast wave is going to be lethal.'

Propelled by the urgency in his tone, she ran for it, keeping one hand on the wall so she could find the alcove and the other hand on Luc's arm. She stumbled over a rock and tumbled to her knees into a pile of something soft and velvety. The clothes from the second barrel. She pushed the bundle into the alcove, while he stacked their packs and the barrels around them.

Luc pushed her down, curling himself around her body and pulling a velvety covering of heavy fabric around their heads. 'Block your ears and pray,' he whispered in her ear, clutching her tightly.

The waiting was the worst part, or so it seemed. When the explosion came, it wasn't the loud bang she expected, but more of a whumping sound. For the first millisecond, she thought *that wasn't so very bad*, but then the blast wave entered the cellar like a derailed freight train. All she could hear was a wall of sound, then nothing but pain and ringing in her ears.

When the shock receded, she realised she was trapped. With a surge of panic, she lashed out, then realised it was only Luc's body on top of her. When he wriggled off, she felt weak with relief that he was alive too. She struggled to sit up and lift the fabric from her face. As soon as she did, she started coughing.

'Stay under the cloak until the dust settles.' Luc flipped the cloak back over them and curled up beside her, holding her head to his chest.

His voice sounded as if it was coming out the end of a very bad phone line, but she caught his meaning and nestled closer to the comfort of his body. She did not know how long they stayed like that, but, eventually, the ringing in her ears ebbed away, leaving a thick silence marred only by the pitter-patter – and occasional thunderous crash – of falling debris.

Luc gradually eased his grip on her. 'Sophie, are you okay?'

She nodded, not wanting to admit just how terrified she was in the face of his apparent calm. 'Yes. Thank you for saving my life.' Even to her still-ringing ears, her voice sounded strained.

'My pleasure.' Luc lifted the edge of the cloak, revealing utter, terrifying darkness. 'Wish I'd grabbed Vincent's torch.'

Sophie felt around for her pack, undoing the clips and reaching into the bottom of it, finding what she was looking for by touch. Relief washed over her, as she switched her spare torch on, although the relief was tempered by what little she could see. Darkness had been transformed into a dense mist of white, swirling chalk dust. Luc's face looked equally ghostly as his eyes widened at the sight of the light.

She turned the torch on the cloak, ripping the silk lining into pieces. With one piece, she gently wiped the dust off his face, before tying another piece as a makeshift mask around his nose and mouth.

'Did I mention that being with you is never dull?' Luc brushed off her face and ran his fingers through her hair, shaking out more dust, before tying her makeshift mask on. He took her hand and helped her to her feet. 'Shall we risk a look around?'

Her legs were shaking as violently as her heart was thumping. 'You might want to get the spare torch out of your pack first.'

The skin around his eyes crinkled into a smile, forming little ridges of white dust. 'You think of everything.'

'I used to do a bit of caving. I always carry a spare torch and batteries, after hearing about a guy who broke his only torch and got trapped underground for days. He was close to madness by the time they found him.' She shivered as she handed him his pack, wishing she hadn't added the last sentence. 'Yours is at the bottom of your pack.'

Luc found it, but didn't turn it on. 'Maybe we should use one torch at a time and keep our packs with us.'

He looked to be on the verge of saying something else, but didn't. There was no need. Sophie didn't have to be a mind reader to know what he was thinking. They could be trapped for a long time and couldn't risk running out of light or being separated from their meagre supplies.

The narrowness of their escape became apparent when they saw the devastation around them. The barrel nearest the exit was peppered with holes and dents, where fragments of stone had blasted into it. As they moved through the cellars, the destruction became increasingly obvious, until they reached the tunnel to the first cellar, which was now completely blocked by a pile of rock. Chalk dust swirled around the rubble, giving it the appearance of a smouldering ruin.

'We're lucky they chose the first tunnel. Most of the blast force would have radiated out, or into the nearer cellars, rather than down to where we were.'

Lucky? The explosion had felt enormous to Sophie. She shuddered to think how much worse it might have been.

They attempted to clear the debris, but it was hopeless with the tools they had. They pulled out a few rocks, but there were plenty more behind, wedged in tightly. Neither of them stated the obvious. In all likelihood, they would need to dig out the entire length of the tunnel to get to the outside world. Impossible without power tools. Even with the right equipment, it might take days.

Sophie started shaking as the full horror of their situation sank in. Now would be a terrific time for some of Luc's trademark calm and logic, before she completely lost her own.

Luc took the torch off her and grasped her trembling fingers in his other hand. 'Seems like the dust has settled a bit.' He swung the torch beam around the cellar. 'Let's check to see if there is any other way out. There might be another cellar system we didn't find, or a new hole created by the explosion.'

Suddenly, his grip tightened on her hand and his body went rigid. Sophie followed the beam of light to the ceiling, seeing a series of gaping cracks across it. Two of the pillars were cracked through as well, one so badly that the top of the pillar was dangling halfway off the bottom.

As they watched, a hail of loose stones rained down the side of the broken pillar. They turned as one and fled back to their refuge, without saying a word. What was there to say? If the whole cellar collapsed, there was almost no hope of survival.

Luc did a quick check of the ceiling and walls of the innermost cellar. 'Not as much obvious instability here, apart from the old rockfall.' He guided her back to the alcove. 'Let's sit for a while and work through our options. With any luck, Armand won't believe that we have gone back to Paris.'

She leaned into his warmth. 'No need to worry about that. Armand will be rallying the rescue squad already. I sent a message to him from my phone, along with a photo of the three of them holding you at gunpoint. I was too far away to get a decent shot, but the urgency of the situation will be clear.'

'Quick thinking. You never cease to amaze me, Sophie.' He put an arm around her and hugged her. 'Where did you disappear to?'

'I fell down an old shaft. The entrance was covered by creepers.'

'You should have stayed hidden.'

'And leave you to be shot? I would never have forgiven myself.' She allowed a few seconds to pass, then added. 'I didn't get much of a chance to look, but the shaft seemed to go in a fair way. If there was an ancient chalk mine already dug into the hill, that might explain why the wine cellars are so unstable.'

'This hill isn't very wide, so there's a chance the old chalk mine might link up with the cellars. We may as well use our time doing a thorough search. Rescue could take a while.'

Great idea. Anything to take her mind off the enormous weight of rock above her. 'I don't know how you stay so calm, Luc, but I'm very grateful for it.'

'I'm glad I appear calm. Believe me, inside I'm a screaming, quivering wreck.'

'Maybe save the screaming for later, after we've checked all possible exits.' Perversely, she felt calmer herself at the thought that Luc was struggling to keep panic under control too.

'That's a promise.' Luc took her hand and helped her to her feet.

Together, they searched the cellar, checking every inch of the wall and ceiling.

As they reached the far side, Sophie stopped and sniffed the air. 'I may be imagining it, but the air seems slightly different here. Can we go back to the rockfall?'

Luc shone the light above the pile of rock, but they could only see a jagged cavity, where a section of the ceiling had collapsed. 'I could have a go at climbing up, but there's not a lot to get a grip on.'

Sophie flicked her torch on. 'Looks too unstable to climb.' She turned one of the empty barrels upside down and clambered up on it. 'Still not high enough to see properly.'

'What if you were on my shoulders?'

'Are you sure you're up to it? That was a fearsome punch in the gut you took.'

'I'll worry about that later, when we're out of here.'

Luc set up three barrels to give them a better base, while Sophie took off her shoes and tied her torch around her neck with the strip of cloth she'd been using as a facemask. With Luc crouching down, she balanced herself on his shoulders, using the pillar as support as he gradually straightened up with a groan.

She examined the cavity as quickly as she could, wishing she'd spent more time in the gym and less at the table. 'Watch out, I'm going to jump down.' She landed near the rim of a barrel, causing it to wobble alarmingly, putting her off balance.

Luc caught her before she fell. 'You're a handy woman to have around. Remind me to invite you along next time I get trapped underground.'

'Not a chance. From now on, I stay above ground level.' She dusted herself down – a pointless exercise, given how thickly coated in chalk dust she was. 'Well, the good news is that there is a source of fresh air. The bad news is that it's no more than a crack. I'd need to be the size of a malnourished mouse to get out that way.'

'If there's fresh air, there's still a chance that there is a way out. Let's keep looking.'

While Sophie put her shoes back on, Luc set off in the opposite direction, starting at the pillar across from the rockfall. When she got up to follow him, she heard a sharp intake of breath.

'Sophie, what do you make of this.'

The excitement in his voice was infectious, but when she looked at the unbroken stretch of solid stone he was pointing to, she began to wonder if an excess of chalk dust, or maybe a touch of hysteria, was affecting his brain.

He took hold of her shoulders and turned her side-on. 'I only noticed it when your torch beam hit it at a sharp angle.'

'Oh, I see what you mean.'

Luc got the crowbar out of his pack and used it to scrape away the chalky film from a person-sized area of rectangular blocks. 'Definitely man-made. The blast must have shaken the surface coating loose. With any luck it has loosened the mortar too.' He prodded the mortar with the end of the crowbar.

'Wait, I've got something better.' She searched his pack for the small mallet and chisel she had thrown in with the rest of the tools, not knowing what they might need.

'Excellent.' Luc tapped the blocks first, then used the chisel to chip out the loose mortar. 'Stand back.' With an almighty swing, he walloped the central block with a two-handed blow of the mallet, sending the block tumbling backward and loosening several others.

The sight of a potential escape route cheered her enough to make an attempt at humour. 'Hey, Luc, can we try to do as little damage as possible? This may be preserved as a historic site one day.'

'Tell that to the guy with the explosives.' He walloped several more times, until there was a sizable window in the wall, which he put his head and the torch through.

When he pulled his head back, he yanked the dust mask off his face, revealing chalk-filled dimples. 'It's another tunnel.'

Sophie let out a whoop and flung her arms around his neck, planting a delighted kiss on his dusty cheek. 'Let's go! I can't wait to get out of here.'

With a little more walloping, the gap was wide enough to crawl through. A short tunnel led to a large, irregularly shaped cavern.

Sophie sniffed the air, which was blessedly dust-free compared to the cellar. 'The air smells fairly fresh. With any luck, that means there's a way out that hasn't collapsed completely.'

'I've never been so pleased to get out of a wine cellar,' Luc said, as he shone his torch around. 'Definitely an old mine. You can see the marks of hand-tools on the walls.' He turned to Sophie and brushed a curl away from her eye. 'We've solved the puzzle of our ancestors, busted a trafficking operation and survived to tell the tale. A pretty good day's work, I'd say.'

'Absolutely. My only regret is that you didn't find any treasure.'

Luc put his hands on her shoulders and whispered, 'Oh, but I did. I've just got to convince her not to run away again.' He reached down and kissed her tentatively.

She put her lips to his ear, feeling him quiver at her touch, then ran her hands slowly down his back. 'I think you're going to have to be more persuasive than that.'

'How about this?' His arms pulled her close, as he kissed her again. Not the kind of airy cheek kiss that French people dispense to anyone remotely familiar, or the kind of kiss you might give a dear friend whose company you enjoy, but the lip-searing kind of kiss that makes everything tingle from tresses to toes.

Her lips responded of their own accord, forgetting her vow to stick to the more sensible 'just friends' status, no matter how much she fancied him. Finally, she pulled away, gasping for breath and feeling as if her whole body was on fire. 'Wow. That was so persuasive, my knees don't seem to be holding me up anymore.'

'I've only just started.' Luc ran his hands through her hair. 'I realise it wouldn't be easy, with our lives and families at opposite ends of the earth, but I've never felt so happy as I've been with you.'

'I feel the same, Luc. But I'd like us to take some time to get to know each other properly, without all the drama of the past few days. Would you come away with me? Travel around France for a week or two, perhaps?'

'There's nothing I would like better.' Luc kissed her again, lightly this time, his lips moving across her forehead and down her cheek to the curve of her neck.

She sighed as every nerve in her body sizzled. After several minutes of bliss, she eased away again. 'Much as I'm enjoying this, perhaps we should look for a way out of here.'

Luc stroked her cheek with his finger, then stooped to pick up their dropped torches. 'I'll go right, you go left. Shout if you find a way out.'

Luc was the first to shout, pipping her by a second. Sophie made her way across the rough floor of the cavern in the direction his voice had come from, but couldn't find him, although she could hear his muffled voice at a distance. Looking up, she saw the entrance to a shaft above her head, with a crumbling set of narrow steps leading up to it.

She sidled up the worn steps carefully, then followed the shaft upwards, squeezing past two rockfalls, until she could see Luc silhouetted against creeper-draped daylight, holding her phone.

Luc turned to her with a smile that made her heart flutter. 'Sorry to desert you. I heard a phone ringing, so I came ahead to investigate.'

Sophie parted the curtain of vegetation, relishing the sensation of sunshine and fresh air on her skin. 'This is the shaft I fell into earlier in the day. I was pretty sure they'd take our phones, so I left mine here, hoping it might help rescuers find us.'

'It gave me quite a start. I thought I was going crazy when I heard the national anthem playing. It was Armand, calling to tell us he'd stopped the three traffickers from escaping, with the help of kitchen hands armed with cleavers, vineyard workers with rakes and secateurs, and a mob of camera-wielding tourists.'

'1789 all over again – the people of France taking up arms against the tyrants.'

'But, thankfully, with no bloodshed. The police are on their way. Armand will be here to pick us up as soon as he can.'

'That's terrific news, but you may want to ask him to hold off for a while. There's something I'd like to show you.'

Sophie led him back down into the mine and across to the far side. 'I saw these just before you called out.' Her torch beam picked out six barrels of a similar type to the ones in the cellar.

Luc looked at the barrels, then at her, dumbstruck.

'It seems our ancestors had a trick or two up their sleeves. Clever idea setting up the other barrels as a decoy.' Sophie handed Luc the crowbar. 'After you, Monsieur Duchamp.'

He continued to stare at the barrels for a few seconds, then strode forward to the first barrel and levered off the lid with far more care than Vincent had shown, placing it on the ground. 'Can you bring the torch closer, please?'

The barrel was packed to the top with straw, but within it, Sophie could see irregular shapes. As Luc carefully lifted the straw away, she saw it was filled with toys, ornaments, books, and childish drawings.

Sophie couldn't help letting out a squeal of sheer delight. 'I always forget that Ernestine was only eleven years old when revolution broke out. I guess this would have been everything that was precious to her and the other children.'

She picked out a set of tin soldiers, no doubt a favourite of the Dauphin. She could see a monkey, which had a mechanical lever, like a wind-up toy. There were even some charming carved horses with jointed legs, very much in the style of the birds Pierre had made for his child and grandchild. To think her ancestor would have played with these very toys way back in the 1780s.

Luc was grinning from ear to ear as he picked up a book. 'Incredible. This really is my idea of treasure.

Can you imagine what Vincent and his men would have said if they'd seen it?'

'I'd have learnt a few more swearwords in French, no doubt, before watching them smash the toys to smithereens.' She put the toys down and leaned over to look at the book, which had 'Ernestine' written in childish letters inside the front cover. 'This is so fantastic. Far better than gold and jewels.'

'Shall we have a look in the other barrels? I don't want to disturb things too much, now we know we are dealing with an important cultural discovery.'

'I think we deserve a peek. After all, none of this would have been found if it hadn't been for us.'

Luc dusted the book off and put it back, then took her in his arms again. 'I bet you didn't expect this when you started delving into your family tree.'

'I was hoping for a little adventure.' She rested her head on his shoulder, feeling a rush of pure joy. 'I think it's fair to say this trip has exceeded expectations by a million orders of magnitude.'

They held each other, enjoying the thrill of their discovery, until the lure of the unopened barrels became too strong to resist.

The second and third barrels were filled with books, ledgers, and diaries, bearing the personal crests of Marie Antoinette and Louis XVI. Luc hung over the barrel with an open mouth, taking deep breaths, obviously overwhelmed by the enormity of the find.

'This lot will keep you busy until you're old and grey.'

'With these diaries, history could be turned on its head, or at the very least, given a whole new perspective. Sophie, can you open the other barrels? I need to sit down for a moment.'

She opened the fourth barrel, finding more gorgeous clothes and shoes, woven with sparkling stones, which must surely be diamonds. The fifth had a high density of straw, hiding delicate vases, ornate clocks, precious ornaments, and embroideries. The sixth barrel made her laugh in delight. She hauled Luc to his feet and showed him.

'Ernestine must have wanted to pack things of special significance to the King. Tools, locks, scientific instruments, maps, books, even a small telescope. Wonderful.'

They stood with their arms around each other, at a loss for words at the abundance of treasures before them. Finally, Luc said, 'Who'd have thought it would end like this?'

She ran her fingers through his hair, which was as stiff and white as an eighteenth-century powdered wig. 'That's not all.' She shone her torch into a recess beyond the barrels, picking out the outline of a lumpy sack.

Luc retrieved it and put it on top of a barrel. The sack was filled with hard, oddly shaped objects and was tightly secured. Luc managed to tease it open without ripping it, while Sophie watched on, wishing he would tear it open, but admiring his patience. When he finally had it open, he shone the torch in and let out a whimper.

When he turned to her, his eyes were glistening. 'Have a look.'

His hands were shaking so much, she had to open it for herself. At first, she couldn't make out what he was being so emotional about. Then it dawned on her that the large, multifaceted stones of red, green and white might well be exactly what they appeared to be – rubies, emeralds and diamonds. And the spiked metal appeared to be shaped like a crown.

She flopped down on the ground with a thump, next to where Luc was trying to get his hyperventilation under control.

'When I was lying awake last night, it struck me that the date of Pierre's visit was quite soon after the theft of the Crown Jewels from the State Treasury. I didn't want to say anything because it was such an incredibly long shot, but now…'

'Oh my god, Luc. This is insane.'

Sophie had no problem imagining what it would be like for him once the news got out. Luc would be swamped with offers from every museum in the country and no doubt besieged by the media for months to come. A find of the magnitude of the lost Crown Jewels of France would be a sensation around the globe.

She would have to fade quietly into the background. Not that she wasn't delighted for him. Really, where was the problem? Going back home had always been the plan, so there was never much chance that their moment of passion would come to anything. Was there? Darn it, why couldn't she have met someone in her real life who made her heart thump as much as he did?

'You've gone quiet, Sophie.'

'It's overwhelming. I know I should be doing a victory dance, but I can't help thinking this discovery is going to cause a media circus. That's not something I could cope with, Luc. But, of course, I am ecstatic for you. You'll be the most famous historian in the world.' She paused. 'So why aren't you dancing?'

He put his arm around her. 'Same reason. I don't want to lose you, Sophie. Maybe we should pretend we didn't find anything.'

She snuggled into him. 'You know that's not an option. But thanks for the thought.'

'We'll find a way, I promise.'

'We should be celebrating the most amazing discovery ever. I'd love to be there when you casually mention to Henri Chevalier that we've found the Crown Jewels, as well as a treasure trove of royal possessions. Henri will never forgive either of us.'

'I can cope with that. In fact, I might just enjoy it. When we get out, I'm going to take you out to the best Michelin-starred restaurant in Reims. We've got a lot to celebrate, Sophie.'

'Definitely, although I think the police might have several hours of questions for us first.' She ran her fingers lightly down his cheek, tracing the contours of his throat to his chest. 'It might have to be a midnight feast on the veranda. Alone. Under the stars.'

'I can't wait. Let's get out of here.'

With a last glance at the barrels, they turned and walked hand-in-hand back to the outside world.

Return to Versailles

Paris, 2019, three months later

Sophie watched from behind the curtains as a buzz of anticipation built in the crowd. After three months of media frenzy, tonight was the gala opening of the exhibition of priceless Crown Jewels and personal items from the household of Louis XVI and Marie Antoinette. What better place than in the breathtaking setting of the Hall of Mirrors at Versailles?

A team of experts from several museums, led by Luc, had worked feverishly to catalogue every item, knowing there would be decades of research to come after the initial euphoria had died down. He was seated on the stage, looking handsome in a bespoke suit, ready to recount their adventure.

Henri Chevalier was on the other side of the stage, as excited as a schoolboy. He had been cleared of all involvement in the trafficking ring and had donated a massive sum to fund the exhibition and research.

Luc was looking around anxiously, resting his hand on the empty seat next to him. Sophie felt a twinge of guilt that she hadn't let him in on the secret, but Martine had been adamant it was better to come as a surprise. She was the organiser of tonight's event and the new curator of the exhibition.

As the museum director adjusted the microphone, a hush fell over the crowd. Dozens of cameras flashed as the director began her welcome speech.

Sophie closed the gap in the curtain and tried not to feel nervous. She had kept out of the spotlight, enjoying her solo travels around Britain and Europe. She knew leaving had been the right decision, as Luc was swamped with work commitments and endless interviews.

Martine slid the diamond-encrusted decorations into Sophie's hair, then adjusted her dress – the same midnight blue dress she had worn to Henri's dinner, which reminded her of Elisabeth's dress from the ship's trunk. The cameo was pinned to the front.

Sophie stroked the loop of pearls around her neck. The necklace had been couriered out from New Zealand under armed guard by security specialists. Her nervousness subsided as she thought about everything her ancestors had been through to keep this heirloom safe. For a moment, it felt as if Ernestine and Elisabeth were standing proudly beside her.

'You look sensational, Sophie,' Martine whispered. 'I'm so grateful to you for getting me the curator's role.'

'You got it on your own merits, Martine.' Luc's daughter was twirling her hair anxiously, so Sophie kissed her cheek and said, 'You'll be amazing.'

'I hope you're able to stay afterwards. Dad won't admit it, but I know he really misses you. Have you talked to him at all since you left?'

'We've been in touch.'

Neither of them had known what would happen to their fledgling relationship after their adventure ended. The decision had been taken out of their hands by the frenzy of activity that followed – the dramatic arrest and trial of the three traffickers who had been plundering French heritage for years – as well as the media hysteria and Luc's heavy workload.

Sophie had missed Luc far more than she cared to admit, even though they had kept in touch via frequent phone calls and messages. When she was recalled to Paris for additional police interviews, they met for dinner. They hadn't made it past the door of the restaurant, before the spark burst into flame again. Her skin blazed at the memory of that night and their subsequent weekends together, the details of which were best not shared with her children or his.

Luc finished his speech, to wild applause. Martine took a deep breath and went through the curtains to announce the official opening of the exhibition. As Sophie peeked out, the lights dimmed, and a series of pictures flashed up on the screens to either side of the stage. Scenes from history, pictures of Louis XVI and Marie Antoinette, and images of the most precious items recovered from the underground cavern. In the centre, above where she was standing, Sophie knew there would be pictures of Ernestine and Marie-Thérèse, and a portrait of Marie Antoinette wearing the famous pearl necklace.

She heard Martine speaking her cue. 'And now, I would like to present the heroine of this extraordinary drama and call on her to officially open this outstanding exhibition of French heritage. Please welcome Sophie West.'

Sophie walked onto the stage to deafening applause from the audience, which turned to gasps of delight when they compared her and the necklace to the projected photos. Out of the corner of her eye, Sophie caught the look of astonishment on Luc's face.

She stepped up to the microphone and read her speech in French, hoping she wasn't butchering their lovely language too badly. She briefly recounted the history of her family and the journey the pearl necklace had made over the past centuries, from the necks of French queens to a humble attic in New Zealand.

'Along the way, I have been privileged to meet many wonderful people, which is reward enough for me. It is my great honour to return this priceless treasure as a gift, back to its rightful place in France.' Sophie took off the pearl necklace and handed it to Martine, in pin-dropping silence. 'I declare this exhibition officially open.'

The hall erupted in thunderous applause and blinding camera flashes, while reporters yelled out questions in a dozen different languages. As soon as she decently could, Sophie gave a final wave and escaped backstage.

Luc was the first to burst through the curtains. He threw his arms around her and kissed her as if they hadn't seen each other for months.

Martine was right behind him, taking in the scene with wide eyes. 'You two! You might have told me.'

Luc eased back on the kiss but didn't let Sophie go. 'And you might have told me what you were planning, Martine. I was worried Sophie hadn't made it tonight.'

Sophie smiled. 'Are you crazy? I wouldn't have missed this for all the champagne in France.'

'You stunned the audience tonight, my darling.'

'I'm a little stunned myself. How often does a woman from the far side of the world get an opportunity to wear a priceless piece of French heritage?'

'Believe me, most people weren't looking at the necklace. Putting you alongside pictures of Ernestine and Marie-Thérèse was a masterstroke.'

'Martine's idea. She's as clever as her father.'

As they smiled into each other's eyes, Martine lunged forward and hugged them both. 'Is there anything else you are keeping from me?'

Luc raised his eyebrow at Sophie.

'I'm about to start a course on cheese tasting here in Paris,' Sophie volunteered. 'And planning to drink more Champagne with a capital C.'

'Armand has promised us free champagne for life, after we arranged for him to have some of the royal possessions on display at the vineyard,' Luc added. 'After that, we're heading to New Zealand. Meet the family, do some hiking, enjoy the Southern Hemisphere sun while it snows in Paris.'

'But what about all the research you have lined up?' Martine asked.

Luc shrugged. 'It'll still be here when we get back.'

'Who are you and what have you done with my father?'

'A minor tweak in priorities, my dear daughter. Now the mystery of Elisabeth is solved, I have to find a new obsession. To my great surprise, it turns out real people can be as fascinating as historical objects.'

Sophie reached up to kiss him. 'Are we going to talk about the past and the future all night, or shall we nab some of that delectable Noiret Champagne before the journalists guzzle it all?'

Luc linked her arm through his as they walked back out onto the stage. 'Talking of the past, I've been reading the Noiret journals in the few spare moments I've had, between working and dreaming about you.'

'Oh?'

'I discovered that Pierre Duchamp and his wife fled back to the vineyard in 1830, when their farm was attacked by the soldiers and Elisabeth escaped with the pearl necklace. Pierre recorded that his wife died soon afterwards, from an infected sword wound and the long-term ill-effects of her time in prison.'

'How tragic–' Sophie stopped dead, as the implications sunk in. 'You mean my crazy prison switch theory could actually be right?'

'What's more, Ernestine had changed her name, so she wouldn't be found after her release from prison.' He looked at her with a hint of mischief in those irresistible eyes.

'Don't keep me in suspense, Luc!'

'She decided to call herself Sophie. Sophie Duchamp. Nice name, don't you think?'

'I do.'

Thank you for reading this story.
If you enjoyed it, I would be grateful if you could
leave a rating or review to help other readers find it.

Read on

A new historical mystery series

The *Penrose & Pyke Mysteries* are set during a remarkable period of social upheaval in 1890s New Zealand, and star Grace Penrose, the granddaughter of Elisabeth and George Penrose from *The Widow's Secret.* The series also features Anne Macmillan, née Godwin, as Grace's aging great-aunt, who is still as feisty as ever.

If you missed the first two books in the French Legacy trilogy …

The Daughter's Promise, a novella, tells the story of Elisabeth Duchamp's escape from France with the pearl necklace.

The Widow's Secret, recounts Elisabeth's voyage to New Zealand, trapped on a sailing ship, where social rivalries and ferocious storms are the least of her worries.

Find out more at https://RosePascoe.com

Historical Characters

All characters in this novel are fictional, apart from:

Bourbon Royal Family

❖ Louis XVI: King from 1774, executed 1793

❖ Marie Antoinette: wife of Louis XVI, executed 1793

❖ Marie-Thérèse: Madame Royale, royal daughter, 1778-1851

❖ Louis-Joseph: royal son and heir (Dauphin), 1781-89

❖ Louis-Charles: royal son, 1785-95 (Dauphin 1789-93, Louis XVII 1793-95)

❖ Sophie: royal daughter, 1786-87

❖ Comte de Provence: brother of Louis XVI (Louis XVIII 1814-1824)

❖ Comte d'Artois: brother of Louis XVI (Charles X 1824-30)

❖ Duc d'Angoulême: son of Comte d'Artois, married Marie-Thérèse 1799

❖ Elisabeth: sister of Louis XVI, executed 1794

Royal Household

❖ Ernestine Lambriquet: born 1778 as Marie-Philippine to Jacques Lambriquet and Philippine Noiret, adopted by Louis XVI and Marie Antoinette in 1788

- ❖ Duchesse de Polignac: favourite of the Queen and children's governess until 1789
- ❖ Madame de Tourzel (Marquise de Tourzel): children's governess 1789-92 (her elderly relative in Paris existed, but is renamed and entirely fictionalised in this story)
- ❖ Pauline de Tourzel: daughter of Madame de Tourzel
- ❖ Madame de Soucy: under-governess 1781-92, daughter of Madame Mackau
- ❖ Madame Campan: Lady-in-Waiting to Marie Antoinette
- ❖ François Huë and Jean-Baptiste Cléry: valets to the Dauphin and King, who continued to serve the family in the Tuileries Palace and Temple Tower
- ❖ Princesse de Lamballe: devoted friend of Marie Antoinette, massacred September 1792

Other characters
- ❖ Louis Philippe, Duc d'Orléans: cousin of Louis XVI, complicit in the revolution, renamed himself Philippe Égalité, executed 1793
- ❖ Louis Philippe, Duc d'Orléans: son of above (King Louis Philippe I 1830-48)
- ❖ Jean Henri Riesener: royal furniture-maker

Historical Notes and References

This novel is a work of fiction. Although many of the characters are well known (and not so well-known) historical figures, their words and actions in this story are derived from my imagination, albeit informed by historical accounts.

However, the plot is built around real events during the French Revolution, based on memoirs from the era, as well as published histories and biographies. The modern-day story (which is entirely fictional) summarises the relevant historical information.

The period was one of the most tumultuous in history and therefore 'the facts' are often uncertain or downright contradictory, varying considerably depending on the narrator's point of view and circumstances, both in what is said and what is left unsaid.

My story is told from the perspective of a young girl who was intimately acquainted with the royal family. Therefore, the point of view is sympathetic to them and limited by her experiences. Thus, there is less emphasis on the very real suffering of the ordinary people before and during the revolution than there would be in a work of non-fiction.

The central figure, Ernestine Lambriquet, was a real person, but little is known of her beyond the tantalising hints drawn together in the fascinating biography of Marie-Thérèse by Susan Nagel.

Ernestine may well have been the daughter of Louis XVI and a chambermaid. Certainly, she was adopted by the royal family, given an extremely valuable pension, lavished with gifts, and lived like a sister to Marie-Thérèse. It is said that she bore a marked resemblance to Marie-Thérèse and the King. She was present at Versailles during the Women's March to the palace on 5 October 1789 but was not in the carriage that took the royal family to Paris. Nevertheless, she lived with them at the Tuileries until the 'Flight to Varennes', when she was sent to her father in the country. After the forced return of the royal family to Paris, Ernestine must have returned too, as she escaped with Madame de Soucy when the Tuileries was overrun and the royal family was arrested. During her escape, she was nearly killed after being mistaken for Marie-Thérèse.

Thus, Ernestine was in an extraordinary position of being an eyewitness to some of history's most shocking events, yet she was considered of such little significance that she can drift more or less unseen around the edges of written history, being mentioned only in passing in key memoirs. Her resemblance to Marie-Thérèse, and the inconsistencies and mysteries

536

surrounding both of their lives, have led to theories involving a switch between the two young women during their escape to Austria in 1795, a theory which has now been dismissed. My novel suggests a fictional alternative – an earlier switch in prison.

The Duchamp family is fictional, as is the plot to hide royal treasures, although the latter was by no means impossible given the chaotic events of the French Revolution. Versailles was effectively abandoned when the royals were forced to go to Paris in October 1789, leaving thousands of priceless articles behind, many of which were sold off by auction years later.

The Crown Jewels were handed over to the National Assembly and stored in the State Treasury, as in the story. The sensational burglary of the Crown Jewels over several nights in September 1792 – astoundingly – actually took place as described. Stolen jewels of enormous value are still coming to light even in modern times, while many of the jewels and regalia remain lost or were destroyed. Many of the personal jewels and valuables belonging to the royal family were entrusted to a number of people and some made it safely out of France and into the hands of the sole survivor, Marie-Thérèse.

I have relied heavily on the excellent book by Susan Nagel, which documents the extraordinary life of Marie-Thérèse. Antonia Fraser's biography of

Marie Antoinette was also filled with interesting and helpful detail. I've used memoirs from the era for additional colour and insight, and included background information from a variety of sources, as listed below.

And finally, my apologies to the fine people of France for taking liberties with your history and culture.

Memoirs

Duchesse d'Angoulême, Madame Elisabeth, Sister of Louis XVI, and Cléry, the King's Valet de Chambre, as translated by Katharine Prescott Wormeley (1912). *The Ruin of a Princess*. New York: The Lamb Publishing Co.
http://digital.library.upenn.edu/women/wormeley/princess/princess.html

Louise Elisabeth de Croy d'Havré, Duchesse de Tourzel (1883) *Mémoires de Madame la Duchesse de Tourzel: Gouvernante des enfants de France pendant les années 1789 à 1795.*
http://www.gutenberg.org/ebooks/33258

Madame Campan. *Memoirs Of The Court Of Marie Antoinette, Queen Of France.*
http://www.gutenberg.org/files/3891

Madame de la Tour du Pin, as edited and translated by Felice Harcourt (1979) *Escape from the Terror: the*

Journal of Madame de la Tour du Pin. The Folio Society, London.

Biography and history
Clarke, Stephen (2018) *The French Revolution and What Went Wrong*. Century, London.
Fraser, Antonia (2001) *Marie Antoinette: the Journey*. Weidenfeld & Nicolson, London.
Hibbert, Christopher (1989) *The Days of The French Revolution*. Penguin, London.
Moorehead, Caroline (2009) *Dancing to the Precipice: Lucie de la Tour du Pin and the French Revolution*. Chatto & Windus, London.
Nagel, Susan (2008) *Marie-Thérèse: the fate of Marie Antoinette's daughter*. Bloomsbury, London.

Life at Versailles
Kisluk-Grosheide, Danielle and Bertrand Rondot (editors) (2018) *Visitors to Versailles from Louis XIV to the French Revolution*. The Metropolitan Museum of Art, New York. Yale University Press.

Delalex, Hélène, Alexandre Maral, Nicholas Milovanovic (2016) *Marie Antoinette*. J. Paul Getty Museum, Los Angeles.

Acknowledgments

Many thanks to the fabulous beta readers who commented on the draft and to the friends and family who provided the support that allowed this novel to be completed in uncertain times.

About the Author

Rose Pascoe writes historical mysteries with a dash of romance, when she isn't plotting real-life adventures. She lives in beautiful New Zealand, land of beaches and mountains, where long walks provide the perfect conditions for dreaming up plots and fickle weather provides the incentive to sit down and write.

After a career in health, justice and social research, her passion is for stories set against a backdrop of social justice. Her heroines are ordinary women, who meet the challenges thrown at them with determination, ingenuity, courage, and humour.

Visit her at: https://RosePascoe.com

Other Books by Rose Pascoe

French Legacy series:

The Daughter's Promise

The Widow's Secret

The Last Child At Versailles

The Penrose & Pyke Mysteries

Murder in the Devil's Half Acre

Murder Most Melancholy

Murder By Vote

Murder in the Moonlight

Murder So Rash

Tinsel and Trickery

Murder Ignited

Murder Over Gold